...fact that the
household is suffering from.
disease should be reported immediat

4. A pupil leaving school during the se
all books belonging to the school h

Date of Issue	Name of Pupil
2/8/74	JACQUELINE WIL
3/6/75	Christine Browne
1975	Ian Sharples

English Short Stories
1888–1937

English Short Stories

1888–1937

Selected by

PHYLLIS M. JONES

OXFORD UNIVERSITY PRESS

LONDON   OXFORD   TORONTO

1973

Oxford University Press

LONDON OXFORD NEW YORK
GLASGOW TORONTO MELBOURNE WELLINGTON
CAPE TOWN IBADAN NAIROBI DAR ES SALAAM LUSAKA ADDIS ABABA
DELHI BOMBAY CALCUTTA MADRAS KARACHI LAHORE DACCA
KUALA LUMPUR SINGAPORE HONG KONG TOKYO

ISBN 0 19 281135 5

First published in the World's Classics, 1939, as
Modern English Short Stories

*First issued as an Oxford University Press paperback
by Oxford University Press, London, 1973*

*Printed in Great Britain
at the University Press, Oxford
by Vivian Ridler
Printer to the University*

Contents

Acknowledgements

THANKS are due to the following for permission to reprint copyright material:

The Trustees of the Hardy Estate, The Macmillan Company of Canada, and Macmillan London and Basingstoke for 'The Three Strangers' from *The Wessex Tales* by Thomas Hardy (Macmillan, 1888).

The author's Executors for 'The Holy Man' from *Unpath'd Waters* by Frank Harris (John Lane, 1913).

The Society of Authors as the literary representative of the Estate of W. W. Jacobs for 'A Garden Plot' from *Light Freights* by W. W. Jacobs (Methuen, 1901).

The Estate of H. G. Wells for 'A Slip under the Microscope' from *The Complete Short Stories of H. G. Wells* (Benn, 1966).

Mrs. Dorothy Cheston Bennett and Chatto and Windus Ltd. for 'The Lion's Share' from *The Grim Smile of the Five Towns* (Chatto & Windus, 1907).

The Literary Executor of W. Somerset Maugham, and William Heinemann Ltd., for 'The Door of Opportunity' from *The Complete Short Stories of W. Somerset Maugham* (Heinemann, 1951).

The author's Executors for 'Fifty Pounds' from *The Field of Mustard* by A. E. Coppard (Jonathan Cape, 1926).

Messrs. Sidgwick & Jackson Ltd. for 'Other Kingdom' from *The Celestial Omnibus* by E. M. Forster (Sidgwick & Jackson, 1911).

The author and Barrie and Jenkins Ltd. for 'Lord Emsworth and the Girl Friend' from *Blandings Castle* (Herbert Jenkins, 1935).

Laurence Pollinger Ltd. and the Estate of the Late Mrs. Frieda Lawrence, and Alfred A. Knopf Inc., for 'The Last Laugh' from *The Complete Short Stories of D. H. Lawrence* (Heinemann, 1955).

The Estate of Stacy Aumonier for 'Juxtapositions' from *Ups and Downs* by Stacy Aumonier (Heinemann, 1931).

viii　　　*ACKNOWLEDGEMENTS*

The Society of Authors as the literary representative of the Estate of Katherine Mansfield for 'Sun and Moon' from *Bliss* by Katherine Mansfield (Constable, 1920).

The Estate of Stella Benson for 'Submarine' from *Collected Short Stories* by Stella Benson (Macmillan, 1936).

Mrs. Laura Huxley and Chatto and Windus Ltd. for 'The Tillotson Banquet' from *Mortal Coils* by Aldous Huxley (Chatto & Windus, 1922).

The author for 'She was Living with his People' from *A Young Man in a Hurry* by T. O. Beachcroft (Boriswood, 1934).

The author and Jonathan Cape Ltd. for 'The Revelation' from *Cut and Come Again* by H. E. Bates (Jonathan Cape, 1935).

The author's Executors and Hope Leresche & Steele for 'The Last Inch' from *The Wisdom of the Simple* by Constance Holme (Oxford University Press, 1937).

The Executors of the Viola Meynell Estate for 'The Pain in the Neck' from *Kissing the Rod* by Viola Meynell (Jonathan Cape, 1937).

The author for 'Joining Charles' from *Joining Charles and other Stories* by Elizabeth Bowen (Constable, 1929).

The author for 'Saturday Afternoon' from *Roaring Tower and Other Short Stories* by Stella Gibbons (Longman, 1937).

THOMAS HARDY

The Three Strangers

Among the few features of agricultural England which retain an appearance but little modified by the lapse of centuries, may be reckoned the high, grassy and furzy downs, coombs, or ewe-leases, as they are indifferently called, that fill a large area of certain counties in the south and south-west. If any mark of human occupation is met with hereon, it usually takes the form of the solitary cottage of some shepherd.

Fifty years ago such a lonely cottage stood on such a down, and may possibly be standing there now. In spite of its loneliness, however, the spot, by actual measurement, was not more than five miles from a county-town. Yet that affected it little. Five miles of irregular upland, during the long inimical seasons, with their sleets, snows, rains, and mists, afford withdrawing space enough to isolate a Timon or a Nebuchadnezzar; much less, in fair weather, to please that less repellent tribe, the poets, philosophers, artists, and others who 'conceive and meditate of pleasant things'.

Some old earthen camp or barrow, some clump of trees, at least some starved fragment of ancient hedge is usually taken advantage of in the erection of these forlorn dwellings. But, in the present case, such a kind of shelter had been disregarded. Higher Crowstairs, as the house was called, stood quite detached and undefended. The only reason for its precise situation seemed to be the crossing of two footpaths at right angles hard by, which may have crossed there and thus for a good five hundred years. Hence the house was exposed to the elements on all sides. But, though the wind up here blew unmistakably when it did blow, and the rain hit hard whenever it fell, the various weathers of the winter season were not quite so formidable on the coomb as they were imagined to be by dwellers on low ground. The raw rimes were not so pernicious as in the hollows, and the frosts were scarcely so severe. When the shepherd and his family who tenanted the house were pitied for their sufferings from the exposure, they said that upon the whole they were less inconvenienced by 'wuzzes and flames' (hoarses and phlegms) than when they had lived by the stream of a snug neighbouring valley.

The night of March 28, 182–, was precisely one of the nights that were wont to call forth these expressions of commiseration. The level rainstorm smote walls, slopes, and hedges like the clothyard shafts of Senlac and Crecy. Such sheep and outdoor animals as had no shelter stood with their buttocks to the winds; while the tails of little birds trying to roost on some scraggy thorn were blown inside-out like umbrellas. The gable-end of the cottage was stained with wet, and the eavesdroppings flapped against the wall. Yet never was commiseration for the shepherd more misplaced. For that cheerful rustic was entertaining a large party in glorification of the christening of his second girl.

The guests had arrived before the rain began to fall, and they were all now assembled in the chief or living room of the dwelling. A glance into the apartment at eight o'clock on this eventful evening would have resulted in the opinion that it was as cosy and comfortable a nook as could be wished for in boisterous weather. The calling of its inhabitant was pro-

claimed by a number of highly-polished sheep-crooks
without stems that were hung ornamentally over the
fireplace, the curl of each shining crook varying from
the antiquated type engraved in the patriarchal pictures of old family Bibles to the most approved
fashion of the last local sheep-fair. The room was
lighted by half-a-dozen candles, having wicks only
a trifle smaller than the grease which enveloped
them, in candlesticks that were never used but at
high-days, holy-days, and family feasts. The lights
were scattered about the room, two of them standing
on the chimney-piece. This position of candles was
in itself significant. Candles on the chimney-piece
always meant a party.

On the hearth, in front of a back-brand to give
substance, blazed a fire of thorns, that crackled 'like
the laughter of the fool'.

Nineteen persons were gathered here. Of these,
five women, wearing gowns of various bright hues,
sat in chairs along the wall; girls shy and not shy
filled the window-bench; four men, including Charley
Jake the hedge-carpenter, Elijah New the parish-
clerk, and John Pitcher, a neighbouring dairyman,
the shepherd's father-in-law, lolled in the settle; a
young man and maid, who were blushing over
tentative *pourparlers* on a life-companionship, sat
beneath the corner-cupboard; and an elderly engaged man of fifty or upward moved restlessly about
from spots where his betrothed was not to the spot
where she was. Enjoyment was pretty general, and
so much the more prevailed in being unhampered
by conventional restrictions. Absolute confidence
in each other's good opinion begat perfect ease,
while the finishing stroke of manner, amounting
to a truly princely serenity, was lent to the majority

by the absence of any expression or trait denoting that they wished to get on in the world, enlarge their minds, or do any eclipsing thing whatever—which nowadays so generally nips the bloom and *bonhomie* of all except the two extremes of the social scale.

Shepherd Fennel had married well, his wife being a dairyman's daughter from a vale at a distance, who brought fifty guineas in her pocket—and kept them there, till they should be required for ministering to the needs of a coming family. This frugal woman had been somewhat exercised as to the character that should be given to the gathering. A sit-still party had its advantages; but an undisturbed position of ease in chairs and settles was apt to lead on the men to such an unconscionable deal of toping that they would sometimes fairly drink the house dry. A dancing-party was the alternative; but this, while avoiding the foregoing objection on the score of good drink, had a counterbalancing disadvantage in the matter of good victuals, the ravenous appetites engendered by the exercise causing immense havoc in the buttery. Shepherdess Fennel fell back upon the intermediate plan of mingling short dances with short periods of talk and singing, so as to hinder any ungovernable rage in either. But this scheme was entirely confined to her own gentle mind: the shepherd himself was in the mood to exhibit the most reckless phases of hospitality.

The fiddler was a boy of those parts, about twelve years of age, who had a wonderful dexterity in jigs and reels, though his fingers were so small and short as to necessitate a constant shifting for the high notes, from which he scrambled back to the first position with sounds not of unmixed purity of tone.

At seven the shrill tweedle-dee of this youngster had begun, accompanied by a booming ground-bass from Elijah New, the parish-clerk, who had thought-fully brought with him his favourite musical instrument, the serpent. Dancing was instantaneous, Mrs. Fennel privately enjoining the players on no account to let the dance exceed the length of a quarter of an hour.

But Elijah and the boy, in the excitement of their position, quite forgot the injunction. Moreover, Oliver Giles, a man of seventeen, one of the dancers, who was enamoured of his partner, a fair girl of thirty-three rolling years, had recklessly handed a new crown-piece to the musicians, as a bribe to keep going as long as they had muscle and wind. Mrs. Fennel, seeing the steam begin to generate on the countenances of her guests, crossed over and touched the fiddler's elbow and put her hand on the serpent's mouth. But they took no notice, and fearing she might lose her character of genial hostess if she were to interfere too markedly, she retired and sat down helpless. And so the dance whizzed on with cumulative fury, the performers moving in their planet-like courses, direct and retrograde, from apogee to peri-gee, till the hand of the well-kicked clock at the bottom of the room had travelled over the circum-ference of an hour.

While these cheerful events were in course of enactment within Fennel's pastoral dwelling, an incident having considerable bearing on the party had occurred in the gloomy night without. Mrs. Fennel's concern about the growing fierceness of the dance corresponded in point of time with the ascent of a human figure to the solitary hill of Higher Crow-stairs from the direction of the distant town. This personage strode on through the rain without a pause, following the little-worn path which, farther on in its course, skirted the shepherd's cottage.

It was nearly the time of full moon, and on this account, though the sky was lined with a uniform sheet of dripping cloud, ordinary objects out-of-doors were readily visible. The sad wan light revealed the lonely pedestrian to be a man of supple frame; his gait suggested that he had somewhat passed the period of perfect and instinctive agility, though not so far as to be otherwise than rapid of motion when occasion required. At a rough guess, he might have been about forty years of age. He appeared tall, but a recruiting sergeant, or other person accustomed to the judging of men's heights by the eye, would have discerned that this was chiefly owing to his gauntness and that he was not more than five-feet-eight or nine.

Notwithstanding the regularity of his tread, there was caution in it, as in that of one who mentally feels his way; and despite the fact that it was not a black coat nor a dark garment of any sort that he wore, there was something about him which suggested that he naturally belonged to the black-coated tribes of men. His clothes were of fustian, and his boots hobnailed, yet in his progress he showed not the mud-accustomed bearing of hobnailed and fustianed peasantry.

By the time that he had arrived abreast of the shepherd's premises the rain came down, or rather came along, with yet more determined violence. The outskirts of the little settlement partially broke the force of wind and rain, and this induced him to stand still. The most salient of the shepherd's domestic erections was an empty sty at the forward corner of his hedgeless garden, for in these latitudes the principle of masking the homelier features of your establishment by a conventional frontage was unknown. The traveller's eye was attracted to this small building by the pallid shine of the wet slates that covered it. He turned aside, and, finding it empty, stood under the pent-roof for shelter.

While he stood, the boom of the serpent within the adjacent house, and the lesser strains of the fiddler, reached the spot as an accompaniment to the surging hiss of the flying rain on the sod, its louder beating on the cabbage leaves of the garden, on the eight or ten beehives just discernible by the path, and its dripping from the eaves into a row of buckets and pans that had been placed under the walls of the cottage. For at Higher Crowstairs, as at all such elevated domiciles, the grand difficulty of housekeeping was an insufficiency of water; and a casual rainfall was utilized by turning out, as catchers, every utensil that the house contained. Some queer stories might be told of the contrivances for economy in suds and dish-waters that are absolutely necessitated in upland habitations during the droughts of summer. But at this season there were no such exigencies; a mere acceptance of what the skies bestowed was sufficient for an abundant store.

At last the notes of the serpent ceased and the house was silent. This cessation of activity aroused the solitary pedestrian from the reverie into which he had lapsed, and, emerging from the shed, with an apparently new intention, he walked up the path to the house-door. Arrived here, his first act was to kneel down on a large stone beside the row of vessels, and to drink a copious draught from one of them. Having quenched his thirst he rose and lifted his hand to knock, but paused with his eye upon the panel. Since the dark surface of the wood revealed absolutely nothing, it was evident that he must be mentally looking through the door, as if he wished to measure thereby all the possibilities that a house of this sort might include, and how they might bear upon the question of his entry.

In his indecision he turned and surveyed the scene around. Not a soul was anywhere visible. The garden-path stretched downward from his feet, gleaming like the track of a snail; the roof of the little well (mostly dry), the well-cover, the top rail of the garden-gate, were varnished with the same dull liquid glaze; while, far away in the vale, a faint whiteness of more than usual extent showed that the rivers were high in the meads. Beyond all this winked a few bleared lamplights through the beating drops— lights that denoted the situation of the county-town from which he had appeared to come. The absence of all notes of life in that direction seemed to clinch his intentions, and he knocked at the door.

Within, a desultory chat had taken the place of movement and musical sound. The hedge-carpenter was suggesting a song to the company, which nobody just then was inclined to undertake, so that the knock afforded a not unwelcome diversion.

'Walk in!' said the shepherd promptly.

The latch clicked upward, and out of the night our pedestrian appeared upon the door-mat. The shepherd arose, snuffed two of the nearest candles, and turned to look at him.

Their light disclosed that the stranger was dark in complexion and not unprepossessing as to feature. His hat, which for a moment he did not remove, hung low over his eyes, without concealing that they were large, open, and determined, moving with a flash rather than a glance round the room. He seemed pleased with his survey, and, baring his shaggy head, said, in a rich deep voice, 'The rain is so heavy, friends, that I ask leave to come in and rest awhile.'

'To be sure, stranger,' said the shepherd. 'And faith, you've been lucky in choosing your time, for we are having a bit of a fling for a glad cause—though, to be sure, a man could hardly wish that glad cause to happen more than once a year.'

'Nor less,' spoke up a woman. 'For 'tis best to get your family over and done with, as soon as you can, so as to be all the earlier out of the fag o't.'

'And what may be this glad cause?' asked the stranger.

'A birth and christening,' said the shepherd.

The stranger hoped his host might not be made unhappy either by too many or too few of such episodes, and being invited by a gesture to a pull at the mug, he readily acquiesced. His manner, which before entering had been so dubious, was now altogether that of a careless and candid man.

'Late to be traipsing athwart this coomb—hey?' said the engaged man of fifty.

'Late it is, master, as you say. I'll take a seat in the chimney-corner, if you have nothing to urge against it, ma'am; for I am a little moist on the side that was next the rain.'

Mrs. Shepherd Fennel assented, and made room for the self-invited comer, who, having got completely inside the chimney-corner, stretched out his legs and his arms with the expansiveness of a person quite at home.

'Yes, I am rather cracked in the vamp,' he said

freely, seeing that the eyes of the shepherd's wife fell upon his boots, 'and I am not well fitted either. I have had some rough times lately, and have been forced to pick up what I can get in the way of wearing, but I must find a suit better fit for working-days when I reach home.'

'One of hereabouts?' she inquired.

'Not quite that—farther up the country.'

'I thought so. And so be I; and by your tongue you come from my neighbourhood.'

'But you would hardly have heard of me,' he said quickly. 'My time would be long before yours, ma'am, you see.'

This testimony to the youthfulness of his hostess had the effect of stopping her cross-examination.

'There is only one thing more wanted to make me happy,' continued the new-comer. 'And that is a little baccy, which I am sorry to say I am out of.'

'I'll fill your pipe,' said the shepherd.

'I must ask you to lend me a pipe likewise.'

'A smoker, and no pipe about 'ee?'

'I have dropped it somewhere on the road.'

The shepherd filled and handed him a new clay pipe, saying, as he did so, 'Hand me your baccy-box—I'll fill that too, now I am about it.'

The man went through the movement of searching his pockets.

'Lost that too?' said his entertainer, with some surprise.

'I am afraid so,' said the man with some confusion. 'Give it to me in a screw of paper.' Lighting his pipe at the candle with a suction that drew the whole flame into the bowl, he resettled himself in the corner and bent his looks upon the faint steam from his damp legs, as if he wished to say no more.

Meanwhile the general body of guests had been taking little notice of this visitor by reason of an absorbing discussion in which they were engaged with the band about a tune for the next dance. The matter being settled, they were about to stand up when an interruption came in the shape of another knock at the door.

At sound of the same the man in the chimney-corner took up the poker and began stirring the brands as if doing it thoroughly were the one aim of his existence; and a second time the shepherd said, 'Walk in!' In a moment another man stood upon the straw-woven door-mat. He, too, was a stranger.

This individual was one of a type radically different from the first. There was more of the commonplace in his manner, and a certain jovial cosmopolitanism sat upon his features. He was several years older than the first arrival, his hair being slightly frosted, his eyebrows bristly, and his whiskers cut back from his cheeks. His face was rather full and flabby, and yet it was not altogether a face without power. A few grog-blossoms marked the neighbourhood of his nose. He flung back his long drab greatcoat, revealing that beneath it he wore a suit of cinder-grey shade throughout, large heavy seals, of some metal or other that would take a polish, dangling from his fob as his only personal ornament. Shaking the water-drops from his low-crowned glazed hat, he said, 'I must ask for a few minutes' shelter, comrades, or I shall be wetted to my skin before I get to Caster-bridge.'

'Make yourself at home, master,' said the shepherd, perhaps a trifle less heartily than on the first occasion. Not that Fennel had the least tinge of niggardliness in his composition; but the room was far from large, spare chairs were not numerous, and damp companions were not altogether desirable at close quarters for the women and girls in their bright-coloured gowns.

However, the second comer, after taking off his greatcoat, and hanging his hat on a nail in one of the ceiling-beams as if he had been specially invited to put it there, advanced and sat down at the table. This had been pushed so closely into the chimney-corner, to give all available room to the dancers, that its inner edge grazed the elbow of the man who had ensconced himself by the fire; and thus the two strangers were brought into close companionship. They nodded to each other by way of breaking the ice of unacquaintance, and the first stranger handed his neighbour the family mug—a huge vessel of brown ware, having its upper edge worn away like a threshold by the rub of whole generations of thirsty lips that had gone the way of all flesh, and bearing the following inscription burnt upon its rotund side in yellow letters:

THERE IS NO FUN
UNTILL I CUM.

The other man, nothing loth, raised the mug to his lips and drank on, and on, and on—till a curious blueness overspread the countenance of the shepherd's wife, who had regarded with no little surprise the first stranger's free offer to the second of what did not belong to him to dispense.

'I knew it!' said the toper to the shepherd with much satisfaction. 'When I walked up your garden before coming in, and saw the hives all of a row, I said to myself, "Where there's bees there's honey, and where there's honey there's mead." But mead of such a truly comfortable sort as this I really didn't expect to meet in my older days.' He took yet another pull at the mug, till it assumed an ominous elevation.

'Glad you enjoy it!' said the shepherd warmly.

'It is goodish mead,' assented Mrs. Fennel, with an absence of enthusiasm which seemed to say that it was possible to buy praise for one's cellar at too heavy a price. 'It is trouble enough to make—and really I hardly think we shall make any more. For honey sells well, and we ourselves can make shift with a drop o' small mead and metheglin for common use from the comb-washings."

'O, but you'll never have the heart!' reproachfully cried the stranger in cinder-grey, after taking up the mug a third time and setting it down empty. 'I love mead, when 'tis old like this, as I love to go to church o' Sundays, or to relieve the needy any day of the week.'

'Ha, ha, ha!' said the man in the chimney-corner, who, in spite of the taciturnity induced by the pipe of tobacco, could not or would not refrain from this slight testimony to his comrade's humour.

Now the old mead of those days, brewed of the purest first-year or maiden honey, four pounds to the gallon—with its due complement of white of eggs, cinnamon, ginger, cloves, mace, rosemary, yeast, and processes of working, bottling, and cellaring—tasted remarkably strong; but it did not taste so strong as it actually was. Hence, presently, the stranger in cinder-grey at the table, moved by its creeping influence, unbuttoned his waistcoat, threw himself back in his chair, spread his legs, and made his presence felt in various ways.

'Well, well, as I say,' he resumed, 'I am going to Casterbridge, and to Casterbridge I must go. I should have been almost there by this time; but the rain drove me into your dwelling, and I'm not sorry for it.'

'You don't live in Casterbridge?' said the shepherd.

'Not as yet; though I shortly mean to move there.'

'Going to set up in trade, perhaps?'

'No, no,' said the shepherd's wife. 'It is easy to see that the gentleman is rich, and don't want to work at anything.'

The cinder-grey stranger paused, as if to consider whether he would accept that definition of himself. He presently rejected it by answering, 'Rich is not quite the word for me, dame. I do work, and I must work. And even if I only get to Casterbridge by midnight I must begin work there at eight to-morrow morning. Yes, het or wet, blow or snow, famine or sword, my day's work to-morrow must be done.'

'Poor man! Then, in spite o' seeming, you be worse off than we?' replied the shepherd's wife.

''Tis the nature of my trade, men and maidens. 'Tis the nature of my trade more than my poverty. . . . But really and truly I must up and off, or I shan't get a lodging in the town.' However, the speaker did not move, and directly added, 'There's time for one more draught of friendship before I go; and I'd perform it at once if the mug were not dry.'

'Here's a mug o' small,' said Mrs. Fennel. 'Small, we call it, though to be sure 'tis only the first wash o' the combs.'

'No,' said the stranger disdainfully. 'I won't spoil your first kindness by partaking o' your second.'

'Certainly not,' broke in Fennel. 'We don't increase and multiply every day, and I'll fill the mug again.' He went away to the dark place under the stairs where the barrel stood. The shepherdess followed him.

'Why should you do this?' she said reproachfully, as soon as they were alone. 'He's emptied it once, though it held enough for ten people; and now he's not contented wi' the small, but must needs call for more o' the strong! And a stranger unbeknown to any of us. For my part, I don't like the look o' the man at all.'

'But he's in the house, my honey; and 'tis a wet night, and a christening. Daze it, what's a cup of mead more or less? There'll be plenty more next bee-burning.'

'Very well—this time, then,' she answered, looking wistfully at the barrel. 'But what is the man's calling, and where is he one of, that he should come in and join us like this?'

'I don't know. I'll ask him again.'

The catastrophe of having the mug drained dry at one pull by the stranger in cinder-grey was effectually guarded against this time by Mrs. Fennel. She poured out his allowance in a small cup, keeping the large one at a discreet distance from him. When he had tossed off his portion the shepherd renewed his inquiry about the stranger's occupation.

The latter did not immediately reply, and the man in the chimney-corner, with sudden demonstrativeness, said, 'Anybody may know my trade—I'm a wheelwright.'

'A very good trade for these parts,' said the shepherd.

'And anybody may know mine—if they've the sense to find it out,' said the stranger in cinder-grey.

'You may generally tell what a man is by his claws,' observed the hedge-carpenter, looking at his own hands. 'My fingers be as full of thorns as an old pin-cushion is of pins.'

The hands of the man in the chimney-corner instinctively sought the shade, and he gazed into the fire as he resumed his pipe. The man at the table took up the hedge-carpenter's remark, and added smartly, 'True; but the oddity of my trade is that, instead of setting a mark upon me, it sets a mark upon my customers.'

No observation being offered by anybody in elucidation of this enigma, the shepherd's wife once more called for a song. The same obstacles presented themselves as at the former time—one had no voice, another had forgotten the first verse. The stranger at the table, whose soul had now risen to a good working temperature, relieved the difficulty by exclaiming that, to start the company, he would sing himself. Thrusting one thumb into the arm-hole of his waistcoat, he waved the other hand in the air, and, with an extemporizing gaze at the shining sheep-crooks above the mantlepiece, began:

> O my trade it is the rarest one,
> > Simple shepherds all—
> My trade is a sight to see;
> For my customers I tie, and take them up on high,
> And waft 'em to a far countree!'

The room was silent when he had finished the verse—with one exception, that of the man in the chimney-corner, who, at the singer's word, 'Chorus!' joined him in a deep bass voice of musical relish—

> And waft 'em to a far countree!

Oliver Giles, John Pitcher the dairyman, the parish-clerk, the engaged man of fifty, the row of young

women against the wall, seemed lost in thought not
of the gayest kind. The shepherd looked medita-
tively on the ground, the shepherdess gazed keenly
at the singer, and with some suspicion; she was
doubting whether this stranger were merely singing
an old song from recollection, or was composing
one there and then for the occasion. All were as
perplexed at the obscure revelation as the guests at
Belshazzar's Feast, except the man in the chimney-
corner, who quietly said, 'Second verse, stranger,'
and smoked on.

The singer thoroughly moistened himself from his
lips inwards, and went on with the next stanza as
requested:

> My tools are but common ones,
>   Simple shepherds all—
> My tools are no sight to see:
> A little hempen string, and a post whereon to swing,
>   Are implements enough for me!

Shepherd Fennel glanced round. There was no
longer any doubt that the stranger was answering
his question rhythmically. The guests one and all
started back with suppressed exclamations. The
young woman engaged to the man of fifty fainted
half-way, and would have proceeded, but finding
him wanting in alacrity for catching her she sat
down trembling.

'O, he's the ——!' whispered the people in the
background, mentioning the name of an ominous
public officer. 'He's come to do it! 'Tis to be at
Casterbridge jail to-morrow—the man for sheep-
stealing—the poor clock-maker we heard of, who
used to live away at Shottsford and had no work to
do—Timothy Summers, whose family were a-starv-
ing, and so he went out of Shottsford by the high-

road, and took a sheep in open daylight, defying the farmer and the farmer's wife and the farmer's lad, and every man jack among 'em. He' (and they nodded towards the stranger of the deadly trade) 'is come from up the country to do it because there's not enough to do in his own county-town, and he's got the place here now our own county man's dead; he's going to live in the same cottage under the prison wall.'

The stranger in cinder-grey took no notice of this whispered string of observations, but again wetted his lips. Seeing that his friend in the chimney-corner was the only one who reciprocated his joviality in any way, he held out his cup towards that appreciative comrade, who also held out his own. They clinked together, the eyes of the rest of the room hanging upon the singer's actions. He parted his lips for the third verse; but at that moment another knock was audible upon the door. This time the knock was faint and hesitating.

The company seemed scared; the shepherd looked with consternation towards the entrance, and it was with some effort that he resisted his alarmed wife's deprecatory glance, and uttered for the third time the welcoming words, 'Walk in!'

The door was gently opened, and another man stood upon the mat. He, like those who had preceded him, was a stranger. This time it was a short, small personage, of fair complexion, and dressed in a decent suit of dark clothes.

'Can you tell me the way to ——?' he began: when, gazing round the room to observe the nature of the company amongst whom he had fallen, his eyes lighted on the stranger in cinder-grey. It was just at the instant when the latter, who had thrown his mind into his song with such a will that he scarcely heeded the interruption, silenced all whispers and inquiries by bursting into his third verse:

> To-morrow is my working day,
> > Simple shepherds all—
> To-morrow is a working day for me:
> For the farmer's sheep is slain, and the lad who did it ta'en,
> > And on his soul may God ha' merc-y!

The stranger in the chimney-corner, waving cups with the singer so heartily that his mead splashed over on the hearth, repeated in his bass voice as before:

> And on his soul may God ha' merc-y!

All this time the third stranger had been standing in the doorway. Finding now that he did not come forward or go on speaking, the guests particularly regarded him. They noticed to their surprise that he stood before them the picture of abject terror—his knees trembling, his hand shaking so violently that the door-latch by which he supported himself rattled audibly: his white lips were parted, and his eyes fixed on the merry officer of justice in the middle of the room. A moment more and he had turned, closed the door, and fled.

'What a man can it be?' said the shepherd.

The rest, between the awfulness of their late discovery and the odd conduct of this third visitor, looked as if they knew not what to think, and said nothing. Instinctively they withdrew farther and farther from the grim gentleman in their midst, whom some of them seemed to take for the Prince of Darkness himself, till they formed a remote circle, an empty space of floor being left between them and him—

> . . . circulus, cujus centrum diabolus.

The room was so silent—though there were more than twenty people in it—that nothing could be heard but the patter of the rain against the window-shutters, accompanied by the occasional hiss of a stray drop that fell down the chimney into the fire, and the steady puffing of the man in the corner, who had now resumed his pipe of long clay.

The stillness was unexpectedly broken. The distant sound of a gun reverberated through the air—apparently from the direction of the county-town.

'Be jiggered!' cried the stranger who had sung the song, jumping up.

'What does that mean?' asked several.

'A prisoner escaped from the jail—that's what it means.'

All listened. The sound was repeated, and none of them spoke but the man in the chimney-corner, who said quietly, 'I've often been told that in this county they fire a gun at such times; but I never heard it till now.'

'I wonder if it is *my* man?' murmured the personage in cinder-grey.

'Surely it is!' said the shepherd involuntarily. 'And surely we've zeed him! That little man who looked in at the door by now, and quivered like a leaf when he zeed ye and heard your song!'

'His teeth chattered, and the breath went out of his body,' said the dairyman.

'And his heart seemed to sink within him like a stone,' said Oliver Giles.

'And he bolted as if he'd been shot at,' said the hedge-carpenter.

'True—his teeth chattered, and his heart seemed to sink; and he bolted as if he'd been shot at,' slowly summed up the man in the chimney-corner.

'I didn't notice it,' remarked the hangman.

'We were all a-wondering what made him run off in such a fright,' faltered one of the women against the wall, 'and now 'tis explained!'

The firing of the alarm-gun went on at intervals, low and sullenly, and their suspicions became a certainty. The sinister gentleman in cinder-grey roused himself. 'Is there a constable here?' he asked, in thick tones. 'If so, let him step forward.'

The engaged man of fifty stepped quavering out from the wall, his betrothed beginning to sob on the back of the chair.

'You are a sworn constable?'

'I be, sir.'

'Then pursue the criminal at once, with assistance, and bring him back here. He can't have gone far.'

'I will, sir, I will—when I've got my staff. I'll go home and get it, and come sharp here, and start in a body.'

'Staff!—never mind your staff; the man'll be gone!'

'But I can't do nothing without my staff—can I, William, and John, and Charles Jake? No; for there's the king's royal crown a painted on en in yaller and gold, and the lion and the unicorn, so as when I raise en up and hit my prisoner, 'tis made a lawful blow thereby. I wouldn't 'tempt to take up a man without my staff—no, not I. If I hadn't the law to gie me courage, why, instead o' my taking up him he might take me up!'

'Now, I'm a king's man myself, and can give you authority enough for this,' said the formidable officer in grey. 'Now then, all of ye, be ready. Have ye any lanterns?'

'Yes—have ye any lanterns?—I demand it!' said the constable.

'And the rest of you able-bodied——'

'Able-bodied men—yes—the rest of ye!' said the constable.

'Have you some good stout staves and pitch-forks——'

'Staves and pitchforks—in the name o' the law! And take 'em in yer hands and go in quest, and do as we in authority tell ye!'

Thus aroused, the men prepared to give chase. The evidence was, indeed, though circumstantial, so convincing, that but little argument was needed to show the shepherd's guests that after what they had seen it would look very much like connivance if they did not instantly pursue the unhappy third stranger, who could not as yet have gone more than a few hundred yards over such uneven country.

A shepherd is always well provided with lanterns; and lighting these hastily and with hurdle-staves in their hands, they poured out of the door, taking a direction along the crest of the hill, away from the town, the rain having fortunately a little abated.

Disturbed by the noise, or possibly by unpleasant dreams of her baptism, the child who had been christened began to cry heart-brokenly in the room overhead. These notes of grief came down through the chinks of the floor to the ears of the women below, who jumped up one by one, and seemed glad of the excuse to ascend and comfort the baby, for the incidents of the last half-hour greatly oppressed them. Thus in the space of two or three minutes the room on the ground-floor was deserted quite.

But it was not for long. Hardly had the sound of footsteps died away when a man returned round the

corner of the house from the direction the pursuers
had taken. Peeping in at the door, and seeing nobody
there, he entered leisurely. It was the stranger of the
chimney-corner, who had gone out with the rest.
The motive of his return was shown by his helping
himself to a cut piece of skimmer-cake that lay on a
ledge beside where he had sat, and which he had
apparently forgotten to take with him. He also
poured out half a cup more mead from the quantity
that remained, ravenously eating and drinking these
as he stood. He had not finished when another
figure came in just as quietly—his friend in cinder-
grey.

'O—you here?' said the latter, smiling. 'I thought
you had gone to help in the capture.' And this
speaker also revealed the object of his return by
looking solicitously round for the fascinating mug
of old mead.

'And I thought you had gone,' said the other, con-
tinuing his skimmer-cake with some effort.

'Well, on second thoughts, I felt there were enough
without me,' said the first confidentially, 'and such
a night as it is, too. Besides, 'tis the business o' the
Government to take care of its criminals—not mine.'

'True; so it is. And I felt as you did, that there
were enough without me.'

'I don't want to break my limbs running over the
humps and hollows of this wild country.'

'Nor I neither, between you and me.'

'These shepherd-people are used to it—simple-
minded souls, you know, stirred up to anything in
a moment. They'll have him ready for me before
the morning, and no trouble to me at all.'

'They'll have him, and we shall have saved ourselves all labour in the matter.'

'True, true. Well, my way is to Casterbridge; and 'tis as much as my legs will do to take me that far. Going the same way?'

'No, I am sorry to say! I have to get home over there' (he nodded indefinitely to the right), 'and I feel as you do, that it is quite enough for my legs to do before bedtime.'

The other had by this time finished the mead in the mug, after which, shaking hands heartily at the door, and wishing each other well, they went their several ways.

In the meantime the company of pursuers had reached the end of the hog's-back elevation which dominated this part of the down. They had decided on no particular plan of action; and, finding that the man of the baleful trade was no longer in their company, they seemed quite unable to form any such plan now. They descended in all directions down the hill, and straightway several of the party fell into the snare set by Nature for all misguided midnight ramblers over this part of the cretaceous formation. The 'lanchets', or flint slopes, which belted the escarpment at intervals of a dozen yards, took the less cautious ones unawares, and losing their footing on the rubbly steep they slid sharply downwards, the lanterns rolling from their hands to the bottom, and there lying on their sides till the horn was scorched through.

When they had again gathered themselves together, the shepherd, as the man who knew the country best, took the lead and guided them round these treacher-ous inclines. The lanterns, which seemed rather to dazzle their eyes and warn the fugitive than to assist them in the exploration, were extinguished, due silence was observed; and in this more rational order they plunged into the vale. It was a grassy, briery, moist defile, affording some shelter to any person who had sought it; but the party perambulated it in vain, and ascended on the other side. Here they wandered apart, and after an interval closed together again to report progress. At the second time of closing in they found themselves near a lonely ash, the single tree on this part of the coomb, probably sown there by a passing bird some fifty years before. And here, standing a little to one side of the trunk, as motionless as the trunk itself, appeared the man they were in quest of, his outline being well defined against the sky beyond. The band noiselessly drew up and faced him.

'Your money or your life!' said the constable sternly to the still figure.

'No, no,' whispered John Pitcher. ''Tisn't our side ought to say that. That's the doctrine of vagabonds like him, and we be on the side of the law.'

'Well, well,' replied the constable impatiently; 'I must say something, mustn't I? and if you had all the weight o' this undertaking upon your mind, perhaps you'd say the wrong thing too!—Prisoner at the bar, surrender, in the name of the Father—the Crown, I mane!'

The man under the tree seemed now to notice them for the first time, and, giving them no opportunity whatever for exhibiting their courage, he strolled slowly towards them. He was, indeed, the little man, the third stranger; but his trepidation had in a great measure gone.

'Well, travellers,' he said, 'did I hear ye speak to me?'

'You did: you've got to come and be our prisoner at once!' said the constable. 'We arrest 'ee on the charge of not biding in Casterbridge jail in a decent proper manner to be hung to-morrow morning. Neighbours, do your duty, and seize the culpet!'

On hearing the charge, the man seemed enlightened, and, saying not another word, resigned himself with preternatural civility to the search-party, who, with their staves in their hands, surrounded him on all sides and marched him back towards the shepherd's cottage.

It was eleven o'clock by the time they arrived. The light shining from the open door, a sound of men's voices within, proclaimed to them as they approached the house that some new events had arisen in their absence. On entering they discovered the shepherd's living room to be invaded by two officers from Casterbridge jail and a well-known magistrate who lived at the nearest country-seat, intelligence of the escape having become generally circulated.

'Gentlemen,' said the constable, 'I have brought back your man—not without risk and danger; but every one must do his duty! He is inside this circle of able-bodied persons, who have lent me useful aid, considering their ignorance of Crown work. Men, bring forward your prisoner!' And the third stranger was led to the light.

'Who is this?' said one of the officials.

'The man,' said the constable.

'Certainly not,' said the turnkey; and the first corroborated his statement.

'But how can it be otherwise?' asked the constable. 'Or why was he so terrified at sight o' the singing instrument of the law who sat there?' Here he related the strange behaviour of the third stranger on entering the house during the hangman's song.

'Can't understand it,' said the officer coolly. 'All I know is that it is not the condemned man. He's quite a different character from this one; a gauntish fellow, with dark hair and eyes, rather good-looking, and with a musical bass voice that if you heard it once you'd never mistake as long as you lived.'

'Why, souls—'twas the man in the chimney-corner!

'Hey—what?' said the magistrate, coming forward after inquiring particulars from the shepherd in the background. 'Haven't you got the man after all?'

'Well, sir,' said the constable, 'he's the man we were in search of, that's true; and yet he's not the man we were in search of. For the man we were in search of was not the man we wanted, sir, if you understand my every-day way; for 'twas the man in the chimney-corner!'

'A pretty kettle of fish altogether!' said the magistrate. 'You had better start for the other man at once.'

The prisoner now spoke for the first time. The mention of the man in the chimney-corner seemed to have moved him as nothing else could do. 'Sir,' he said, stepping forward to the magistrate, 'take no more trouble about me. The time is come when I may as well speak. I have done nothing; my crime is that the condemned man is my brother. Early this afternoon I left home at Shottsford to tramp it all the way to Casterbridge jail to bid him farewell. I was benighted, and called here to rest and ask the way. When I opened the door I saw before me the very man, my brother, that I thought to see in the condemned cell at Casterbridge. He was in this chimney-corner; and jammed close to him, so that he could not have got out if he had tried, was the executioner who'd come to take his life, singing a song about it and not knowing that it was his victim who was close by, joining in to save appearances. My brother looked a glance of agony at me, and I knew he meant, "Don't reveal what you see; my life depends on it." I was so terror-struck that I could hardly stand, and, not knowing what I did, I turned and hurried away.'

The narrator's manner and tone had the stamp of truth, and his story made a great impression on all around. 'And do you know where your brother is at the present time?' asked the magistrate.

'I do not. I have never seen him since I closed this door.'

'I can testify to that, for we've been between ye ever since,' said the constable.

'Where does he think to fly to?—what is his occupation?'

'He's a watch-and-clock-maker, sir.'

''A said 'a was a wheelwright—a wicked rogue,' said the constable.

'The wheels of clocks and watches he meant, no doubt,' said Shepherd Fennel. 'I thought his hands were palish for's trade.'

'Well, it appears to me that nothing can be gained by retaining this poor man in custody,' said the magistrate; 'your business lies with the other, unquestionably.'

And so the little man was released off-hand; but he looked nothing the less sad on that account, it being beyond the power of magistrate or constable to raze out the written troubles in his brain, for they concerned another whom he regarded with more solicitude than himself. When this was done, and the man had gone his way, the night was found to be so far advanced that it was deemed useless to renew the search before the next morning.

Next day, accordingly, the quest for the clever sheep-stealer became general and keen, to all appearance at least. But the intended punishment was cruelly disproportioned to the transgression, and the sympathy of a great many country-folk in that district was strongly on the side of the fugitive. Moreover, his marvellous coolness and daring in hob-and-nobbing with the hangman, under the unprecedented circumstances of the shepherd's party, won their admiration. So that it may be questioned if all those who ostensibly made themselves so busy in exploring woods and fields and lanes were quite so thorough when it came to the private examination of their own lofts and outhouses. Stories were afloat of a mysterious figure being occasionally seen in some old overgrown trackway or other, remote from turnpike roads; but when a search was instituted in any of these suspected quarters nobody was found. Thus the days and weeks passed without tidings.

In brief, the bass-voiced man of the chimney-corner was never recaptured. Some said that he went across the sea, others that he did not, but buried himself in the depths of a populous city. At any rate the gentleman in cinder-grey never did his morning's work at Casterbridge, nor met anywhere at all, for business purposes, the genial comrade with whom he had passed an hour of relaxation in the lonely house on the coomb.

The grass has long been green on the graves of Shepherd Fennel and his frugal wife; the guests who made up the christening party have mainly followed their entertainers to the tomb; the baby in whose honour they had all met is a matron in the sere and yellow leaf. But the arrival of the three strangers at the shepherd's that night, and the details connected therewith, is a story as well known as ever in the country about Higher Crowstairs.

FRANK HARRIS

The Holy Man (*after Tolstoy*)

Paul, the eldest son of Count Stroganoff, was only thirty-two when he was made a Bishop: he was the youngest dignitary in the Greek Church, yet his diocese was among the largest: it extended for hundreds of miles along the shore of the Caspian. Even as a youth Paul had astonished people by his sincerity and gentleness, and the honours paid to him seemed to increase his lovable qualities.

Shortly after his induction he set out to visit his whole diocese in order to learn the needs of the people. On this pastoral tour he took with him two older priests in the hope that he might profit by their experience. After many disappointments he was forced to admit that they could only be used as aids to memory, or as secretaries; for they could not even understand his passionate enthusiasm. The life of Christ was the model the young Bishop set before himself, and he took joy in whatever pain or fatigue his ideal involved. His two priests thought it unbecoming in a Bishop to work so hard and to be so careless of 'dignity and state', by which they meant ease and good living. At first they grumbled a good deal at the work and with apparent reason, for, indeed, the Bishop forgot himself in his mission, and as the tour went on his body seemed to waste away in the fire of his zeal.

After he had come to the extreme southern point of his diocese he took ship and began to work his way north along the coast, in order to visit all the fishing villages.

One afternoon, after a hard morning's work, he was seated on deck resting. The little ship lay becalmed a long way from the shore, for the water was shallow and the breeze had died down in the heat of the day.

There had been rain-clouds over the land, but suddenly the sun came out hotly and the Bishop caught sight of some roofs glistening rosy-pink in the sunshine a long way off.

'What place is that?' he asked the Captain.

'Krasnavodsk, I think it is called,' replied the Captain after some hesitation, 'a little nest between the mountains and the sea; a hundred souls perhaps in all.'

(Men are commonly called 'souls' in Russia as they are called 'hands' in England.)

'One hundred souls,' repeated the Bishop, 'shut away from the world; I must visit Krasnavodsk.'

The priests shrugged their shoulders but said nothing; they knew it was no use objecting or complaining. But this time the Captain came to their aid.

'It's twenty-five versts away,' he said, 'and the sailors are done up. You'll be able to get in easily enough, but coming out again against the sea-breeze will take hard rowing.'

'To-morrow is Sunday,' rejoined the Bishop, 'and the sailors will be able to rest all day. Please, Captain, tell them to get out the boat. I wouldn't ask for myself,' he added in a low voice.

The Captain understood; the boat was got out, and under her little lug-sail reached the shore in a couple of hours.

Lermontoff, the big helmsman, stepped at once into the shallow water and carried the Bishop on his back up the beach so that he shouldn't get wet. The two priests got to land as best they could.

At the first cottage the Bishop asked an old man, who was cutting sticks, where the church was.

'Church,' repeated the peasant, 'there isn't one.'

'Haven't you any pope, any priest here?' inquired the Bishop.

'What's that?'

'Surely,' replied the Bishop, 'you have some one here who visits the dying and prays with them, some one who attends to the sick women and children?'

'Oh, yes,' cried the old man, straightening himself; 'we have a holy man.'

'Holy man?' repeated the Bishop, 'who is he?'

'Oh, a good man, a saint,' replied the old peasant, 'he does everything for any one in need.'

'Is he a Christian?'

'I don't think so,' the old man rejoined, shaking his head, 'I've never heard that name.'

'Do you pay him for his services?' asked the Bishop.

'No, no,' was the reply, 'he would not take anything.'

'How does he live?' the Bishop probed farther.

'Like the rest of us he works in his little garden.'

'Show me where he lives: will you?' said the Bishop gently, and at once the old man put down his axe and led the way among the scattered huts.

In a few moments they came to the cottage standing in a square of cabbages. It was just like the other cottages in the village, poverty-stricken and weather-worn, wearing its patches without thought of concealment.

The old man opened the door:

'Some visitors for you, Ivanushka,' he said, standing aside to let the Bishop and his priests pass in.

The Bishop saw before him a broad, thin man of about sixty, dressed half like a peasant, half like a fisherman; he wore the usual sheepskin and high fisherman's boots. The only noticeable thing in his appearance was the way his silver hair and beard contrasted with the dark tan of his skin; his eyes were clear, blue, and steady.

'Come in, Excellency,' he said, 'come in,' and he hastily dusted a stool with his sleeve for the Bishop and placed it for him with a low bow.

'Thank you,' said the Bishop, taking the seat, 'I am somewhat tired, and the rest will be grateful. But be seated, too,' he added, for the 'holy man' was standing before him bowed in an attitude of respectful attention. Without a word Ivan drew up a stool and sat down.

'I was surprised,' the Bishop began, 'to find you have no church here, and no priest; the peasant who showed us the way did not even know what "Christian" meant.'

The holy man looked at him with his patient eyes, but said nothing, so the Bishop went on:

'You're a Christian: are you not?'

'I have not heard that name before,' said the holy man.

The Bishop lifted his eyebrows in surprise.

'Why then do you attend to the poor and ailing in their need?' he argued; 'why do you help them?'

The holy man looked at him for a moment, and then replied quietly:

'I was helped when I was young and needed it.'

'But what religion have you?' asked the Bishop.

'Religion,' the old man repeated, wonderingly, 'what is religion?'

'We call ourselves Christians,' the Bishop began, 'because Jesus, the founder of our faith, was called Christ. Jesus was the Son of God, and came down from heaven with the Gospel of Good Tidings; He taught men that they were the children of God, and that God is love.'

The face of the old man lighted up and he leaned forward eagerly:

'Tell me about Him, please.'

The Bishop told him the story of Jesus, and when he came to the end the old man cried:

'What a beautiful story! I've never heard or imagined such a story.'

'I intend,' said the Bishop, 'as soon as I get home again, to send you a priest, and he will establish a church here where you can worship God, and he will teach you the whole story of the suffering and death of the divine Master.'

'That will be good of you,' cried the old man, warmly, 'we shall be very glad to welcome him.'

The Bishop was touched by the evident sincerity of his listener.

'Before I go,' he said, 'and I shall have to go soon, because it will take us some hours to get out to the ship again, I should like to tell you the prayer that Jesus taught His disciples.'

'I should like very much to hear it,' the old man said quietly.

'Let us kneel down then,' said the Bishop, 'as a sign of reverence, and repeat it after me, for we are all brethren together in the love of the Master;' and saying this he knelt down, and the old man immediately knelt down beside him and clasped his hands as the Bishop clasped his and repeated the sentences as they dropped from the Bishop's lips.

'Our Father, which art in heaven, hallowed be Thy name.'

When the old man had repeated the words, the Bishop went on:

'Thy kingdom come. Thy will be done in earth as it is in heaven.'

The fervour with which the old man repeated the words 'Thy will be done in earth, as it is in heaven' was really touching.

The Bishop continued:

'Give us this day our daily bread. And forgive us our debts,[1] as we forgive our debtors.'

'Give . . . give——,' repeated the old man, having apparently forgotten the words.

'Give us this day our daily bread,' repeated the Bishop, 'and forgive us our debts as we forgive our debtors.'

'Give and forgive,' said the old man at length . . . 'Give and forgive,' and the Bishop seeing that his memory was weak took up the prayer again:

'And lead us not into temptation, but deliver us from evil.'

Again the old man repeated the words with an astonishing fervour, 'And lead us not into temptation, but deliver us from evil.'

And the Bishop concluded:

'For Thine is the kingdom, and the power, and the glory, for ever. Amen.'

The old man's voice had an accent of loving and passionate sincerity as he said 'For thine is the

[1] This form of the Lord's Prayer is evidently taken from Matthew.

kingdom, and the power and the beauty, for ever and ever. Amen.'

The Bishop rose to his feet and his host followed his example, and when he held out his hand the old man clasped it in both his, saying:

'How can I ever thank you for telling me that beautiful story of Christ; how can I ever thank you enough for teaching me His prayer?'

As one in an ecstasy he repeated the words: 'Thy kingdom come. Thy will be done in earth as it is in heaven. . . '

Touched by his reverent, heartfelt sincerity, the Bishop treated him with great kindness; he put his hand on his shoulder and said:

'As soon as I get back I will send you a priest, who will teach you more, much more than I have had time to teach you; he will indeed tell you all you want to know of our religion—the love by which we live, the hope in which we die.' Before he could stop him the old man had bent his head and kissed the Bishop's hand; the tears stood in his eyes as he did him reverence.

He accompanied the Bishop to the water's edge, and, seeing the Bishop hesitate on the brink waiting for the steersman to carry him to the boat, the 'holy man' stooped and took the Bishop in his arms and strode with him through the water and put him gently on the cushioned seat in the sternsheets as if he had been a little child, much to the surprise of the Bishop and of Lermontoff, who said as if to himself:

'That fellow's as strong as a young man.'

For a long time after the boat had left the shore the old man stood on the beach waving his hands to the Bishop and his companions; but when they were well out to sea, on the second tack, he turned and went up to his cottage and disappeared from their sight.

A little later the Bishop, turning to his priests, said:

'What an interesting experience! What a wonderful old man! Didn't you notice how fervently he said the Lord's Prayer?'

'Yes,' replied the younger priest indifferently,' he was trying to show off, I thought.'

'No, no,' cried the Bishop. 'His sincerity was manifest and his goodness too. Did you notice that he said "give and forgive" instead of just repeating the words? And if you think of it, "give us this day our daily bread and forgive us our debts as we forgive our debtors" seems a little like a bargain. I'm not sure that the simple word "give and forgive" is not better, more in the spirit of Jesus?'

The younger priest shrugged his shoulders as if the question had no interest for him.

'Perhaps that's what the old man meant?' questioned the Bishop after a pause.

But as neither of the priests answered him, he went on, as if thinking aloud:

'At the end again he used the word "beauty" for "glory". I wonder was that unconscious? In any case an extraordinary man and good, I am sure, out of sheer kindness and sweetness of nature, as many men are good in Russia. No wonder our *moujiks* call it "Holy Russia"; no wonder, when you can find men like that.'

'They are as ignorant as pigs,' cried the other priests, 'not a soul in the village can either read or write: they are heathens, barbarians. They've never even heard of Christ and don't know what religion means.'

The Bishop looked at them and said nothing; seemingly he preferred his own thoughts.

It was black night when they came to the ship, and at once they all went to their cabins to sleep; for the day had been very tiring.

The Bishop had been asleep perhaps a couple of hours when he was awakened by the younger priest shaking him and saying:

'Come on deck quickly, quickly, Excellency, something extraordinary's happening, a light on the sea and no one can make out what it is!'

'A light,' exclaimed the Bishop, getting out of bed and beginning to draw on his clothes.

'Yes, a light on the water,' repeated the priest; 'but come quickly, please; the Captain sent me for you.'

When the Bishop reached the deck, the Captain was standing with his night-glass to his eyes, looking over the waste of water to leeward, where, indeed, a light could be seen flickering close to the surface of the sea; it appeared to be a hundred yards or so away.

'What is it?' cried the Bishop, astonished by the fact that all the sailors had crowded round and were staring at the light.

'What is it?' repeated the Captain gruffly, for he was greatly moved; 'it's a man with a grey beard; he has a lantern in his right hand, and he's walking on the water.'

'But no one can walk on the water,' said the Bishop gently. 'It would be a miracle,' he added, in a tone of remonstrance.

'Miracle or not,' retorted the Captain, taking the glass from his eyes, 'that's what I see, and the man'll be here soon, for he's coming towards us. Look, you,' and he handed the glass to one of the sailors as he spoke.

The light still went on swaying about as if indeed it were being carried in the hand of a man. The sailor had hardly put the night-glass to his eyes, when he cried out:

'That's what it is!—a man walking on the water . . . it's the "holy man" who carried your Excellency on board the boat this afternoon.'

'God help us!' cried the priests, crossing themselves.

'He'll be here in a moment or two,' added the sailor, 'he's coming quickly,' and, indeed, almost at once the old man came to them from the water and stepped over the low bulwark on to the deck.

At this the priests went down on their knees, thinking it was some miracle, and the sailors, including the Captain, followed their example, leaving the Bishop standing awe-stricken and uncertain in their midst.

The 'holy man' came forward, and, stretching out his hands, said:

'I'm afraid I've disturbed you, Excellency: but soon after you left me, I found I had forgotten part of that beautiful prayer and I could not bear you to go away and think me careless of all you had taught me, and so I came to ask you to help my memory just once more.' . . .

'I remember the first part of the prayer and the last words as if I had been hearing it all my life and knew it in my soul, but the middle has escaped me.' . . .

'I remember "Our Father, which art in heaven, Hallowed be Thy name. Thy kingdom come. Thy will be done in earth as it is in heaven," and then all I can remember is, "Give and forgive," and the end,

"And lead us not into temptation, but deliver us from evil. For Thine is the kingdom, and the power and the beauty for ever and ever. Amen."

'But I've forgotten some words in the middle: won't you tell me the middle again?'

'How did you come to us?' asked the Bishop in awed wonderment. 'How did you walk on the water?'

'Oh, that's easy,' replied the old man, 'any one can do that; whatever you love and trust in this world loves you in return. We love the water that makes everything pure and sweet for us, and is never tired of cleansing, and the water loves us in return; any one can walk on it; but won't you teach me that beautiful prayer, the prayer Jesus taught His disciples?'

The Bishop shook his head, and in a low voice, as if to himself, said:

'I don't think I can teach you anything about Jesus the Christ. You know a great deal already. I only wish——'

A Garden Plot

THE able-bodied men of the village were at work, the children were at school singing the multiplication-table lullaby, while the wives and mothers at home nursed the baby with one hand and did the housework with the other. At the end of the village an old man past work sat at a rough deal table under the creaking signboard of the Cauliflower, gratefully drinking from a mug of ale supplied by a chance traveller who sat opposite him.

The shade of the elms was pleasant and the ale good. The traveller filled his pipe and, glancing at the dusty hedges and the white road baking in the sun, called for the mugs to be refilled, and pushed his pouch towards his companion. After which he paid a compliment to the appearance of the village.

'It ain't what it was when I was a boy,' quavered the old man, filling his pipe with trembling fingers. 'I mind when the grindstone was stuck just outside the winder o' the forge instead o' being one side as it now is; and as for the shop winder—it's twice the size it was when I was a young 'un.'

He lit his pipe with the scientific accuracy of a smoker of sixty years' standing, and shook his head solemnly as he regarded his altered birthplace. Then his colour heightened and his dim eyes flashed.

'It's the people about 'ere 'as changed more than the place 'as,' he said, with sudden fierceness; 'there's a set o' men about here nowadays as are no good to anybody; reg'lar raskels. And if you've the mind to listen I can tell you of one or two as couldn't be beat in London itself.

'There's Tom Adams for one. He went and started wot 'e called a Benevolent Club. Threepence a week each we paid agin sickness or accident, and Tom was secretary. Three weeks arter the club was started he caught a chill and was laid up for a month. He got back to work a week, and then 'e sprained something in 'is leg; and arter that was well 'is inside went wrong. We didn't think much of it at first, not understanding figures; but at the end o' six months the club hadn't got a farthing, and they was in Tom's debt one pound seventeen-and-six.

'He isn't the only one o' that sort in the place, either. There was Herbert Richardson. He went to town, and came back with the idea of a Goose Club for Christmas. We paid twopence a week into that for pretty near ten months, and then Herbert went back to town again, and all we 'ear of 'im, through his sister, is that he's still there and doing well, and don't know when he'll be back.

'But the artfullest and worst man in this place— and that's saying a good deal, mind you—is Bob Pretty. Deep is no word for 'im. There's no way of being up to 'im. It's through 'im that we lost our Flower Show; and, if you'd like to 'ear the rights o' that, I don't suppose there's anybody in this place as knows as much about it as I do—barring Bob hisself that is, but 'e wouldn't tell it to you as plain as I can.

'We'd only 'ad the Flower Show one year, and little anybody thought that the next one was to be the last. The first year you might smell the place a mile off in the summer, and on the day of the show people came from a long way round, and brought money to spend at the Cauliflower and other places.

'It was started just after we got our new parson, and Mrs. Pawlett, the parson's wife, 'is name being Pawlett, thought as she'd encourage men to love their 'omes and be better 'usbands by giving a prize every year for the best cottage garden. Three pounds was the prize, and a metal teapot with writing on it.

'As I said, we only 'ad it two years. The fust year the garden as got it was a picter, and Bill Chambers, 'im as won the prize, used to say as 'e was out o' pocket by it, taking 'is time and the money 'e spent on flowers. Not as we believed that, you understand, 'specially as Bill did 'is very best to get it the next year, too. 'E didn't get it, and though p'r'aps most of us was glad 'e didn't, we was all very surprised at the way it turned out in the end.

'The Flower Show was to be 'eld on the 5th o' July, just as a'most everything about here was at its best. On the 15th of June Bill Chambers's garden seemed to be leading, but Peter Smith and Joe Gubbins and Sam Jones and Henery Walker was almost as good, and it was understood that more than one of 'em had got a surprise which they'd produce at the last moment, too late for the others to copy. We used to sit up here of an evening at this Cauliflower public-house and put money on it. I put mine on Henery Walker, and the time I spent in 'is garden 'elping 'im is a sin and a shame to think of.

'Of course some of 'em used to make fun of it, and Bob Pretty was the worst of 'em all. He was always a lazy, good-for-nothing man, and 'is garden was a disgrace. He'd chuck down any rubbish in it: old bones, old tins, bits of an old bucket, anything to make it untidy. He used to larf at 'em awful about their gardens and about being took up by the parson's wife. Nobody ever see 'im do any work, real 'ard work, but the smell from 'is place at dinner-time was always nice, and I believe that he knew more about game than the parson hisself did.

'It was the day arter this one I'm speaking about, the 16th o' June, that the trouble all began, and it came about in a very eggstrordinary way. George English, a quiet man getting into years, who used when 'e was younger to foller the sea, and whose only misfortin was that 'e was a brother-in-law o' Bob Pretty's, his sister marrying Bob while 'e was at sea and knowing nothing about it, 'ad a letter come from a mate of his who 'ad gone to Australia to live. He'd 'ad letters from Australia before, as we all knew from Miss Wicks at the post office, but this one upset him altogether. He didn't seem like to know what to do about it.

'While he was wondering Bill Chambers passed. He always did pass George's house about that time in the evening, it being on 'is way 'ome, and he saw George standing at 'is gate with a letter in 'is 'and looking very puzzled.

'"Evenin', George," ses Bill.

'"Evenin'," ses George.

'"Not bad news, I 'ope?" ses Bill, noticing 'is manner, and thinking it was strange.

'"No," ses George. "I've just 'ad a very eggstrordinary letter from Australia," he ses, "that's all."

'Bill Chambers was always a very inquisitive sort o' man, and he stayed and talked to George until George, arter fust making him swear oaths that 'e wouldn't tell a soul, took 'im inside and showed 'im the letter.

'It was more like a story-book than a letter. George's mate, John Biggs by name, wrote to say that an uncle of his who had just died, on 'is deathbed told him that thirty years ago he 'ad been in this very village, staying at this 'ere very Cauliflower, whose beer we're drinking now. In the night, when everybody was asleep, he got up and went quiet-like and buried a bag of five hundred and seventeen sovereigns and one half-sovereign in one of the cottage gardens till 'e could come for it agin. He didn't say 'ow he come by the money, and, when Bill spoke about that, George English said that, knowing the man, he was afraid 'e 'adn't come by it honest, but anyway his friend John Biggs wanted it, and, wot was more, 'ad asked 'im in the letter to get it for 'im.

'"And wot I'm to do about it, Bill," he ses, "I don't know. All the directions he gives is, that 'e thinks it was the tenth cottage on the right-'and side of the road, coming down from the Cauliflower. He thinks it's the tenth, but 'e's not quite sure. Do you think I'd better make it known and offer a reward of ten shillings, say, to any one who finds it?"

'"No," ses Bill, shaking 'is 'ead. "I should hold on a bit if I was you, and think it over. I shouldn't tell another single soul, if I was you."

'"I b'lieve you're right," ses George. "John Biggs would never forgive me if I lost that money for 'im. You'll remember about it keeping secret, Bill?"

'Bill swore he wouldn't tell a soul, and 'e went off 'ome and 'ad his supper, and then 'e walked up the road to the Cauliflower and back, and then up and back again, thinking over what George 'ad been telling 'im, and noticing, what 'e'd never taken the trouble to notice before, that 'is very house was the tenth one from the Cauliflower.

'Mrs. Chambers woke up at two o'clock next morning and told Bill to get up farther, and then found 'e wasn't there. She was rather surprised at first, but she didn't think much of it, and thought, what happened to be true, that 'e was busy in the garden, it being a light night. She turned over and went to sleep again, and at five when she woke up she could distinctly 'ear Bill working 'is 'ardest. Then she went to the winder and nearly dropped as she saw Bill in his shirt and trousers digging away like mad. A quarter of the garden was all dug up, and she shoved open the winder and screamed out to know what 'e was doing.

'Bill stood up straight and wiped 'is face with his shirt-sleeve and started digging again, and then his wife just put something on and rushed downstairs as fast as she could go.

'"What on earth are you a-doing of, Bill?" she screams.

'"Go indoors," ses Bill, still digging.

'"Have you gone mad?" she ses, half crying.

'Bill just stopped to throw a lump of mould at her, and then went on digging till Henery Walker who also thought 'e 'ad gone mad, and didn't want to stop 'im too soon, put 'is 'ead over the 'edge and asked 'im the same thing.

'"Ask no questions and you'll 'ear no lies, and keep your ugly face your own side of the 'edge," ses Bill. "Take it indoors and frighten the children with," he ses. "I don't want it staring at me."

'Henery walked off offended, and Bill went on with his digging. He wouldn't go to work, and 'e 'ad his breakfast in the garden, and his wife spent all the morning in the front answering the neighbour's questions and begging of 'em to go in and say something to Bill. One of 'em did go, and came back a'most directly and stood there for hours telling diff'rent people wot Bill 'ad said to '*er*, and asking whether 'e couldn't be locked up for it.

'By tea-time Bill was dead-beat, and that stiff he could 'ardly raise 'is bread and butter to his mouth. Several o' the chaps looked in in the evening, but all they could get out of 'im was, that it was a new way o' cultivating 'is garden 'e 'ad just 'eard of, and that those who lived the longest would see the most. By night-time 'e'd nearly finished the job, and 'is garden was just ruined.

'Afore people 'ad done talking about Bill, I'm blest if Peter Smith didn't go and cultivate 'is garden in exactly the same way. The parson and 'is wife was away on their 'oliday, and nobody could say a word. The curate who 'ad come over to take 'is place for a time, and who took the names of people for the Flower Show, did point out to 'im that he was spoiling 'is chances, but Peter was so rude to 'im that he didn't stay long enough to say much.

'When Joe Gubbins started digging up 'is garden people began to think they were all bewitched, and I went round to see Henery Walker to tell 'im wot a fine chance 'e'd got, and to remind 'im that I'd put another ninepence on 'im the night before. All 'e said was: "More fool you." and went on digging a 'ole in his garden big enough to put a 'ouse in.

'In a fortnight's time there wasn't a garden worth looking at in the place, and it was quite clear there'd be no Flower Show that year, and of all the silly, bad-tempered men in the place them as 'ad dug up their pretty gardens was the wust.

'It was just a few days before the day fixed for the Flower Show, and I was walking up the road when I see Joe and Henery Walker and one or two more

leaning over Bob Pretty's fence and talking to 'im.
I stopped too, to see what they were looking at and
found they was watching Bob's two boys a-weeding
of 'is garden. It was a disgraceful, untidy sort of
place, as I said before, with a few marigolds and
nasturtiums, and sich-like put in anywhere, and Bob
was walking up and down smoking of 'is pipe and
watching 'is wife hoe atween the plants and cut off
dead marigold blooms.

'"That's a pretty garden you've got there, Bob,"
ses Joe, grinning.

'"I've seen wuss," ses Bob.

'"Going in for the Flower Show, Bob?" ses
Henery, with a wink at us.

'"O' course I am," ses Bob, 'olding 'is 'ead up;
"my marigolds ought to pull me through," he ses.

'Henery wouldn't believe it at fust, but when he
saw Bob show 'is missus 'ow to pat the path down
with the back o' the spade and hold the nails for 'er
while she nailed a climbing nasturtium to the fence,
he went off and fetched Bill Chambers and one or
two others, and they all leaned over the fence
breathing their 'ardest and a-saying of all the nasty
things to Bob they could think of.

'"It's the best-kep' garden in the place," ses Bob.
"I ain't afraid o' your new way o' cultivating flowers,
Bill Chambers. Old-fashioned ways suit me best; I
learnt 'ow to grow flowers from my father."

'"You ain't 'ad the cheek to give your name in,
Bob?" ses Sam Jones, staring.

'Bob didn't answer 'im. "Pick those bits o' grass
out o' the path, old gal," he ses to 'is wife; "they
look untidy, and untidiness I can't abear."

'He walked up and down smoking 'is pipe and
pretending not to notice Henery Walker, wot 'ad

moved farther along the fence, and was staring at some drabble-tailed-looking geraniums as if 'e'd seen 'em afore but wasn't quite sure where.

'"Admiring my geraniums, Henery?" ses Bob at last.

'"Where'd you get 'em?" ses Henery, 'ardly able to speak.

'"My florist's," says Bob in a off-hand manner.

'"Your *wot*?" asks Henery.

'"My florist," ses Bob.

'"And who might 'e be when 'e's at home?" asked Henery.

'"'Tain't so likely I'm going to tell you that," ses Bob. "Be reasonable, Henery, and ask yourself whether it's likely I should tell you 'is name. Why, I've never seen sich fine geraniums afore. I've been nursing 'em inside all the summer, and just planted 'em out."

'"About two days arter I threw mine over my back fence," ses Henery Walker, speaking very slowly.

'"Ho," ses Bob, surprised. "I didn't know you 'ad any geraniums, Henery. I thought you was digging for gravel this year."

'Henery didn't answer him. Not because 'e didn't want to, mind you, but because he couldn't.

'"That one," ses Bob, pointing to a broken geranium with the stem of 'is pipe, "is a 'Dook o' Wellington,' and that white one there is wot I'm going to call 'Pretty's Pride.' That fine marigold over there, wot looks like a sunflower, is called 'Golden Dreams.'"

'"Come along, Henery," ses Bill Chambers, bursting, "come and get something to take the taste out of your mouth."

'"I'm sorry I can't offer you a flower for your

button-'ole," ses Bob, perlitely, "but it's getting so near the Flower Show now I can't afford it. If you chaps only knew wot pleasure was to be 'ad sitting among your innercent flowers, you wouldn't want to go to the public-house so often."

'He shook 'is 'ead at 'em, and telling his wife to give the "Dook o' Wellington" a mug of water, sat down in the chair agin and wiped the sweat off 'is brow.

'Bill Chambers did a bit o' thinking as they walked up the road, and by and by 'e turns to Joe Gubbins and 'e ses:

'"Seen anything o' George English lately, Joe?"

'"*Yes*," ses Joe.

'"Seems to me we all 'ave," ses Sam Jones.

'None of 'em liked to say wot was in their minds, 'aving all seen George English and swore pretty strong not to tell his secret, and none of 'em liking to own up that they'd been digging up their gardens to get money as 'e'd told 'em about. But presently Bill Chambers ses: "Without telling no secrets or breaking no promises, Joe, supposing a certain 'ouse was mentioned in a certain letter from forrin parts, wot 'ouse was it?"

'"Supposing it was so," ses Joe, careful, too; "the second 'ouse, counting the Cauliflower."

'"The ninth 'ouse, you mean," ses Henery Walker sharply.

'"Second 'ouse in Mill Lane, you mean," ses Sam Jones, wot lived there.

'Then they all see 'ow they'd been done, and that they wasn't, in a manner o' speaking, referring to the same letter. They came up and sat 'ere where we're sitting now, all dazed-like. It wasn't only the chance o' losing the prize that upset 'em, but they'd wasted their time and ruined their gardens and got called mad by the other folks. Henery Walker's state o' mind was dreadful for to see, and he kep' thinking of 'orrible things to say to George English, and then being afraid they wasn't strong enough.

'While they was talking who should come along but George English hisself! He came right up to the table, and they all sat back on the bench and stared at 'im fierce, and Henery Walker crinkled 'is nose at him.

'"Evening," he ses, but none of 'em answered 'im; they all looked at Henery to see wot 'e was going to say.

'"Wot's up?" ses George in surprise.

'"*Gardens*," ses Henery.

'"So I've 'eard," ses George.

'He shook his 'ead and looked at them sorrowful and severe at the same time.

'"So I 'eard, and I couldn't believe my ears till I went and looked for myself," he ses, "and wot I want to say is this: you know wot I'm referring to. If any man 'as found wot don't belong to him 'e knows who to give it to. It ain't wot I should 'ave expected of men wot's lived in the same place as *me* for years. Talk about honesty," 'e ses, shaking 'is 'ead agin, "I should like to see a little of it."

'Peter Smith opened his mouth to speak, and 'ardly knowing wot 'e was doing took a pull at 'is beer at the same time, and if Sam Jones 'adn't been by to thump 'im on the back I b'lieve he'd ha' died there and then.

'"Mark my words," ses George English, speaking very slow and solemn, "there'll be no blessing on it. Whoever's made 'is fortune by getting up and digging 'is garden over won't get no real benefit from it. He may wear a black coat and new trousers on Sunday, but 'e won't be 'appy. I'll go and get my little taste 'o beer somewhere else," 'e ses. "I can't breathe here."

'He walked off before any one could say a word; Bill Chambers dropped 'is pipe and smashed it. Henery Walker sat staring after 'im with 'is mouth wide open, and Sam Jones, who was always one to take advantage, drank 'is own beer under the firm belief that it was Joe's.

'"I shall take care that Mrs. Pawlett 'ears o' this," ses Henery at last.

'"And be asked wot you dug your garden up for," ses Joe, "and 'ave to explain that you broke your promise to George. Why, she'd talk at us for years and years."

'"And parson 'ud preach a sermon about it," ses Sam; "where's your sense, Henery?"

'"We should be the larfing-stock for miles round," ses Bill Chambers. "If anybody wants to know, I dug my garden up to enrich the soil for next year, and also to give some other chap a chance of the prize."

'Peter Smith 'as always been a unfortunit man; he's got the name for it. He was just 'aving another drink as Bill said that, and this time we all thought 'e'd gorn. He did hisself.

'Mrs. Pawlett and the parson came 'ome next day, an' 'er voice got that squeaky with surprise it was painful to listen to her. All the chaps stuck to the tale that they'd dug their garden up to give the others a chance, and Henery Walker, 'e went farther and said it was owing to a sermon on unselfishness wot the curate 'ad preached three weeks afore. He 'ad a nice little red-covered 'ymn-book the next day with "From a friend" wrote in it.

'All things considered, Mrs. Pawlett was for doing away with the Flower Show that year and giving two prizes next year instead, but one or two other chaps, encouraged by Bob's example, 'ad given in their names too, and they said it wouldn't be fair to their wives. All the gardens but one was worse than Bob's, the men not having started till later than wot 'e did, and not being able to get their geraniums from 'is florist. The only better garden was Ralph Thomson's, who lived next door to 'im, but two nights afore the Flower Show 'is pig got walking in its sleep. Ralph said it was a mystery to 'im 'ow the pig could ha' got out; it must ha' put its foot through a hole too small for it, and turned the button of its door, and then climbed over a four-foot fence. He told Bob 'e wished the pig could speak, but Bob said that that was sinful and unchristian of 'im, and that most likely if it could, it would only call 'im a lot o' bad names, and ask 'im why he didn't feed it properly.

'There was quite a crowd on Flower Show day following the judges. First of all, to Bill Chambers's astonishment and surprise, they went to 'is place and stood on the 'eaps in 'is garden judging 'em, while Bill peeped at 'em through the kitchen winder 'arf crazy. They went to every garden in the place, until one of the young ladies got tired of it, and asked Mrs. Pawlett whether they was there to judge cottage gardens or earthquakes.

'Everybody 'eld their breaths that evening in the schoolroom when Mrs. Pawlett got up on the platform and took a slip of paper from one of the judges. She stood a moment waiting for silence, and then 'eld up her 'and to stop what she thought was clapping at the back, but which was two or three wimmin who 'ad 'ad to take their crying babies out, trying to quiet 'em in the porch. Then Mrs. Pawlett put 'er glasses on her nose and just read out, short and sweet, that the prize of three sovereigns and a metal teapot for the best-kept cottage garden 'ad been won by Mr. Robert Pretty.

'One or two people patted Bob on the back as 'e walked up the middle to take the prize; then one or two more did, and Bill Chambers's pat was the 'eartiest of 'em all. Bob stopped and spoke to 'im about it.

'You would 'ardly think that Bob 'ud have the cheek to stand up there and make a speech, but 'e did. He said it gave 'im great pleasure to take the teapot and the money, and the more pleasure because 'e felt that 'e had earned 'em. He said that if 'e told 'em all 'e'd done to make sure o' the prize they'd be surprised. He said that 'e'd been like Ralph Thomson's pig, up early and late.

'He stood up there talking as though 'e was never going to leave off, and said that 'e hoped as 'is example would be a benefit to 'is neighbours. Some of 'em seemed to think that digging was everything, but 'e could say with pride that 'e 'adn't put a spade to 'is garden for three years until a week ago, and then not much.

'He finished 'is remarks by saying that 'e was going to give a tea-party up at the Cauliflower to christen the teapot, where 'e'd be pleased to welcome all friends. Quite a crowd got up and followed 'im out then, instead o' waiting for the dissolving views, and came back 'arf an hour arterwards, saying that until they'd got as far as the Cauliflower they'd no idea as Bob was so pertickler who 'e mixed with.

'That was the last Flower Show we ever 'ad in Claybury, Mrs. Pawlett and the judges meeting the

tea-party coming 'ome, and 'aving to get over a gate
into a field, to let it pass. What with that and Mrs.
Pawlett tumbling over something farther up the
road, which turned out to be the teapot, smelling
strongly of beer, the Flower Show was given up,
and the parson preached three Sundays running on
the sin of beer-drinking to children who'd never
'ad any and wimmen who couldn't get it.'

H. G. WELLS

A Slip under the Microscope

Outside the laboratory windows was a watery-grey fog, and within a close warmth and the yellow light of the green-shaded gas lamps that stood two to each table down its narrow length. On each table stood a couple of glass jars containing the mangled vestiges of the crayfish, mussels, frogs, and guineapigs upon which the students had been working, and down the side of the room, facing the windows, were shelves bearing bleached dissections in spirits, surmounted by a row of beautifully executed anatomical drawings in whitewood frames and overhanging a row of cubical lockers. All the doors of the laboratory were panelled with blackboard, and on these were the half-erased diagrams of the previous day's work. The laboratory was empty, save for the demonstrator, who sat near the preparation-room door, and silent, save for a low, continuous murmur, and the clicking of the rocker microtome at which he was working. But scattered about the room were traces of numerous students: hand-bags, polished boxes of instruments, in one place a large drawing covered by newspaper, and in another a prettily bound copy of *News from Nowhere*, a book oddly at variance with its surroundings. These things had been put down hastily as the students had arrived and hurried at once to secure their seats in the adjacent lecture theatre. Deadened by the closed door, the measured accents of the professor sounded as a featureless muttering.

Presently, faint through the closed windows came

the sound of the Oratory clock striking the hour of eleven. The clicking of the microtome ceased, and the demonstrator looked at his watch, rose, thrust his hands into his pockets, and walked slowly down the laboratory towards the lecture theatre door. He stood listening for a moment, and then his eye fell on the little volume by William Morris. He picked it up, glanced at the title, smiled, opened it, looked at the name on the fly-leaf, ran the leaves through with his hand, and put it down. Almost immediately the even murmur of the lecturer ceased, there was a sudden burst of pencils rattling on the desks in the lecture theatre, a stirring, a scraping of feet, and a number of voices speaking together. Then a firm footfall approached the door, which began to open, and stood ajar as some indistinctly heard question arrested the new-comer.

The demonstrator turned, walked slowly back past the microtome, and left the laboratory by the preparation-room door. As he did so, first one, and then several students carrying notebooks entered the laboratory from the lecture theatre, and distributed themselves among the little tables, or stood in a group about the doorway. They were an exceptionally heterogeneous assembly, for while Oxford and Cambridge still recoil from the blushing prospect of mixed classes, the College of Science anticipated America in the matter years ago—mixed socially too, for the prestige of the College is high, and its scholarships, free of any age limit, dredge deeper even than do those of the Scotch universities. The class numbered one-and-twenty, but some remained in the theatre questioning the professor, copying the blackboard diagrams before they were washed off, or examining the special specimens he had produced to illustrate the day's teaching. Of the nine who had come into the laboratory three were girls, one of whom, a little fair woman wearing spectacles and dressed in greyish-green, was peering out of the window at the fog, while the other two, both whole-some-looking, plain-faced schoolgirls, unrolled and put on the brown holland aprons they wore while dissecting. Of the men, two went down the laboratory to their places, one a pallid, dark-bearded man, who had once been a tailor; the other a pleasant-featured, ruddy young man of twenty, dressed in a well-fitting brown suit; young Wedderburn, the son of Wedderburn the eye specialist. The others formed a little knot near the theatre door. One of these, a dwarfed, spectacled figure with a hunch back, sat on a bent wood stool; two others, one a short, dark youngster and the other a flaxen-haired, reddish-complexioned young man, stood leaning side by side against the slate sink, while the fourth stood facing them, and maintained the larger share of the conversation.

This last person was named Hill. He was a sturdily built young fellow, of the same age as Wedderburn; he had a white face, dark grey eyes, hair of an indeterminate colour, and prominent, irregular features. He talked rather louder than was needful and thrust his hands deeply into his pockets. His collar was frayed and blue with the starch of a careless laundress, his clothes were evidently ready-made, and there was a patch on the side of his boot near the toe. And as he talked or listened to the others, he glanced now and again towards the lecture theatre door. They were discussing the depressing perora-tion of the lecture they had just heard, the last lecture it was in the introductory course in zoology.

'From ovum to ovum is the goal of the higher vertebrata,' the lecturer had said in his melancholy tones, and so had neatly rounded off the sketch of comparative anatomy he had been developing. The spectacled hunchback had repeated it with noisy appreciation, had tossed it towards the fair-haired student with an evident provocation, and had started one of those vague, rambling discussions on generalities so unaccountably dear to the student mind all the world over.

'That is our goal, perhaps—I admit it, as far as science goes,' said the fair-haired student, rising to the challenge. 'But there are things above science.'

'Science,' said Hill confidently, 'is systematic knowledge. Ideas that don't come into the system— must anyhow—be loose ideas.' He was not quite sure whether that was a clever saying or a fatuity until his hearers took it seriously.

'The thing I cannot understand,' said the hunchback, at large, 'is whether Hill is a materialist or not.'

'There is one thing above matter,' said Hill promptly, feeling he made a better point this time, aware, too, of some one in the doorway behind him, and raising his voice a trifle for her benefit, 'and that is, the delusion that there is something above matter.'

'So we have your gospel at last,' said the fair student. 'It's all a delusion, is it? All our aspirations to lead something more than dogs' lives, all our work for anything beyond ourselves. But see how inconsistent you are. Your socialism, for instance. Why do you trouble about the interests of the race? Why do you concern yourself about the beggar in the gutter? Why are you bothering yourself to lend that book'—he indicated William Morris by a movement of the head—'to every one in the lab.?'

'Girl,' said the hunchback indistinctly, and glanced guiltily over his shoulder.

The girl in brown, with the brown eyes, had come into the laboratory, and stood on the other side of the table behind him, with her rolled-up apron in one hand, looking over her shoulder, listening to the discussion. She did not notice the hunchback, because she was glancing from Hill to his interlocutor. Hill's consciousness of her presence betrayed itself to her only in his studious ignoring of the fact; but she understood that, and it pleased her. 'I see no reason,' said he, 'why a man should live like a brute because he knows of nothing beyond matter, and does not expect to exist a hundred years hence.'

'Why shouldn't he?' said the fair-haired student.

'Why *should* he?' said Hill.

'What inducement has he?'

'That's the way with all you religious people. It's all a business of inducements. Cannot a man seek after righteousness for righteousness' sake?'

There was a pause. The fair man answered, with a kind of vocal padding, 'But—you see—inducement—when I said inducement,' to gain time. And then the hunchback came to his rescue and inserted a question. He was a terrible person in the debating society with his questions, and they invariably took one form—a demand for a definition. 'What's your definition of righteousness?' said the hunchback at this stage.

Hill experienced a sudden loss of complacency at this question, but even as it was asked, relief came in the person of Brooks, the laboratory attendant, who entered by the preparation-room door, carrying a number of freshly killed guineapigs by their hind legs. 'This is the last batch of material this session,' said the youngster who had not previously spoken. Brooks advanced up the laboratory, smacking down a couple of guineapigs at each table. The rest of the class, scenting the prey from afar, came crowding in by the lecture theatre door, and the discussion perished abruptly as the students who were not already in their places hurried to them to secure the choice of a specimen. There was a noise of keys rattling on split rings as lockers were opened and dissecting instruments taken out. Hill was already standing by his table, and his box of scalpels was sticking out of his pocket. The girl in brown came a step towards him, and leaning over his table said softly, 'Did you see that I returned your book, Mr. Hill?'

During the whole scene she and the book had been vividly present in his consciousness; but he made a clumsy pretence of looking at the book and seeing it for the first time. 'Oh yes,' he said, taking it up. 'I see. Did you like it?'

'I want to ask you some questions about it—some time.'

'Certainly,' said Hill. 'I shall be glad.' He stopped awkwardly. 'You liked it?' he said.

'It's a wonderful book. Only some things I don't understand.'

Then suddenly the laboratory was hushed by a curious braying noise. It was the demonstrator. He was at the blackboard ready to begin the day's instruction, and it was his custom to demand silence by a sound midway between the 'Er' of common intercourse and the blast of a trumpet. The girl in brown slipped back to her place: it was immediately in front of Hill's, and Hill, forgetting her forthwith, took a notebook out of the drawer of his table, turned over its leaves hastily, drew a stumpy pencil from his pocket, and prepared to make a copious note of the coming demonstration. For demonstrations and lectures are the sacred text of the College students. Books, saving only the Professor's own, you may—it is even expedient to—ignore.

Hill was the son of a Landport cobbler and had been hooked by a chance blue paper the authorities had thrown out to the Landport Technical College. He kept himself in London on his allowance of a guinea a week, and found that, with proper care, this also covered his clothing allowance, an occasional waterproof collar, that is; and ink and needles and cotton and such-like necessaries for a man about town. This was his first year and his first session, but the brown old man in Landport had already got himself detested in many public-houses by boasting of his son, 'the Professor.' Hill was a vigorous youngster, with a serene contempt for the clergy of all denominations, and a fine ambition to reconstruct the world. He regarded his scholarship as a brilliant opportunity. He had begun to read at seven, and had read steadily whatever came in his way, good or bad, since then. His worldly experience had been limited to the island of Portsea, and acquired chiefly in the wholesale boot factory in which he had worked by day, after passing the seventh standard of the Board school. He had a considerable gift of speech, as the College Debating Society, which met amidst the crushing machines and mine models in the metallurgical theatre downstairs, already recognized—recognized by a violent battering of desks whenever he rose. And he was just at that fine emotional age when life opens at the end of a narrow pass like a broad valley at one's feet, full of the promise of wonderful discoveries and tremendous achievements. And his own limitations, save that he knew that he knew neither Latin nor French, were all unknown to him.

At first his interest had been divided pretty equally between his biological work at the College and social and theological theorizing, an employment which he took in deadly earnest. Of a night, when the big museum library was not open, he would sit on the bed of his room in Chelsea with his coat and a muffler on, and write out the lecture notes and revise his dissection memoranda until Thorpe called him out by a whistle—the landlady objected to open the door to attic visitors—and then the two would go prowling about the shadowy, shiny, gas-lit streets, talking, very much in the fashion of the sample just given, of the God Idea and Righteousness and Carlyle and the Reorganization of Society. And in the midst of it all, Hill, arguing not only for Thorpe but for the casual passer-by, would lose the thread of his argument glancing at some pretty painted face that looked meaningly at him as he passed. Science and Righteousness! But once or twice lately there had been signs that a third interest was creeping into his life, and he had found his attention wandering from the fate of the mesoblastic somites or the probable meaning of the blastopore, to the thought of the girl with the brown eyes who sat at the table before him.

She was a paying student; she descended inconceivable social altitudes to speak to him. At the thought of the education she must have had, and the accomplishments she must possess, the soul of Hill became abject within him. She had spoken to him first over a difficulty about the alisphenoid of a rabbit's skull, and he had found that, in biology at least, he had no reason for self-abasement. And from that, after the manner of young people starting from any starting-point, they got to generalities, and while Hill attacked her upon the question of socialism,— some instinct told him to spare her a direct assault upon her religion—she was gathering resolution to undertake what she told herself was his æsthetic education. She was a year or two older than he, though the thought never occurred to him. The loan of *News from Nowhere* was the beginning of a series of cross loans. Upon some absurd first principle of his, Hill had never 'wasted time' upon poetry, and it seemed an appalling deficiency to her. One day in the lunch hour, when she chanced upon him alone in the little museum where the skeletons were arranged, shamefully eating the bun that constituted his midday meal, she retreated, and returned to lend him, with a slightly furtive air, a volume of Browning. He stood sideways towards her and took the book rather clumsily, because he was holding the bun in the other hand. And in the retrospect his voice lacked the cheerful clearness he could have wished.

That occurred after the examination in comparative anatomy, on the day before the College turned out its students and was carefully locked up by the officials for the Christmas holidays. The excitement of cramming for the first trial of strength had for a little while dominated Hill to the exclusion of his other interests. In the forecasts of the result in which every one indulged he was surprised to find that no one regarded him as a possible competitor for the Harvey Commemoration Medal, of which this and the two subsequent examinations disposed. It was about this time that Wedderburn, who so far had lived inconspicuously on the uttermost margin of Hill's perceptions, began to take on the appearance of an obstacle. By a mutual agreement, the nocturnal prowlings with Thorpe ceased for the three weeks before the examination, and his landlady pointed out that she really could not supply so much lamp oil at the price. He walked to and fro from the College with little slips of mnemonics in his hand, lists of crayfish appendages, rabbits' skull-bones, and vertebrate nerves, for example, and became a positive nuisance to foot passengers in the opposite direction.

But, by a natural reaction, Poetry and the girl with the brown eyes ruled the Christmas holiday. The pending results of the examination became such a secondary consideration that Hill marvelled at his father's excitement. Even had he wished it, there was no comparative anatomy to read in Landport, and he was too poor to buy books, but the stock of poets in the library was extensive, and Hill's attack was magnificently sustained. He saturated himself with the fluent numbers of Longfellow and Tennyson, and fortified himself with Shakespeare; found a kindred soul in Pope and a master in Shelley, and heard and fled the siren voices of Eliza Cook and Mrs. Hemans. But he read no more Browning, because he hoped for the loan of other volumes from Miss Haysman when he returned to London.

He walked from his lodgings to the College with that volume of Browning in his shiny black bag and his mind teeming with the finest general propositions about poetry. Indeed, he framed first this little speech and then that with which to grace the return. The morning was an exceptionally pleasant one for London; there was a clear hard frost and undeniable blue in the sky, a thin haze softened every outline,

and warm shafts of sunlight struck between the house
blocks and turned the sunny side of the street to
amber and gold. In the hall of the College he pulled
off his glove and signed his name with fingers so stiff
with cold that the characteristic dash under the
signature he cultivated became a quivering line. He
imagined Miss Haysman about him everywhere. He
turned at the staircase, and there, below, he saw a
crowd struggling at the foot of the notice-board.
This, possibly, was the biology list. He forgot
Browning and Miss Haysman for the moment and
joined the scrimmage. And at last, with his cheek
flattened against the sleeve of the man on the step
above him, he read the list—

Class I

H. J. Somers Wedderburn
William Hill

and thereafter followed a second class that is outside
our present sympathies. It was characteristic that he
did not trouble to look for Thorpe on the physics list,
but backed out of the struggle at once, and in a
curious emotional state between pride over common
second-class humanity and acute disappointment at
Wedderburn's success, went on his way upstairs.
At the top, as he was hanging up his coat in the
passage, the zoological demonstrator, a young man
from Oxford who secretly regarded him as a
blatant 'mugger' of the very worst type, offered his
heartiest congratulations.

At the laboratory door Hill stopped for a second
to get his breath, and then entered. He looked
straight up the laboratory and saw all five girl
students grouped in their places, and Wedderburn,
the once retiring Wedderburn, leaning rather grace-

fully against the window, playing with the blind tassel and talking apparently to the five of them. Now, Hill could talk bravely enough and even overbearingly to one girl, and he could have made a speech to a roomful of girls, but this business of standing at ease and appreciating, fencing, and returning quick remarks round a group was, he knew, altogether beyond him. Coming up the staircase his feelings for Wedderburn had been generous, a certain admiration perhaps, a willingness to shake his hand conspicuously and heartily as one who had fought but the first round. But before Christmas Wedderburn had never gone up to that end of the room to talk. In a flash Hill's mist of vague excitement condensed abruptly to a vivid dislike of Wedderburn. Possibly his expression changed. As he came up to his place, Wedderburn nodded carelessly to him, and the others glanced round. Miss Haysman looked at him and away again, the faintest touch of her eyes. 'I can't agree with you, Mr. Wedderburn,' she said.

'I must congratulate you on your first class, Mr. Hill,' said the spectacled girl in green, turning round and beaming at him.

'It's nothing,' said Hill, staring at Wedderburn and Miss Haysman talking together, and eager to hear what they talked about.

'We poor folks in the second class don't think so,' said the girl in spectacles.

What was it Wedderburn was saying? Something about William Morris! Hill did not answer the girl in spectacles, and the smile died out of his face. He could not hear, and failed to see how he could 'cut in'. Confound Wedderburn! He sat down, opened his bag, hesitated whether to return the volume of Browning forthwith, in the sight of all, and instead drew out his new notebooks for the short course in elementary botany that was now beginning, and which would terminate in February. As he did so, a fat heavy man with a white face and pale grey eyes—Bindon, the professor of botany, who came up from Kew for January and February—came in by the lecture theatre door, and passed, rubbing his hands together and smiling, in silent affability down the laboratory.

In the subsequent six weeks Hill experienced some very rapid and curiously complex emotional developments. For the most part he had Wedderburn in focus—a fact that Miss Haysman never suspected. She told Hill (for in the comparative privacy of the museum she talked a good deal to him of socialism and Browning and general propositions) that she had met Wedderburn at the house of some people she knew, and 'he's inherited his cleverness; for his father, you know, is the great eye specialist.'

'*My* father is a cobbler,' said Hill, quite irrelevantly, and perceived the want of dignity even as he said it. But the gleam of jealousy did not offend her. She conceived herself the fundamental source of it. He suffered bitterly from a sense of Wedderburn's unfairness, and a realization of his own handicap. Here was this Wedderburn had picked up a prominent man for a father, and instead of his losing so many marks on the score of that advantage, it was counted to him for righteousness! And while Hill had to introduce himself and talk to Miss Haysman clumsily over mangled guineapigs in the laboratory, this Wedderburn, in some backstairs way, had access to her social altitudes, and could converse in a polished argot that Hill understood perhaps, but felt incapable of speaking. Not, of course, that he wanted to. Then it seemed to Hill that for Wedderburn to come there day after day with cuffs unfrayed, neatly tailored, precisely barbered, quietly perfect, was in itself an ill-bred, sneering sort of proceeding. Moreover, it was a stealthy thing for Wedderburn to behave insignificantly for a space, to mock modesty, to lead Hill to fancy that he himself was beyond dispute the man of the year, and then suddenly to dart in front of him, and incontinently to swell up in this fashion. In addition to these things, Wedderburn displayed an increasing disposition to join in any conversational grouping that included Miss Haysman; and would venture, and indeed seek occasion, to pass opinions derogatory to socialism and atheism. He goaded Hill to incivilities by neat, shallow, and exceedingly effective personalities about the socialist leaders, until Hill hated Bernard Shaw's graceful egotisms, William Morris's limited editions and luxurious wall-papers, and Walter Crane's charmingly absurd ideal working men, about as much as he hated Wedderburn. The dissertations in the laboratory, that had been his glory in the previous term, became a danger, degenerated into inglorious tussles with Wedderburn, and Hill kept to them only out of an obscure perception that his honour was involved. In the debating society Hill knew quite clearly that, to a thunderous accompaniment of banged desks, he could have pulverized Wedderburn. Only Wedderburn never attended the debating society to be pulverized, because—nauseous affectation!—he 'dined late.'

You must not imagine that these things presented themselves in quite such a crude form to Hill's perception. Hill was a born generalizer. Wedderburn to him was not so much an individual obstacle as a type, the salient angle of a class. The economic theories that, after infinite ferment, had shaped themselves in Hill's mind, became abruptly concrete at the contact. The world became full of easy-mannered, graceful, gracefully-dressed, conversationally dexterous, finally shallow Wedderburn's, Bishops Wedderburn, Wedderburn M.P.'s, Professors Wedderburn, Wedderburn landlords, all with finger-bowl shibboleths and epigrammatic cities of refuge from a sturdy debater. And every one ill-clothed or ill-dressed, from the cobbler to the cab-runner, was, to Hill's imagination, a man and a brother, a fellow-sufferer. So that he became, as it were, a champion of the fallen and oppressed, albeit to outward seeming only a self-assertive, ill-mannered young man, and an unsuccessful champion at that. Again and again a skirmish over the afternoon tea that the girl students had inaugurated left Hill with flushed cheeks and a tattered temper, and the debating society noticed a new quality of sarcastic bitterness in his speeches.

You will understand now how it was necessary, if only in the interests of humanity, that Hill should demolish Wedderburn in the forthcoming examination and outshine him in the eyes of Miss Haysman; and you will perceive, too, how Miss Haysman fell into some common feminine misconceptions. The Hill-Wedderburn quarrel, for in his unostentatious way Wedderburn reciprocated Hill's ill-veiled rivalry, became a tribute to her indefinable charm: she was the Queen of Beauty in a tournament of scalpels and stumpy pencils. To her confidential friend's secret annoyance, it even troubled her conscience, for she was a good girl, and painfully aware, through Ruskin and contemporary fiction, how entirely men's

activities are determined by women's attitudes. And
if Hill never by any chance mentioned the topic of
love to her, she only credited him with the finer
modesty for that omission.

So the time came on for the second examination,
and Hill's increasing pallor confirmed the general
rumour that he was working hard. In the aërated
bread shop near South Kensington Station you
would see him, breaking his bun and sipping his
milk with his eyes intent upon a paper of closely
written notes. In his bedroom there were propositions about buds and stems round his looking-glass,
a diagram to catch his eye, if soap should chance to
spare it, above his washing basin. He missed several
meetings of the debating society, but he found
the chance encounters with Miss Haysman in the
spacious ways of the adjacent art museum, or in
the little museum at the top of the College, or in the
College corridors, more frequent and very restful.
In particular, they used to meet in a little gallery full
of wrought-iron chests and gates near the art library,
and there Hill used to talk, under the gentle stimulus
of her flattering attention, of Browning and his
personal ambitions. A characteristic she found remarkable in him was his freedom from avarice. He
contemplated quite calmly the prospect of living all
his life on an income below a hundred pounds a year.
But he was determined to be famous, to make,
recognizably in his own proper person, the world a
better place to live in. He took Bradlaugh and John
Burns for his leaders and models, poor, even im-
pecunious, great men. But Miss Haysman thought
that such lives were deficient on the æsthetic side, by
which, though she did not know it, she meant good
wall-paper and upholstery, pretty books, tasteful

clothes, concerts, and meals nicely cooked and respectfully served.

At last came the day of the second examination, and the professor of botany, a fussy, conscientious man, rearranged all the tables in a long narrow laboratory to prevent copying, and put his demonstrator on a chair on a table (where he felt, he said, like a Hindoo god), to see all the cheating, and stuck a notice outside the door, 'Door closed', for no earthly reason that any human being could discover. And all the morning from ten till one the quill of Wedderburn shrieked defiance at Hill's, and the quills of the others chased their leaders in a tireless pack, and so also it was in the afternoon. Wedderburn was a little quieter than usual, and Hill's face was hot all day and his overcoat bulged with textbooks and notebooks against the last moment's revision. And the next day, in the morning and in the afternoon, was the practical examination, when sections had to be cut and slides identified. In the morning Hill was depressed because he knew he had cut a thick section, and in the afternoon came the mysterious slip.

It was just the kind of thing that the botanical professor was always doing. Like the income tax, it offered a premium to the cheat. It was a preparation under the microscope, a little glass slip, held in its place on the stage of the instrument by light steel clips, and the inscription set forth that the slip was not to be moved. Each student was to go in turn to it, sketch it, write in his book of answers what he considered it to be, and return to his place. Now, to move such a slip is a thing one can do by a chance movement of the finger, and in a fraction of a second. The professor's reason for decreeing that the slip

should not be moved depended on the fact that the
object he wanted identified was characteristic of a
certain tree stem. In the position in which it was
placed it was a difficult thing to recognize, but once
the slip was moved so as to bring other parts of
the preparation into view, its nature was obvious
enough.

Hill came to this, flushed from a contest with
staining re-agents, sat down on the little stool before
the microscope, turned the mirror to get the best
light, and then, out of sheer habit, shifted the slip.
At once he remembered the prohibition, and, with
an almost continuous motion of his hands, moved it
back, and sat paralysed with astonishment at his
action.

Then, slowly, he turned his head. The professor
was out of the room; the demonstrator sat aloft on
his impromptu rostrum, reading the *Q. Jour. Mi.
Sci.*; the rest of the examinees were busy, and with
their backs to him. Should he own up to the accident
now? He knew quite clearly what the thing was.
It was a lenticel, a characteristic preparation from
the elder-tree. His eyes roved over his intent fellow-
students and Wedderburn suddenly glanced over his
shoulder at him with a queer expression in his eyes.
The mental excitement that had kept Hill at an
abnormal pitch of vigour these two days gave way
to a curious nervous tension. His book of answers
was beside him. He did not write down what the
thing was, but with one eye at the microscope he
began making a hasty sketch of it. His mind was full
of this grotesque puzzle in ethics that had suddenly
been sprung upon him. Should he identify it? or
should he leave this question unanswered? In that
case Wedderburn would probably come out first in

the second result. How could he tell now whether he might not have identified the thing without shifting it? It was possible that Wedderburn had failed to recognize it, of course. Suppose Wedderburn too had shifted the slide? He looked up at the clock. There were fifteen minutes in which to make up his mind. He gathered up his book of answers and the coloured pencils he used in illustrating his replies and walked back to his seat.

He read through his manuscript, and then sat thinking and gnawing his knuckle. It would look queer now if he owned up. He *must* beat Wedderburn. He forgot the examples of those starry gentlemen, John Burns and Bradlaugh. Besides, he reflected, the glimpse of the rest of the slip he had had was after all quite accidental, forced upon him by chance, a kind of providential revelation rather than an unfair advantage. It was not nearly so dishonest to avail himself of that as it was of Broome, who believed in the efficacy of prayer, to pray daily for a first-class. 'Five minutes more,' said the demonstrator, folding up his paper and becoming observant. Hill watched the clock hands until two minutes remained; then he opened the book of answers, and, with hot ears and an affectation of ease, gave his drawing of the lenticel its name.

When the second pass list appeared, the previous positions of Wedderburn and Hill were reversed and the spectacled girl in green, who knew the demonstrator in private life (where he was practically human), said that in the result of the two examinations taken together Hill had the advantage of a mark—167 to 166 out of a possible 200. Every one admired Hill in a way, though the suspicion of 'mugging' clung to him. But Hill was to find congratulations and Miss Haysman's enhanced opinion of him, and even the decided decline in the crest of Wedderburn, tainted by an unhappy memory. He felt a remarkable access of energy at first, and the note of a democracy marching to triumph returned to his debating society speeches; he worked at his comparative anatomy with tremendous zeal and effect, and he went on with his æsthetic education. But through it all, a vivid little picture was continually coming before his mind's eye—of a sneakish person manipulating a slide.

No human being had witnessed the act, and he was cocksure that no higher power existed to see it; but for all that it worried him. Memories are not dead things, but alive; they dwindle in disuse, but they harden and develop in all sorts of queer ways if they are being continually fretted. Curiously enough, though at the time he perceived clearly that the shifting was accidental, as the days wore on his memory became confused about it, until at last he was not sure—although he assured himself that he *was* sure—whether the movement had been absolutely involuntary. Then it is possible that Hill's dietary was conducive to morbid conscientiousness; a breakfast frequently eaten in a hurry, a midday bun, and, at such hours after five as chanced to be convenient, such meat as his means determined, usually in a chop-house in a back street off the Brompton Road. Occasionally he treated himself to threepenny or ninepenny classics, and they usually represented a suppression of potatoes or chops. It is indisputable that outbreaks of self-abasement and emotional revival have a distinct relation to periods of scarcity. But apart from this influence on the feelings, there was in Hill a distinct aversion to falsity that the blasphemous Landport cobbler had inculcated by strap and tongue from his earliest years. Of one fact about professed atheists I am convinced; they may be—they usually are—fools, void of subtlety, revilers of holy institutions, brutal speakers, and mischievous knaves, but they lie with difficulty. If it were not so, if they had the faintest grasp of the idea of compromise, they would simply be liberal churchmen. And, moreover, this memory poisoned his regard for Miss Haysman. For she now so evidently preferred him to Wedderburn that he felt sure he cared for her, and began reciprocating her attentions by timid marks of personal regard; at one time he even bought a bunch of violets, carried it about in his pocket, and produced it with a stumbling explanation, withered and dead, in the gallery of old iron. It poisoned, too, the denunciation of capitalist dishonesty that had been one of his life's pleasures. And lastly, it poisoned his triumph in Wedderburn. Previously he had been Wedderburn's superior in his own eyes, and had raged simply at a want of recognition. Now he began to fret at the darker suspicion of positive inferiority. He fancied he found justifications for his position in Browning, but they vanished on analysis. At last—moved, curiously enough, by exactly the same motive forces that had resulted in his dishonesty—he went to Professor Bindon, and made a clean breast of the whole affair. As Hill was a paid student, Professor Bindon did not ask him to sit down, and he stood before the professor's desk as he made his confession.

'It's a curious story,' said Professor Bindon, slowly realizing how the thing reflected on himself, and then letting his anger rise,—'A most remarkable story. I can't understand your doing it, and I can't

understand this avowal. You're a type of student
—Cambridge men would never dream—I suppose
I ought to have thought—Why *did* you cheat?'

'I didn't cheat,' said Hill.

'But you have just been telling me you did.'

'I thought I explained—'

'Either you cheated or you did not cheat.'—

'I said my motion was involuntary.'

'I am not a metaphysician, I am a servant of
science—of fact. You were told not to move the slip.
You did move the slip. If that is not cheating—'

'If I was a cheat,' said Hill, with the note of
hysterics in his voice, 'should I come here and tell
you?'

'Your repentance, of course, does you credit,' said
Professor Bindon, 'but it does not alter the original
facts.'

'No, sir,' said Hill, giving in in utter self-abasement.

'Even now you cause an enormous amount of
trouble. The examination list will have to be revised.'

'I suppose so, sir.'

'Suppose so? Of course it must be revised. And
I don't see how I can conscientiously pass you.'

'Not pass me?' said Hill. 'Fail me?'

'It's the rule in all examinations. Or where should
we be? What else did you expect? You don't want
to shirk the consequences of your own acts?'

'I thought, perhaps'—said Hill. And then, 'Fail
me? I thought, as I told you, you would simply
deduct the marks given for that slip.'

'Impossible!' said Bindon. 'Besides, it would still
leave you above Wedderburn. Deduct only the
marks—Preposterous! The Departmental Regulations distinctly say—'

'But it's my own admission, sir.'

'The Regulations say nothing whatever of the manner in which the matter comes to light. They simply provide—'

'It will ruin me. If I fail this examination, they won't renew my scholarship.'

'You should have thought of that before.'

'But, sir, consider all my circumstances—'

'I cannot consider anything. Professors in this College are machines. The Regulations will not even let us recommend our students for appointments. I am a machine, and you have worked me. I have to do—'

'It's very hard, sir.'

'Possibly it is.'

'If I am to be failed this examination, I might as well go home at once.'

'That is as you think proper.' Bindon's voice softened a little; he perceived he had been unjust, and, provided he did not contradict himself, he was disposed to amelioration. 'As a private person,' he said, 'I think this confession of yours goes far to mitigate your offence. But you have set the machinery in motion, and now it must take its course. I—I am really sorry you gave way.'

A wave of emotion prevented Hill from answering. Suddenly, very vividly, he saw the heavily-lined face of the old Landport cobbler, his father. 'Good God! What a fool I have been!' he said hotly and abruptly.

'I hope,' said Bindon, 'that it will be a lesson to you.'

But, curiously enough, they were not thinking of quite the same indiscretion.

There was a pause.

'I would like a day to think, sir, and then I will let

you know—about going home, I mean,' said Hill, moving towards the door.

The next day Hill's place was vacant. The spectacled girl in green was, as usual, first with the news. Wedderburn and Miss Haysman were talking of a performance of *The Meistersingers* when she came up to them.

'Have you heard?' she said.

'Heard what?'

'There was cheating in the examination.'

'Cheating!' said Wedderburn, with his face suddenly hot. 'How?'

'That slide'—

'Moved? Never!'

'It was. That slide that we weren't to move'—

'Nonsense!' said Wedderburn. 'Why! How could they find out? Who do they say—?'

'It was Mr. Hill.'

'*Hill!*'

'Mr. Hill!'

'Not—surely not the immaculate Hill?' said Wedderburn, recovering.

'I don't believe it,' said Miss Haysman. 'How do you know?'

'I *didn't*,' said the girl in spectacles. 'But I know it now for a fact. Mr. Hill went and confessed to Professor Bindon himself.'

'By Jove!' said Wedderburn. 'Hill of all people. But I am always inclined to distrust these philanthropists-on-principle'—

'Are you quite sure?' said Miss Haysman, with a catch in her breath.

'Quite. It's dreadful, isn't it? But, you know, what can you expect? His father is a cobbler.'

Then Miss Haysman astonished the girl in spectacles.

'I don't care. I will not believe it,' she said, flushing darkly under her warm-tinted skin. 'I will not believe it until he has told me so himself—face to face. I would scarcely believe it then,' and abruptly she turned her back on the girl in spectacles, and walked to her own place.

'It's true, all the same,' said the girl in spectacles, peering and smiling at Wedderburn.

But Wedderburn did not answer her. She was indeed one of those people who seemed destined to make unanswered remarks.

ARNOLD BENNETT

The Lion's Share

I

IN the Five Towns the following history is related
by those who know it as something side-splittingly
funny—as one of the best jokes that ever occurred
in a district devoted to jokes. And I, too, have
hitherto regarded it as such. But upon my soul, now
that I come to write it down, it strikes me as being,
after all, a pretty grim tragedy. However, you shall
judge, and laugh or cry as you please.

It began in the little house of Mrs. Carpole, up
at Bleakridge, on the hill between Bursley and
Hanbridge. Mrs. Carpole was the second Mrs.
Carpole, and her husband was dead. She had a
stepson, Horace, and a son of her own, Sidney.
Horace is the hero, or the villain, of the history.
On the day when the unfortunate affair began he
was nineteen years old, and a model youth. Not
only was he getting on in business, not only did he
give half his evenings to the study of the chemistry
of pottery and the other half to various secretaryships
in connexion with the Wesleyan Methodist Chapel
and Sunday-school, not only did he save money, not
only was he a comfort to his stepmother and a sort
of uncle to Sidney, not only was he an early riser,
a total abstainer, a non-smoker, and a good listener;
but, in addition to the practice of these manifold and
rare virtues, he found time, even at that tender age,
to pay his tailor's bill promptly and to fold his
trousers in the same crease every night—so that he

always looked neat and dignified. Strange to say, he made no friends. Perhaps he was just a thought too perfect for a district like the Five Towns; a sin or so might have endeared him to the entire neighbour-hood. Perhaps his loneliness was due to his imperfect sense of humour, or perhaps to the dull, unsmiling heaviness of his somewhat flat features.

Sidney was quite a different story. Sidney, to use his mother's phrase, was a little jockey. His years were then eight. Fair-haired and blue-eyed, as most little jockeys are, he had a smile and a scowl that were equally effective in tyrannizing over both his mother and Horace, and he was beloved by every-body. Women turned to look at him in the street. Unhappily, his health was not good. He was afflicted by a slight deafness, which, however, the doctor said he would grow out of; the doctor predicted for him a lusty manhood. In the meantime, he caught every disease that happened to be about, and nearly died of each one. His latest acquisition had been scarlet fever. Now one afternoon, after he had 'peeled' and his room had been disinfected and he was begin-ning to walk again, Horace came home and decided that Sidney should be brought downstairs for tea as a treat, to celebrate his convalescence, and that he, Horace, would carry him downstairs. Mrs. Carpole was delighted with the idea, and Sidney also, except that Sidney did not want to be carried downstairs—he wanted to walk down.

'I think it will be better for him to walk, Horace dear,' said Mrs. Carpole, in her thin, plaintive voice. 'He can, quite well. And you know how clumsy you are. Supposing you were to fall!'

Horace, nevertheless, in pursuance of his pro-gramme of being uncle to Sidney, was determined to carry Sidney. And carry Sidney he did, despite warnings and kickings. At least he carried him as far as the turn in the steep stairs, at which point he fell, just as his stepmother had feared, and Sidney with him. The half-brothers arrived on the ground floor in company, but Horace, with his eleven stone two, was on top, and the poor suffering little convalescent lay moveless and insensible.

It took the doctor forty minutes to bring him to, and all the time the odour of grilled herrings, which formed part of the uneaten tea, made itself felt through the house like a Satanic comment on the spectacle of human life. The scene was dreadful at first. The agony then passed. There were no bruises on the boy, not a mark, and in a couple of hours he seemed to be perfectly himself. Horace breathed again, and thanked Heaven it was no worse. His gratitude to Heaven was, however, slightly premature, for in the black middle of the night poor Sidney was seized with excruciating pains in the head, and the doctor lost four hours' sleep. These pains returned at intervals of a few days, and naturally the child's convalescence was retarded. Then Horace said that Mrs. Carpole should take Sidney to Buxton for a fortnight, and he paid all the expenses of the trip out of his savings. He was desolated, utterly stricken; he said he should never forgive himself. Sidney improved, slowly.

II

After several months, during which Horace had given up all his limited spare time to the superintendence of the child's first steps in knowledge, Sidney was judged to be sufficiently strong to go to school, and it was arranged that he should attend

the Endowed School at the Wedgwood Institution.
Horace accompanied him thither on the opening
day of the term—it was an inclement morning in
January—and left the young delicate sprig, apparently joyous and content, to the care of his masters
and the mercy of his companions. But Sidney came
home for dinner weeping—weeping in spite of his
new mortar-board cap, his new satchel, his new box
of compasses, and his new books. His mother kept
him at home in the afternoon, and by the evening
another of those terrible attacks had supervened.
The doctor and Horace and Mrs. Carpole once
more lost much precious sleep. The mysterious
malady continued. School was out of the question.

And when Sidney took the air, in charge of his
mother, everybody stopped to sympathize with him
and to stroke his curls and call him a poor dear, and
also to commiserate Mrs. Carpole. As for Horace,
Bursley tried to feel sorry for Horace, but it only
succeeded in showing Horace that it was hiding a
sentiment of indignation against him. Each friendly
face as it passed Horace in the street said, without
words, 'There goes the youth who probably ruined
his young stepbrother's life. And through sheer
obstinacy too! He dropped the little darling in spite
of warnings and protests, and then fell on the top of
him. Of course, he didn't do it on purpose, but——'

The doctor mentioned Greatorex of Manchester,
the celebrated brain specialist. And Horace took
Sidney to Manchester. They had to wait an hour
and a quarter to see Greatorex, his well-known con-
sulting rooms in John Dalton Street being crowded
with imperfect brains; but their turn came at last,
and they found themselves in Greatorex's presence.
Greatorex was a fat man, with the voice of a thin

man, who seemed to spend the whole of his career in the care of his finger-nails.

'Well, my little fellow,' said Greatorex, 'don't cry.' (For Sidney was already crying.) And then to Horace, in a curt tone: 'What is it?'

And Horace was obliged to humiliate himself and relate the accident in detail, together with all that had subsequently happened.

'Yes, yes, yes, yes!' Greatorex would punctuate the recital, and when tired of 'yes' he would say 'Hum, hum, hum, hum!'

When he had said 'hum' seventy-two times he suddenly remarked that his fee was three guineas, and told Horace to strengthen Sidney all he could, not to work him too hard, and to bring him back in a year's time.

Horace paid the money, Greatorex emitted a final 'hum,' and then the stepbrothers were whisked out by an expeditious footman. The experience cost Horace over four pounds and the loss of a day's time. And the worst was that Sidney had a violent attack that very night.

School being impossible for him, Sidney had intermittent instruction from professors of both sexes at home. But he learnt practically nothing except the banjo. Horace had to buy him a banjo: it cost the best part of a ten-pound note; still, Horace could do no less. Sidney's stature grew rapidly; his general health certainly improved, yet not completely; he always had a fragile, interesting air. Moreover, his deafness did not disappear: there were occasions when it was extremely pronounced. And he was never quite safe from those attacks in the head. He spent a month or six weeks each year in the expensive bracing atmosphere of some seaside resort, and altogether he was decidedly a heavy drain on Horace's resources. People were aware of this, and they said that Horace ought to be happy that he was *in a position* to spend money freely on his poor brother. Had not the doctor predicted, before the catastrophe due to Horace's culpable negligence, that Sidney would grow into a strong man, and that his deafness would leave him? The truth was, one never knew the end of those accidents in infancy! Further, was not Sidney's sad condition slowly killing his mother? It was whispered about that, since the disaster, Sidney had not been *quite* sound mentally. Was not the mere suspicion of this enough to kill any mother?

And, as a fact, Mrs. Carpole did die. She died of a quinsy, doubtless aggravated by Sidney's sad condition.

Not long afterwards Horace came into a small fortune from his maternal grandfather. But poor Sidney did not come into any fortune, and people somehow illogically inferred that Horace had not behaved quite nicely in coming into a fortune while his suffering invalid brother, whom he had so deeply harmed, came into nothing. Even Horace had compunctions due to the visitations of a similar idea. And with part of the fortune he bought a house with a large garden up at Toft End, the highest hill of the hilly Five Towns, so that Sidney might have the benefit of the air. He also engaged a housekeeper and servants. With the remainder of the fortune he obtained a partnership in the firm of earthenware manufacturers for whom he had been acting as highly-paid manager.

Sidney reached the age of eighteen, and was most effective to look upon, his bright hair being still curly and his eyes a wondrous blue and his form elegant; and the question of Sidney's future arose. His health was steadily on the up grade. The deafness had quite disappeared. He had inclinations towards art, and had already amused himself by painting some beautiful vases. So it was settled that he should enter Horace's works on the art side, with a view to becoming, ultimately, art director. Horace gave him three pounds a week, in order that he might feel perfectly independent, and, to the same end, Sidney paid Horace seven-and-sixpence a week for board and lodging. But the change of life upset the youth's health again. After only two visits to the works he had a grave recurrence of the head-attacks, and he was solemnly exhorted not to apply himself too closely to business. He therefore took several half-holidays a week, and sometimes a whole one. And even when he put in one of his full days he would arrive at the works three hours after Horace, and restore the balance by leaving an hour earlier. The entire town watched over him as a mother watches over a son. The notion that he was not *quite* right in the pate gradually died away, and everybody was thankful for that, though it was feared an untimely grave might be his portion.

III

She was a nice girl: the nicest girl that Horace had ever met with, because her charming niceness included a faculty of being really serious about serious things—and yet she could be deliciously gay. In short, she was a revelation to Horace. And her name was Ella, and she had come one year to spend some weeks with Mrs. Penkethman, the widowed headmistress of the Wesleyan Day School, who was her cousin. Mrs. Penkethman and Ella had been holidaying together in France; their arrival in Bursley naturally coincided with the reopening of the school in August for the autumn term.

Now at this period Horace was rather lonely in his large house and garden; for Sidney, in pursuit of health, had gone off on a six weeks' cruise round Holland, Finland, Norway, and Sweden, in one of those Atlantic liners which, translated like Enoch without dying, become in their old age 'steam-yachts,' with fine names apt to lead to confusion with the private yacht of the Tsar of Russia. Horace had offered him the trip, and Horace was also paying his weekly salary as usual.

So Horace, who had always been friendly with Mrs. Penkethman, grew now more than ever friendly with Mrs. Penkethman. And Mrs. Penkethman and Ella were inseparable. The few aristocrats left in Bursley in September remarked that Horace knew what he was about, as it was notorious that Ella had the most solid expectations. But as a matter of fact Horace did not know what he was about, and he never once thought of Ella's expectations. He was simply, as they say in Bursley, knocked silly by Ella. He honestly imagined her to be the wonderfullest woman on the earth's surface, with her dark eyes and her expressive sympathetic gestures, and her alternations of seriousness and gaiety. It astounded him that a girl of twenty-one could have thought so deeply upon life as she had. The inexplicable thing was that she looked up to *him*. She evidently admired *him*. He wanted to tell her that she was quite wrong about him, much too kind in her estimate of him—that really he was a very ordinary man indeed. But another instinct prevented him from thus undeceiving her.

And one Saturday afternoon, the season being late September, Horace actually got those two women up to tea in his house and garden. He had not dared to dream of such bliss. He had hesitated long before asking them to come, and in asking them he had blushed and stammered: the invitation had seemed to him to savour of audacity. But, bless you! they had accepted with apparent ecstasy. They gave him to think that they had genuinely wanted to come. And they came extra-specially dressed—visions, lilies of the field. And as the day was quite warm, tea was served in the garden, and everybody admired the view; and there was no restraint, no awkwardness. In particular Ella talked with an ease and a distinction that enchanted Horace, and almost made him talk with ease and distinction too. He said to himself that, seeing he had only known her a month, he was getting on amazingly. He said to himself that his good luck passed belief.

Then there was a sound of cab-wheels on the other side of the garden-wall, and presently Horace heard the housekeeper complimenting Sidney on his good looks, and Sidney asking the housekeeper to lend him three shillings to pay the cabman. The golden youth had returned without the slightest warning from his cruise. The tea trio, at the lower end of the garden, saw him standing in the porch, tanned, curly, graceful, and young. Horace half rose, and then sat down again. Ella stared hard.

'That must be your brother,' she said.

'Yes, that's Sid,' Horace answered; and then, calling out loudly: 'Come down here, Sid, and tell them to bring another cup and saucer.'

'Right you are, old man,' Sidney shouted. 'You see I'm back. What! Mrs. Penkethman, is that you?' He came down the central path of the garden like a Narcissus.

'He *does* look delicate,' said Ella under her breath to Horace. Tears came to her eyes.

Naturally Ella knew all about Sidney. She enjoyed the entire confidence of Mrs. Penkethman, and what Mrs. Penkethman didn't know of the private history of the upper classes in Bursley did not amount to very much.

These were nearly the last words that Ella spoke to Horace that afternoon. The introduction was made, and Sidney slipped into the party as comfortably as he slipped into everything, like a candle slipping into a socket. But nevertheless Ella talked no more. She just stared at Sidney, and listened to him. Horace was proud that Sidney had made such an impression on her; he was glad that she showed no aversion to Sidney, because, in the event of Horace's marriage, where would Sidney live, if not with Horace and Horace's wife? Still, he could have wished that Ella would continue to display her conversational powers.

Presently Sidney lighted a cigarette. He was of those young men whose delicate mouths seem to have been fashioned for the nice conduct of a cigarette. And he had a way of blowing out the smoke that secretly ravished every feminine beholder. Horace still held to his boyhood's principles; but he envied Sidney a little.

At the conclusion of the festivity these two women naturally could not be permitted to walk home alone. And, naturally, also, the four could not walk abreast on the narrow pavements. Horace went first with

Mrs. Penkethman. He was mad with anxiety to appropriate Ella, but he dared not. It would not have been quite correct; it would have been, as they say in Bursley, too thick. Besides, there was the question of age. Horace was over thirty, and Mrs. Penkethman was also—over thirty; whereas Sidney was twenty-one, and so was Ella. Hence Sidney walked behind with Ella and the procession started in silence. Horace did not look round too often— that would not have been quite proper—but whenever he did look round the other couple had lagged farther and farther behind, and Ella seemed perfectly to have recovered her speech. At length he looked round, and lo! they had not turned the last corner; and they arrived at Mrs. Penkethman's cottage at Hillport a quarter of an hour after their elders.

IV

The wedding cost Horace a large sum of money. You see, he could not do less than behave handsomely by the bride, owing to his notorious admiration for her; and of course the bridegroom needed setting up. Horace practically furnished their home for them out of his own pocket; it was not to be expected that Sidney should have resources. Further, Sidney as a single man, paying seven-and-six a week for board and lodging, could no doubt struggle along upon three pounds weekly. But Sidney as a husband, with the nicest girl in the world to take care of, and house-rent to pay, could not possibly perform the same feat. Although he did no more work at the manufactory—Horace could not have been so unbrotherly as to demand it—Horace paid him eight pounds a week instead of three.

And the affair cost Horace a good deal besides

money. But what could Horace do? He decidedly would not have wished to wreck the happiness of two young and beautiful lives, even had he possessed the power to do so. And he did not possess the power. Those two did not consult Horace before falling in love. They merely fell in love, and there was end of it—and an end of Horace too! Horace had to suffer. He did suffer.

Perhaps it was for his highest welfare that other matters came to monopolize his mind. One sorrow drives out another. If you sit on a pin you are apt to forget that you have the toothache. The earthenware manufactory was not going well. Plenty of business was being done, but not at the right prices. Crushed between the upper and nether millstones of the McKinley Tariff and German competition, Horace, in company with other manufacturers, was breathing out his life's blood in the shape of capital. The truth was that he had never had enough capital. He had heavily mortgaged the house at Toft End in order to purchase his partners' shares in the business and have the whole undertaking to himself, and he profoundly regretted it. He needed every penny that he could collect; the strictest economy was necessary if he meant to survive the struggle. And here he was paying eight pounds a week to a personage purely ornamental, after having squandered hundreds in rendering that personage comfortable! The situation was dreadful.

You may ask, Why did he not explain the situation to Sidney? Well, partly because he was too kind, and partly because he was too proud, and partly because Sidney would not have understood. Horace fought on, keeping up a position in the town and hoping that miracles would occur.

Then Ella's expectations were realized. Sidney and she had some twenty thousand pounds to play with. And they played the most agreeable games. But not in Bursley. No. They left Horace in Bursley and went to Llandudno for a spell. Horace envied them, but he saw them off at the station as an elder brother should, and tipped the porters.

Certainly he was relieved of the formality of paying eight pounds a week to his brother. But this did not help him much. The sad fact was that 'things' (by which is meant fate, circumstances, credit, and so on) had gone too far. It was no longer a question of eight pounds a week; it was a question of final ruin.

Surely he might have borrowed money from Sidney? Sidney had no money; the money was Ella's, and Horace could not have brought himself to borrow money from a woman—from Ella, from a heavenly creature who always had a soothing sympathetic word for him. That would have been to take advantage of Ella. No, if you suggest such a thing, you do not know Horace.

I stated in the beginning that he had no faults. He was therefore absolutely honest. And he called his creditors together while he could yet pay them twenty shillings in the pound. It was a noble act, rare enough in the Five Towns and in other parts of England. But he received no praise for it. He had only done what every man in his position ought to do. If Horace had failed for ten times the sum that his debts actually did amount to, and then paid two shillings in the pound instead of twenty, he would have made a stir in the world and been looked up to as no ordinary man of business.

Having settled his affairs in this humdrum, idiotic manner, Horace took a third-class return to Llandudno. Sidney and Ella were staying at the hydro with the strange Welsh name, and he found Sidney lolling on the sunshiny beach in front of the hydro discoursing on the banjo to himself. When asked where his wife was, Sidney replied that she was lying down, and was obliged to rest as much as possible.

Horace, ashamed to trouble this domestic idyl, related his misfortunes as airily as he could.

And Sidney said he was awfully sorry, and had no notion how matters stood, and could he do anything for Horace? If so, Horace might——

'No,' said Horace. 'I'm all right. I've very fortunately got an excellent place as manager in a big new manufactory in Germany.' (This is how we deal with German competition in the Five Towns.)

'Germany?' cried Sidney.

'Yes,' said Horace; 'and I start the day after to-morrow.'

'Well,' said Sidney, 'at any rate you'll stay the night.'

'Thanks,' said Horace, 'you're very kind. I will.'

So they went into the hydro together, Sidney caressing his wonderful new pearl-inlaid banjo; and Horace talked in low tones to Ella as she lay on the sofa. He convinced Ella that his departure to Germany was the one thing he had desired all his life, because it was not good that Ella should be startled, shocked, or grieved.

They dined well.

But in the night Sidney had a recurrence of his old illness—a bad attack; and Horace sat up through dark hours, fetched the doctor, and bought things at the chemist's. Towards morning Sidney was better. And Horace, standing near the bed, gazed at his stepbrother and tried in his stupid way to read the secrets beneath that curly hair. But he had no success. He caught himself calculating how much Sidney had cost him, at periods of his career when he could ill spare money; and, having caught himself, he was angry with himself for such baseness. At eight o'clock he ventured to knock at Ella's door and explain to her that Sidney had not been quite well. She had passed a peaceful night, for he had, of course, refrained from disturbing her.

He was not quite sure whether Sidney had meant him to stay at the hydro as his guest, so he demanded a bill, paid it, said good-bye, and left for Bonn-on-the-Rhine. He was very exhausted and sleepy. Happily the third-class carriages on the London & North-Western are pretty comfortable. Between Chester and Crewe he had quite a doze, and dreamed that he had married Ella after all, and that her twenty thousand pounds had put the earthenware business on a footing of magnificent and splendid security.

V

A few months later Horace's house and garden at Toft End were put up to auction by arrangement with his mortgagee and his trade-creditors. And Sidney was struck with the idea of buying the place. The impression was that it would go cheap. Sidney said it would be a pity to let the abode pass out of the family. Ella said that the idea of buying it was a charming one, because in the garden it was that she had first met her Sidney. So the place was duly bought, and Sidney and Ella went to live there.

Several years elapsed.

Then one day little Horace was informed that his uncle Horace, whom he had never seen, was coming to the house on a visit, and that he must be a good boy, and polite to his uncle, and all the usual sort of thing.

And in effect Horace the elder did arrive in the afternoon. He found no one to meet him at the station, or at the garden gate of the pleasaunce that had once been his, or even at the front door. A pert parlour-maid told him that her master and mistress were upstairs in the nursery, and that he was requested to go up. And he went up, and to be sure Sidney met him at the top of the stairs, banjo in hand, cigarette in mouth, smiling, easy and elegant as usual—not a trace of physical weakness in his face or form. And Horace was jocularly ushered into the nursery and introduced to his nephew. Ella had changed. She was no longer slim, and no longer gay and serious by turns. She narrowly missed being stout, and she was continuously gay, like Sidney. The child was also gay. Everybody was glad to see Horace, but nobody seemed deeply interested in Horace's affairs. As a fact he had done rather well in Germany, and had now come back to England in order to assume a working partnership in a small potting concern at Hanbridge. He was virtually beginning life afresh. But what concerned Sidney and Ella was themselves and their offspring. They talked incessantly about the infinitesimal details of their daily existence, and the alterations which they had made, or meant to make, in the house and garden. And occasionally Sidney thrummed a tune on the banjo to amuse the infant. Horace had expected them to be curious about Germany and his life in Germany. But not a bit! He might have come in from the next street and left them only yesterday, for all the curiosity they exhibited.

'Shall we go down to the drawing-room and have tea, eh?' said Ella.

'Yes, let's go and kill the fatted calf,' said Sidney.

And strangely enough, inexplicably enough, Horace did feel like a prodigal.

Sidney went off with the precious banjo, and Ella picked up sundry belongings without which she never travelled about the house.

'You carry me downstairs, unky?' the little nephew suggested, with an appealing glance at his new uncle.

'No,' said Horace, 'I'm dashed if I do!'

H. H. MUNRO ['SAKI']

The Open Window

'My aunt will be down presently, Mr. Nuttel,' said a very self-possessed young lady of fifteen; 'in the meantime you must try and put up with me.'

Framton Nuttel endeavoured to say the correct something which should duly flatter the niece of the moment without unduly discounting the aunt that was to come. Privately he doubted more than ever whether these formal visits on a succession of total strangers would do much towards helping the nerve cure which he was supposed to be undergoing.

'I know how it will be,' his sister had said when he was preparing to migrate to this rural retreat; 'you will bury yourself down there and not speak to a living soul, and your nerves will be worse than ever from moping. I shall just give you letters of introduction to all the people I know there. Some of them, as far as I can remember, were quite nice.'

Framton wondered whether Mrs. Sappleton, the lady to whom he was presenting one of the letters of introduction, came into the nice division.

'Do you know many of the people round here?' asked the niece, when she judged that they had had sufficient silent communion.

'Hardly a soul,' said Framton. 'My sister was staying here, at the rectory, you know, some four years ago, and she gave me letters of introduction to some of the people here.'

He made the last statement in a tone of distinct regret.

'Then you know practically nothing about my aunt?' pursued the self-possessed young lady.

'Only her name and adress,' admitted the caller. He was wondering whether Mrs. Sappleton was in the married or widowed state. An undefinable something about the room seemed to suggest masculine habitation.

'Her great tragedy happened just three years ago,' said the child; 'that would be since your sister's time.'

'Her tragedy?' asked Framton; somehow in this restful country spot tragedies seemed out of place.

'You may wonder why we keep that window wide open on an October afternoon,' said the niece, indicating a large French window that opened on to a lawn.

'It is quite warm for the time of the year,' said Framton; 'but has that window got anything to do with the tragedy?'

'Out through that window, three years ago to a day, her husband and her two young brothers went off for their day's shooting. They never came back. In crossing the moor to their favourite snipe-shooting ground they were all three engulfed in a treacherous piece of bog. It had been that dreadful wet summer, you know, and places that were safe in other years gave way suddenly without warning. Their bodies were never recovered. That was the dreadful part of it.' Here the child's voice lost its self-possessed note and became falteringly human. 'Poor aunt always thinks that they will come back some day, they and the little brown spaniel that was lost with them, and walk in at that window just as they used to do. That is why the window is kept open every evening till it is quite dusk. Poor dear aunt, she has often told me how they went out, her husband with his white water-proof coat over his arm, and Ronnie, her youngest brother, singing, 'Bertie, why do you bound?' as he always did to tease her, because she said it got on her nerves. Do you know, sometimes on still, quiet evenings like this, I almost get a creepy feeling that they will all walk in through that window—'

She broke off with a little shudder. It was a relief to Framton when the aunt bustled into the room with a whirl of apologies for being late in making her appearance.

'I hope Vera has been amusing you?' she said.

'She has been very interesting,' said Framton.

'I hope you don't mind the open window,' said Mrs. Sappleton briskly; 'my husband and brothers will be home directly from shooting, and they always come in this way. They've been out for snipe in the marshes to-day, so they'll make a fine mess over my poor carpets. So like you men-folk, isn't it?'

She rattled on cheerfully about the shooting and the scarcity of birds, and the prospects for duck in the winter. To Framton it was all purely horrible. He made a desperate but only partially successful effort to turn the talk on to a less ghastly topic; he was conscious that his hostess was giving him only a fragment of her attention, and her eyes were constantly straying past him to the open window and the lawn beyond. It was certainly an unfortunate coincidence that he should have paid his visit on this tragic anniversary.

'The doctors agree in ordering me complete rest, an absence of mental excitement, and avoidance of anything in the nature of violent physical exercise,' announced Framton, who laboured under the toler-ably widespread delusion that total strangers and

chance acquaintances are hungry for the least detail
of one's ailments and infirmities, their cause and
cure. 'On the matter of diet they are not so much in
agreement,' he continued.

'No?' said Mrs. Sappleton, in a voice which only
replaced a yawn at the last moment. Then she suddenly brightened into alert attention—but not to
what Framton was saying.

'Here they are at last!' she cried. 'Just in time
for tea, and don't they look as if they were muddy
up to the eyes!'

Framton shivered slightly and turned towards the
niece with a look intended to convey sympathetic
comprehension. The child was staring out through
the open window with dazed horror in her eyes. In a
chill shock of nameless fear Framton swung round
in his seat and looked in the same direction.

In the deepening twilight three figures were
walking across the lawn towards the window; they
all carried guns under their arms, and one of them
was additionally burdened with a white coat hung
over his shoulders. A tired brown spaniel kept close
at their heels. Noiselessly they neared the house, and
then a hoarse young voice chanted out of the dusk:
'I said, Bertie, why do you bound?'

Framton grabbed wildly at his stick and hat; the
hall-door, the gravel-drive, and the front gate were
dimly noted stages in his headlong retreat. A cyclist
coming along the road had to run into the hedge to
avoid imminent collision.

'Here we are, my dear,' said the bearer of the white
mackintosh, coming in through the window; 'fairly
muddy, but most of it's dry. Who was that who
bolted out as we came up?'

'A most extraordinary man, a Mr. Nuttel,' said

Mrs. Sappleton; 'could only talk about his illnesses, and dashed off without a word of good-bye or apology when you arrived. One would think he had seen a ghost.'

'I expect it was the spaniel,' said the niece calmly; 'he told me he had a horror of dogs. He was once hunted into a cemetery somewhere on the banks of the Ganges by a pack of pariah dogs, and had to spend the night in a newly dug grave with the creatures snarling and grinning and foaming just above him. Enough to make any one lose their nerve.'

Romance at short notice was her speciality.

H. H. MUNRO ['SAKI']

The Music on the Hill

Sylvia Seltoun ate her breakfast in the morning-room at Yessney with a pleasant sense of ultimate victory, such as a fervent Ironside might have permitted himself on the morrow of Worcester fight. She was scarcely pugnacious by temperament, but belonged to that more successful class of fighters who are pugnacious by circumstance. Fate had willed that her life should be occupied with a series of small struggles, usually with the odds slightly against her, and usually she had just managed to come through winning. And now she felt that she had brought her hardest and certainly her most important struggle to a successful issue. To have married Mortimer Seltoun, 'Dead Mortimer' as his more intimate enemies called him, in the teeth of the cold hostility of his family, and in spite of his unaffected indifference to women, was indeed an achievement that had needed some determination and adroitness to carry through; yesterday she had brought her victory to its concluding stage by wrenching her husband away from Town and its group of satellite watering-places and 'settling him down', in the vocabulary of her kind, in this remote wood-girt manor farm which was his country house.

'You will never get Mortimer to go,' his mother had said carpingly, 'but if he once goes he'll stay; Yessney throws almost as much a spell over him as Town does. One can understand what holds him to Town, but Yessney—' and the dowager had shrugged her shoulders.

There was a sombre almost savage wildness about Yessney that was certainly not likely to appeal to town-bred tastes, and Sylvia, notwithstanding her name, was accustomed to nothing much more sylvan than 'leafy Kensington'. She looked on the country as something excellent and wholesome in its way, which was apt to become troublesome if you encouraged it overmuch. Distrust of town-life had been a new thing with her, born of her marriage with Mortimer, and she had watched with satisfaction the gradual fading of what she called 'the Jermyn-Street-look' in his eyes as the woods and heather of Yessney had closed in on them yesternight. Her will-power and strategy had prevailed; Mortimer would stay.

Outside the morning-room windows was a triangular slope of turf, which the indulgent might call a lawn, and beyond its low hedge of neglected fuchsia bushes a steeper slope of heather and bracken dropped down into cavernous combes overgrown with oak and yew. In its wild open savagery there seemed a stealthy linking of the joy of life with the terror of unseen things. Sylvia smiled complacently as she gazed with a School-of-Art appreciation at the landscape, and then of a sudden she almost shuddered.

'It is very wild,' she said to Mortimer, who had joined her; 'one could almost think that in such a place the worship of Pan had never quite died out.'

'The worship of Pan never has died out,' said Mortimer. 'Other newer gods have drawn aside his votaries from time to time, but he is the Nature-God to whom all must come back at last. He has been called the Father of all the Gods, but most of his children have been stillborn.'

Sylvia was religious in an honest, vaguely devo-

tional kind of way, and did not like to hear her
beliefs spoken of as mere aftergrowths, but it was
at least something new and hopeful to hear Dead
Mortimer speak with such energy and conviction on
any subject.

'You don't really believe in Pan?' she asked
incredulously.

'I've been a fool in most things,' said Mortimer
quietly, 'but I'm not such a fool as not to believe in
Pan when I'm down here. And if you're wise you
won't disbelieve in him too boastfully while you're
in his country.'

It was not till a week later, when Sylvia had exhausted the attractions of the woodland walks round
Yessney, that she ventured on a tour of inspection
of the farm buildings. A farm-yard suggested in her
mind a scene of cheerful bustle, with churns and flails
and smiling dairymaids, and teams of horses drinking
knee-deep in duck-crowded ponds. As she wandered
among the gaunt grey buildings of Yessney manor
farm her first impression was one of crushing stillness
and desolation, as though she had happened on some
lone deserted homestead long given over to owls and
cobwebs; then came a sense of furtive watchful
hostility, the same shadow of unseen things that
seemed to lurk in the wooded combes and coppices.
From behind heavy doors and shuttered windows
came the restless stamp of hoof or rasp of chain
halter, and at times a muffled bellow from some
stalled beast. From a distant corner a shaggy dog
watched her with intent unfriendly eyes; as she drew
near it slipped quietly into its kennel, and slipped
out again as noiselessly when she had passed by.
A few hens, questing for food under a rick, stole
away under a gate at her approach. Sylvia felt that

if she had come across any human beings in this
wilderness of barn and byre they would have fled
wraith-like from her gaze. At last, turning a corner
quickly, she came upon a living thing that did not
fly from her. Astretch in a pool of mud was an
enormous sow, gigantic beyond the town-woman's
wildest computation of swine-flesh, and speedily alert
to resent and if necessary repel the unwonted intru-
sion. It was Sylvia's turn to make an unobtrusive
retreat. As she threaded her way past rickyards
and cowsheds and long blank walls, she started
suddenly at a strange sound—the echo of a boy's
laughter, golden and equivocal. Jan, the only boy
employed on the farm, a tow-headed, wizen-faced
yokel, was visibly at work on a potato clearing
half-way up the nearest hill-side, and Mortimer,
when questioned, knew of no other probable or
possible begetter of the hidden mockery that had
ambushed Sylvia's retreat. The memory of that un-
traceable echo was added to her other impressions
of a furtive sinister 'something' that hung around
Yessney.

Of Mortimer she saw very little; farm and woods
and trout-streams seemed to swallow him up from
dawn till dusk. Once, following the direction she
had seen him take in the morning, she came to an
open space in a nut copse, further shut in by huge
yew trees, in the centre of which stood a stone
pedestal surmounted by a small bronze figure of a
youthful Pan. It was a beautiful piece of workman-
ship, but her attention was chiefly held by the fact
that a newly cut bunch of grapes had been placed as
an offering at its feet. Grapes were none too plentiful
at the manor house, and Sylvia snatched the bunch
angrily from the pedestal. Contemptuous annoyance

dominated her thoughts as she strolled slowly home-
ward, and then gave way to a sharp feeling of something that was very near fright; across a thick tangle
of undergrowth a boy's face was scowling at her,
brown and beautiful, with unutterably evil eyes. It
was a lonely pathway, all pathways round Yessney
were lonely for the matter of that, and she sped
forward without waiting to give a closer scrutiny to
this sudden apparition. It was not till she had
reached the house that she discovered that she had
dropped the bunch of grapes in her flight.

'I saw a youth in the wood to-day,' she told
Mortimer that evening, 'brown-faced and rather
handsome, but a scoundrel to look at. A gipsy lad,
I suppose.'

'A reasonable theory,' said Mortimer, 'only there
aren't any gipsies in these parts at present.'

'Then who was he?' asked Sylvia, and as Mortimer appeared to have no theory of his own, she
passed on to recount her finding of the votive
offering.

'I suppose it was your doing,' she observed; 'it's
a harmless piece of lunacy, but people would think
you dreadfully silly if they knew of it.'

'Did you meddle with it in any way?' asked
Mortimer.

'I—I threw the grapes away. It seemed so silly,'
said Sylvia, watching Mortimer's impassive face for
a sign of annoyance.

'I don't think you were wise to do that,' he said
reflectively. 'I've heard it said that the Wood Gods
are rather horrible to those who molest them.'

'Horrible perhaps to those that believe in them,
but you see I don't,' retorted Sylvia.

'All the same,' said Mortimer in his even, dispassionate tone, 'I should avoid the woods and orchards if I were you, and give a wide berth to the horned beasts on the farm.'

It was all nonsense, of course, but in that lonely wood-girt spot nonsense seemed able to rear a bastard brood of uneasiness.

'Mortimer,' said Sylvia suddenly, 'I think we will go back to Town some time soon.'

Her victory had not been so complete as she had supposed; it had carried her on to ground that she was already anxious to quit.

'I don't think you will ever go back to Town,' said Mortimer. He seemed to be paraphrasing his mother's prediction as to himself.

Sylvia noted with dissatisfaction and some self-contempt that the course of her next afternoon's ramble took her instinctively clear of the network of woods. As to the horned cattle, Mortimer's warning was scarcely needed, for she had always regarded them as of doubtful neutrality at the best: her imagination unsexed the most matronly dairy cows and turned them into bulls liable to 'see red' at any moment. The ram who fed in the narrow paddock below the orchards she had adjudged, after ample and cautious probation, to be of docile temper; to-day, however, she decided to leave his docility untested, for the usually tranquil beast was roaming with every sign of restlessness from corner to corner of his meadow. A low, fitful piping, as of some reedy flute, was coming from the depth of a neighbouring copse, and there seemed to be some subtle connexion between the animal's restless pacing and the wild music from the wood. Sylvia turned her steps in an upward direction and climbed the heather-clad slopes that stretched in rolling shoulders high above

Yessney. She had left the piping notes behind her, but across the wooded combes at her feet the wind brought her another kind of music, the straining bay of hounds in full chase. Yessney was just on the outskirts of the Devon-and-Somerset country, and the hunted deer sometimes came that way. Sylvia could presently see a dark body, breasting hill after hill, and sinking again and again out of sight as he crossed the combes, while behind him steadily swelled that relentless chorus, and she grew tense with the excited sympathy that one feels for any hunted thing in whose capture one is not directly interested. And at last he broke through the outermost line of oak scrub and fern and stood panting in the open, a fat September stag carrying a well-furnished head. His obvious course was to drop down to the brown pools of Undercombe, and thence make his way towards the red deer's favoured sanctuary, the sea. To Sylvia's surprise, however, he turned his head to the upland slope and came lumbering resolutely onward over the heather. 'It will be dreadful,' she thought, 'the hounds will pull him down under my very eyes.' But the music of the pack seemed to have died away for a moment, and in its place she heard again that wild piping, which rose now on this side, now on that, as though urging the failing stag to a final effort. Sylvia stood well aside from his path, half hidden in a thick growth of whortle bushes, and watched him swing stiffly upward, his flanks dark with sweat, the coarse hair on his neck showing light by contrast. The pipe music shrilled suddenly around her, seeming to come from the bushes at her very feet, and at the same moment the great beast slewed round and bore directly down upon her. In an instant her pity for the hunted animal was changed to wild terror at her own danger; the thick heather roots mocked her scrambling efforts at flight, and she looked frantically downward for a glimpse of oncoming hounds. The huge antler spikes were within a few yards of her, and in a flash of numbing fear she remembered Mortimer's warning, to beware of horned beasts on the farm. And then with a quick throb of joy she saw that she was not alone; a human figure stood a few paces aside, knee-deep in the whortle bushes.

'Drive it off!' she shrieked. But the figure made no answering movement.

The antlers drove straight at her breast, the acrid smell of the hunted animal was in her nostrils, but her eyes were filled with the horror of something she saw other than her oncoming death. And in her ears rang the echo of a boy's laughter, golden and equivocal.

W. SOMERSET MAUGHAM

The Door of Opportunity

THEY got a first-class carriage to themselves. It was lucky, because they were taking a good deal in with them, Alban's suit-case and a hold-all, Anne's dressing-case and her hat-box. They had two trunks in the van, containing what they wanted immediately, but all the rest of their luggage Alban had put in the care of an agent who was to take it up to London and store it till they had made up their minds what to do. They had a lot, pictures and books, curios that Alban had collected in the East, his guns and saddles. They had left Sondurah for ever. Alban, as was his way, tipped the porter generously and then went to the bookstall and bought papers. He bought *The New Statesman* and *The Nation*, and *The Tatler* and *The Sketch*, and the last number of *The London Mercury*. He came back to the carriage and threw them on the seat.

'It's only an hour's journey,' said Anne.

'I know, but I wanted to buy them. I've been starved so long. Isn't it grand to think that to-morrow morning we shall have to-morrow's *Times* and *The Express* and *The Mail*?'

She did not answer and he turned away, for he saw coming towards them two persons, a man and his wife, who had been fellow-passengers from Singapore.

'Get through the customs all right?' he cried to them cheerily.

The man seemed not to hear, for he walked straight on, but the woman answered.

'Yes, they never found the cigarettes.'

She saw Anne, gave her a friendly little smile, and passed on. Anne flushed.

'I was afraid they'd want to come in here,' said Alban. 'Let's have the carriage to ourselves if we can.'

She looked at him curiously.

'I don't think you need worry,' she answered. 'I don't think any one will come in.'

He lit a cigarette and lingered at the carriage door. On his face was a happy smile. When they had passed through the Red Sea and found a sharp wind in the Canal, Anne had been surprised to see how much the men who had looked presentable enough in the white ducks in which she had been accustomed to see them, were changed when they left them off for warmer clothes. They looked like nothing on earth then. Their ties were awful and their shirts all wrong. They wore grubby flannel trousers and shabby old golf-coats that had too obviously been bought off the nail, or blue serge suits that betrayed the provincial tailor. Most of the passengers had got off at Marseilles, but a dozen or so, either because after a long period in the East they thought the trip through the Bay would do them good, or, like themselves, for economy's sake, had gone all the way to Tilbury, and now several of them walked along the platform. They wore solar topis or double-brimmed terais, and heavy greatcoats, or else shapeless soft hats or bowlers, not too well brushed, that looked too small for them. It was a shock to see them. They looked suburban and a trifle second-rate. But Alban had already a London look. There was not a speck of dust on his smart greatcoat, and his black Homburg hat looked brand-new. You would never have guessed that he had not been home for three years. His collar fitted closely round his neck and his foulard tie was neatly tied. As Anne looked at him she could not but think how good-looking he was. He was just under six feet tall, and slim, and he wore his clothes well and his clothes were well cut. He had fair hair, still thick, and blue eyes and the faintly yellow skin common to men of that complexion after they have lost the pink-and-white freshness of early youth. There was no colour in his cheeks. It was a fine head, well set on rather a long neck, with a somewhat prominent Adam's apple; but you were more impressed with the distinction than with the beauty of his face. It was because his features were so regular, his nose so straight, his brow so broad that he photographed so well. Indeed, from his photographs you would have thought him extremely handsome. He was not that, perhaps because his eyebrows and his eyelashes were pale and his lips thin, but he looked very intellectual. There was refinement in his face and a spirituality that was oddly moving. That was how you thought a poet should look; and when Anne became engaged to him she told her girl friends who asked her about him that he looked like Shelley. He turned to her now with a little smile in his blue eyes. His smile was very attractive.

'What a perfect day to land in England!'

It was October. They had steamed up the Channel on a grey sea under a grey sky. There was not a breath of wind. The fishing boats seemed to rest on the placid water as though the elements had for ever forgotten their old hostility. The coast was incredibly green, but with a bright cosy greenness quite unlike the luxuriant, vehement verdure of Eastern jungles. The red towns they passed here and there were

comfortable and homelike. They seemed to welcome
the exiles with a smiling friendliness. And when they
drew into the estuary of the Thames they saw the
rich levels of Essex and in a little while Chalk Church
on the Kentish shore, lonely in the midst of weather-
beaten trees, and beyond it the woods of Cobham.
The sun, red in a faint mist, set on the marshes, and
night fell. In the station the arc-lamps shed a light
that spotted the darkness with cold hard patches.
It was good to see the porters lumbering about in
their grubby uniforms and the stationmaster fat and
important in his bowler hat. The stationmaster
blew a· whistle and waved his arm. Alban stepped
into the carriage and seated himself in the corner
opposite to Anne. The train started.

'We're due in London at six-ten,' said Alban.
'We ought to get to Jermyn Street by seven. That'll
give us an hour to bath and change and we can get
to the Savoy for dinner by eight-thirty. A bottle of
pop to-night, my pet, and a slap-up dinner.' He gave
a chuckle. 'I heard the Strouds and the Maundys
arranging to meet at the Trocadero Grill-Room.'

He took up the papers and asked if she wanted
any of them. Anne shook her head.

'Tired?' he smiled.

'No.'

'Excited?'

In order not to answer she gave a little laugh. He
began to look at the papers, starting with the pub-
lishers' advertisements, and she was conscious of the
intense satisfaction it was to him to feel himself
through them once more in the middle of things.
They had taken in those same papers in Sondurah,
but they arrived six weeks old, and though they kept
them abreast of what was going on in the world that

interested them both, they emphasized their exile.
But these were fresh from the press. They smelt
different. They had a crispness that was almost
voluptuous. He wanted to read them all at once.
Anne looked out of the window. The country was
dark, and she could see little but the lights of their
carriage reflected on the glass, but very soon the
town encroached upon it, and then she saw little
sordid houses, mile upon mile of them, with a light
in a window here and there, and the chimneys made
a dreary pattern against the sky. They passed
through Barking and East Ham and Bromley—it was
silly that the name on the platform as they went
through the station should give her such a tremor—
and then Stepney. Alban put down his papers.

'We shall be there in five minutes now.'

He put on his hat and took down from the racks
the things the porter had put in them. He looked at
her with shining eyes and his lips twitched. She saw
that he was only just able to control his emotion.
He looked out of the window, too, and they passed
over brightly lighted thoroughfares, close packed
with tram-cars, buses, and motor-vans, and they saw
the streets thick with people. What a mob! The
shops were all lit up. They saw the hawkers with
their barrows at the curb. 'London,' he said.

He took her hand and gently pressed it. His smile
was so sweet that she had to say something. She
tried to be facetious.

'Does it make you feel all funny inside?'

'I don't know if I want to cry or if I want to be
sick.'

Fenchurch Street. He lowered the window and
waved his arm for a porter. With a grinding of
brakes the train came to a standstill. A porter

opened the door and Alban handed him out one
package after another. Then in his polite way,
having jumped out, he gave his hand to Anne to
help her down to the platform. The porter went to
fetch a barrow and they stood by the pile of their
luggage. Alban waved to two passengers from the
ship who passed them. The man nodded stiffly.

'What a comfort it is that we shall never have to
be civil to those awful people any more,' said Alban
lightly.

Anne gave him a quick glance. He was really
incomprehensible. The porter came back with his
barrow, the luggage was put on and they followed
him to collect their trunks. Alban took his wife's
arm and pressed it.

'The smell of London. By God, it's grand.'

He rejoiced in the noise and the bustle and the
crowd of people who jostled them; the radiance of
the arc-lamps and the black shadows they cast, sharp
but full-toned, gave him a sense of elation. They got
out into the street and the porter went off to get
them a taxi. Alban's eyes glittered as he looked at
the buses and the policemen trying to direct the
confusion. His distinguished face bore a look of
something like inspiration. The taxi came. Their
luggage was stowed away and piled up beside the
driver, Alban gave the porter half a crown, and they
drove off. They turned down Gracechurch Street
and in Cannon Street were held up by a block in the
traffic. Alban laughed out loud.

'What's the matter?' said Anne.

'I'm so excited.'

They went along the Embankment. It was relatively quiet there. Taxis and cars passed them.
The bells of the trams were music in his ears. At

Westminster Bridge they cut across Parliament Square and drove through the green silence of St. James's Park. They had engaged a room at a hotel just off Jermyn Street. The reception clerk took them upstairs and a porter brought up their luggage. It was a room with twin beds and a bathroom.

'This looks all right,' said Alban. 'It'll do us till we can find a flat or something.'

He looked at his watch.

'Look here, darling, we shall only fall over one another if we try to unpack together. We've got oodles of time and it'll take you longer to get straight and dress than me. I'll clear out. I want to go to the club and see if there's any mail for me. I've got my dinner-jacket in my suit-case and it'll only take me twenty minutes to have a bath and dress. Does that suit you?'

'Yes. That's all right.'

'I'll be back in an hour.'

'Very well.'

He took out of his pocket the little comb he always carried and passed it through his long fair hair. Then he put on his hat. He gave himself a glance in the mirror.

'Shall I turn on the bath for you?'

'No, don't bother.'

'All right. So long.'

He went out.

When he was gone Anne took her dressing-case and her hat-box and put them on the top of her trunk. Then she rang the bell. She did not take off her hat. She sat down and lit a cigarette. When a servant answered the bell she asked for the porter. He came. She pointed to the luggage.

'Will you take those things and leave them in the

hall for the present. I'll tell you what to do with them presently.'

'Very good, ma'am.'

She gave him a florin. He took the trunk out and the other packages and closed the door behind him. A few tears slid down Anne's cheeks, but she shook herself; she dried her eyes and powdered her face. She needed all her calm. She was glad that Alban had conceived the idea of going to his club. It made things easier and gave her a little time to think them out.

Now that the moment had come to do what she had for weeks determined, now that she must say the terrible things she had to say, she quailed. Her heart sank. She knew exactly what she meant to say to Alban, she had made up her mind about that long ago, and had said the very words to herself a hundred times, three or four times a day every day of the long journey from Singapore, but she was afraid that she would grow confused. She dreaded an argument. The thought of a scene made her feel slightly sick. It was something at all events to have an hour in which to collect herself. He would say she was heartless and cruel and unreasonable. She could not help it.

'No, no, no,' she cried aloud.

She shuddered with horror. And all at once she saw herself again in the bungalow, sitting as she had been sitting when the whole thing started. It was getting on towards tiffin time and in a few minutes Alban would be back from the office. It gave her pleasure to reflect that it was an attractive room for him to come back to, the large veranda which was their parlour, and she knew that though they had been there eighteen months he was still alive to the

success she had made of it. The jalousies were drawn
now against the midday sun and the mellowed light
filtering through them gave an impression of cool
silence. Anne was house-proud, and though they
were moved from district to district according to
the exigencies of the Service and seldom stayed anywhere very long, at each new post she started with
new enthusiasm to make their house cosy and charming. She was very modern. Visitors were surprised
because there were no knick-knacks. They were
taken aback by the bold colour of her curtains and
could not at all make out the tinted reproductions of
pictures by Marie Laurencin and Gauguin in silvered
frames which were placed on the walls with such
cunning skill. She was conscious that few of
them quite approved and the good ladies of Port
Wallace and Pemberton thought such arrangements
odd, affected, and out of place; but this left her calm.
They would learn. It did them good to get a bit of a
jolt. And now she looked round the long, spacious
veranda with the complacent sigh of the artist
satisfied with his work. It was gay. It was bare.
It was restful. It refreshed the spirit and gently
excited the fancy. Three immense bowls of yellow
cannas completed the colour scheme. Her eyes
lingered for a moment on the book-shelves filled with
books; that was another thing that disconcerted the
colony, all the books they had, and strange books
too, heavy they thought them for the most part; and
she gave them a little affectionate look as though
they were living things. Then she gave the piano
a glance. A piece of music was still open on the
rack, it was something of Debussy, and Alban had
been playing it before he went to the office.

Her friends in the colony had condoled with her

when Alban was appointed D.O. at Daktar, for it
was the most isolated district in Sondurah. It was
connected with the town which was the head-quarters
of the government neither by telegraph nor telephone.
But she liked it. They had been there some time
and she hoped they would remain till Alban went
home on leave in another twelve months. It was as
large as an English county, with a long coast-line,
and the sea was dotted with little islands. A broad,
winding river ran through it and on each side of this
stretched hills densely covered with virgin forest.
The station, a good way up the river, consisted of a
row of Chinese shops and a native village nestling
amid coconut trees, the District Office, the D.O.'s
bungalow, the Clerk's quarters, and the barracks.
Their only neighbours were the manager of a rubber
estate a few miles up the river and the manager and
his assistant, Dutchmen both, of a timber camp on
one of the river's tributaries. The rubber estate's
launch went up and down twice a month and was
their only means of regular communication with the
outside world. But though they were lonely they
were not dull. Their days were full. Their ponies
waited for them at dawn and they rode while the
day was still fresh and in the bridle-paths through
the jungle lingered the mystery of the tropical night.
They came back, bathed, changed and had breakfast,
and Alban went to the office. Anne spent the morning writing letters and working. She had fallen in
love with the country from the first day she arrived
in it and had taken pains to master the common
language spoken. Her imagination was inflamed by
the stories she heard of love and jealousy and death.
She was told romantic tales of a time that was only
just past. She sought to steep herself in the lore of

those strange people. Both she and Alban read a great deal. They had for the country a considerable library and new books came from London by nearly every mail. Little that was noteworthy escaped them. Alban was fond of playing the piano. For an amateur he played very well. He had studied rather seriously, and he had an agreeable touch and a good ear; he could read music with ease, and it was always a pleasure to Anne to sit by him and follow the score when he tried something new. But their great delight was to tour the district. Sometimes they would be away for a fortnight at a time. They would go down the river in a prahu and then sail from one little island to another, bathe in the sea, and fish, or else row upstream till it grew shallow and the trees on either bank were so close to one another that you only saw a slim strip of sky between. Here the boatmen had to pole and they would spend the night in a native house. They bathed in a river pool so clear that you could see the sand shining silver at the bottom; and the spot was so lovely, so peaceful and remote, that you felt you could stay there for ever. Sometimes, on the other hand, they would tramp for days along the jungle paths, sleeping under canvas, and notwithstanding the mosquitoes that tormented them and the leeches that sucked their blood, enjoy every moment. Whoever slept so well as on a camp bed? And then there was the gladness of getting back, the delight in the comfort of the well-ordered establishment, the mail that had arrived with letters from home, and all the papers and the piano.

Alban would sit down to it then, his fingers itching to feel the keys, and in what he played, Stravinsky, Ravel, Darius Milhaud, she seemed to feel that he put in something of his own, the sounds of the jungle at night, dawn over the estuary, the starry nights, and the crystal clearness of the forest pools.

Sometimes the rain fell in sheets for days at a time. Then Alban worked at Chinese. He was learning it so that he could communicate with the Chinese of the country in their own language, and Anne did the thousand-and-one things for which she had not had time before. Those days brought them even more closely together; they always had plenty to talk about, and when they were occupied with their separate affairs they were pleased to feel in their bones that they were near to one another. They were wonderfully united. The rainy days that shut them up within the walls of the bungalow made them feel as if they were one body in face of the world.

On occasion they went to Port Wallace. It was a change, but Anne was always glad to get home. She was never quite at her ease there. She was conscious that none of the people they met liked Alban. They were very ordinary people, middle-class and suburban and dull, without any of the intellectual interests that made life so full and varied to Alban and her, and many of them were narrow-minded and ill-natured; but since they had to pass the better part of their lives in contact with them, it was tiresome that they should feel so unkindly towards Alban. They said he was conceited. He was always very pleasant with them, but she was aware that they resented his cordiality. When he tried to be jovial they said he was putting on airs, and when he chaffed them they thought he was being funny at their expense.

Once they stayed at Government House, and Mrs.

Hannay, the Governor's wife, who liked her, talked to her about it. Perhaps the Governor had suggested that she should give Anne a hint.

'You know, my dear, it's a pity your husband doesn't try to be more come-hither with people. He's very intelligent; don't you think it would be better if he didn't let others see he knows it quite so clearly? My husband said to me only yesterday: of course I know Alban Torel is the cleverest young man in the Service, but he does manage to put my back up more than any one I know. I am the Governor, but when he talks to me he always gives me the impression that he looks upon me as a damned fool.'

The worst of it was that Anne knew how low an opinion Alban had of the Governor's parts.

'He doesn't mean to be superior,' Anne answered, smiling. 'And he really isn't in the least conceited. I think it's only because he has a straight nose and high cheek-bones.'

'You know, they don't like him at the club. They call him Powder-Puff Percy.'

Anne flushed. She had heard that before and it made her very angry. Her eyes filled with tears.

'I think it's frightfully unfair.'

Mrs. Hannay took her hand and gave it an affectionate little squeeze.

'My dear, you know I don't want to hurt your feelings. Your husband can't help rising very high in the Service. He'd make things so much easier for himself if he were a little more human. Why doesn't he play football?'

'It's not his game. He's always only too glad to play tennis.'

'He doesn't give that impression. He gives the

impression that there's no one here who's worth his
while to play with.'

'Well, there isn't,' said Anne, stung.

Alban happened to be an extremely good tennis-
player. He had played a lot of tournaments in
England and Anne knew that it gave him a grim
satisfaction to knock those beefy, hearty men all
over the court. He could make the best of them look
foolish. He could be maddening on the tennis court
and Anne was aware that sometimes he could not
resist the temptation.

'He does play to the gallery, doesn't he?' said
Mrs. Hannay.

'I don't think so. Believe me, Alban has no idea
he isn't popular. As far as I can see he's always
pleasant and friendly with everybody.'

'It's then he's most offensive,' said Mrs. Hannay
dryly.

'I know people don't like us very much,' said
Anne, smiling a little. 'I'm very sorry, but really I
don't know what we can do about it.'

'Not you, my dear,' cried Mrs. Hannay. 'Everybody adores you. That's why they put up with your
husband. My dear, who could help liking you?'

'I don't know why they should adore me,' said
Anne.

But she did not say it quite sincerely. She was
deliberately playing the part of the dear little woman
and within her she bubbled with amusement. They
disliked Alban because he had such an air of distinction, and because he was interested in art and literature; they did not understand these things and so
thought them unmanly; and they disliked him
because his capacity was greater than theirs. They
disliked him because he was better bred than they.

They thought him superior; well, he was superior, but not in the sense they meant. They forgave her because she was an ugly little thing. That was what she called herself, but she wasn't that, or if she was it was with an ugliness that was most attractive. She was like a little monkey, but a very sweet little monkey and very human. She had a neat figure. That was her best point. That and her eyes. They were very large, of a deep brown, liquid and shining; they were full of fun, but they could be tender on occasion with a charming sympathy. She was dark, her frizzy hair was almost black, and her skin was swarthy; she had a small fleshy nose, with large nostrils, and much too big a mouth. But she was alert and vivacious. She could talk with a show of real interest to the ladies of the colony about their husbands and their servants and their children in England, and she could listen appreciatively to the men who told her stories that she had often heard before. They thought her a jolly good sort. They did not know what clever fun she made of them in private. It never occurred to them that she thought them narrow, gross, and pretentious. They found no glamour in the East because they looked at it vulgarly with material eyes. Romance lingered at their threshold and they drove it away like an importunate beggar. She was aloof. She repeated to herself Landor's line:

'Nature I loved, and next to nature, art.'

She reflected on her conversation with Mrs. Hannay, but on the whole it left her unconcerned. She wondered whether she should say anything about it to Alban; it had always seemed a little odd to her that he should be so little aware of his unpopularity; but she was afraid that if she told him of it he would

become self-conscious. He never noticed the cold-
ness of the men at the club. He made them feel shy
and therefore uncomfortable. His appearance then
caused a sort of awkwardness, but he, happily insensible, was breezily cordial to all and sundry. The
fact was that he was strangely unconscious of other
people. She was in a class by herself, she and a little
group of friends they had in London, but he could
never quite realize that the people of the colony, the
government officials and the planters and their wives,
were human beings. They were to him like pawns in
a game. He laughed with them, chaffed them, and
was amiably tolerant of them; with a chuckle Anne
told herself that he was rather like the master of a
preparatory school taking little boys out on a picnic
and anxious to give them a good time.

She was afraid it wasn't much good telling Alban.
He was incapable of the dissimulation which, she
happily realized, came so easily to her. What was
one to do with these people? The men had come
out to the colony as lads from second-rate schools,
and life had taught them nothing. At fifty they had
the outlook of hobbledehoys. Most of them drank
a great deal too much. They read nothing worth
reading. Their ambition was to be like everybody
else. Their highest praise was to say that a man was
a damned good sort. If you were interested in the
things of the spirit you were a prig. They were eaten
up with envy of one another and devoured by petty
jealousies. And the women, poor things, were
obsessed by petty rivalries. They made a circle that
was more provincial than any in the smallest town in
England. They were prudish and spiteful. What
did it matter if they did not like Alban? They would
have to put up with him because his ability was so

great. He was clever and energetic. They could not
say that he did not do his work well. He had been
successful in every post he had occupied. With his
sensitiveness and his imagination he understood the
native mind and he was able to get the natives to do
things that no one in his position could. He had a
gift for languages, and he spoke all the local dialects.
He not only knew the common tongue that most of
the government officials spoke, but was acquainted
with the niceties of the language and on occasion
could make use of a ceremonial speech that flattered
and impressed the chiefs. He had a gift for organiza-
tion. He was not afraid of responsibility. In due
course he was bound to be made a Resident. Alban
had some interest in England; his father was a
brigadier-general killed in the War, and though he
had no private means he had influential friends. He
spoke of them with pleasant irony.

'The great advantage of democratic government,'
he said, 'is that merit, with influence to back it, can
be pretty sure of receiving its due reward.'

Alban was so obviously the ablest man in the
service that there seemed no reason why he should
not eventually be made Governor. Then, thought
Anne, his air of superiority, of which they complained, would be in place. They would accept him
as their master and he would know how to make
himself respected and obeyed. The position she
foresaw did not dazzle her. She accepted it as a right.
It would be fun for Alban to be Governor and for
her to be the Governor's wife. And what an opportunity! They were sheep, the government servants
and the planters; when Government House was the
seat of culture they would soon fall into line. When
the best way to the Governor's favour was to be

intelligent, intelligence would become the fashion. She and Alban would cherish the native arts and collect carefully the memorials of a vanished past. The country would make an advance it had never dreamed of. They would develop it, but along lines of order and beauty. They would instil into their subordinates a passion for that beautiful land and a loving interest in these romantic races. They would make them realize what music meant. They would cultivate literature. They would create beauty. It would be the golden age.

Suddenly she heard Alban's footstep. Anne awoke from her day-dream. All that was far away in the future. Alban was only a District Officer yet and what was important was the life they were living now. She heard Alban go into the bath-house and splash water over himself. In a minute he came in. He had changed into a shirt and shorts. His fair hair was still wet.

'Tiffin ready?' he asked.

'Yes.'

He sat down at the piano and played the piece that he had played in the morning. The silvery notes cascaded coolly down the sultry air. You had an impression of a formal garden with great trees and elegant pieces of artificial water and of leisurely walks bordered with pseudo-classical statues. Alban played with an exquisite delicacy. Lunch was announced by the head boy. He rose from the piano. They walked into the dining-room hand in hand. A punkah lazily fanned the air. Anne gave the table a glance. With its bright-coloured tablecloth and the amusing plates it looked very gay.

'Anything exciting at the office this morning?' she asked.

'No, nothing much. A buffalo case. Oh, and Prynne has sent along to ask me to go up to the estate. Some coolies have been damaging the trees and he wants me to come along and look into it.'

Prynne was manager of the rubber estate up the river and now and then they spent a night with him. Sometimes when he wanted a change he came down to dinner and slept at the D.O.'s bungalow. They both liked him. He was a man of five-and-thirty, with a red face with deep furrows in it, and very black hair. He was quite uneducated, but cheerful and easy, and being the only Englishman within two days' journey they could not but be friendly with him. He had been a little shy of them at first. News spreads quickly in the East and long before they arrived in the district he heard that they were high-brows. He did not know what he would make of them. He probably did not know that he had charm, which makes up for many more commendable quali-ties, and Alban with his almost feminine sensibilities was peculiarly susceptible to this. He found Alban much more human than he expected, and of course Anne was stunning. Alban played rag-time for him, which he would not have done for the Governor, and played dominoes with him. When Alban was making his first tour of the district with Anne, and suggested that they would like to spend a couple of nights on the estate, he had thought it as well to warn him that he lived with a native woman and had two children by her. He would do his best to keep them out of Anne's sight, but he could not send them away, there was nowhere to send them. Alban laughed.

'Anne isn't that sort of woman at all. Don't dream of hiding them. She loves children.'

Anne quickly made friends with the shy, pretty

little native woman and soon was playing happily
with the children. She and the girl had long confidential chats. The children took a fancy to her.
She brought them lovely toys from Port Wallace.
Prynne, comparing her smiling tolerance with the
disapproving acidity of the other white women of
the colony, described himself as knocked all of a
heap. He could not do enough to show his delight
and gratitude.

'If all highbrows are like you,' he said, 'give me
highbrows every time.'

He hated to think that in another year they would
leave the district for good and the chances were that,
if the next D.O. was married, his wife would think it
dreadful that, rather than live alone, he had a native
woman to live with him and, what was more, was
much attached to her.

But there had been a good deal of discontent on
the estate of late. The coolies were Chinese and
infected with communist ideas. They were dis-
orderly. Alban had been obliged to sentence several
of them for various crimes to terms of imprison-
ment.

'Prynne tells me that as soon as their term is up
he's going to send them all back to China and get
Javanese instead,' said Alban. 'I'm sure he's right.
They're much more amenable.'

'You don't think there's going to be any serious
trouble?'

'Oh, no. Prynne knows his job and he's a pretty
determined fellow. He wouldn't put up with any
nonsense and with me and our policemen to back
him up I don't imagine they'll try any monkey tricks.'
He smiled. 'The iron hand in the velvet glove.'

The words were barely out of his mouth when a

sudden shouting arose. There was a commotion and the sound of steps. Loud voices and cries.

'Tuan, Tuan.'

'What the devil's the matter?'

Alban sprang from his chair and went swiftly on to the veranda. Anne followed him. At the bottom of the steps was a group of natives. There was the sergeant, and three or four policemen, boatmen and several men from the kampong.

'What is it?' called Alban.

Two or three shouted back in answer. The sergeant pushed others aside and Alban saw lying on the ground a man in a shirt and khaki shorts. He ran down the steps. He recognized the man as the assistant manager of Prynne's estate. He was a half-caste. His shorts were covered with blood and there was clotted blood all over one side of his face and head. He was unconscious.

'Bring him up here,' called Anne.

Alban gave an order. The man was lifted up and carried on to the veranda. They laid him on the floor and Anne put a pillow under his head. She sent for water and for the medicine chest in which they kept things for emergency.

'Is he dead?' asked Alban.

'No.'

'Better try to give him some brandy.'

The boatmen brought ghastly news. The Chinese coolies had risen suddenly and attacked the manager's office. Prynne was killed and the assistant manager, Oakley by name, had escaped only by the skin of his teeth. He had come upon the rioters when they were looting the office, he had seen Prynne's body thrown out of the window, and had taken to his heels. Some of the Chinese saw him and gave chase. He ran for the river and was wounded as he jumped into the launch. The launch managed to put off before the Chinese could get on board and they had come down-stream for help as fast as they could go. As they went they saw flames rising from the office buildings. There was no doubt that the coolies had burned down everything that would burn.

Oakley gave a groan and opened his eyes. He was a little, dark-skinned man, with flattened features and thick coarse hair. His great native eyes were filled with terror.

'You're all right,' said Anne. 'You're quite safe.'

He gave a sigh and smiled. Anne washed his face and swabbed it with antiseptics. The wound on his head was not serious.

'Can you speak yet?' said Alban.

'Wait a bit,' she said. 'We must look at his leg.'

Alban ordered the sergeant to get the crowd out of the veranda. Anne ripped up one leg of the shorts. The material was clinging to the coagulated wound.

'I've been bleeding like a pig,' said Oakley.

It was only a flesh wound. Alban was clever with his fingers, and though the blood began to flow again they stanched it. Alban put on a dressing and a bandage. The sergeant and a policeman lifted Oakley on to a long chair. Alban gave him a brandy and soda, and soon he felt strong enough to speak. He knew no more than the boatmen had already told. Prynne was dead and the estate was in flames.

'And the girl and the children?' asked Anne.

'I don't know.'

'Oh, Alban.'

'I must turn out the police. Are you sure Prynne is dead?'

'Yes, sir. I saw him.'

'Have the rioters got fire-arms?'

'I don't know, sir.'

'How d'you mean, you don't know?' Alban cried irritably. 'Prynne had a gun, hadn't he?'

'Yes, sir.'

'There must have been more on the estate. You had one, didn't you? The head overseer had one.'

The half-caste was silent. Alban looked at him sternly.

'How many of those damned Chinese are there?'

'A hundred and fifty.'

Anne wondered that he asked so many questions. It seemed waste of time. The important thing was to collect coolies for the transport up-river, prepare the boats and issue ammunition to the police.

'How many policemen have you got, sir?' asked Oakley.

'Eight and the sergeant.'

'Could I come too? That would make ten of us. I'm sure I shall be all right now I'm bandaged.'

'I'm not going,' said Alban.

'Alban, you must,' cried Anne. She could not believe her ears.

'Nonsense. It would be madness. Oakley's obviously useless. He's sure to have a temperature in a few hours. He'd only be in the way. That leaves nine guns. There are a hundred and fifty Chinese and they've got fire-arms and all the ammunition in the world.'

'How d'you know?'

'It stands to reason they wouldn't have started a show like this unless they had. It would be idiotic to go.'

Anne stared at him with open mouth. Oakley's eyes were puzzled.

'What are you going to do?'

'Well, fortunately we've got the launch. I'll send it to Port Wallace with a request for reinforcements.'

'But they won't be here for two days at least.'

'Well, what of it? Prynne's dead and the estate burned to the ground. We couldn't do any good by going up now. I shall send a native to reconnoitre so that we can find out exactly what the rioters are doing.' He gave Anne his charming smile. 'Believe me, my pet, the rascals won't lose anything by waiting a day or two for what's coming to them.'

Oakley opened his mouth to speak, but perhaps he hadn't the nerve. He was a half-caste assistant manager and Alban, the D.O., represented the power of the Government. But the man's eyes sought Anne's and she thought she read in them an earnest and personal appeal.

'But in two days they're capable of committing the most frightful atrocities,' she cried. 'It's quite unspeakable what they may do.'

'Whatever damage they do they'll pay for. I promise you that.'

'Oh, Alban, you can't sit still and do nothing. I beseech you to go yourself at once.'

'Don't be so silly. I can't quell a riot with eight policemen and a sergeant. I haven't got the right to take a risk of that sort. We'd have to go in boats. You don't think we could get up unobserved. The lalang along the banks is perfect cover and they could just take pot shots at us as we came along. We shouldn't have a chance.'

'I'm afraid they'll only think it weakness if nothing is done for two days, sir,' said Oakley.

'When I want your opinion I'll ask for it,' said Alban acidly. 'So far as I can see when there was danger the only thing you did was to cut and run. I can't persuade myself that your assistance in a crisis would be very valuable.'

The half-caste reddened. He said nothing more. He looked straight in front of him with troubled eyes.

'I'm going down to the office,' said Alban. 'I'll just write a short report and send it down the river by launch at once.'

He gave an order to the sergeant, who had been standing all this time stiffly at the top of the steps. He saluted and ran off. Alban went into a little hall they had to get his topi. Anne swiftly followed him.

'Alban, for God's sake listen to me a minute,' she whispered.

'I don't want to be rude to you, darling, but I am pressed for time. I think you'd much better mind your own business.'

'You can't do nothing, Alban. You must go. Whatever the risk.'

'Don't be such a fool,' he said angrily.

He had never been angry with her before. She seized his hand to hold him back.

'I tell you I can do no good by going.'

'You don't know. There's the woman and Prynne's children. We must do something to save them. Let me come with you. They'll kill them.'

'They've probably killed them already.'

'Oh, how can you be so callous! If there's a chance of saving them it's your duty to try.'

'It's my duty to act like a reasonable human being. I'm not going to risk my life and my policemen's for the sake of a native woman and her half-caste brats. What sort of a damned fool do you take me for?'

'They'll say you were afraid.'

'Who?'

'Every one in the colony.'

He smiled disdainfully.

'If you only knew what a complete contempt I have for the opinion of every one in the colony.'

She gave him a long searching look. She had been married to him for eight years and she knew every expression of his face and every thought in his mind. She stared into his blue eyes as if they were open windows. She suddenly went quite pale. She dropped his hand and turned away. Without another word she went back on to the veranda. Her ugly little monkey face was a mask of horror.

Alban went to his office, wrote a brief account of the facts, and in a few minutes the motor launch was pounding down the river.

The next two days were endless. Escaped natives brought them news of happenings on the estate. But from their excited and terrified stories it was impossible to get an exact impression of the truth. There had been a good deal of bloodshed. The head overseer had been killed. They brought wild tales of cruelty and outrage. Anne could hear nothing of Prynne's woman and the two children. She shuddered when she thought of what might have been their fate. Alban collected as many natives as he could. They were armed with spears and swords. He commandeered boats. The situation was serious, but he kept his head. He felt that he had done all that was possible and nothing remained but for him to carry on normally. He did his official work. He played the piano a great deal. He rode with Anne in the early morning. He appeared to have forgotten that they had had the first serious difference of opinion in the whole of their married life. He took it that Anne had accepted the wisdom of his decision. He was as amusing, cordial, and gay with her as he had always been. When he spoke of the rioters it was with grim irony: when the time came to settle matters a good many of them would wish they had never been born.

'What'll happen to them?' asked Anne.

'Oh, they'll hang.' He gave a shrug of distaste. 'I hate having to be present at executions. It always makes me feel rather sick.'

He was very sympathetic to Oakley, whom they had put to bed and whom Anne was nursing. Perhaps he was sorry that in the exasperation of the moment he had spoken to him offensively, and he went out of his way to be nice to him.

Then on the afternoon of the third day, when they were drinking their coffee after luncheon, Alban's quick ears caught the sound of a motor boat approaching. At the same moment a policeman ran up to say that the Government launch was sighted.

'At last,' cried Alban.

He bolted out of the house. Anne raised one of the jalousies and looked out at the river. Now the sound was quite loud and in a moment she saw the boat come round the bend. She saw Alban on the landing-stage. He got into a prahu and as the launch dropped her anchor he went on board. She told Oakley that the reinforcements had come.

'Will the D.O. go up with them when they attack?' he asked her.

'Naturally,' said Anne coldly.

'I wondered.'

Anne felt a strange feeling in her heart. For the

last two days she had had to exercise all her self-control not to cry. She did not answer. She went out of the room.

A quarter of an hour later Alban returned to the bungalow with the captain of constabulary who had been sent with twenty Sikhs to deal with the rioters. Captain Stratton was a little red-faced man with a red moustache and bow legs, very hearty and dashing, whom she had met often at Port Wallace.

'Well, Mrs. Torel, this is a pretty kettle of fish,' he cried, as he shook hands with her, in a loud jolly voice. 'Here I am, with my army all full of pep and ready for a scrap. Up, boys, and at 'em. Have you got anything to drink in this benighted place?'

'Boy,' she cried, smiling.

'Something long and cool and faintly alcoholic, and then I'm ready to discuss the plan of campaign.'

His breeziness was very comforting. It blew away the sullen apprehension that seemed ever since the disaster to brood over the lost peace of the bungalow. The boy came in with a tray and Stratton mixed himself a stengah. Alban put him in possession of the facts. He told them clearly, briefly, and with precision.

'I must say I admire you,' said Stratton. 'In your place I should never have been able to resist the temptation to take my eight cops and have a whack at the blighters myself.'

'I thought it was a perfectly unjustifiable risk to take.'

'Safety first, old boy, eh, what?' said Stratton jovially. 'I'm jolly glad you didn't. It's not often we get the chance of a scrap. It would have been a dirty trick to keep the whole show to yourself.'

Captain Stratton was all for steaming straight up

the river and attacking at once, but Alban pointed
out to him the inadvisability of such a course. The
sound of the approaching launch would warn the
rioters. The long grass at the river's edge offered
them cover and they had enough guns to make a
landing difficult. It seemed useless to expose the
attacking force to their fire. It was silly to forget
that they had to face a hundred and fifty desperate
men and it would be easy to fall into an ambush.
Alban expounded his own plan. Stratton listened to
it. He nodded now and then. The plan was evidently
a good one. It would enable them to take the rioters
on the rear, surprise them, and in all probability
finish the job without a single casualty. He would
have been a fool not to accept it.

'But why didn't you do that yourself?' asked
Stratton.

'With eight men and a sergeant?'

Stratton did not answer.

'Anyhow it's not a bad idea and we'll settle on it.
It gives us plenty of time, so with your permission,
Mrs. Torel, I'll have a bath.'

They set out at sunset, Captain Stratton and his
twenty Sikhs, Alban with his policemen and the
natives he had collected. The night was dark and
moonless. Trailing behind them were the dug-outs
that Alban had gathered together and into which
after a certain distance they proposed to transfer
their force. It was important that no sound should
give warning of their approach. After they had gone
for about three hours by launch they took to the
dug-outs and in them silently paddled up stream.
They reached the border of the vast estate and
landed. Guides led them along a path so narrow that
they had to march in single file. It had been long

unused and the going was heavy. They had twice to
ford a stream. The path led them circuitously to the
rear of the coolie lines, but they did not wish to reach
them till nearly dawn and presently Stratton gave the
order to halt. It was a long cold wait. At last the
night seemed to be less dark; you did not see the
trunks of the trees, but were vaguely sensible of them
against its darkness. Stratton had been sitting with
his back to a tree. He gave a whispered order to a
sergeant and in a few minutes the column was once
more on the march. Suddenly they found themselves
on a road. They formed fours. The dawn broke and
in the ghostly light the surrounding objects were
wanly visible. The column stopped on a whispered
order. They had come in sight of the coolie lines.
Silence reigned in them. The column crept on again
and again halted. Stratton, his eyes shining, gave
Alban a smile.

'We've caught the blighters asleep.'

He lined up his men. They inserted cartridges in
their guns. He stepped forward and raised his hand.
The carbines were pointed at the coolie lines.

'Fire.'

There was a rattle as the volley of shots rang out.
Then suddenly there was a tremendous din and the
Chinese poured out, shouting and waving their arms,
but in front of them, to Alban's utter bewilderment,
bellowing at the top of his voice and shaking his fist
at them, was a white man.

'Who the hell's that?' cried Stratton.

A very big, very fat man, in khaki trousers and a
singlet, was running towards them as fast as his fat
legs would carry him and as he ran shaking both
fists at them and yelling:

'*Smerige flikkers! Vervloekte ploerten!*

'My God, it's Van Hasseldt,' said Alban.

This was the Dutch manager of the timber camp which was situated on a considerable tributary of the river about twenty miles away.

'What the hell do you think you're doing?' he puffed as he came up to them.

'How the hell did you get here?' asked Stratton in turn.

He saw that the Chinese were scattering in all directions and gave his men instructions to round them up. Then he turned again to Van Hasseldt.

'What's it mean?'

'Mean? Mean?' shouted the Dutchman furiously. 'That's what I want to know. You and your damned policemen. What do you mean by coming here at this hour in the morning and firing a damned volley? Target practice? You might have killed me. Idiots!'

'Have a cigarette,' said Stratton.

'How did you get here, Van Hasseldt?' asked Alban again, very much at sea. 'This is the force they've sent from Port Wallace to quell the riot.'

'How did I get here? I walked. How did you think I got here? Riot be damned. I quelled the riot. If that's what you came here for you can take your damned policemen home again. A bullet came within a foot of my head.'

'I don't understand,' said Alban.

'There's nothing to understand,' spluttered Van Hasseldt, still fuming. 'Some coolies came to my estate and said the chinks had killed Prynne and burned the bally place down, so I took my assistant and my head overseer and a Dutch friend I had staying with me and came over to see what the trouble was.'

Captain Stratton opened his eyes wide.

'Did you just stroll in as if it was a picnic?' he asked.

'Well, you don't think after all the years I've been in this country I'm going to let a couple of hundred chinks put the fear of God into me? I found them all scared out of their lives. One of them had the nerve to pull a gun on me and I blew his bloody brains out. And the rest surrendered. I've got the leaders tied up. I was going to send a boat down to you this morning to come up and get them.'

Stratton stared at him for a minute and then burst into a shout of laughter. He laughed till the tears ran down his face. The Dutchman looked at him angrily, then began to laugh too; he laughed with the big belly laugh of a very fat man and his coils of fat heaved and shook. Alban watched them sullenly. He was very angry.

'What about Prynne's girl and the kids?' he asked.

'Oh, they got away all right.'

It just showed how wise he had been not to let himself be influenced by Anne's hysteria. Of course the children had come to no harm. He never thought they would.

Van Hasseldt and his little party started back for the timber camp, and as soon after as possible Stratton embarked his twenty Sikhs and leaving Alban with his sergeant and his policemen to deal with the situation departed for Port Wallace. Alban gave him a brief report for the Governor. There was much for him to do. It looked as though he would have to stay for a considerable time; but since every house on the estate had been burned to the ground and he was obliged to install himself in the coolie lines he thought it better that Anne should not join him. He sent her a note to that effect. He was glad to be able to reassure her of the safety of poor Prynne's girl. He set to work at once to make his preliminary inquiry. He examined a host of witnesses. But a week later he received an order to go to Port Wallace at once. The launch that brought it was to take him and he was able to see Anne on the way down for no more than an hour. Alban was a trifle vexed.

'I don't know why the Governor can't leave me to get things straight without dragging me off like this. It's extremely inconvenient.'

'Oh, well, the Government never bothers very much about the convenience of its subordinates, does it?' smiled Anne.

'It's just red-tape. I would offer to take you along, darling, only I shan't stay a minute longer than I need. I want to get my evidence together for the Sessions Court as soon as possible. I think in a country like this it's very important that justice should be prompt.'

When the launch came into Port Wallace one of the harbour police told him that the harbour-master had a chit for him. It was from the Governor's secretary and informed him that His Excellency desired to see him as soon as convenient after his arrival. It was ten in the morning. Alban went to the club, had a bath and shaved, and then in clean ducks, his hair neatly brushed, he called a rickshaw and told the boy to take him to the Governor's office. He was at once shown into the secretary's room. The secretary shook hands with him.

'I'll tell H.E. you're here,' he said. Won't you sit down?'

The secretary left the room and in a little while came back.

'H.E. will see you in a minute. Do you mind if I get on with my letters?'

Alban smiled. The secretary was not exactly come-hither. He waited, smoking a cigarette, and amused himself with his own thoughts. He was making a good job of the preliminary inquiry. It interested him. Then an orderly came in and told Alban that the Governor was ready for him. He rose from his seat and followed him into the Governor's room.

'Good morning, Torel.'

'Good morning, sir.'

The Governor was sitting at a large desk. He nodded to Alban and motioned to him to take a seat. The Governor was all grey. His hair was grey, his face, his eyes; he looked as though the tropical suns had washed the colour out of him; he had been in the country for thirty years and had risen one by one through all the ranks of the Service; he looked tired and depressed. Even his voice was grey. Alban liked him because he was quiet; he did not think him clever, but he had an unrivalled knowledge of the country, and his great experience was a very good substitute for intelligence. He looked at Alban for a full moment without speaking and the odd idea came to Alban that he was embarrassed. He very nearly gave him a lead.

'I saw Van Hasseldt yesterday,' said the Governor suddenly.

'Yes, sir?'

'Will you give me your account of the occurrences at the Alud Estate and of the steps you took to deal with them.'

Alban had an orderly mind. He was self-possessed. He marshalled his facts well and was able to state them with precision. He chose his words with care and spoke them fluently.

'You had a sergeant and eight policemen. Why did you not immediately go to the scene of the disturbance?'

'I thought the risk was unjustifiable.'

A thin smile was outlined on the Governor's grey face.

'If the officers of this Government had hesitated to take unjustifiable risks it would never have become a province of the British Empire.'

Alban was silent. It was difficult to talk to a man who spoke obvious nonsense.

'I am anxious to hear your reasons for the decision you took.'

Alban gave them coolly. He was quite convinced of the rightness of his action. He repeated, but more fully, what he had said in the first place to Anne. The Governor listened attentively.

'Van Hasseldt, with his manager, a Dutch friend of his, and a native overseer, seems to have coped with the situation very efficiently,' said the Governor.

'He had a lucky break. That doesn't prevent him from being a damned fool. It was madness to do what he did.'

'Do you realize that by leaving a Dutch planter to do what you should have done yourself, you have covered the Government with ridicule?'

'No, sir.'

'You've made yourself a laughing-stock in the whole colony.'

Alban smiled.

'My back is broad enough to bear the ridicule of persons to whose opinion I am entirely indifferent.'

'The utility of a Government official depends very

largely on his prestige, and I'm afraid his prestige is likely to be inconsiderable when he lies under the stigma of cowardice.'

Alban flushed a little.

'I don't quite know what you mean by that, sir.'

'I've gone into the matter very carefully. I've seen Captain Stratton, and Oakley, poor Prynne's assistant, and I've seen Van Hasseldt. I've listened to your defence.'

'I didn't know that I was defending myself, sir.'

'Be so good as not to interrupt me. I think you committed a grave error of judgement. As it turns out the risk was very small, but whatever it was, I think you should have taken it. In such matters promptness and firmness are essential. It is not for me to conjecture what motive led you to send for a force of constabulary and do nothing till they came. I am afraid, however, that I consider that your usefulness in the Service is no longer very great.'

Alban looked at him with astonishment.

'But would you have gone under the circumstances?' he asked him.

'I should.'

Alban shrugged his shoulders.

'Don't you believe me?' rapped out the Governor.

'Of course I believe you, sir. But perhaps you will allow me to say that if you had been killed the colony would have suffered an irreparable loss.'

The Governor drummed on the table with his fingers. He looked out of the window and then looked again at Alban. When he spoke it was not unkindly.

'I think you are unfitted by temperament for this rather rough-and-tumble life, Torel. If you'll take my advice you'll go home. With your abilities I feel sure that you'll soon find an occupation much better suited to you.'

'I'm afraid I don't understand what you mean, sir.'

'Oh, come, Torel, you're not stupid. I'm trying to make things easy for you. For your wife's sake as well as for your own I do not wish you to leave the colony with the stigma of being dismissed from the Service for cowardice. I'm giving you the opportunity of resigning.'

'Thank you very much, sir. I'm not prepared to avail myself of the opportunity. If I resign I admit that I committed an error and that the charge you make against me is justified. I don't admit it.'

'You can please yourself. I have considered the matter very carefully and I have no doubt about it in my mind. I am forced to discharge you from the Service. The necessary papers will reach you in due course. Meanwhile you will return to your post and hand over to the officer appointed to succeed you on his arrival.'

'Very good, sir,' replied Alban, a twinkle of amusement in his eyes. 'When do you desire me to return to my post?'

'At once.'

'Have you any objection to my going to the club and having tiffin before I go?'

The Governor looked at him with surprise. His exasperation was mingled with an unwilling admiration.

'Not at all. I'm sorry, Torel, that this unhappy incident should have deprived the Government of a servant whose zeal has always been so apparent and whose tact, intelligence, and industry seemed to point him out in the future for very high office.'

'Your Excellency does not read Schiller, I suppose.

You are probably not acquainted with his celebrated line: *mit der Dummheit kämpfen die Götter selbst vergebens.*'

'What does it mean?'

'Roughly: against stupidity the gods themselves battle in vain.'

'Good morning.'

With his head in the air, a smile on his lips, Alban left the Governor's office. The Governor was human, and he had the curiosity to ask his secretary later in the day if Alban Torel had really gone to the club.

'Yes, sir. He had tiffin there.'

'It must have wanted some nerve.'

Alban entered the club jauntily and joined the group of men standing at the bar. He talked to them in the breezy, cordial tone he always used with them. It was designed to put them at their ease. They had been discussing him ever since Stratton had come back to Port Wallace with his story, sneering at him and laughing at him, and all that had resented his superciliousness, and they were the majority, were triumphant because his pride had had a fall. But they were so taken aback at seeing him now, so confused to find him as confident as ever, that it was they who were embarrassed.

One man, though he knew perfectly, asked him what he was doing in Port Wallace.

'Oh, I came about the riot on the Alud Estate. H.E. wanted to see me. He does not see eye to eye with me about it. The silly old ass has fired me. I'm going home as soon as he appoints a D.O. to take over.'

There was a moment of awkwardness. One, more kindly disposed than the others, said:

'I'm awfully sorry.'

Alban shrugged his shoulders.

'My dear fellow, what can you do with a perfect damned fool? The only thing is to let him stew in his own juice.'

When the Governor's secretary had told his chief as much of this as he thought discreet, the Governor smiled.

'Courage is a queer thing. I would rather have shot myself than go to the club just then and face all those fellows.'

A fortnight later, having sold to the incoming D.O. all the decorations that Anne had taken so much trouble about, with the rest of their things in packing-cases and trunks, they arrived at Port Wallace to await the local steamer that was to take them to Singapore. The padre's wife invited them to stay with her, but Anne refused; she insisted that they should go to the hotel. An hour after their arrival she received a very kind little letter from the Governor's wife asking her to go and have tea with her. She went. She found Mrs. Hannay alone, but in a minute the Governor joined them. He expressed his regret that she was leaving and told her how sorry he was for the cause.

'It's very kind of you to say that,' said Anne, smiling gaily, 'but you mustn't think I take it to heart. I'm entirely on Alban's side. I think what he did was absolutely right and if you don't mind my saying so I think you've treated him most unjustly.'

'Believe me, I hated having to take the step I took.'

'Don't let's talk about it,' said Anne.

'What are your plans when you get home?' asked Mrs. Hannay.

Anne began to chat brightly. You would have thought she had not a care in the world. She seemed in great spirits at going home. She was jolly and amusing and made little jokes. When she took leave of the Governor and his wife she thanked them for all their kindness. The Governor escorted her to the door.

The next day but one, after dinner, they went on board the clean and comfortable little ship. The padre and his wife saw them off. When they went into their cabin they found a large parcel on Anne's bunk. It was addressed to Alban. He opened it and saw that it was an immense powder-puff.

'Hullo, I wonder who sent us this?' he said, with a laugh. 'It must be for you, darling.'

Anne gave him a quick look. She went pale. The brutes! How could they be so cruel? She forced herself to smile.

'It's enormous, isn't it? I've never seen such a large powder-puff in my life.'

But when he had left the cabin and they were out at sea, she threw it passionately overboard.

And now, now that they were back in London and Sondurah was nine thousand miles away, she clenched her hands as she thought of it. Somehow, it seemed the worst thing of all. It was so wantonly unkind to send that absurd object to Alban, Powder-puff Percy; it showed such a petty spite. Was that their idea of humour? Nothing had hurt her more and even now she felt that it was only by holding on to herself that she could prevent herself from crying. Suddenly she started, for the door opened and Alban came in. She was still sitting in the chair in which he had left her.

'Hullo, why haven't you dressed?' He looked about the room. 'You haven't unpacked.'

'No.'

'Why on earth not?'

'I'm not going to unpack. I'm not going to stay here. I'm leaving you.'

'What are you talking about?'

'I've stuck it out till now. I made up my mind I would till we got home. I set my teeth, I've borne more than I thought it possible to bear, but now it's finished. I've done all that could be expected of me. We're back in London now and I can go.'

He looked at her in utter bewilderment.

'Are you mad, Anne?'

'Oh, my God, what I've endured! The journey to Singapore, with all the officers knowing, and even the Chinese stewards. And at Singapore, the way people looked at us at the hotel, and the sympathy I had to put up with, the bricks they dropped and their embarrassment when they realized what they'd done. My God, I could have killed them. That interminable journey home. There wasn't a single passenger on the ship who didn't know. The contempt they had for you and the kindness they went out of their way to show me. And you so self-complacent and so pleased with yourself, seeing nothing, feeling nothing. You must have the hide of a rhinoceros. The misery of seeing you so chatty and agreeable. Pariahs, that's what we were. You seemed to ask them to snub you. How can any one be so shameless?'

She was flaming with passion. Now that at last she need not wear the mask of indifference and pride that she had forced herself to assume she cast aside all reserve and all self-control. The words poured from her trembling lips in a virulent stream.

'My dear, how can you be so absurd?' he said good-naturedly, smiling. 'You must be very nervous and high-strung to have got such ideas in your head. Why didn't you tell me? You're like a country bumpkin who comes to London and thinks every one is staring at him. Nobody bothered about us and if they did what on earth did it matter? You ought to have more sense than to bother about what a lot of fools say. And what do you imagine they were saying?'

'They were saying you'd been fired.'

'Well, that was true,' he laughed.

'They said you were a coward.'

'What of it?'

'Well, you see, that was true too.'

He looked at her for a moment reflectively. His lips tightened a little.

'And what makes you think so?' he asked acidly.

'I saw it in your eyes, that day the news came, when you refused to go to the estate and I followed you into the hall when you went to fetch your topi. I begged you to go, I felt that whatever the danger you must take it, and suddenly I saw the fear in your eyes. I nearly fainted with the horror.'

'I should have been a fool to risk my life to no purpose. Why should I? Nothing that concerned me was at stake. Courage is the obvious virtue of the stupid. I don't attach any particular importance to it.'

'How do you mean that nothing that concerned you was at stake? If that's true then your whole life is a sham. You've given away everything you stood for, everything we both stand for. You've let all of us down. We did set ourselves up on a pinnacle, we did think ourselves better than the rest of them because we loved literature and art and music, we weren't content to live a life of ignoble jealousies and vulgar tittle-tattle, we did cherish the things of the spirit, and we loved beauty. It was our food and drink. They laughed at us and sneered at us. That was inevitable. The ignorant and the common naturally hate and fear those who are interested in things they don't understand. We didn't care. We called them Philistines. We despised them and we had a right to despise them. Our justification was that we were better and nobler and wiser and braver than they were. And you weren't better, you weren't nobler, you weren't braver. When the crisis came you slunk away like a whipped cur with his tail between his legs. You of all people hadn't the right to be a coward. They despise *us* now and they have the right to despise us. Us and all we stood for. Now they can say that art and beauty are all rot; when it comes to a pinch people like us always let you down. They never stopped looking for a chance to turn and rend us and you gave it to them. They can say that they always expected it. It's a triumph for them. I used to be furious because they called you Powder-Puff Percy. Did you know they did?'

'Of course. I thought it very vulgar, but it left me entirely indifferent.'

'It's funny that their instinct should have been so right.'

'Do you mean to say you've been harbouring this against me all these weeks? I should never have thought you capable of it.'

'I couldn't let you down when every one was against you. I was too proud for that. Whatever happened I swore to myself that I'd stick to you till we got home. It's been torture.'

'Don't you love me any more?'

'Love you? I loathe the very sight of you.'

'Anne.'

'God knows I loved you. For eight years I worshipped the ground you trod on. You were everything to me. I believed in you as some people believe in God. When I saw the fear in your eyes that day, when you told me that you weren't going to risk your life for a kept woman and her half-caste brats, I was shattered. It was as though some one had wrenched my heart out of my body and trampled on it. You killed my love there and then, Alban. You killed it stone-dead. Since then when you've kissed me I've had to clench my hands so as not to turn my face away. The mere thought of anything else makes me feel physically sick. I loathe your complacence and your frightful insensitiveness. Perhaps I could have forgiven it if it had been just a moment's weakness and if afterwards you'd been ashamed. I should have been miserable, but I think my love was so great that I should only have felt pity for you. But you're incapable of shame. And now I believe in nothing. You're only a silly, pretentious vulgar poseur. I would rather be the wife of a second-rate planter so long as he had the common human virtues of a man than the wife of a fake like you.'

He did not answer. Gradually his face began to discompose. Those handsome, regular features of his horribly distorted and suddenly he broke out into loud sobs. She gave a little cry.

'Don't, Alban, don't.'

'Oh, darling, how can you be so cruel to me? I adore you. I'd give my whole life to please you. I can't live without you.'

She put out her arms as though to ward off a blow.

'No, no, Alban, don't try to move me. I can't. I must go. I can't live with you any more. It would be frightful. I can never forget. I must tell you the truth, I have only contempt for you and repulsion.'

He sank down at her feet and tried to cling to her knees. With a gasp she sprang up and he buried his head in the empty chair. He cried painfully with sobs that tore his chest. The sound was horrible. The tears streamed from Anne's eyes and, putting her hands to her ears to shut out that dreadful, hysterical sobbing, blindly stumbling she rushed to the door and ran out.

A. E. COPPARD

Fifty Pounds

After tea Philip Repton and Eulalia Burnes discussed their gloomy circumstances. Repton was the precarious sort of London journalist, a dark deliberating man, lean and drooping, full of genteel unprosperity, who wrote articles about *Single Tax, Diet and Reason, The Futility of this, that, and the other,* or *The Significance of the other, that, and this*; all done with a bleak care and signed P. Stick Repton. Eulalia was brown-haired and hardy, undeliberating and intuitive; she had been milliner, clerk, domestic help, and something in a canteen; and P. Stick Repton had, as one commonly says, picked her up at a time when she was drifting about London without a penny in her purse, without even a purse, and he had not yet put her down.

'I can't understand! It's sickening, monstrous!' Lally was fumbling with a match before the penny gas-fire, for when it was evening, in September, it always got chilly on a floor so high up. Their flat was a fourth-floor one and there were—O, fifteen thousand stairs! Out of the window and beyond the chimneys you could see the long glare from lights in High Holborn, and hear the hums and hoots of buses. And that was a comfort.

'Lower! Turn it lower!' yelled Philip. The gas had ignited with an astounding thump; the kneeling Lally had thrown up her hands and dropped the matchbox, saying 'Damn' in the same tone as one might say Good morning to a milkman.

'You shouldn't do it, you know,' grumbled Repton.

'You'll blow us to the deuce.' And that was just like Lally, that was Lally all over, always: the gas, the nobs of sugar in his tea, the way she . . . and the, the . . . O dear, dear! In their early life together, begun so abruptly and illicitly six months before, her simple hidden beauties had delighted him by their surprises; they had peered and shone brighter, had waned and recurred; she was less the one star in his universe than a faint galaxy.

This room of theirs was a dingy room, very small but very high. A lanky gas-tube swooped from the middle of the ceiling towards the middle of the table-cloth as if burning to discover whether that was pink or saffron or fawn—and it *was* hard to tell—but on perceiving that the cloth, whatever its tint, was disturbingly spangled with dozens of cup-stains and several large envelopes, the gas-tube in the violence of its disappointment contorted itself abruptly, assumed a lateral bend, and put out its tongue of flame at an oleograph of Mona Lisa which hung above the fire-place.

Those envelopes were the torment to Lally; they were the sickening, monstrous manifestations which she could not understand. There were always some of them lying there, or about the room, bulging with manuscripts that no editors—they *couldn't* have perused them—wanted; and so it had come to the desperate point when, as Lally was saying, something had to be done about things. Repton had done all *he* could; he wrote unceasingly, all day, all night, but all his projects insolvently withered, and morning, noon, and evening brought his manuscripts back as unwanted as snow in summer. He was depressed and baffled and weary. And there was simply nothing else he could do, nothing in the world. Apart from his own wonderful gift he was useless, Lally knew, and he was being steadily and stupidly murdered by those editors. It was weeks since they had eaten a proper meal. Whenever they obtained any real nice food now, they sat down to it silently, intently, and destructively. As far as Lally could tell there seemed to be no prospect of any such meals again in life or time, and the worst of it all was Philip's pride—he was actually too proud to ask any one for assistance! Not that he would be too proud to accept help if it were offered to him: O no, if it came he would rejoice at it! But still, he had that nervous shrinking pride that coiled upon itself, and he would not ask; he was like a wounded animal that hid its woe far away from the rest of the world. Only Lally knew his need, but why could not other people see it— those villainous editors! His own wants were so modest and he had a generous mind.

'Phil,' Lally said, seating herself at the table. Repton was lolling in a wicker arm-chair beside the gas-fire. 'I'm not going on waiting and waiting any longer, I must go and get a job. Yes, I must. We get poorer and poorer. We can't go on like it any longer, there's no use, and I can't bear it.'

'No, no, I can't have that, my dear. . . .'

'But I will!' she cried. 'O, why are you so proud?'

'Proud! Proud!' He stared into the gas-fire, his tired arms hanging limp over the arms of the chair. 'You don't understand. There are things the flesh has to endure, and things the spirit too must endure. . . .' Lally loved to hear him talk like that; and it was just as well, for Repton was much given to such discoursing. Deep in her mind was the conviction that he had simple access to profound, almost unimaginable, wisdom. 'It isn't pride, it is just that there is a certain order in life, in my life, that it would not do for. I could not bear it, I could never rest: I can't explain that, but just believe it, Lally.' His head was empty but unbowed; he spoke quickly and finished almost angrily. 'If only I had money! It's not for myself. I can stand all this, any amount of it. I've done so before, and I shall do again and again I've no doubt. But I have to think of you.'

That was fiercely annoying. Lally got up and went and stood over him.

'Why are you so stupid? I can think for myself and fend for myself. I'm not married to you. You have your pride, but I can't starve for it. And I've a pride, too, I'm a burden to you. If you won't let me work now while we're together, then I must leave you and work for myself.'

'Leave! Leave me now? When things are so bad?' His white face gleamed his perturbation up at her. 'O well, go, go.' But then, mournfully moved, he took her hands and fondled them. 'Don't be a fool, Lally; it's only a passing depression, this; I've known worse before, and it never lasts long, something turns up, always does. There's good and bad in it all, but there's more goodness than anything else. You see.'

'I don't want to wait for ever, even for goodness. I don't believe in it, I never see it, never feel it, it is no use to me. I could go and steal, or walk the streets, or do any dirty thing—easily. What's the good of goodness if it isn't any use?'

'But, but,' Repton stammered, 'what's the use of bad, if it isn't any better?'

'I mean . . .' began Lally.

'You don't mean anything, my dear girl.'

'I mean, when you haven't any choice it's no use talking moral, or having pride, it's stupid. O, my darling'—she slid down to him and lay against his breast—'it's not you, you are everything to me; that's why it angers me so, this treatment of you, all hard blows and no comfort. It will never be any different, I feel it will never be different now, and it terrifies me.'

'Pooh!' Repton kissed her and comforted her: she was his beloved. 'When things are wrong with us our fancies take their tone from our misfortunes, badness, evil. I sometimes have a queer stray feeling that one day I shall be hanged. Yes, I don't know what for, what *could* I be hanged for? And, do you know, at other times I've had a kind of intuition that one day I shall be—what do you think?—Prime Minister of the country! Yes, well, you can't reason against such things. I know what I should do, I've my plans, I've even made a list of the men for my Cabinet. Yes, well, there you are!'

But Lally had made up her mind to leave him; she would leave him for a while and earn her own living. When things took a turn for the better she would join him again. She told him this. She had friends who were going to get her some work.

'But what are you going to do, Lally, I . . . '

'I'm going away to Glasgow,' said she.

'Glasgow? He had heard things about Glasgow! Good heavens!'

'I've some friends there,' the girl went on steadily. She had got up and was sitting on the arm of his chair. 'I wrote to them last week. They can get me a job almost any when, and I can stay with them. They want me to go—they've sent the money for my fare. I think I shall have to go.'

'You don't love me then!' said the man.

Lally kissed him.

'But *do* you? Tell me!'

'Yes, my dear,' said Lally, 'of course.'

An uneasiness possessed him; he released her moodily. Where was their wild passion flown to? She was staring at him intently, then she tenderly said: 'My love, don't you be melancholy, don't take it to heart so. I'd cross the world to find you a pin.'

'No, no, you musn't do that,' he exclaimed idiotically. At her indulgent smile he grimly laughed too, and then sank back in his chair. The girl stood up and went about the room doing vague nothings, until he spoke again.

'So you are tired of me?'

Lally went to him steadily and knelt down by his chair. 'If I was tired of you, Phil, I'd kill myself.'

Moodily he ignored her. 'I suppose it had to end like this. But I've loved you desperately.' Lally was now weeping on his shoulder, and he began to twirl a lock of her rich brown hair absently with his fingers as if it were a seal on a watch chain. 'I'd been thinking we might as well get married, as soon as things had turned round.'

'I'll come back, Phil,'—she clasped him so tenderly—'as soon as you want me.'

'But you are not really going?'

'Yes,' said Lally.

'You're not to go!'

'I wouldn't go if . . . if anything . . . if you had any luck. But as we are now I must go away, to give you a chance. You see that, darling Phil?'

'You're not to go; I object. I just love you, Lally, that's all, and of course I want to keep you here.'

'Then what are we to do?'

'I . . . don't . . . know. Things drop out of the sky.
But we must be together. You're not to go.'

Lally sighed: he was stupid. And Repton began
to turn over in his mind the dismal knowledge that
she had taken this step in secret, she had not told him
while she was trying to get to Glasgow. Now here
she was with the fare, and as good as gone! Yes, it
was all over.

'When do you propose to go?'

'Not for a few days, nearly a fortnight.'

'Good God,' he moaned. Yes, it was all over
then. He had never dreamed that this would be the
end, that she would be the first to break away.
He had always envisaged a tender scene in which
he could tell her, with dignity and gentle humour,
that . . . Well, he never had quite hit upon the
words he would use, but that was the kind of setting.
And now, here she was with her fare to Glasgow,
her heart turned towards Glasgow, and she as good
as gone to Glasgow! No dignity, no gentle humour
—in fact he was enraged—sullen but enraged; he
boiled furtively. But he said with mournful calm:

'I've so many misfortunes, I suppose I can bear
this, too.' Gloomy and tragic he was.

'Dear, darling Phil, it's for your own sake I'm
going.'

Repton sniffed derisively. 'We are always mis-
taken in the reasons for our commonest actions;
Nature derides us all. You are sick of me; I can't
blame you.'

Eulalia was so moved that she could only weep
again. Nevertheless she wrote to her friends in
Glasgow promising to be with them by a stated date.

Towards the evening of the following day, at a

time when she was alone, a letter arrived addressed to herself. It was from a firm of solicitors in Cornhill inviting her to call upon them. A flame leaped up in Lally's heart: it might mean the offer of some work which would keep her in London after all! If only it were so she would accept it on the spot, and Philip would have to be made to see the reasonability of it. But at the office in Cornhill a more astonishing outcome awaited her. There she showed her letter to a little office boy with scarcely any finger-nails and very little nose, and he took it to an elderly man who had a superabundance of both. Smiling affably the long-nosed man led her upstairs into the sombre den of a gentleman who had some white hair and a lumpy yellow complexion. Having put to her a number of questions relating to her family history, and appearing to be satisfied and not at all surprised by her answers, this gentleman revealed to Lally the overpowering tidings that she was entitled to a legacy of eighty pounds by the will of a forgotten and recently deceased aunt. Subject to certain formalities, proofs of identity and so forth, he promised Lally the possession of the money within about a week.

Lally's descent to the street, her emergence into the clamouring atmosphere, her walk along to Holborn, were accomplished in a state of blessedness and trance, a trance in which life became a thousand times aerially enlarged, movement was a delight, and thought a rapture. She would give all the money to Philip, and if he very much wanted it she would even marry him now. Perhaps, though, she would save ten pounds of it for herself. The other seventy would keep them for . . . it was impossible to say how long it would keep them. They could have a little holiday somewhere in the country together, he was so worn and weary. Perhaps she had better not tell Philip anything at all about it until her lovely money was really in her hand. Nothing in life, at least nothing about money, was ever certain; something horrible might happen at the crucial moment and the money be snatched from her very fingers. O, she would go mad then! So for some days she kept her wonderful secret.

Their imminent separation had given Repton a tender sadness that was very moving. 'Eulalia,' he would say; for he had suddenly adopted the formal version of her name: 'Eulalia, we've had a great time together, a wonderful time, there will never be anything like it again.' She often shed tears, but she kept the grand secret still locked in her heart. Indeed, it occurred to her very forcibly that even now his stupid pride might cause him to reject her money altogether. Silly, silly Philip! Of course it would have been different if they had married; he would naturally have taken it then, and really, it would have *been* his. She would have to think out some dodge to overcome his scruples. Scruples were *such* a nuisance, but then it was very noble of him: there were not many men who wouldn't take money from a girl they were living with.

Well, a week later she was summoned again to the office in Cornhill and received from the white-haired gentleman a cheque for eighty pounds drawn on the Bank of England to the order of Eulalia Burnes. Miss Burnes desired to cash the cheque straightway, so the large-nosed elderly clerk was deputed to accompany her to the Bank of England close by and assist in procuring the money.

'A very nice errand!' exclaimed that gentleman as they crossed to Threadneedle Street past the Royal Exchange. Miss Burnes smiled her acknowledgement, and he began to tell her of other windfalls that had been disbursed in his time—but vast sums, very great persons—until she began to infer that Blackbean, Carp, and Ransome were universal dispensers of heavenly largesse.

'Yes, but,' said the clerk, hawking a good deal from an affliction of catarrh, 'I never got any myself, and never will. If I did, do you know what I would do with it?' But at that moment they entered the portals of the bank, and in the excitement of the business, Miss Burnes forgot to ask the clerk how he would use a legacy, and thus she possibly lost a most valuable slice of knowledge. With one fifty-pound note and six five-pound notes clasped in her handbag she bade good-bye to the long-nosed clerk, who shook her fervently by the hand and assured her that Blackbean, Carp, and Ransome would be delighted at all times to undertake any commissions on her behalf. Then she fled along the pavement, blithe as a bird, until she was breathless with her flight. Presently she came opposite the window of a typewriting agency. Tripping airily into its office she laid a scrap of paper before a lovely Hebe who was typing there.

'I want this typed, if you please,' said Lally.

The beautiful typist read the words on the scrap of paper and stared at the heiress.

'I don't want any address to appear,' said Lally; 'just a plain sheet, please.'

A few moments later she received a neatly typed page folded in an envelope, and after paying the charge she hurried off to a District Messenger office. Here she addressed the envelope in a disguised hand to *P. Stick Repton, Esq.*, at their address in Holborn. She read the typed letter through again:

Dᴇᴀʀ Sɪʀ,

In common with many others I entertain the greatest admiration for your literary abilities, and I therefore beg you to accept this tangible expression of that admiration from a constant reader of your articles who, for purely private reasons, desires to remain anonymous.

Your very sincere
WELLWISHER.

Placing the fifty-pound note upon the letter Lally carefully folded them together and put them both into the envelope. The attendant then gave it to a uniformed lad, who sauntered off whistling very casually, somewhat to Lally's alarm—he looked so small and careless to be entrusted with fifty pounds. Then Lally went out, changed one of her five-pound notes and had a lunch—half-crown, but it was worth it. O, how enchanting and exciting London was! In two days more she would have been gone: now she would have to write off at once to her Glasgow friends and tell them she had changed her mind, that she was now settled in London. O, how enchanting and delightful! And to-night he would take her out to dine in some fine restaurant, and they would do a theatre. She did not really want to marry Phil, they had got on so well without it, but if he wanted that too she did not mind—much. They would go away into the country for a whole week. What money would do! Marvellous! And looking round the restaurant she felt sure that no other woman there, no matter how well-dressed, had as much as thirty pounds in her handbag.

Returning home in the afternoon she became conscious of her own betraying radiance; very demure and subdued and usual she would have to be, or he might guess the cause of it. Though she danced up the long flights of stairs, she entered their room quietly, but the sight of Repton staring out of the window, forlorn as a drowsy horse, overcame her and she rushed to embrace him, crying 'Darling!'

'Hullo, hullo!' he smiled.

'I'm so fond of you, Phil dear.'

'But . . . but you're deserting me!'

'O no,' she cried archly; 'I'm not—not deserting you.'

'All right.' Repton shrugged his shoulders, but he seemed happier. He did not mention the fifty pounds then: perhaps it had not come yet—or perhaps he was thinking to surprise her.

'Let's go for a walk, it's a screaming lovely day,' said Lally.

'O, I dunno.' He yawned and stretched. 'Nearly tea-time, isn't it?'

'Well, we . . . ' Lally was about to suggest having tea out somewhere, but she bethought herself in time. 'I suppose it is. Yes, it is.'

So they stayed in for tea. No sooner was tea over than Repton remarked that he had an engagement somewhere. Off he went, leaving Lally disturbed and anxious. Why had he not mentioned the fifty pounds? Surely it had not gone to the wrong address? This suspicion once formed, Lally soon became certain, tragically sure, that she had mis-addressed the envelope herself. A conviction that she had put No. 17 instead of No. 71 was almost overpowering, and she fancied that she hadn't even put London on the envelope—but Glasgow. That was impossible, though, but—O, the horror!—somebody else was enjoying their fifty pounds. The girl's

fears were not allayed by the running visit she paid to
the messenger office that evening, for the rash imp
who had been entrusted with her letter had gone
home and therefore could not be interrogated until
the morrow. By now she was sure that he had blun-
dered; he had been so casual with an important
letter like that! Lally never did, and never would
again, trust any little boys who wore their hats so
much on one side, were so glossy with hair-oil, and
went about whistling just to madden you. She
burned to ask where the boy lived, but in spite of her
desperate desire she could not do so. She dared not,
it would expose her to . . . to something or other she
could only feel, not name; you had to keep cool, to
let nothing, not even curiosity, master you.

Hurrying home again, though hurrying was not
her custom, and there was no occasion for it, she
wrote the letter to her Glasgow friends. Then it
crossed her mind that it would be wiser not to post
the letter that night; better wait until the morning,
after she had discovered what the horrible little
messenger had done with her letter. Bed was a poor
refuge from her thoughts, but she accepted it, and
when Phil came home she was not sleeping. While he
undressed he told her of the lecture he had been to,
something about Agrarian Depopulation it was, but
even after he had stretched himself beside her, he did
not speak about the fifty pounds. Nothing, not even
curiosity, should master her, and so she calmed
herself, and in time fitfully slept.

At breakfast next morning he asked her what she
was going to do that day.

'O,' replied Lally offhandedly, 'I've a lot of things
to see to, you know; I must go out. I'm sorry the
porridge is so awful this morning, Phil, but . . .'

'Awful?' he broke in. 'But it's nicer than usual! Where are you going? I thought—our last day, you know—we might go out somewhere together.'

'Dear Phil!' Lovingly she stretched out a hand to be caressed across the table. 'But I've several things to do. I'll come back early, eh?' She got up and hurried round to embrace him.

'All right,' he said. 'Don't be long.'

Off went Lally to the messenger office, at first as happy as a bird, but on approaching the building the old tremors assailed her. Inside the room was the cocky little boy who bade her 'Good morning' with laconic assurance. Lally at once questioned him, and when he triumphantly produced a delivery book she grew limp with her suppressed fear, one fear above all others. For a moment she did not want to look at it: Truth hung by a hair, and as long as it so hung she might swear it was a lie. But there it was, written right across the page, an entry of a letter delivered, signed for in the well-known hand, *P. Stick Repton.* There was no more doubt, only a sharp indignant agony as if she had been stabbed with a dagger of ice.

'O yes, thank you,' said Lally calmly. 'Did you hand it to him yourself?'

'Yes'm,' replied the boy, and he described Philip.

'Did he open the letter?'

'Yes'm.'

'There was no answer?'

'No'm.'

'All right.' Fumbling in her bag, she added: 'I think I've got a sixpence for you.'

Out in the street again she tremblingly chuckled to herself. 'So that is what he is like, after all. Cruel and mean!' He was going to let her go and keep the

money in secret to himself! How despicable! Cruel
and mean, cruel and mean. She hummed it to herself: 'Cruel and mean, cruel and mean!' It eased her
tortured bosom. 'Cruel and mean!' And he was waiting at home for her, waiting with a smile for their last
day together. It would *have* to be their last day. She
tore up the letter to her Glasgow friends, for now she
must go to them. So cruel and mean! Let him wait!
A 'bus stopped beside her and she stepped on to it,
climbing to the top and sitting there while the air
chilled her burning features. The 'bus made a long
journey to Plaistow. She knew nothing of Plaistow,
she wanted to know nothing of Plaistow, but she did
not care where the 'bus took her; she only wanted
to keep moving, and moving away, as far away as
possible from Holborn and from him, and not once
let those hovering tears fall down.

From Plaistow she turned and walked back as far
as the Mile End Road. Thereabouts, wherever she
went she met clergymen, dozens of them. There
must be a conference, about charity or something,
Lally thought. With a vague desire to confide her
trouble to some one, she observed them; it would
relieve the strain. But there was none she could tell
her sorrow to, and failing that, when she came to a
neat restaurant she entered it and consumed a fish.
Just beyond her three sleek parsons were lunching,
sleek and pink; bald, affable, consoling men, all very
much alike.

'I saw Carter yesterday,' she heard one say. Lally
liked listening to the conversation of strangers, and
she had often wondered what clergymen talked about
among themselves.

'What, Carter! Indeed. Nice fellow Carter. How
was he?'

'Carter loves preaching, you know!' cried the third.

'O yes, he loves preaching!'

'Ha ha ha, yes.'

'Ha ha ha, oom.'

'Awf'ly good preacher, though.'

'Yes, awf'ly good.'

'And he's awf'ly good at comic songs, too.'

'Yes?'

'Yes!'

Three glasses of water, a crumbling of bread, a silence suggestive of prayer.

'How long has he been married?'

'Twelve years,' returned the cleric who had met Carter.

'O, twelve years!'

'I've only been married twelve years myself,' said the oldest of them.

'Indeed!'

'Yes, I tarried very long.'

'Ha, ha, ha, yes.'

'Ha, ha, ha, oom.'

'Er . . . have you any family?'

'No.'

Very delicate and dainty in handling their food they were; very delicate and dainty.

'My rectory is a magnificent old house,' continued the recently married one. 'Built originally 1700. Burnt down. Rebuilt 1784.'

'Indeed!'

'Humph!'

'Seventeen bedrooms and two delightful tennis courts.'

'O, well done!' the others cried, and then they all fell with genteel gusto upon a pale blancmange.

From the restaurant the girl sauntered about for a while, and then there was a cinema wherein, seated warm and comfortable in the twitching darkness, she partially stilled her misery. Some nervous fancy kept her roaming in that district for most of the evening. She knew that if she left it she would go home, and she did not want to go home. The naphtha lamps of the booths at Mile End were bright and distracting, and the hum of the evening business was good despite the smell. A man was weaving sweet-stuffs from a pliant roll of warm toffee that he wrestled with as the athlete wrestles with the python. There were stalls with things of iron, with fruit or fish, pots and pans, leather, string, nails. Watches for use—or for ornament—what d'ye lack? A sailor told naughty stories while selling bunches of green grapes out of barrels of cork dust which he swore he had stolen from the Queen of Honolulu. People clamoured for them both. You could buy back numbers of the comic papers at four a penny, rolls of linoleum for very little more—and use either for the others' purpose.

'At thrippence per foot, mesdames,' cried the sweating cheapjack, lashing himself into ecstatic furies, 'that's a piece of fabric weft and woven with triple-strength Andalusian jute, double-hot-pressed with rubber from the island of Pagama, and stencilled by an artist as poisoned his grandfather's cook. That's a piece of fabric, mesdames, as the king of heaven himself wouldn't mind to put down in his parlour—if he had the chance. Do I ask thrippence a foot for that piece of fabric? Mesdames, I was never a daring chap.'

Lally watched it all, she looked and listened; then looked and did not see, listened and did not hear.

Her misery was not the mere disappointment of love, not that kind of misery alone; it was the crushing of an ideal in which love had had its home, a treachery cruel and mean. The sky of night, so smooth, so bestarred, looked wrinkled through her screen of unshed tears; her sorrow was a wild cloud that troubled the moon with darkness.

In miserable desultory wandering she had spent her day, their last day, and now, returning to Holborn in the late evening, she suddenly began to hurry, for a new possibility had come to lighten her dejection. Perhaps, after all, so whimsical he was, he was keeping his 'revelation' until the last day, or even the last hour, when (nothing being known to her, as he imagined) all hopes being gone and they had come to the last kiss, he would take her in his arms and laughingly kill all grief, waving the succour of a flimsy bank-note like a flag of triumph. Perhaps even, in fact surely, that was why he wanted to take her out to-day! O, what a blind, wicked, stupid girl she was, and in a perfect frenzy of bubbling faith she panted homewards for his revealing sign.

From the pavement below she could see that their room was lit. Weakly she climbed the stairs and opened the door. Phil was standing up, staring so strangely at her. Helplessly and half-guilty she began to smile. Without a word said he came quickly to her and crushed her in his arms, her burning silent man, loving and exciting her. Lying against his breast in that constraining embrace, their passionate disaster was gone, her doubts were flown; all perception of the feud was torn from her and deeply drowned in a gulf of bliss. She was aware only of the consoling delight of their reunion, of his amorous kisses, of his tongue tingling the soft down on her upper lip that she disliked and he admired. All the soft wanton endearments that she so loved to hear him speak were singing in her ears, and then he suddenly swung and lifted her up, snapped out the gaslight, and carried her off to bed.

Life that is born of love feeds on love; if the wherewithal be hidden, how shall we stay our hunger? The galaxy may grow dim, or the stars drop in a wandering void; you can neither keep them in your hands nor crumble them in your mind.

What was it Phil had once called her? Numskull! After all it was his own fifty pounds, she had given it to him freely, it was his to do as he liked with. A gift was a gift, it was poor spirit to send money to any one with the covetous expectation that it would return to you. She would surely go to-morrow.

The next morning he awoke her early, and kissed her.

'What time does your train go?' said he.

'Train!' Lally scrambled from his arms and out of bed.

A fine day, a glowing day. O bright, sharp air! Quickly she dressed, and went into the other room to prepare their breakfast. Soon he followed, and they ate silently together, although whenever they were near each other he caressed her tenderly. Afterwards she went into the bedroom and packed her bag; there was nothing more to be done, he was beyond hope. No woman waits to be sacrificed, least of all those who sacrifice themselves with courage and a quiet mind. When she was ready to go she took her portmanteau into the sitting-room; he, too, made to put on his hat and coat.

'No,' murmured Lally, 'you're not to come with me.'

'Pooh, my dear!' he protested; 'nonsense.'

'I won't have you come,' cried Lally with an asperity that impressed him.

'But you can't carry that bag to the station by yourself!'

'I shall take a taxi.' She buttoned her gloves.

'My dear!' His humorous deprecation annoyed her.

'O, bosh!' Putting her gloved hands around his neck she kissed him coolly. 'Good-bye. Write to me often. Let me know how you thrive, won't you, Phil? And'— a little waveringly—'love me always.' She stared queerly at the two dimples in his cheeks; each dimple was a nest of hair that could never be shaved.

'Lally darling, beloved girl! I never loved you more than now, this moment. You are more precious than ever to me.'

At that, she knew her moment of sardonic revelation had come—but she dared not use it, she let it go. She could not so deeply humiliate him by revealing her knowledge of his perfidy. A compassionate divinity smiles at our puny sins. She knew his perfidy, but to triumph in it would defeat her own pride. Let him keep his gracious, mournful airs to the last, false though they were. It was better to part so, better from such a figure than from an abject scarecrow, even though both were the same inside. And something capriciously reminded her, for a flying moment, of elephants she had seen swaying with the grand movement of tidal water— and groping for monkey-nuts.

Lally tripped down the stairs alone. At the end of the street she turned for a last glance. There he was, high up in the window, waving good-byes. And she waved back at him.

E. M. FORSTER

Other Kingdom

I

'"*Quem*, whom; *fugis*, are you avoiding; *ah demens*, you silly ass; *habitarunt di quoque*, gods too have lived in; *silvas*, the woods." Go ahead!'

I always brighten the classics—it is part of my system—and therefore I translated *demens* by 'silly ass'. But Miss Beaumont need not have made a note of the translation, and Ford, who knows better, need not have echoed after me. 'Whom are you avoiding, you silly ass, gods too have lived in the woods.'

'Ye—es,' I replied, with scholarly hesitation. 'Ye—es. *Silvas*—woods, wooded spaces, the country generally. Yes. *Demens*, of course, is *de—mens*. "Ah, witless fellow! Gods, I say, even gods have dwelt in the woods ere now."'

'But I thought gods always lived in the sky,' said Mrs. Worters, interrupting our lesson for I think the third-and-twentieth time.

'Not always,' answered Miss Beaumont. As she spoke she inserted 'witless fellow' as an alternative to 'silly ass'.

'I always thought they lived in the sky.'

'Oh, no, Mrs. Worters,' the girl repeated. 'Not always.' And finding her place in the note-book she read as follows: 'Gods. Where. Chief deities—Mount Olympus. Pan—most places, as name implies. Oreads—mountains. Sirens, Tritons, Nereids—water (salt). Naiads—water (fresh). Satyrs, Fauns, &c.—woods. Dryads—trees.'

'Well, dear, you have learnt a lot. And will you now tell me what good it has done you?'

'It has helped me—' faltered Miss Beaumont. She was very earnest over her classics. She wished she could have said what good they had done her.

Ford came to her rescue. 'Of course it's helped you. The classics are full of tips. They teach you how to dodge things.'

I begged my young friend not to dodge his Virgil lesson.

'But they do!' he cried. 'Suppose that long-haired brute Apollo wants to give you a music lesson. Well, out you pop into the laurels. Or Universal Nature comes along. You aren't feeling particularly keen on Universal Nature, so you turn into a reed.'

'Is Jack mad?' asked Mrs. Worters.

But Miss Beaumont had caught the allusions— which were quite ingenious I must admit. 'And Crœsus?' she inquired. 'What was it one turned into to get away from Crœsus?'

I hastened to tidy up her mythology. 'Midas, Miss Beaumont, not Crœsus. And he turns you— you don't turn yourself: he turns you into gold.'

'There's no dodging Midas,' said Ford.

'Surely—' said Miss Beaumont. She had been learning Latin not quite a fortnight, but she would have corrected the Regius Professor.

He began to tease her. 'Oh, there's no dodging Midas! He just comes, he touches you, and you pay him several thousand per cent. at once. You're gold—a young golden lady—if he touches you.'

'I won't be touched!' she cried, relapsing into her habitual frivolity.

'Oh, but he'll touch you.'

'He shan't!'

'He will.'

'He shan't!'

'He will.'

Miss Beaumont took up her Virgil and smacked Ford over the head with it.

'Evelyn! Evelyn!' said Mrs. Worters. 'Now you are forgetting yourself. And you also forget my question. What good has Latin done you?'

'Mr. Ford—what good has Latin done you?'

'Mr. Inskip—what good has Latin done us?'

So I was let in for the classical controversy. The arguments for the study of Latin are perfectly sound, but they are difficult to remember, and the afternoon sun was hot, and I needed my tea. But I had to justify my existence as a coach, so I took off my eye-glasses and breathed on them and said, 'My dear Ford, what a question!'

'It's all right for Jack,' said Mrs. Worters. 'Jack has to pass his entrance examination. But what's the good of it for Evelyn? None at all.'

'No, Mrs. Worters,' I persisted, pointing my eye-glasses at her. 'I cannot agree. Miss Beaumont is—in a sense—new to our civilization. She is entering it, and Latin is one of the subjects in her entrance examination also. No one can grasp modern life without some knowledge of its origins.'

'But why should she grasp modern life?' said the tiresome woman.

'Well, there you are!' I retorted, and shut up my eye-glasses with a snap.

'Mr. Inskip, I am not there. Kindly tell me what's the good of it all. Oh, I've been through it myself: Jupiter, Venus, Juno, I know the lot of them. And many of the stories not at all proper.'

'Classical education,' I said drily, 'is not entirely

confined to classical mythology. Though even the
mythology has its value. Dreams if you like, but
there is value in dreams.'

'I too have dreams,' said Mrs. Worters, 'but I am
not so foolish as to mention them afterwards.'

Mercifully we were interrupted. A rich virile voice
close behind us said, 'Cherish your dreams!' We
had been joined by our host, Harcourt Worters—
Mrs. Worters' son, Miss Beaumont's fiancé, Ford's
guardian, my employer: I must speak of him as
Mr. Worters.

'Let us cherish our dreams!' he repeated. 'All
day I've been fighting, haggling, bargaining. And to
come out on to this lawn and see you all learning
Latin, so happy, so passionless, so Arcadian——'

He did not finish the sentence, but sank into the
chair next to Miss Beaumont, and possessed himself of
her hand. As he did so she sang: 'Áh yoù sílly àss
góds lìve in woóds!'

'What have we here?' said Mr. Worters with a
slight frown.

With the other hand she pointed to me.

'Virgil—' I stammered. 'Colloquial translation——'

'Oh, I see; a colloquial translation of poetry.'
Then his smile returned. 'Perhaps if gods live in
woods, that is why woods are so dear. I have just
bought Other Kingdom Copse!'

Loud exclamations of joy. Indeed, the beeches in
that copse are as fine as any in Hertfordshire. Moreover, it, and the meadow by which it is approached,
have always made an ugly notch in the rounded
contours of the Worters estate. So we were all very
glad that Mr. Worters had purchased Other Kingdom. Only Ford kept silent, stroking his head where

the Virgil had hit it, and smiling a little to himself as he did so.

'Judging from the price I paid, I should say there was a god in every tree. But price, this time, was no object.' He glanced at Miss Beaumont.

'You admire beeches, Evelyn, do you not?'

'I forget always which they are. Like this?'

She flung her arms up above her head, close together, so that she looked like a slender column. Then her body swayed and her delicate green dress quivered over it with the suggestion of countless leaves.

'My dear child!' exclaimed her lover.

'No: that is a silver birch,' said Ford.

'Oh, of course. Like this, then.' And she twitched up her skirts so that for a moment they spread out in great horizontal layers, like the layers of a beech.

We glanced at the house, but none of the servants were looking. So we laughed, and said she ought to go on the variety stage.

'Ah, this is the kind I like!' she cried, and practised the beech-tree again.

'I thought so,' said Mr. Worters. 'I thought so. Other Kingdom Copse is yours.'

'Mine——?' She had never had such a present in her life. She could not realize it.

'The purchase will be drawn up in your name. You will sign the deed. Receive the wood, with my love. It is a second engagement ring.'

'But is it—is it mine? Can I—do what I like there?'

'You can,' said Mr. Worters, smiling.

She rushed at him and kissed him. She kissed Mrs. Worters. She would have kissed myself and

Ford if we had not extruded elbows. The joy of possession had turned her head.

'It's mine! I can walk there, work there, live there. A wood of my own! Mine for ever.'

'Yours, at all events, for ninety-nine years.'

'Ninety-nine years?' I regret to say there was a tinge of disappointment in her voice.

'My dear child! Do you expect to live longer?'

'I suppose I can't,' she replied, and flushed a little. 'I don't know.'

'Ninety-nine seems long enough to most people. I have got this house, and the very lawn you are standing on, on a lease of ninety-nine years. Yet I call them my own, and I think I am justified. Am I not?'

'Oh, yes.'

'Ninety-nine years is practically for ever. Isn't it?'

'Oh, yes. It must be.'

Ford possesses a most inflammatory note-book. Outside it is labelled 'Private', inside it is headed 'Practically a book'. I saw him make an entry in it now, 'Eternity: practically ninety-nine years'.

Mr. Worters, as if speaking to himself, now observed: 'My goodness! My goodness! How land has risen! Perfectly astounding.'

I saw that he was in need of a Boswell, so I said: 'Has it, indeed?'

'My dear Inskip. Guess what I could have got that wood for ten years ago! But I refused. Guess why.'

We could not guess why.

'Because the transaction would not have been straight.' A most becoming blush spread over his face as he uttered the noble word. 'Not straight. Straight legally. But not morally straight. We were to force the hands of the man who owned it. I refused. The others—decent fellows in their way— told me I was squeamish. I said, "Yes. Perhaps I am. My name is plain Harcourt Worters—not a well-known name if you go outside the City and my own country, but a name which, where it is known, carries, I flatter myself, some weight. And I will not sign my name to this. That is all. Call me squeamish if you like. But I will not sign. It is just a fad of mine. Let us call it a fad."' He blushed again. Ford believes that his guardian blushes all over— that if you could strip him and make him talk nobly he would look like a boiled lobster. There is a picture of him in this condition in the note-book.

'So the man who owned it then didn't own it now?' said Miss Beaumont, who had followed the narrative with some interest.

'Oh, no!' said Mr. Worters.

'Why no!' said Mrs. Worters absently, as she hunted in the grass for her knitting-needle. 'Of course not. It belongs to the widow.'

'Tea!' cried her son, springing vivaciously to his feet. 'I see tea and I want it. Come, mother. Come along, Evelyn. I can tell you it's no joke, a hard day in the battle of life. For life is practically a battle. To all intents and purposes a battle. Except for a few lucky fellows who can read books, and so avoid the realities. But I——'

His voice died away as he escorted the two ladies over the smooth lawn and up the stone steps to the terrace, on which the footman was placing tables and little chairs and a silver kettle-stand. More ladies came out of the house. We could just hear their shouts of excitement as they also were told of the purchase of Other Kingdom.

I like Ford. The boy has the makings of a scholar and—though for some reason he objects to the word —of a gentleman. It amused me now to see his lip curl with the vague cynicism of youth. He cannot understand the footman and the solid silver kettle-stand. They make him cross. For he has dreams— not exactly spiritual dreams: Mr. Worters is the man for those—but dreams of the tangible and the actual: robust dreams, which take him, not to heaven, but to another earth. There are no footmen in this other earth, and the kettle-stands, I suppose, will not be made of silver, and I know that everything is to be itself, and not practically something else. But what this means, and, if it means anything, what the good of it is, I am not prepared to say. For though I have just said 'there is value in dreams', I only said it to silence old Mrs. Worters.

'Go ahead, man! We can't have tea till we've got through something.'

He turned his chair away from the terrace, so that he could sit looking at the meadows and at the stream that runs through the meadows, and at the beech-trees of Other Kingdom that rise beyond the stream. Then, most gravely and admirably, he began to construe the Eclogues of Virgil.

II

Other Kingdom Copse is just like any other beech copse, and I am therefore spared the fatigue of describing it. And the stream in front of it, like many other streams, is not crossed by a bridge in the right place, and you must either walk round a mile or else you must paddle. Miss Beaumont suggested that we should paddle.

Mr. Worters accepted the suggestion tumultuously. It only became evident gradually that he was not going to adopt it.

'What fun! what fun! We will paddle to your kingdom. If only—if only it wasn't for the tea-things.'

'But you can carry the tea-things on your back.'

'Why, yes! so I can. Or the servants could.'

'Harcourt—no servants. This is my picnic, and my wood. I'm going to settle everything. I didn't tell you: I've got all the food. I've been in the village with Mr. Ford.'

'In the village——?'

'Yes. We got biscuits and oranges and half a pound of tea. That's all you'll have. He carried them up. And he'll carry them over the stream. I want you just to lend me some tea-things—not the best ones. I'll take care of them. That's all.'

'Dear creature. . . .'

'Evelyn,' said Mrs. Worters, 'how much did you and Jack pay for that tea?'

'For the half-pound, tenpence.'

Mrs. Worters received the announcement in gloomy silence.

'Mother!' cried Mr. Worters. 'Why, I forgot! How could we go paddling with mother?'

'Oh, but, Mrs. Worters, we could carry you over.'

'Thank you, dearest child. I am sure you could.'

'Alas! alas! Evelyn. Mother is laughing at us. She would sooner die than be carried. And alas! there are my sisters, and Mrs. Osgood: she has a cold, tiresome woman. No: we shall have to go round by the bridge.'

'But some of us——' began Ford. His guardian cut him short with a quick look.

So we went round—a procession of eight. Miss

Beaumont led us. She was full of fun—at least so I
thought at the time, but when I reviewed her speeches
afterwards I could not find in them anything amusing. It was all this kind of thing: 'Single file! Pretend
you're in church and don't talk. Mr. Ford, turn out
your toes. Harcourt—at the bridge throw to the
Naiad a pinch of tea. She has a headache. She has
had a headache for nineteen hundred years.' All
that she said was quite stupid. I cannot think why I
liked it at the time.

As we approached the copse she said, 'Mr.
Inskip, sing, and we'll sing after you: Áh yoù sílly
àss góds live in woóds.' I cleared my throat and gave
out the abominable phrase, and we all chanted it as
if it were a litany. There was something attractive
about Miss Beaumont. I was not surprised that
Harcourt had picked her out of 'Ireland' and had
brought her home, without money, without con-
nexions, almost without antecedents, to be his bride.
It was daring of him, but he knew himself to be
a daring fellow. She brought him nothing; but
that he could afford, he had so vast a surplus of
spiritual and commercial goods. 'In time,' I heard
him tell his mother, 'in time Evelyn will repay me
a thousandfold.' Meanwhile there was something
attractive about her. If it were my place to like
people, I could have liked her very much.

'Stop singing!' she cried. We had entered the
wood. 'Welcome, all of you.' We bowed. Ford,
who had not been laughing, bowed down to the
ground. 'And now be seated. Mrs. Worters—will
you sit there—against that tree with a green trunk?
It will show up your beautiful dress.'

'Very well, dear, I will,' said Mrs. Worters.

'Anna—there. Mr. Inskip next to her. Then Ruth

and Mrs. Osgood. Oh, Harcourt—do sit a little
forward, so that you'll hide the house. I don't want
to see the house at all.'

'I won't!' laughed her lover, 'I want my back
against a tree, too.'

'Miss Beaumont,' asked Ford, 'where shall I sit?'
He was standing at attention, like a soldier.

'Oh, look at all these Worters!' she cried, 'and
one little Ford in the middle of them!' For she
was at that state of civilization which appreciates
a pun.

'Shall I stand, Miss Beaumont? Shall I hide the
house from you if I stand?'

'Sit down, Jack, you baby!' cried his guardian,
breaking in with needless asperity. 'Sit down!'

'He may just as well stand if he will,' said she.
'Just pull back your soft hat, Mr. Ford. Like a halo.
Now you hide even the smoke from the chimneys.
And it makes you look beautiful.'

'Evelyn! Evelyn! You are too hard on the boy.
You'll tire him. He's one of those bookworms. He's
not strong. Let him sit down.'

'Aren't you strong?' she asked.

'I am strong!' he cried. It is quite true. Ford has
no right to be strong, but he is. He never did his
dumb-bells or played in his school fifteen. But the
muscles came. He thinks they came while he was
reading Pindar.

'Then you may just as well stand, if you will.'

'Evelyn! Evelyn! childish, selfish maiden! If poor
Jack gets tired I will take his place. Why don't you
want to see the house? Eh?'

Mrs. Worters and the Miss Worters moved
uneasily. They saw that their Harcourt was not
quite pleased. Theirs not to question why. It was

for Evelyn to remove his displeasure, and they glanced at her.

'Well, why don't you want to see your future home? I must say—though I practically planned the house myself—that it looks very well from here. I like the gables. Miss! Answer me!'

I felt for Miss Beaumont. A home-made gable is an awful thing, and Harcourt's mansion looked like a cottage with the dropsy. But what would she say?

She said nothing.

'Well?'

It was as if he had never spoken. She was as merry, as smiling, as pretty as ever, and she said nothing. She had not realized that a question requires an answer.

For us the situation was intolerable. I had to save it by making a tactful reference to the view, which, I said, reminded me a little of the country near Veii. It did not—indeed it could not, for I have never been near Veii. But it is part of my system to make classical allusions. And at all events I saved the situation.

Miss Beaumont was serious and rational at once. She asked me the date of Veii. I made a suitable answer.

'I do like the classics,' she informed us. 'They are so natural. Just writing down things.'

'Ye—es,' said I. 'But the classics have their poetry as well as their prose. They're more than a record of facts.'

'Just writing down things,' said Miss Beaumont, and smiled as if the silly definition pleased her.

Harcourt had recovered himself. 'A very just criticism,' said he. 'It is what I always feel about

the ancient world. It takes us but a very little way.
It only writes things down.'

'What do you mean?' asked Evelyn.

'I mean this—though it is presumptuous to speak
in the presence of Mr. Inskip. This is what I mean.
The classics are not everything. We owe them an
enormous debt; I am the last to undervalue it; I, too,
went through them at school. They are full of
elegance and beauty. But they are not everything.
They were written before men began to really feel.'
He coloured crimson. 'Hence, the chilliness of
classical art—its lack of—of a something. Whereas
later things—Dante—a Madonna of Raphael—some
bars of Mendelssohn——.' His voice tailed reverently away. We sat with our eyes on the ground, not
liking to look at Miss Beaumont. It is a fairly open
secret that she also lacks a something. She has not
yet developed her soul.

The silence was broken by the still small voice of
Mrs. Worters saying that she was faint with hunger.

The young hostess sprang up. She would let none
of us help her: it was her party. She undid the
basket and emptied out the biscuits and oranges
from their bags, and boiled the kettle and poured out
the tea, which was horrible. But we laughed and
talked with the frivolity that suits the open air, and
even Mrs. Worters expectorated her flies with a
smile. Over us all there stood the silent, chivalrous
figure of Ford, drinking tea carefully lest it should
disturb his outline. His guardian, who is a wag,
chaffed him and tickled his ankles and calves.

'Well, this is nice!' said Miss Beaumont. 'I am
happy.'

'Your wood, Evelyn!' said the ladies.

'Her wood for ever!' cried Mr. Worters. 'It is

an unsatisfactory arrangement, a ninety-nine years' lease. There is no feeling of permanency. I reopened negotiations. I have bought her the wood for ever— all right, dear, all right: don't make a fuss.'

'But I must!' she cried. 'For everything's perfect! Every one so kind—and I didn't know most of you a year ago. Oh, it is so wonderful—and now a wood— a wood of my own—a wood for ever. All of you coming to tea with me here! Dear Harcourt—dear people—and just where the house would come and spoil things, there is Mr. Ford!'

'Ha! ha!' laughed Mr. Worters, and slipped his hand up round the boy's ankle. What happened I do not know, but Ford collapsed on to the ground with a sharp cry. To an outsider it might have sounded like a cry of anger or pain. We, who knew better, laughed uproariously.

'Down he goes! Down he goes!' And they struggled playfully, kicking up the mould and the dry leaves.

'Don't hurt my wood!' cried Miss Beaumont.

Ford gave another sharp cry. Mr. Worters withdrew his hand. 'Victory!' he exclaimed. 'Evelyn! behold the family seat!' But Miss Beaumont, in her butterfly fashion, had left us, and was strolling away into her wood.

We packed up the tea-things and then split into groups. Ford went with the ladies. Mr. Worters did me the honour to stop by me.

'Well!' he said, in accordance with his usual formula, 'and how go the classics?'

'Fairly well.'

'Does Miss Beaumont show any ability?'

'I should say that she does. At all events she has enthusiasm.'

'You do not think it is the enthusiasm of a child? I will be frank with you, Mr. Inskip. In many ways Miss Beaumont's practically a child. She has everything to learn: she acknowledges as much herself. Her new life is so different—so strange. Our habits—our thoughts—she has to be initiated into them all.'

I saw what he was driving at, but I am not a fool, and I replied: 'And how can she be initiated better than through the classics?'

'Exactly, exactly,' said Mr. Worters. In the distance we heard her voice. She was counting the beech-trees. 'The only question is—this Latin and Greek—what will she do with it? Can she make anything of it? Can she—well, it's not as if she will ever have to teach it to others.'

'That is true.' And my features might have been observed to become undecided.

'Whether, since she knows so little—I grant you she has enthusiasm. But ought one not to divert her enthusiasm—say to English literature? She scarcely knows her Tennyson at all. Last night in the conservatory I read her that wonderful scene between Arthur and Guinevere. Greek and Latin are all very well, but I sometimes feel we ought to begin at the beginning.'

'You feel,' said I, 'that for Miss Beaumont the classics are something of a luxury.'

'A luxury. That is the exact word, Mr. Inskip. A luxury. A whim. It is all very well for Jack Ford. And here we come to another point. Surely she keeps Jack back? Her knowledge must be elementary.'

'Well, her knowledge *is* elementary: and I must say that it's difficult to teach them together. Jack has read a good deal, one way and another, whereas

Miss Beaumont, though diligent and enthusias-
tic——'

'So I have been feeling. The arrangement is
scarcely fair on Jack?'

'Well, I must admit——'

'Quite so. I ought never to have suggested it. It
must come to an end. Of course, Mr. Inskip, it shall
make no difference to you, this withdrawal of a
pupil.'

'The lessons shall cease at once, Mr. Worters.'

Here she came up to us. 'Harcourt, there are
seventy-eight trees. I have had such a count.'

He smiled down at her. Let me remember to say
that he is tall and handsome, with a strong chin and
liquid brown eyes, and a high forehead and hair not
at all grey. Few things are more striking than a
photograph of Mr. Harcourt Worters.

'Seventy-eight trees?'

'Seventy-eight.'

'Are you pleased?'

'Oh, Harcourt——!'

I began to pack up the tea-things. They both saw
and heard me. It was their own fault if they did not
go farther.

'I'm looking forward to the bridge,' said he. 'A
rustic bridge at the bottom, and then, perhaps, an
asphalt path from the house over the meadow, so
that in all weathers we can walk here dry-shod.
The boys come into the wood—look at all these
initials—and I thought of putting a simple fence, to
prevent any one but ourselves——'

'Harcourt!'

'A simple fence,' he continued, 'just like what I
have put round my garden and the fields. Then at
the other side of the copse, away from the house, I

would put a gate and have keys—two keys, I think—
one for me and one for you—not more; and I would
bring the asphalt path——'

'But Harcourt——'

'But Evelyn!'

'I—I—I——'

'You—you—you——?'

'I—I don't want an asphalt path.'

'No? Perhaps you are right. Cinders perhaps.
Yes. Or even gravel.'

'But Harcourt—I don't want a path at all. I—I—
can't afford a path.'

He gave a roar of triumphant laughter. 'Dearest!
As if you were going to be bothered? The path's
part of my present.'

'The wood is your present,' said Miss Beaumont.
'Do you know—I don't care for the path. I'd rather
always come as we came to-day. And I don't want a
bridge. No—nor a fence either. I don't mind the
boys and their initials. They and the girls have
always come up to Other Kingdom and cut their
names together in the bark. It's called the Fourth
Time of Asking. I don't want it to stop.'

'Ugh!' He pointed to a large heart transfixed by
an arrow. 'Ugh! Ugh!' I suspect that he was
gaining time.

'They cut their names and go away, and when
the first child is born they come again and deepen
the cuts. So for each child. That's how you know:
the initials that go right through to the wood are the
fathers and mothers of large families, and the
scratches in the bark that soon close up are boys and
girls who were never married at all.'

'You wonderful person! I've lived here all my
life and never heard a word of this. Fancy folk-lore

in Hertfordshire! I must tell the Archdeacon: he will be delighted——'

'And Harcourt, I don't want this to stop.'

'My dear girl, the villagers will find other trees! There's nothing particular in Other Kingdom.'

'But——'

'Other Kingdom shall be for us. You and I alone. Our initials only.' His voice sank to a whisper.

'I don't want it fenced in.' Her face was turned to me; I saw that it was puzzled and frightened. 'I hate fences. And bridges. And all paths. It is my wood. Please: you gave me the wood.'

'Why, yes!' he replied, soothing her. But I could see that he was angry. 'Of course. But aha! Evelyn, the meadow's mine; I have a right to fence there— between my domain and yours!'

'Oh, fence me out if you like! Fence me out as much as you like! But never in. Oh, Harcourt, never in. I must be on the outside, I must be where any one can reach me. Year by year—while the initials deepen—the only thing worth feeling—and at last they close up—but one has felt them.'

'Our initials!' he murmured, seizing upon the one word which he had understood and which was useful to him. 'Let us carve our initials now. You and I—a heart if you like it, and an arrow and everything. H. W.—E. B.'

'H. W.,' she repeated, 'and E. B.'

He took out his penknife and drew her away in search of an unsullied tree. 'E. B., Eternal Blessing. Mine! Mine! My haven from the world! My temple of purity. Oh, the spiritual exaltation—you cannot understand it, but you will! Oh, the seclusion of Paradise. Year after year alone together, all in all to each other—year after year, soul to soul, E. B., Everlasting Bliss!'

He stretched out his hand to cut the initials. As he did so she seemed to awake from a dream. 'Harcourt!' she cried, 'Harcourt! What's that? What's that red stuff on your finger and thumb?

III

Oh, My goodness! Oh, all ye goddesses and gods! Here's a mess. Mr. Worters has been reading Ford's inflammatory note-book.

'It is my own fault,' said Ford. 'I should have labelled it 'Practically Private.' How could he know he was not meant to look inside?'

I spoke out severely, as an employee should. 'My dear boy, none of that. The label came unstuck. That was why Mr. Worters opened the book. He never suspected it was private. See—the label's off.'

'Scratched off,' Ford retorted grimly, and glanced at his ankle.

I affected not to understand. 'The point is this. Mr. Worters is thinking the matter over for four-and-twenty hours. If you take my advice you will apologize before that time elapses.'

'And if I don't?'

'You know your own affairs of course. But don't forget that you are young and practically ignorant of life, and that you have scarcely any money of your own. As far as I can see, your career practically depends on the favour of Mr. Worters. You have laughed at him. He does not like being laughed at. It seems to me that your course is obvious.'

'Apology?'

'Complete.'

'And if I don't?'

'Departure.'

He sat down on the stone steps and rested his head on his knees. On the lawn below us was Miss Beaumont, draggling about with some croquet balls. Her lover was out in the meadow, superintending the course of the asphalt path. For the path is to be made, and so is the bridge, and the fence is to be built round Other Kingdom after all. In time Miss Beaumont saw how unreasonable were her objections. Of her own accord, one evening in the drawing-room, she gave her Harcourt permission to do what he liked. 'That wood looks nearer,' said Ford.

'The inside fences have gone: that brings it nearer. But my dear boy—you must settle what you're going to do.'

'How much has he read?'

'Naturally he only opened the book. From what you showed me of it, one glance would be enough.'

'Did he open at the poems?'

'Poems?'

'Did he speak of the poems?'

'No. Were they about him?'

'They were not about him.'

'Then it wouldn't matter if he saw them.'

'It is sometimes a compliment to be mentioned,' said Ford, looking up at me. The remark had a stinging fragrance about it—such a fragrance as clings to the mouth after admirable wine. It did not taste like the remark of a boy. I was sorry that my pupil was likely to wreck his career; and I told him again that he had better apologize.

'I won't speak of Mr. Worters' claim for an apology. That's an aspect on which I prefer not to touch. The point is, if you don't apologize, you go—where?'

'To an aunt at Peckham.'

I pointed to the pleasant, comfortable landscape, full of cows and carriage-horses out at grass and civil retainers. In the midst of it stood Mr. Worters, radiating energy and wealth, like a terrestrial sun. 'My dear Ford—don't be heroic! Apologize.'

Unfortunately I raised my voice a little, and Miss Beaumont heard me, down on the lawn.

'Apologize?' she cried. 'What about?' And as she was not interested in the game, she came up the steps towards us, trailing her croquet mallet behind her. Her walk was rather listless. She was toning down at last.

'Come indoors!' I whispered. 'We must get out of this.'

'Not a bit of it!' said Ford.

'What is it?' she asked, standing beside him on the step.

He swallowed something as he looked up at her. Suddenly I understood. I knew the nature and the subject of his poems. I was not so sure now that he had better apologize. The sooner he was kicked out of the place the better.

In spite of my remonstrances, he told her about the book, and her first remark was: 'Oh, do let me see it!' She had no 'proper feeling' of any kind. Then she said: 'But why do you both look so sad?'

'We are awaiting Mr. Worters' decision,' said I.

'Mr. Inskip! What nonsense! Do you suppose Harcourt'll be angry?'

'Of course he is angry, and rightly so.'

'But why?'

'Ford has laughed at him.'

'But what's that!' And for the first time there was anger in her voice. 'Do you mean to say he'll punish some one who laughs at him? Why, for what else—for whatever reason are we all here? Not to laugh at each other! I laugh at people all day. At Mr. Ford. At you. And so does Harcourt. Oh, you've misjudged him! He won't—he couldn't be angry with people who laughed.'

'Mine is not nice laughter,' said Ford. 'He could not well forgive me.'

'You're a silly boy.' She sneered at him. 'You don't know Harcourt. So generous in every way. Why, he'd be as furious as I should be if you apologized. Mr. Inskip, isn't that so?'

'He has every right to an apology, I think.'

'Right? What's a right? You use too many new words. "Rights"—"apologies"—"society"— "position"—I don't follow it. What are we all here for, anyhow?'

Her discourse was full of trembling lights and shadows—frivolous one moment, the next moment asking why Humanity is here. I did not take the Moral Science Tripos, so I could not tell her.

'One thing I know—and that is that Harcourt isn't as stupid as you two. He soars above conventions. He doesn't care about "rights" and "apologies". He knows that all laughter is nice, and that the other nice things are money and the soul and so on.'

The soul and so on! I wonder that Harcourt out in the meadows did not have an apoplectic fit.

'Why, what a poor business your life would be,' she continued, 'if you all kept taking offence and apologizing! Forty million people in England and all of them touchy! How one would laugh if it was true! Just imagine!' And she did laugh. 'Look at Harcourt though. He knows better. He isn't petty like that. Mr. Ford! He isn't petty like that. Why, what's wrong with your eyes?'

He rested his head on his knees again, and we could see his eyes no longer. In dispassionate tones she informed me that she thought he was crying. Then she tapped him on the hair with her mallet and said: 'Cry-baby! Cry-cry-baby! Crying about nothing!' and ran laughing down the steps. 'All right!' she shouted from the lawn. 'Tell the cry-baby to stop. I'm going to speak to Harcourt!'

We watched her go in silence. Ford had scarcely been crying. His eyes had only become large and angry. He used such swear-words as he knew, and then got up abruptly and went into the house. I think he could not bear to see her disillusioned. I had no such tenderness, and it was with considerable interest that I watched Miss Beaumont approach her lord.

She walked confidently across the meadow, bowing to the workmen as they raised their hats. Her languor had passed, and with it her suggestion of 'tone'. She was the same crude, unsophisticated person that Harcourt had picked out of Ireland— beautiful and ludicrous in the extreme, and—if you go in for pathos—extremely pathetic.

I saw them meet, and soon she was hanging on his arm. The motion of his hand explained to her the construction of bridges. Twice she interrupted him: he had to explain everything again. Then she got in her word, and what followed was a good deal better than a play. Their two little figures parted and met and parted again, she gesticulating, he most

pompous and calm. She pleaded, she argued and
—if satire can carry half a mile—she tried to be
satirical. To enforce one of her childish points she
made two steps back. Splash! She was floundering
in the little stream.

That was the *dénouement* of the comedy. Harcourt
rescued her, while the workmen crowded round in
an agitated chorus. She was wet quite as far as her
knees, and muddy over her ankles. In this state she
was conducted towards me, and in time I began
to hear words; 'Influenza—a slight immersion—
clothes are of no consequence beside health—pray,
dearest, don't worry—yes, it must have been a shock
—bed! bed! I insist on bed! Promise? Good girl.
Up the steps to bed then.'

They parted on the lawn, and she came obediently
up the steps. Her face was full of terror and bewilderment.

'So you've had a wetting, Miss Beaumont!'

'Wetting? Oh, yes. But, Mr. Inskip—I don't
understand: I've failed.'

I expressed surprise.

'Mr. Ford is to go—at once. I've failed.'

'I'm sorry.'

'I've failed with Harcourt. He's offended. He
won't laugh. He won't let me do what I want.
Latin and Greek began it: I wanted to know about
gods and heroes and he wouldn't let me: then I
wanted no fence round Other Kingdom and no
bridge and no path—and look! Now I ask that
Mr. Ford, who has done nothing, shan't be punished
for it—and he is to go away for ever.'

'Impertinence is not "nothing," Miss Beaumont.'
For I must keep in with Harcourt.

'Impertinence is nothing!' she cried. 'It doesn't

exist. It's a sham, like "claims" and "position" and "rights". It's part of the great dream.'

'What "great dream"?' I asked, trying not to smile.

'Tell Mr. Ford—here comes Harcourt; I must go to bed. Give my love to Mr. Ford, and tell him "to guess". I shall never see him again, and I won't stand it. Tell him to guess. I am sorry I called him a cry-baby. He was not crying like a baby. He was crying like a grown-up person, and now I have grown up too.'

I judged it right to repeat this conversation to my employer.

IV

The bridge is built, the fence finished, and Other Kingdom lies tethered by a ribbon of asphalt to our front door. The seventy-eight trees therein certainly seem nearer, and during the windy nights that followed Ford's departure we could hear their branches sighing, and would find in the morning that beech-leaves had been blown right up against the house. Miss Beaumont made no attempt to go out, much to the relief of the ladies, for Harcourt had given the word that she was not to go out unattended, and the boisterous weather deranged their petticoats. She remained indoors, neither reading nor laughing, and dressing no longer in green, but in brown.

Not noticing her presence, Mr. Worters looked in one day and said with a sigh of relief: 'That's all right. The circle's completed.'

'Is it indeed!' she replied.

'You there, you quiet little mouse? I only meant that our lords, the British workmen, have at last condescended to complete their labours, and have rounded us off from the world. I—in the end I was a naughty, domineering tyrant, and disobeyed you. I didn't have the gate out at the farther side of the copse. Will you forgive me?'

'Anything, Harcourt, that pleases you, is certain to please me.'

The ladies smiled at each other, and Mr. Worters said: 'That's right, and as soon as the wind goes down we'll all progress together to your wood, and take possession of it formally, for it didn't really count that last time.'

'No, it didn't really count that last time,' Miss Beaumont echoed.

'Evelyn says this wind never will go down,' remarked Mrs. Worters. 'I don't know how she knows.'

'It will never go down, as long as I am in the house.'

'Really?' he said gaily. 'Then come out now, and send it down with me.'

They took a few turns up and down the terrace. The wind lulled for a moment, but blew fiercer than ever during lunch. As we ate, it roared and whistled down the chimney at us, and the trees of Other Kingdom frothed like the sea. Leaves and twigs flew from them, and a bough, a good-sized bough, was blown on to the smooth asphalt path, and actually switchbacked over the bridge, up the meadow, and across our very lawn. (I venture to say 'our', as I am now staying on as Harcourt's secretary.) Only the stone steps prevented it from reaching the terrace and perhaps breaking the dining-room window. Miss Beaumont sprang up and, napkin in hand, ran out and touched it.

'Oh, Evelyn——' the ladies cried.

'Let her go,' said Mr. Worters tolerantly. 'It certainly is a remarkable incident, remarkable. We must remember to tell the Archdeacon about it.'

'Harcourt,' she cried, with the first hint of returning colour in her cheeks, 'mightn't we go up to the copse after lunch, you and I?'

Mr. Worters considered.

'Of course, not if you don't think best.'

'Inskip, what's your opinion?'

I saw what his own was, and cried, 'Oh, let's go!' though I detest the wind as much as any one.

'Very well. Mother, Anna, Ruth, Mrs. Osgood—we'll all go.'

And go we did, a lugubrious procession; but the gods were good to us for once, for as soon as we were started, the tempest dropped, and there ensued an extraordinary calm. After all, Miss Beaumont was something of a weather prophet. Her spirits improved every minute. She tripped in front of us along the asphalt path, and ever and anon turned round to say to her lover some gracious or alluring thing. I admired her for it. I admire people who know on which side their bread's buttered.

'Evelyn, come here!'

'Come here yourself.'

'Give me a kiss.'

'Come and take it then.'

He ran after her, and she ran away, while all our party laughed melodiously.

'Oh, I am so happy!' she cried. 'I think I've everything I want in all the world. Oh dear, those last few days indoors! But oh, I am so happy now!' She had changed her brown dress for the old flowing green one, and she began to do her skirt dance in the open meadow, lit by sudden gleams of the sunshine.

It was really a beautiful sight, and Mr. Worters did not correct her, glad perhaps that she should recover her spirits, even if she lost her tone. Her feet scarcely moved, but her body so swayed and her dress spread so gloriously around her, that we were transported with joy. She danced to the song of a bird that sang passionately in Other Kingdom, and the river held back its waves to watch her (one might have supposed), and the winds lay spellbound in their cavern, and the great clouds spellbound in the sky. She danced away from our society and our life, back, back, through the centuries till houses and fences fell and the earth lay wild to the sun. Her garment was as foliage upon her, the strength of her limbs as boughs, her throat the smooth upper branch that salutes the morning or glistens to the rain. Leaves move, leaves hide it as hers was hidden by the motion of her hair. Leaves move again and it is ours, as her throat was ours again when, parting the tangle, she faced us crying, 'Oh!' crying, 'Oh Harcourt! I never was so happy. I have all that there is in the world.'

But he, entrammelled in love's ecstasy, forgetting certain Madonnas of Raphael, forgetting, I fancy, his soul, sprang to inarm her with, 'Evelyn! Eternal Bliss! Mine to eternity! Mine!' and she sprang away. Music was added and she sang, 'Oh Ford! oh Ford, among all these Worters, I am coming through you to my Kingdom. Oh Ford, my lover while I was a woman, I will never forget you, never, as long as I have branches to shade you from the sun,' and, singing, crossed the stream.

Why he followed her so passionately, I do not know. It was play, she was in his own domain which a fence surrounds, and she could not possibly escape him. But he dashed round by the bridge as if all their love was at stake, and pursued her with fierceness up the hill. She ran well, but the end was a foregone conclusion, and we only speculated whether he would catch her outside or inside the copse. He gained on her inch by inch; now they were in the shadow of the trees; he had practically grasped her, he had missed; she had disappeared into the trees themselves, he following.

'Harcourt is in high spirits,' said Mrs. Osgood, Anna, and Ruth.

'Evelyn!' we heard him shouting within.

We proceeded up the asphalt path.

'Evelyn! Evelyn!'

'He's not caught her yet, evidently.'

'Where are you, Evelyn?'

'Miss Beaumont must have hidden herself rather cleverly.'

'Look here,' cried Harcourt, emerging, 'have you seen Evelyn?'

'Oh, no, she's certainly inside.'

'So I thought.'

'Evelyn must be dodging round one of the trunks. You go this way, I that. We'll soon find her.'

We searched, gaily at first, and always with a feeling that Miss Beaumont was close by, that the delicate limbs were just behind this bole, the hair and the drapery quivering among those leaves. She was beside us, above us; here was her footstep on the purple-brown earth—her bosom, her neck—she was everywhere and nowhere. Gaiety turned to irritation, irritation to anger and fear. Miss Beaumont was apparently lost. 'Evelyn! Evelyn!' we continued to cry. 'Oh, really, it is beyond a joke.'

Then the wind arose, the more violent for its lull,

and we were driven into the house by a terrific storm. We said, 'At all events she will come back now.' But she did not come, and the rain hissed and rose up from the dry meadows like incense smoke, and smote the quivering leaves to applause. Then it lightened. Ladies screamed, and we saw Other Kingdom as one who claps the hands, and heard it as one who roars with laughter in the thunder. Not even the Archdeacon can remember such a storm. All Harcourt's seedlings were ruined, and the tiles flew off his gables right and left. He came to me presently with a white, drawn face, saying: 'Inskip, can I trust you?'

'You can, indeed.'

'I have long suspected it; she has eloped with Ford.'

'But how——' I gasped.

'The carriage is ready—we'll talk as we drive.' Then, against the rain he shouted: 'No gate in the fence, I know, but what about a ladder? While I blunder, she's over the fence, and he——'

'But you were so close. There was not the time.'

'There is time for anything,' he said venomously, 'where a treacherous woman is concerned. I found her no better than a savage, I trained her, I educated her. But I'll break them both. I can do that; I'll break them soul and body.'

No one can break Ford now. The task is impossible. But I trembled for Miss Beaumont.

We missed the train. Young couples had gone by it, several young couples, and we heard of more young couples in London, as if all the world were mocking Harcourt's solitude. In desperation we sought the squalid suburb that is now Ford's home. We swept past the dirty maid and the terrified aunt, swept upstairs, to catch him if we could red-handed. He was seated at the table, reading the *Œdipus Coloneus* of Sophocles.

'That won't take in me!' shouted Harcourt. 'You've got Miss Beaumont with you, and I know it.'

'No such luck,' said Ford.

He stammered with rage. 'Inskip—you hear that? "No such luck"! Quote the evidence against him. I can't speak.'

So I quoted her song. '"Oh Ford! Oh Ford, among all these Worters, I am coming through you to my Kingdom! Oh Ford, my lover while I was a woman, I will never forget you, never, as long as I have branches to shade you from the sun." Soon after that, we lost her.'

'And—and on another occasion she sent a message of similar effect. Inskip, bear witness. He was to "guess" something.'

'I have guessed it,' said Ford.

'So you practically——'

'Oh, no, Mr. Worters, you mistake me. I have not practically guessed. I have guessed. I could tell you if I chose, but it would be no good, for she has not practically escaped you. She has escaped you absolutely, for ever and ever, as long as there are branches to shade men from the sun.'

P. G. WODEHOUSE
Lord Emsworth and the Girl Friend

THE day was so warm, so fair, so magically a thing of sunshine and blue skies and bird-song that any one acquainted with Clarence, ninth Earl of Emsworth, and aware of his liking for fine weather, would have pictured him going about the place on this summer morning with a beaming smile and an uplifted heart. Instead of which, humped over the breakfast table, he was directing at a blameless kippered herring a look of such intense bitterness that the fish seemed to sizzle beneath it. For it was August Bank Holiday, and Blandings Castle on August Bank Holiday became, in his lordship's opinion, a miniature Inferno.

This was the day when his park and grounds broke out into a noisome rash of swings, roundabouts, marquees, toy balloons, and paper bags; when a tidal wave of the peasantry and its squealing young engulfed those haunts of immemorial peace. On August Bank Holiday he was not allowed to potter pleasantly about his gardens in an old coat: forces beyond his control shoved him into a stiff collar and a top-hat and told him to go out and be genial. And in the cool of the quiet evenfall they put him on a platform and made him make a speech. To a man with a day like that in front of him fine weather was a mockery.

His sister, Lady Constance Keeble, looked brightly at him over the coffee-pot.

'What a lovely morning!' she said.

Lord Emsworth's gloom deepened. He chafed at being called upon—by this woman of all others—to behave as if everything was for the jolliest in the jolliest of all possible worlds. But for his sister Constance and her hawk-like vigilance, he might, he thought, have been able at least to dodge the top-hat.

'Have you got your speech ready?'

'Yes.'

'Well, mind you learn it by heart this time and don't stammer and dodder as you did last year.'

Lord Emsworth pushed plate and kipper away. He had lost his desire for food.

'And don't forget you have to go to the village this morning to judge the cottage gardens.'

'All right, all right, all right,' said his lordship testily. 'I've not forgotten.'

'I think I will come to the village with you. There are a number of those Fresh Air London children staying there now, and I must warn them to behave properly when they come to the Fête this afternoon. You know what London children are. McAllister says he found one of them in the gardens the other day, picking his flowers.'

At any other time the news of this outrage would, no doubt, have affected Lord Emsworth profoundly. But now, so intense was his self-pity, he did not even shudder. He drank coffee with the air of a man who regretted that it was not hemlock.

'By the way, McAllister was speaking to me again last night about that gravel path through the yew alley. He seems very keen on it.'

'Glug!' said Lord Emsworth—which, as any philologist will tell you, is the sound which peers of the realm make when stricken to the soul while drinking coffee.

Concerning Glasgow, that great commercial and manufacturing city in the county of Lanarkshire in Scotland, much has been written. So lyrically does the Encyclopædia Britannica deal with the place that it covers twenty-seven pages before it can tear itself away and go on to Glass, Glastonbury, Glatz, and Glauber. The only aspect of it, however, which immediately concerns the present historian is the fact that the citizens it breeds are apt to be grim, dour, persevering, tenacious men; men with red whiskers who know what they want and mean to get it. Such a one was Angus McAllister, head-gardener at Blandings Castle.

For years Angus McAllister had set before himself as his earthly goal the construction of a gravel path through the Castle's famous yew alley. For years he had been bringing the project to the notice of his employer, though in any one less whiskered the latter's unconcealed loathing would have caused embarrassment. And now, it seemed, he was at it again.

'Gravel path!' Lord Emsworth stiffened through the whole length of his stringy body. Nature, he had always maintained, intended a yew alley to be carpeted with a mossy growth. And, whatever Nature felt about it, he personally was dashed if he was going to have men with Clydeside accents and faces like dissipated potatoes coming along and mutilating that lovely expanse of green velvet. 'Gravel path, indeed! Why not asphalt? Why not a few hoardings with advertisements of liver pills and a filling-station? That's what the man would really like.'

Lord Emsworth felt bitter, and when he felt bitter he could be terribly sarcastic.

'Well, I think it is a very good idea,' said his sister.

'One could walk there in wet weather then. Damp moss is ruinous to shoes.'

Lord Emsworth rose. He could bear no more of this. He left the table, the room, and the house and, reaching the yew alley some minutes later, was revolted to find it infested by Angus McAllister in person. The head-gardener was standing gazing at the moss like a high priest of some ancient religion about to stick the gaff into the human sacrifice.

'Morning, McAllister,' said Lord Emsworth coldly.

'Good morrrrning, your lorrudsheep.'

There was a pause. Angus McAllister, extending a foot that looked like a violin-case, pressed it on the moss. The meaning of the gesture was plain. It expressed contempt, dislike, a generally anti-moss spirit: and Lord Emsworth, wincing, surveyed the man unpleasantly through his pince-nez. Though not often given to theological speculation, he was wondering why Providence, if obliged to make head-gardeners, had found it necessary to make them so Scotch. In the case of Angus McAllister, why, going a step farther, have made him a human being at all? All the ingredients of a first-class mule simply thrown away. He felt that he might have liked Angus McAllister if he had been a mule.

'I was speaking to her leddyship yesterday.'

'Oh?'

'About the gravel path I was speaking to her leddyship.'

'Oh?'

'Her leddyship likes the notion fine.'

'Indeed! Well . . .'

Lord Emsworth's face had turned a lively pink, and he was about to release the blistering words which were forming themselves in his mind when suddenly he caught the head-gardener's eye and paused. Angus McAllister was looking at him in a peculiar manner, and he knew what that look meant. Just one crack, his eye was saying—in Scotch, of course—just one crack out of you and I tender my resignation. And with a sickening shock it came home to Lord Emsworth how completely he was in this man's clutches.

He shuffled miserably. Yes, he was helpless. Except for that kink about gravel paths, Angus McAllister was a head-gardener in a thousand, and he needed him. He could not do without him. That, unfortunately, had been proved by experiment. Once before, at the time when they were grooming for the Agricultural Show that pumpkin which had subsequently romped home so gallant a winner, he had dared to flout Angus McAllister. And Angus had resigned, and he had been forced to plead—yes, plead—with him to come back. An employer cannot hope to do this sort of thing and still rule with an iron hand. Filled with the coward rage that dares to burn but does not dare to blaze, Lord Emsworth coughed a cough that was undisguisedly a bronchial white flag.

'I'll—er—I'll think it over, McAllister.'

'Mphm.'

'I have to go to the village now. I will see you later.'

'Mphm.'

'Meanwhile, I will—er—think it over.'

'Mphm.'

The task of judging the floral displays in the cottage gardens of the little village of Blandings

Parva was one to which Lord Emsworth had looked forward with pleasurable anticipation. It was the sort of job he liked. But now, even though he had managed to give his sister Constance the slip and was free from her threatened society, he approached the task with a downcast spirit. It is always unpleasant for a proud man to realize that he is no longer captain of his soul; that he is to all intents and purposes ground beneath the number twelve heel of a Glaswegian head-gardener; and, brooding on this, he judged the cottage gardens with a distrait eye. It was only when he came to the last on his list that anything like animation crept into his demeanour.

This, he perceived, peering over its rickety fence, was not at all a bad little garden. It demanded closer inspection. He unlatched the gate and pottered in. And a dog, dozing behind a water-butt, opened one eye and looked at him. It was one of those hairy, nondescript dogs, and its gaze was cold, wary, and suspicious, like that of a stockbroker who thinks someone is going to play the confidence trick on him.

Lord Emsworth did not observe the animal. He had pottered to a bed of wallflowers and now, stooping, he took a sniff at them.

As sniffs go, it was an innocent sniff, but the dog for some reason appeared to read into it criminality of a high order. All the indignant householder in him woke in a flash. The next moment the world had become full of hideous noises, and Lord Emsworth's preoccupation was swept away in a passionate desire to save his ankles from harm.

As these chronicles of Blandings Castle have already shown, he was not at his best with strange dogs. Beyond saying 'Go away, sir!' and leaping to and fro with an agility surprising in one of his years, he had accomplished little in the direction of a reasoned plan of defence when the cottage door opened and a girl came out.

'Hoy!' cried the girl.

And on the instant, at the mere sound of her voice, the mongrel, suspending hostilities, bounded at the new-comer and writhed on his back at her feet with all four legs in the air. The spectacle reminded Lord Emsworth irresistibly of his own behaviour when in the presence of Angus McAllister.

He blinked at his preserver. She was a small girl, of uncertain age—possibly twelve or thirteen, though a combination of London fogs and early cares had given her face a sort of wizened motherliness which in some odd way caused his lordship from the first to look on her as belonging to his own generation. She was the type of girl you see in back streets carrying a baby nearly as large as herself and still retaining sufficient energy to lead one little brother by the hand and shout recrimination at another in the distance. Her cheeks shone from recent soaping, and she was dressed in a velveteen frock which was obviously the pick of her wardrobe. Her hair, in defiance of the prevailing mode, she wore drawn tightly back into a short pigtail.

'Er—thank you,' said Lord Emsworth.

'Thank you, sir,' said the girl.

For what she was thanking him, his lordship was not able to gather. Later, as their acquaintance ripened, he was to discover that this strange gratitude was a habit with his new friend. She thanked everybody for everything. At the moment, the mannerism surprised him. He continued to blink at her through his pince-nez.

Lack of practice had rendered Lord Emsworth a

little rusty in the art of making conversation to members of the other sex. He sought in his mind for topics.

'Fine day.'

'Yes, sir. Thank you, sir.'

'Are you'—Lord Emsworth furtively consulted his list—'are you the daughter of—ah—Ebenezer Sprockett?' he asked, thinking, as he had often thought before, what ghastly names some of his tenantry possessed.

'No, sir. I'm from London, sir.'

'Ah? London, eh? Pretty warm it must be there.' He paused. Then, remembering a formula of his youth: 'Er—been out much this Season?'

'No, sir.'

'Everybody out of town now, I suppose? What part of London?'

'Drury Line, sir.'

'What's your name? Eh, what?'

'Gladys, sir. Thank you, sir. This is Ern.'

A small boy had wandered out of the cottage, a rather hard-boiled specimen with freckles, bearing surprisingly in his hand a large and beautiful bunch of flowers. Lord Emsworth bowed courteously and with the addition of this third party to the *tête-à-tête* felt more at his ease.

'How do you do,' he said. 'What pretty flowers.'

With her brother's advent, Gladys, also, had lost diffidence and gained conversational aplomb.

'A treat, ain't they?' she agreed eagerly. 'I got 'em for 'im up at the big 'ahse. Coo! The old josser the plice belongs to didn't arf chase me. 'E found me picking 'em and 'e sharted somefin at me and come runnin' after me, but I copped 'im on the shin wiv a stone and 'e stopped to rub it and I come away.'

Lord Emsworth might have corrected her impression that Blandings Castle and its gardens belonged to Angus McAllister, but his mind was so filled with admiration and gratitude that he refrained from doing so. He looked at the girl almost reverently. Not content with controlling savage dogs with a mere word, this super-woman actually threw stones at Angus McAllister—a thing which he had never been able to nerve himself to do in an association which had lasted nine years—and, what was more, copped him on the shin with them. What nonsense, Lord Emsworth felt, the papers talked about the Modern Girl. If this was a specimen, the Modern Girl was the highest point the sex had yet reached.

'Ern,' said Gladys, changing the subject, 'is wearin' 'air-oil todiy.'

Lord Emsworth had already observed this and had, indeed, been moving to windward as she spoke.

'For the Feet,' explained Gladys.

'For the feet?' It seemed unusual.

'For the Feet in the pork this afternoon.'

'Oh, you are going to the Fête?'

'Yes, sir, thank you, sir.'

For the first time, Lord Emsworth found himself regarding that grisly social event with something approaching favour.

'We must look out for one another there,' he said cordially. 'You will remember me again? I shall be wearing'—he gulped—'a top-hat.'

'Ern's going to wear a stror penamaw that's been give 'im.'

Lord Emsworth regarded the lucky young devil with frank envy. He rather fancied he knew that panama. It had been his constant companion for some six years and then had been torn from him by

his sister Constance and handed over to the vicar's
wife for her rummage-sale.

He sighed.

'Well, good-bye.'

'Good-bye, sir. Thank you, sir.'

Lord Emsworth walked pensively out of the
garden and, turning into the little street, encountered
Lady Constance.

'Oh, there you are, Clarence.'

'Yes,' said Lord Emsworth, for such was the case.

'Have you finished judging the gardens?'

'Yes.'

'I am just going into this end cottage here. The
vicar tells me there is a little girl from London
staying there. I want to warn her to behave this
afternoon. I have spoken to the others.'

Lord Emsworth drew himself up. His pince-nez
were slightly askew, but despite this his gaze was
commanding and impressive.

'Well, mind what you say,' he said authoritatively.
'None of your district-visiting stuff, Constance.'

'What do you mean?'

'You know what I mean. I have the greatest
respect for the young lady to whom you refer. She
behaved on a certain recent occasion—on two recent
occasions—with notable gallantry and resource, and
I won't have her ballyragged. Understand that!'

The technical title of the orgy which broke out
annually on the first Monday in August in the park
of Blandings Castle was the Blandings Parva School
Treat, and it seemed to Lord Emsworth, wanly
watching the proceedings from under the shadow of
his top-hat, that if this was the sort of thing schools
looked on as pleasure he and they were mentally

poles apart. A function like the Blandings Parva
School Treat blurred his conception of Man as
Nature's Final Word.

The decent sheep and cattle to whom this park
normally belonged had been hustled away into
regions unknown, leaving the smooth expanse of turf
to children whose vivacity scared Lord Emsworth
and adults who appeared to him to have cast aside
all dignity and every other noble quality which goes
to make a one hundred per cent. British citizen. Look
at Mrs. Rossiter over there, for instance, the wife
of Jno. Rossiter, Provisions, Groceries, and Home-
Made Jams. On any other day of the year, when you
met her, Mrs. Rossiter was a nice, quiet, docile
woman who gave at the knees respectfully as you
passed. To-day, flushed in the face and with her
bonnet on one side, she seemed to have gone completely native. She was wandering to and fro drinking lemonade out of a bottle and employing her
mouth, when not so occupied, to make a devastating
noise with what he believed was termed a squeaker.

The injustice of the thing stung Lord Emsworth.
This park was his own private park. What right had
people to come and blow squeakers in it? How
would Mrs. Rossiter like it if one afternoon he
suddenly invaded her neat little garden in the High
Street and rushed about over her lawn, blowing a
squeaker?

And it was always on these occasions so infernally
hot. July might have ended in a flurry of snow, but
directly the first Monday in August arrived and he
had to put on a stiff collar out came the sun, blazing
with tropic fury.

Of course, admitted Lord Emsworth, for he was a
fair-minded man, this cut both ways. The hotter the

day, the more quickly his collar lost its starch and
ceased to spike him like a javelin. This afternoon,
for instance, it had resolved itself almost immediately
into something which felt like a wet compress.
Severe as were his sufferings, he was compelled to
recognize that he was that much ahead of the game.

A masterful figure loomed at his side.

'Clarence!'

Lord Emsworth's mental and spiritual state was
now such that not even the advent of his sister Constance could add noticeably to his discomfort.

'Clarence, you look a perfect sight.'

'I know I do. Who wouldn't in a rig-out like this?
Why in the name of goodness you always insist . . .'

'Please don't be childish, Clarence. I cannot
understand the fuss you make about dressing for
once in your life like a reasonable English gentleman
and not like a tramp.'

'It's this top-hat. It's exciting the children.'

'What on earth do you mean, exciting the children?'

'Well, all I can tell you is that just now, as I was
passing the place where they're playing football—
Football! In weather like this!—a small boy called
out something derogatory and threw a portion of a
coco-nut at it.'

'If you will identify the child,' said Lady Constance warmly, 'I will have him severely punished.'

'How the dickens,' replied his lordship with equal
warmth, 'can I identify the child? They all look
alike to me. And if I did identify him, I would shake
him by the hand. A boy who throws coco-nuts at
top-hats is fundamentally sound in his views. And
stiff collars . . .'

'Stiff! That's what I came to speak to you about.

Are you aware that your collar looks like a rag? Go
in and change it at once.'

'But, my dear Constance . . .'

'At once, Clarence. I simply cannot understand
a man having so little pride in his appearance. But
all your life you have been like that. I remember
when we were children . . .'

Lord Emsworth's past was not of such a purity
that he was prepared to stand and listen to it being
lectured on by a sister with a good memory.

'Oh, all right, all right, all right,' he said. 'I'll
change it, I'll change it.'

'Well, hurry. They are just starting tea.'

Lord Emsworth quivered.

'Have I got to go into that tea-tent?'

'Of course you have. Don't be so ridiculous. I do
wish you would realize your position. As master of
Blandings Castle . . .'

A bitter, mirthless laugh from the poor peon
thus ludicrously described drowned the rest of the
sentence.

It always seemed to Lord Emsworth, in analysing
these entertainments, that the August Bank Holiday
Saturnalia at Blandings Castle reached a peak of re-
pulsiveness when tea was served in the big marquee.
Tea over, the agony abated, to become acute once
more at the moment when he stepped to the edge of
the platform and cleared his throat and tried to
recollect what the deuce he had planned to say to
the goggling audience beneath him. After that, it
subsided again and passed until the following August.

Conditions during the tea hour, the marquee
having stood all day under a blazing sun, were
generally such that Shadrach, Meshach, and Abed-

nego, had they been there, could have learned
something new about burning fiery furnaces. Lord
Emsworth, delayed by the revision of his toilet, made
his entry when the meal was half over and was
pleased to find that his second collar almost instan-
taneously began to relax its iron grip. That, however,
was the only gleam of happiness which was to be
vouchsafed him. Once in the tent, it took his experienced eye but a moment to discern that the
present feast was eclipsing in frightfulness all its
predecessors.

Young Blandings Parva, in its normal form, tended
rather to the stolidly bovine than the riotous. In all
villages, of course, there must of necessity be an
occasional tough egg—in the case of Blandings Parva
the names of Willie Drake and Thomas (Rat-Face)
Blenkiron spring to the mind—but it was seldom
that the local infants offered anything beyond the
power of a curate to control. What was giving the
present gathering its striking resemblance to a
reunion of *sans-culottes* at the height of the French
Revolution was the admixture of the Fresh Air
London visitors.

About the London child, reared among the tin
cans and cabbage stalks of Drury Lane and Clare
Market, there is a breezy insouciance which his
country cousin lacks. Years of back-chat with
annoyed parents and relatives have cured him of any
tendency he may have had towards shyness, with the
result that when he requires anything he grabs for it,
and when he is amused by any slight peculiarity in
the personal appearance of members of the governing
classes he finds no difficulty in translating his
thoughts into speech. Already, up and down the
long tables, the curate's unfortunate squint was

coming in for hearty comment, and the front teeth of one of the school-teachers ran it a close second for popularity. Lord Emsworth was not, as a rule, a man of swift inspirations, but it occurred to him at this juncture that it would be a prudent move to take off his top-hat before his little guests observed it and appreciated its humorous possibilities.

The action was not, however, necessary. Even as he raised his hand a rock cake, singing through the air like a shell, took it off for him.

Lord Emsworth had had sufficient. Even Constance, unreasonable woman though she was, could hardly expect him to stay and beam genially under conditions like this. All civilized laws had obviously gone by the board and Anarchy reigned in the marquee. The curate was doing his best to form a provisional government consisting of himself and the two school-teachers, but there was only one man who could have coped adequately with the situation and that was King Herod, who—regrettably—was not among those present. Feeling like some aristocrat of the old régime sneaking away from the tumbril, Lord Emsworth edged to the exit and withdrew.

Outside the marquee the world was quieter, but only comparatively so. What Lord Emsworth craved was solitude, and in all the broad park there seemed to be but one spot where it was to be had. This was a red-tiled shed, standing beside a small pond, used at happier times as a lounge or retiring-room for cattle. Hurrying thither, his lordship had just begun to revel in the cool, cow-scented dimness of its interior when from one of the dark corners, causing him to start and bite his tongue, there came the sound of a subdued sniff.

He turned. This was persecution. With the whole park to mess about in, why should an infernal child invade this one sanctuary of his? He spoke with angry sharpness. He came of a line of warrior ancestors and his fighting blood was up.

'Who's that?'

'Me, sir. Thank you, sir.'

Only one person of Lord Emsworth's acquaintance was capable of expressing gratitude for having been barked at in such a tone. His wrath died away and remorse took its place. He felt like a man who in error has kicked a favourite dog.

'God bless my soul!' he exclaimed. 'What in the world are you doing in a cow-shed?'

'Please, sir, I was put.'

'Put? How do you mean, put? Why?'

'For pinching things, sir.'

'Eh? What? Pinching things? Most extra-ordinary. What did you—er—pinch?'

'Two buns, two jem-sengwiches, two apples, and a slicer cake.'

The girl had come out of her corner and was standing correctly at attention. Force of habit had caused her to intone the list of the purloined articles in the sing-song voice in which she was wont to recite the multiplication-table at school, but Lord Emsworth could see that she was deeply moved. Tear-stains glistened on her face, and no Emsworth had ever been able to watch unstirred a woman's tears. The ninth Earl was visibly affected.

'Blow your nose,' he said, hospitably extending his handkerchief.

'Yes, sir. Thank you, sir.'

'What did you say you had pinched? Two buns . . .'

'. . . Two jem-sengwiches, two apples, and a slicer cake.'

'Did you eat them?'

'No, sir. They wasn't for me. They was for Ern.'

'Ern? Oh, ah, yes. Yes, to be sure. For Ern, eh?'

'Yes, sir.'

'But why the dooce couldn't Ern have—er—pinched them for himself? Strong, able-bodied young feller, I mean.'

Lord Emsworth, a member of the old school, did not like this disposition on the part of the modern young man to shirk the dirty work and let the woman pay.

'Ern wasn't allowed to come to the treat, sir.'

'What! Not allowed? Who said he musn't?'

'The lidy, sir.'

'What lidy?'

'The one that come in just after you'd gorn this morning.'

A fierce snort escaped Lord Emsworth. Constance! What the devil did Constance mean by taking it upon herself to revise his list of guests without so much as a . . . Constance, eh? He snorted again. One of these days Constance would go too far.

'Monstrous!' he cried.

'Yes, sir.'

'High-handed tyranny, by Gad. Did she give any reason?'

'The lidy didn't like Ern biting 'er in the leg, sir.'

'Ern bit her in the leg?'

'Yes, sir. Pliying 'e was a dorg. And the lidy was cross and Ern wasn't allowed to come to the treat, and I told 'im I'd bring 'im back somefing nice.'

Lord Emsworth breathed heavily. He had not

supposed that in these degenerate days a family like this existed. The sister copped Angus McAllister on the shin with stones, the brother bit Constance in the leg. . . . It was like listening to some grand old saga of the exploits of heroes and demigods.

'I thought if I didn't 'ave nothing myself it would make it all right.'

'Nothing?' Lord Emsworth started. 'Do you mean to tell me you have not had tea?'

'No, sir. Thank you, sir. I thought if I didn't 'ave none, then it would be all right Ern 'aving what I would 'ave 'ad if I 'ad 'ave 'ad.'

His lordship's head, never strong, swam a little. Then it resumed its equilibrium. He caught her drift.

'God bless my soul!' said Lord Emsworth. 'I never heard anything so monstrous and appalling in my life. Come with me immediately.'

'The lidy said I was to stop 'ere, sir.'

Lord Emsworth gave vent to his loudest snort of the afternoon.

'Confound the lidy!'

'Yes, sir. Thank you, sir.'

Five minutes later Beach, the butler, enjoying a siesta in the housekeeper's room, was roused from his slumbers by the unexpected ringing of a bell. Answering its summons, he found his employer in the library, and with him a surprising young person in a velveteen frock, at the sight of whom his eyebrows quivered and, but for his iron self-restraint, would have risen.

'Beach!'

'Your lordship?'

'This young lady would like some tea.'

'Very good, your lordship.'

'Buns, you know. And apples, and jem—I mean jam-sandwiches, and cake, and that sort of thing.'

'Very good, your lordship.'

'And she has a brother, Beach.'

'Indeed, your lordship?'

'She will want to take some stuff away for him.' Lord Emsworth turned to his guest. 'Ernest would like a little chicken, perhaps?'

'Coo!'

'I beg your pardon?'

'Yes, sir. Thank you, sir.'

'And a slice or two of ham?'

'Yes, sir. Thank you, sir.'

'And—he has no gouty tendency?'

'No, sir. Thank you, sir.'

'Capital! Then a bottle of that new lot of port, Beach. It's some stuff they've sent me down to try,' explained his lordship. 'Nothing special, you understand,' he added apologetically, 'but quite drinkable. I should like your brother's opinion of it. See that all that is put together in a parcel, Beach, and leave it on the table in the hall. We will pick it up as we go out.'

A welcome coolness had crept into the evening air by the time Lord Emsworth and his guest came out of the great door of the castle. Gladys, holding her host's hand and clutching the parcel, sighed contentedly. She had done herself well at the tea-table. Life seemed to have nothing more to offer.

Lord Emsworth did not share this view. His spacious mood had not yet exhausted itself.

'Now, is there anything else you can think of that Ernest would like?' he asked. 'If so, do not hesitate to mention it. Beach, can you think of anything?'

The butler, hovering respectfully, was unable to do so.

'No, your lordship. I ventured to add—on my own responsibility, your lordship—some hard-boiled eggs and a pot of jam to the parcel.'

'Excellent! You are sure there is nothing else?'

A wistful look came into Gladys's eyes.

'Could he 'ave some flarze?'

'Certainly,' said Lord Emsworth. 'Certainly, certainly, certainly. By all means. Just what I was about to suggest my—er—what *is* flarze?'

Beach, the linguist, interpreted.

'I think the young lady means flowers, your lordship.'

'Yes, sir. Thank you, sir. Flarze.'

'Oh?' said Lord Emsworth. 'Oh? Flarze?' he said slowly. 'Oh, ah, yes. Yes. I see. H'm!'

He removed his pince-nez, wiped them thoughtfully, replaced them, and gazed with wrinkling forehead at the gardens that stretched gaily out before him. Flarze! It would be idle to deny that those gardens contained flarze in full measure. They were bright with Achillea, Bignonia Radicans, Campanula, Digitalis, Euphorbia, Funkia, Gypsophila, Helianthus, Iris, Liatris, Monarda, Phlox Drummondii, Salvia, Thalictrum, Vinca and Yucca. But the devil of it was that Angus McAllister would have a fit if they were picked. Across the threshold of this Eden the ginger whiskers of Angus McAllister lay like a flaming sword.

As a general rule, the procedure for getting flowers out of Angus McAllister was as follows. You waited till he was in one of his rare moods of complaisance, then you led the conversation gently round to the subject of interior decoration, and then, choosing your moment, you asked if he could possibly spare a few to be put in vases. The last thing you thought of doing was to charge in and start helping yourself.

'I—er— . . .' said Lord Emsworth.

He stopped. In a sudden blinding flash of clear vision he had seen himself for what he was—the spineless, unspeakably unworthy descendant of ancestors who, though they may have had their faults, had certainly known how to handle employees. It was 'How now, varlet!' and 'Marry come up, thou malapert knave!' in the days of previous Earls of Emsworth. Of course, they had possessed certain advantages which he lacked. It undoubtedly helped a man in his dealings with the domestic staff to have, as they had had, the rights of the high, the middle, and the low justice—which meant, broadly, that if you got annoyed with your head-gardener you could immediately divide him into four head-gardeners with a battle-axe and no questions asked—but even so, he realized that they were better men than he was and that, if he allowed craven fear of Angus McAllister to stand in the way of this delightful girl and her charming brother getting all the flowers they required, he was not worthy to be the last of their line.

Lord Emsworth wrestled with his tremors.

'Certainly, certainly, certainly,' he said, though not without a qualm. 'Take as many as you want.'

And so it came about that Angus McAllister, crouched in his potting-shed like some dangerous beast in its den, beheld a sight which first froze his blood and then sent it boiling through his veins. Flitting to and fro through his sacred gardens, picking his sacred flowers, was a small girl in a velveteen frock. And—which brought apoplexy a step closer—it was the same small girl who two days before had copped him on the shin with a stone. The stillness of the summer evening was shattered by a roar that sounded like boilers exploding, and Angus McAllister came out of the potting-shed at forty-five miles per hour.

Gladys did not linger. She was a London child, trained from infancy to bear herself gallantly in the presence of alarms and excursions, but this excursion had been so sudden that it momentarily broke her nerve. With a horrified yelp she scuttled to where Lord Emsworth stood and, hiding behind him, clutched the tails of his morning-coat.

'Oo-er!' said Gladys.

Lord Emsworth was not feeling so frightfully good himself. We have pictured him a few moments back drawing inspiration from the nobility of his ancestors and saying, in effect, 'That for McAllister!' but truth now compels us to admit that this hardy attitude was largely due to the fact that he believed the head-gardener to be a safe quarter of a mile away among the swings and roundabouts of the Fête. The spectacle of the man charging vengefully down on him with gleaming eyes and bristling whiskers made him feel like a nervous English infantryman at the battle of Bannockburn. His knees shook and the soul within him quivered.

And then something happened, and the whole aspect of the situation changed.

It was, in itself, quite a trivial thing, but it had an astoundingly stimulating effect on Lord Emsworth's morale. What happened was that Gladys, seeking further protection, slipped at this moment a small, hot hand into his.

It was a mute vote of confidence, and Lord Emsworth intended to be worthy of it.

'He's coming,' whispered his lordship's Inferiority Complex agitatedly.

'What of it?' replied Lord Emsworth stoutly.

'Tick him off,' breathed his lordship's ancestors in his other ear.

'Leave it to me,' replied Lord Emsworth.

He drew himself up and adjusted his pince-nez. He felt filled with a cool masterfulness. If the man tendered his resignation, let him tender his damned resignation.

'Well, McAllister?' said Lord Emsworth coldly.

He removed his top-hat and brushed it against his sleeve.

'What is the matter, McAllister?'

He replaced his top-hat.

'You appear agitated, McAllister.'

He jerked his head militantly. The hat fell off. He let it lie. Freed from its loathsome weight he felt more masterful than ever. It had just needed that to bring him to the top of his form.

'This young lady,' said Lord Emsworth, 'has my full permission to pick all the flowers she wants, McAllister. If you do not see eye to eye with me in this matter, McAllister, say so and we will discuss what you are going to do about it, McAllister. These gardens, McAllister, belong to me, and if you do not —er—appreciate that fact you will, no doubt, be able to find another employer—ah—more in tune with your views. I value your services highly, McAllister, but I will not be dictated to in my own garden, McAllister. Er—dash it,' added his lordship, spoiling the whole effect.

A long moment followed in which Nature stood still, breathless. The Achillea stood still. So did the Bignonia Radicans. So did the Campanula, the

Digitalis, the Euphorbia, the Funkia, the Gypsophila, the Helianthus, the Iris, the Liatris, the
Monarda, the Phlox Drummondii, the Salvia, the
Thalictrum, the Vinca, and the Yucca. From far off
in the direction of the park there sounded the happy
howls of children who were probably breaking
things, but even these seemed hushed. The evening
breeze had died away.

Angus McAllister stood glowering. His attitude
was that of one sorely perplexed. So might the early
bird have looked if the worm ear-marked for its
breakfast had suddenly turned and snapped at it.
It had never occurred to him that his employer would
voluntarily suggest that he sought another position,
and now that he had suggested it Angus McAllister
disliked the idea very much. Blandings Castle was
in his bones. Elsewhere, he would feel an exile.
He fingered his whiskers, but they gave him no
comfort.

He made his decision. Better to cease to be a
Napoleon than be a Napoleon in exile.

'Mphm,' said Angus McAllister.

'Oh, and by the way, McAllister,' said Lord
Emsworth, 'that matter of the gravel path through
the yew alley. I've been thinking it over, and I
won't have it. Not on any account. Mutilate my
beautiful moss with a beastly gravel path? Make
an eyesore of the loveliest spot in one of the finest
and oldest gardens in the United Kingdom? Certainly not. Most decidedly not. Try to remember,
McAllister, as you work in the gardens of Blandings
Castle, that you are not back in Glasgow, laying out
recreation grounds. That is all, McAllister. Er—
dash it—that is all.'

'Mphm,' said Angus McAllister.

He turned. He walked away. The potting-shed swallowed him up. Nature resumed its breathing. The breeze began to blow again. And all over the gardens birds who had stopped on their high note carried on according to plan.

Lord Emsworth took out his handkerchief and dabbed with it at his forehead. He was shaken, but a novel sense of being a man among men thrilled him. It might seem bravado, but he almost wished—yes, dash it, he almost wished—that his sister Constance would come along and start something while he felt like this.

He had his wish.

'Clarence!'

Yes, there she was, hurrying towards him up the garden path. She, like McAllister, seemed agitated. Something was on her mind.

'Clarence!'

'Don't keep saying "Clarence!" as if you were a dashed parrot,' said Lord Emsworth haughtily. 'What the dickens is the matter, Constance?'

'Matter? Do you know what the time is? Do you know that everybody is waiting down there for you to make your speech?'

Lord Emsworth met her eye sternly.

'I do not,' he said. 'And I don't care. I'm not going to make any dashed speech. If you want a speech, let the vicar make it. Or make it yourself. Speech! I never heard such dashed nonsense in my life.' He turned to Gladys. 'Now, my dear,' he said, 'if you will just give me time to get out of these infernal clothes and this ghastly collar and put on something human, we'll go down to the village and have a chat with Ern.'

D. H. LAWRENCE

The Last Laugh

THERE was a little snow on the ground, and the church clock had just struck midnight. Hampstead in the night of winter for once was looking pretty, with clean white earth and lamps for moon, and dark sky above the lamps.

A confused little sound of voices, a gleam of hidden yellow light. And then the garden door of a tall, dark Georgian house suddenly opened, and three people confusedly emerged. A girl in a dark blue coat and fur turban, very erect: a fellow with a little dispatch-case, slouching: a thin man with a red beard, bareheaded, peering out of the gateway down the hill that swung in a curve downwards towards London.

'Look at it! A new world!' cried the man in the beard, ironically, as he stood on the step and peered out.

'No, Lorenzo! It's only whitewash!' cried the young man in the overcoat. His voice was handsome, resonant, plangent, with a weary sardonic touch. As he turned back his face was dark in shadow.

The girl with the erect, alert head, like a bird, turned back to the two men.

'What was that?' she asked, in her quick, quiet voice.

'Lorenzo says it's a new world. I say it's only whitewash,' cried the man in the street.

She stood still and lifted her woolly, gloved finger. She was deaf and was taking it in.

Yes, she had got it. She gave a quick, chuckling laugh, glanced very quickly at the man in the bowler hat, then back at the man in the stucco gateway, who was grinning like a satyr and waving good-bye.

'Good-bye, Lorenzo!' came the resonant, weary cry of the man in the bowler hat.

'Good-bye!' came the sharp, night-bird call of the girl.

The green gate slammed, then the inner door. The two were alone in the street, save for the policeman at the corner. The road curved steeply downhill.

'You'd better mind how you *step*!' shouted the man in the bowler hat, leaning near the erect, sharp girl, and slouching in his walk. She paused a moment, to make sure what he had said.

'Don't mind me, I'm quite all right. Mind yourself!' she said quickly. At that very moment he gave a wild lurch on the slippery snow, but managed to save himself from falling. She watched him, on tiptoes of alertness. His bowler hat bounced away in the thin snow. They were under a lamp near the curve. As he ducked for his hat he showed a bald spot, just like a tonsure, among his dark, thin, rather curly hair. And when he looked up at her, with his thick black brows sardonically arched, and his rather hooked nose self-derisive, jamming his hat on again, he seemed like a satanic young priest. His face had beautiful lines, like a faun, and a doubtful martyred expression. A sort of faun on the Cross, with all the malice of the complication.

'Did you hurt yourself?' she asked, in her quick, cool, unemotional way.

'No!' he shouted derisively.

'Give me the machine, won't you?' she said, holding out her woolly hand. 'I believe I'm safer.'

'Do you *want* it?' he shouted.

'Yes, I'm sure I'm safer.'

He handed her the little brown dispatch-case, which was really a Marconi listening machine for her deafness. She marched erect as ever. He shoved his hands deep in his overcoat pockets and slouched along beside her, as if he wouldn't make his legs firm. The road curved down in front of them, clean and pale with snow under the lamps. A motor-car came churning up. A few dark figures slipped away into the dark recesses of the houses, like fishes among rocks above a sea-bed of white sand. On the left was a tuft of trees sloping upwards into the dark.

He kept looking around, pushing out his finely shaped chin and his hooked nose as if he were listening for something. He could still hear the motor-car climbing on to the Heath. Below was the yellow, foul-smelling glare of the Hampstead Tube station. On the right the trees.

The girl, with her alert pink-and-white face, looked at him sharply, inquisitively. She had an odd nymph-like inquisitiveness, sometimes like a bird, sometimes a squirrel, sometimes a rabbit: never quite like a woman. At last he stood still, as if he would go no farther. There was a curious, baffled grin on his smooth, cream-coloured face.

'James,' he said loudly to her, leaning towards her ear. 'Do you hear somebody *laughing*?'

'Laughing?' she retorted quickly. 'Who's laughing?'

'I don't know. *Somebody!*' he shouted, showing his teeth at her in a very odd way.

'No, I hear nobody,' she announced.

'But it's most *extraordinary*!' he cried, his voice slurring up and down. 'Put on your machine.'

'Put it on?' she retorted. 'What for?'

'To see if you can *hear* it,' he cried.

'Hear what?'

'The *laughing*. Somebody laughing. It's most *extraordinary*.'

She gave her odd little chuckle and handed him her machine. He held it while she opened the lid and attached the wires, putting the band over her head and the receivers at her ears, like a wireless operator. Crumbs of snow fell down the cold darkness. She switched on: little yellow lights in glass tubes shone in the machine. She was connected, she was listening. He stood with his head ducked, his hands shoved down in his overcoat pockets.

Suddenly he lifted his face and gave the weirdest, slightly neighing laugh, uncovering his strong, spaced teeth and arching his black brows, and watching her with queer, gleaming, goat-like eyes.

She seemed a little dismayed.

'There!' he said. 'Didn't you hear it?'

'I heard *you*!' she said, in a tone which conveyed that *that* was enough.

'But didn't you hear *it*?' he cried, unfurling his lips oddly again.

'No!' she said.

He looked at her vindictively, and stood again with ducked head. She remained erect, her fur hat in her hand, her fine bobbed hair banded with the machine-band and catching crumbs of snow, her odd, bright-eyed, deaf nymph's face lifted with blank listening.

'There!' he cried, suddenly jerking up his gleaming face. 'You mean to tell me you can't——' He was looking at her almost diabolically. But something else was too strong for him. His face wreathed with

a startling, peculiar smile, seeming to gleam, and
suddenly the most extraordinary laugh came bursting
out of him, like an animal laughing. It was a strange,
neighing sound, amazing in her ears. She was
startled, and switched her machine quieter.

A large form loomed up: a tall, clean-shaven
young policeman.

'A radio?' he asked laconically.

'No, it's my machine. I'm deaf!' said Miss James
quickly and distinctly. She was not the daughter of
a peer for nothing.

The man in the bowler hat lifted his face and
glared at the fresh-faced young policeman with a
peculiar white glare in his eyes.

'Look here!' he said distinctly. 'Did you hear
some one laughing?'

'Laughing? I heard you, sir.'

'No, *not* me.' He gave an impatient jerk of his
arm, and lifted his face again. His smooth, creamy
face seemed to gleam, there were subtle curves of
derisive triumph in all its lines. He was careful not
to look directly at the young policeman. 'The most
extraordinary laughter I ever heard,' he added,
and the same touch of derisive exultation sounded
in his tones.

The policeman looked down on him cogitatingly.

'It's perfectly all right,' said Miss James coolly.
'He's not drunk. He just hears something that
we don't hear.'

'Drunk!' echoed the man in the bowler hat, in
profoundly amused derision. 'If I were merely
drunk——' And off he went again in the wild,
neighing, animal laughter, while his averted face
seemed to flash.

At the sound of the laughter something roused in

the blood of the girl and of the policeman. They stood nearer to one another, so that their sleeves touched and they looked wonderingly across at the man in the bowler hat. He lifted his black brows at them.

'Do you mean to say you heard nothing?' he asked.

'Only you,' said Miss James.

'Only you, sir!' echoed the policeman.

'What was it like?' asked Miss James.

'Ask me to *describe* it!' retorted the young man, in extreme contempt. 'It's the most marvellous sound in the world.'

And truly he seemed wrapped up in a new mystery.

'Where does it come from?' asked Miss James, very practical.

'*Apparently*,' he answered in contempt, 'from over there.' And he pointed to the trees and bushes inside the railings over the road.

'Well, let's go and see!' she said. 'I can carry my machine and go on listening.'

The man seemed relieved to get rid of the burden. He shoved his hands in his pockets again and sloped off across the road. The policeman, a queer look flickering on his fresh young face, put his hand round the girl's arm carefully and subtly, to help her. She did not lean at all on the support of the big hand, but she was interested, so she did not resent it. Having held herself all her life intensely aloof from physical contact, and never having let any man touch her, she now, with a certain nymph-like voluptuous-ness, allowed the large hand of the young policeman to support her as they followed the quick wolf-like figure of the other man across the road uphill. And she could feel the presence of the young policeman, through all the thickness of his dark-blue uniform, as something young and alert and bright.

When they came up to the man in the bowler hat, he was standing with his head ducked, his ears pricked, listening beside the iron rail inside which grew big black holly-trees tufted with snow, and old, ribbed, silent English elms.

The policeman and the girl stood waiting. She was peering into the bushes with the sharp eyes of a deaf nymph, deaf to the world's noises. The man in the bowler hat listened intensely. A lorry rolled down-hill, making the earth tremble.

'There!' cried the girl, as the lorry rumbled darkly past. And she glanced round with flashing eyes at her policeman, her fresh soft face gleaming with startled life. She glanced straight into the puzzled, amused eyes of the young policeman. He was just enjoying himself.

'Don't you see?' she said, rather imperiously.

'What is it, Miss?' answered the policeman.

'I mustn't point,' she said. 'Look where I look.'

And she looked away with brilliant eyes, into the dark holly bushes. She must see something, for she smiled faintly, with subtle satisfaction, and she tossed her erect head in all the pride of vindication. The policeman looked at her instead of into the bushes. There was a certain brilliance of triumph and vindication in all the poise of her slim body.

'I always knew I should see him,' she said triumphantly to herself.

'Whom do you see?' shouted the man in the bowler hat.

'Don't you see him too?' she asked, turning round her soft, arch, nymph-like face anxiously. She was anxious for the little man to see.

'No, I see nothing. What do you see, James?' cried the man in the bowler hat, insisting.

'A man.'

'Where?'

'There. Among the holly bushes.'

'Is he there now?'

'No! He's gone.'

'What sort of a man?'

'I don't know.'

'What did he look like?'

'I can't tell you.'

But at that instant the man in the bowler hat turned suddenly, and the arch, triumphant look flew to his face.

'Why, he must be *there*!' he cried, pointing up the grove. 'Don't you hear him laughing? He must be behind those trees.'

And his voice, with curious delight, broke into a laugh again, as he stood and stamped his feet on the snow, and danced to his own laughter, ducking his head. Then he turned away and ran swiftly up the avenue lined with old trees.

He slowed down as a door at the end of a garden path, white with untouched snow, suddenly opened, and a woman in a long-fringed black shawl stood in the light. She peered out into the night. Then she came down to the low garden gate. Crumbs of snow still fell. She had dark hair and a tall dark comb.

'Did you knock at my door?' she asked of the man in the bowler hat.

'I? No!'

'Somebody knocked at my door.'

'Did they? Are you sure? They can't have done. There are no footmarks in the snow.'

'Nor are there!' she said. 'But somebody knocked and called something.'

'That's very curious,' said the man. 'Were you expecting some one?'

'No. Not exactly expecting any one. Except that one is always expecting Somebody, you know.' In the dimness of the snow-lit night he could see her making big, dark eyes at him.

'Was it some one laughing?' he said.

'No. It was no one laughing, exactly. Some one knocked, and I ran to open, hoping as one always hopes, you know——'

'What?'

'Oh—that something wonderful is going to happen.'

He was standing close to the low gate. She stood on the opposite side. Her hair was dark, her face seemed dusky, as she looked up at him with her dark meaningful eyes.

'Did you wish some one would come?' he asked.

'Very much,' she replied, in her plangent Jewish voice. She must be a Jewess.

'No matter who?' he said, laughing.

'So long as it was a man I could like,' she said in a low, meaningful, falsely shy voice.

'Really!' he said. 'Perhaps after all it was I who knocked—without knowing.'

'I think it was,' she said. 'It must have been.'

'Shall I come in?' he asked, putting his hand on the little gate.

'Don't you think you'd better?' she replied.

He bent down, unlatching the gate. As he did so the woman in the black shawl turned, and, glancing over her shoulder, hurried back to the house, walking unevenly in the snow, on her high-heeled shoes. The man hurried after her, hastening like a hound to catch up.

Meanwhile the girl and the policeman had come up. The girl stood still when she saw the man in the bowler hat going up the garden walk after the woman in the black shawl with the fringe.

'Is he going in?' she asked quickly.

'Looks like it, doesn't it?' said the policeman.

'Does he know that woman?'

'I can't say. I should say he soon will,' replied the policeman.

'But who is she?'

'I couldn't say who she is.'

The two dark, confused figures entered the lighted doorway, then the door closed on them.

'He's gone,' said the girl outside on the snow. She hastily began to pull off the band of her telephone-receiver, and switched off her machine. The tubes of secret light disappeared, she packed up the little leather case. Then, pulling on her soft fur cap, she stood once more ready.

The slightly martial look which her long, dark-blue, military-seeming coat gave her was intensified, while the slightly anxious, bewildered look of her face had gone. She seemed to stretch herself, to stretch her limbs free. And the inert look had left her full soft cheeks. Her cheeks were alive with the glimmer of pride and a new dangerous surety.

She looked quickly at the tall young policeman. He was clean-shaven, fresh-faced, smiling oddly under his helmet, waiting in subtle patience a few yards away. She saw that he was a decent young man, one of the waiting sort.

The second of ancient fear was followed at once in her by a blithe, unaccustomed sense of power.

'Well!' she said. 'I should say it's no use waiting.'
She spoke decisively.

'You don't have to wait for him, do you?' asked
the policeman.

'Not at all. He's much better where he is.' She
laughed an odd, brief laugh. Then glancing over her
shoulder, she set off down the hill, carrying her little
case. Her feet felt light, her legs felt long and strong.
She glanced over her shoulder again. The young
policeman was following her, and she laughed to
herself. Her limbs felt so lithe and so strong, if she
wished she could easily run faster than he. If she
wished she could easily kill him, even with her
hands.

So it seemed to her. But why kill him? He was a
decent young fellow. She had in front of her eyes the
dark face among the holly bushes, with the brilliant,
mocking eyes. Her breast felt full of power, and her
legs felt long and strong and wild. She was surprised
herself at the strong, bright, throbbing sensation
beneath her breasts, a sensation of triumph and of
rosy anger. Her hands felt keen on her wrists. She
who had always declared she had not a muscle in
her body! Even now, it was not muscle, it was a sort
of flame.

Suddenly it began to snow heavily, with fierce
frozen puffs of wind. The snow was small, in frozen
grains, and hit sharp on her face. It seemed to whirl
round her as if she herself were whirling in a cloud.
But she did not mind. There was a flame in her,
her limbs felt flamey and strong, amid the whirl.

And the whirling, snowy air seemed full of
presences, full of strange unheard voices. She was
used to the sensation of noises taking place which
she could not hear. This sensation became very

strong.   She felt something was happening in the wild air.

The London air was no longer heavy and clammy, saturated with ghosts of the unwilling dead. A new, clean tempest swept down from the Pole, and there were noises.

Voices were calling. In spite of her deafness she could hear some one, several voices, calling and whistling, as if many people were hallooing through the air:

'He's come back! Aha! He's come back!'

There was a wild, whistling, jubilant sound of voices in the storm of snow. Then obscured lightning winked through the snow in the air.

'Is that thunder and lightning?' she asked of the young policeman, as she stood still, waiting for his form to emerge through the veil of whirling snow.

'Seems like it to me,' he said.

And at that very moment the lightning blinked again, and the dark, laughing face was near her face, it almost touched her cheek.

She started back, but a flame of delight went over her.

'There!' she said. 'Did you see that?'

'It lightened,' said the policeman.

She was looking at him almost angrily. But then the clean, fresh animal look of his skin, and the tame animal look in his frightened eyes amused her, she laughed her low, triumphant laugh. He was obviously afraid, like a frightened dog that sees something uncanny.

The storm suddenly whistled louder, more violently, and, with a strange noise like castanets, she seemed to hear voices clapping and crying:

'He is here! He's come back!'

She nodded her head gravely.

The policeman and she moved on side by side. She lived alone in a little stucco house in a side street down the hill. There was a church and a grove of trees and then the little old row of houses. The wind blew fiercely, thick with snow. Now and again a taxi went by, with its lights showing weirdly. But the world seemed empty, uninhabited save by snow and voices.

As the girl and the policeman turned past the grove of trees near the church, a great whirl of wind and snow made them stand still, and in the wild confusion they heard a whirling of sharp, delighted voices, something like seagulls, crying:

'He's here! He's here!'

'Well, I'm jolly glad he's back,' said the girl calmly.

'What's that?' said the nervous policeman, hovering near the girl.

The wind let them move forward. As they passed along the railings it seemed to them the doors of the church were open, and the windows were out, and the snow and the voices were blowing in a wild career all through the church.

'How extraordinary that they left the church open!' said the girl.

The policeman stood still. He could not reply.

And as they stood they listened to the wind and the church full of whirling voices all calling confusedly.

'*Now* I hear the laughing,' she said suddenly.

It came from the church: a sound of low, subtle, endless laughter, a strange, naked sound.

'Now I hear it!' she said.

But the policeman did not speak. He stood

cowed, with his tail between his legs, listening to the strange noises in the church.

The wind must have blown out one of the windows, for they could see the snow whirling in volleys through the black gap, and whirling inside the church like a dim light. There came a sudden crash, followed by a burst of chuckling, naked laughter. The snow seemed to make a queer light inside the building, like ghosts moving, big and tall.

There was more laughter, and a tearing sound. On the wind, pieces of paper, leaves of books, came whirling among the snow through the dark window. Then a white thing, soaring like a crazy bird, rose up on the wind as if it had wings, and lodged on a black tree outside, struggling. It was the altar-cloth.

There came a bit of gay, trilling music. The wind was running over the organ-pipes like pan-pipes, quickly up and down. Snatches of wild, gay, trilling music and bursts of the naked low laughter.

'Really!' said the girl. 'This is most extraordinary. Do you hear the music and the people laughing?'

'Yes, I hear somebody on the organ!' said the policeman.

'And do you get the puff of warm wind? Smelling of spring. Almond blossom, that's what it is! A most marvellous scent of almond blossom. *Isn't* it an extraordinary thing!'

She went on triumphantly past the church, and came to the row of little old houses. She entered her own gate in the little railed entrance.

'Here I am!' she said finally. 'I'm home now. Thank you very much for coming with me.'

She looked at the young policeman. His whole

body was white as a wall with snow, and in the vague light of the arc-lamp from the street his face was humble and frightened.

'Can I come in and warm myself a bit?' he asked humbly. She knew it was fear rather than cold that froze him. He was in mortal fear.

'Well!' she said. 'Stay down in the sitting-room if you like. But don't come upstairs, because I am alone in the house. You can make up the fire in the sitting-room, and you can go when you are warm.'

She left him on the big, low couch before the fire, his face bluish and blank with fear. He rolled his blue eyes after her as she left the room. But she went up to her bedroom, and fastened her door.

In the morning she was in her studio upstairs in her little house, looking at her own paintings and laughing to herself. Her canaries were talking and shrilly whistling in the sunshine that followed the storm. The cold snow outside was still clean, and the white glare in the air gave the effect of much stronger sunshine than actually existed.

She was looking at her own paintings, and chuckling to herself over their comicalness. Suddenly they struck her as absolutely absurd. She quite enjoyed looking at them, they seemed to her so grotesque. Especially her self-portrait, with its nice brown hair and its slightly opened rabbit-mouth and its baffled, uncertain rabbit eyes. She looked at the painted face and laughed in a long, rippling laugh, till the yellow canaries like faded daffodils almost went mad in an effort to sing louder. The girl's long, rippling laugh sounded through the house uncannily.

The housekeeper, a rather sad-faced young woman of a superior sort—nearly all people in England are of the superior sort, superiority being an English ailment—came in with an inquiring and rather disap-proving look.

'Did you call, Miss James?' she asked loudly.

'No. No, I didn't call. Don't shout, I can hear quite well,' replied the girl.

The housekeeper looked at her again.

'You knew there was a young man in the sitting-room?' she said.

'No. Really!' cried the girl. 'What, the young policeman? I'd forgotten all about him. He came in in the storm to warm himself. Hasn't he gone?'

'No, Miss James.'

'How extraordinary of him! What time is it? Quarter to nine! Why didn't he go when he was warm? I must go and see him, I suppose.'

'He says he's lame,' said the housekeeper censori-ously and loudly.

'Lame! That's extraordinary. He certainly wasn't last night. But don't shout. I can hear quite well.'

'Is Mr. Marchbanks coming in to breakfast, Miss James?' said the housekeeper, more and more cen-sorious.

'I couldn't say. But I'll come down as soon as mine is ready. I'll be down in a minute, anyhow, to see the policeman. Extraordinary that he is still here.'

She sat down before her window, in the sun, to think awhile. She could see the snow outside, the bare, purplish trees. The air all seemed rare and different. Suddenly the world had become quite different: as if some skin or integument had broken, as if the old, mouldering London sky had crackled and rolled back, like an old skin, shrivelled, leaving an absolutely new blue heaven.

'It really is extraordinary!' she said to herself. 'I

certainly saw that man's face. What a wonderful face
it was! I shall never forget it. Such laughter! He
laughs longest who laughs last. He certainly will
have the last laugh. I like him for that: he will laugh
last. Must be some one really extraordinary! How
very nice to be the one to laugh last. He certainly
will. What a wonderful being! I suppose I must call
him a being. He's not a person exactly.

'But how wonderful of him to come back and alter
all the world immediately! *Isn't* that extraordinary.
I wonder if he'll have altered Marchbanks. Of course
Marchbanks never *saw* him. But he heard him.
Wouldn't that do as well, I wonder!—I *wonder!*'

She went off into a muse about Marchbanks.
She and he were *such* friends. They had been friends
like that for almost two years. Never lovers. Never
that at all. But *friends*.

And after all, she had been in love with him: in her
head. This seemed now so funny to her: that she
had been, in her head, so much in love with him.
After all, life was too absurd.

Because now she saw herself and him as such
a funny pair. He so funnily taking life terribly
seriously, especially his own life. And she so ridicu-
lously *determined* to save him from himself. Oh,
how absurd! *Determined* to save him from himself,
and wildly in love with him in the effort. The determination to save him from himself.

Absurd! Absurd! Absurd! Since she had seen the
man laughing among the holly-bushes—*such* extraordinary, wonderful laughter—she had seen her
own ridiculousness. Really, what fantastic silliness,
saving a man from himself! Saving anybody. What
fantastic silliness! How much more amusing and
lively to let a man go to perdition in his own way.

Perdition was more amusing than salvation anyhow, and a much better place for most men to go to.

She had never been in love with any man, and only spuriously in love with Marchbanks. She saw it quite plainly now. After all, what nonsense it all was, this being-in-love business. Thank goodness she had never made the humiliating mistake.

No, the man among the holly-bushes had made her see it all so plainly: the ridiculousness of being in love, the *infra dig.* business of chasing a man or being chased by a man.

'Is love *really* so absurd and *infra dig.*?' she said aloud to herself.

'Why, of course!' came a deep, laughing voice.

She started round, but nobody was to be seen.

'I expect it's that man again!' she said to herself. 'It really *is* remarkable, you know. I consider it's a remarkable thing that I never really wanted a man, *any* man. And there I am over thirty. It *is* curious. Whether it's something wrong with me, or right with me, I can't say. I don't know till I've proved it. But I believe, if that man kept on laughing something would happen to me.'

She smelt the curious smell of almond blossom in the room, and heard the distant laugh again.

'I do wonder why Marchbanks went with that woman last night—that Jewish-looking woman. Whatever could he want of her?—or she him? So strange, as if they both had made up their minds to something! How extraordinarily puzzling life is! So messy, it all seems.

'Why does nobody ever laugh in life like that man? He *did* seem so wonderful. So scornful! And so proud! And so real! With those laughing, scornful, amazing eyes, just laughing and disappearing again.

I can't imagine him chasing a Jewish-looking woman.
Or chasing any woman, thank goodness. It's all *so*
messy. My policeman would be messy if one would
let him: like a dog. I do dislike dogs, really I do.
And men do seem so doggy!——'

But even while she mused, she began to laugh
again to herself with a long, low chuckle. How
wonderful of that man to come and laugh like that
and make the sky crack and shrivel like an old skin!
Wasn't he wonderful! Wouldn't it be wonderful if
he just touched her. Even touched her. She felt, if
he touched her, she herself would emerge new and
tender out of an old, hard skin. She was gazing
abstractedly out of the window.

'There he comes, just now,' she said abruptly.
But she meant Marchbanks, not the laughing man.

There he came, his hands still shoved down in his
overcoat pockets, his head still rather furtively
ducked, in the bowler hat, and his legs still rather
shambling. He came hurrying across the road, not
looking up, deep in thought, no doubt. Thinking
profoundly, with agonies of agitation, no doubt
about his last night's experience. It made her
laugh.

She, watching from the window above, burst into
a long laugh, and the canaries went off their heads
again.

He was in the hall below. His resonant voice was
calling, rather imperiously:

'James! Are you coming down?'

'No,' she called. 'You come up.'

He came up two at a time, as if his feet were a bit
savage with the stairs for obstructing him.

In the doorway he stood staring at her with a
vacant, sardonic look, his grey eyes moving with a

queer light. And she looked back at him with a curious, rather haughty carelessness.

'Don't you want your breakfast?' she asked. It was his custom to come and take breakfast with her each morning.

'No,' he answered loudly. 'I went to a tea-shop.'

'Don't shout,' she said. 'I can hear you quite well.'

He looked at her with mockery and a touch of malice.

'I believe you always could,' he said, still loudly.

'Well, anyway, I can now, so you needn't shout,' she replied.

And again his grey eyes, with the queer, grey phosphorescent gleam in them, lingered malignantly on her face.

'Don't look at me,' she said calmly. 'I know all about everything.'

He burst into a pouf of malicious laughter.

'Who taught you—the policeman?' he cried.

'Oh, by the way, he must be downstairs! No, he was only incidental. So, I suppose, was the woman in the shawl. Did you stay all night?'

'Not entirely. I came away before dawn. What did you do?'

'Don't shout. I came home long before dawn.' And she seemed to hear the long, low laughter.

'Why, what's the matter!' he said curiously. 'What have you been doing?'

'I don't quite know. Why?—are you going to call me to account?'

'Did you hear that laughing?'

'Oh, yes. And many more things. And saw things too.'

'Have you seen the paper?'

'No. Don't shout, I can hear.'

'There's been a great storm, blew out the windows and doors of the church outside here, and pretty well wrecked the place.'

'I saw it. A leaf of the church Bible blew right in my face: from the Book of Job——' She gave a low laugh.

'But what else did you see?' he cried loudly.

'I saw *him.*'

'Who?'

'Ah, that I can't say.

'But what was he like?'

'That I can't tell you. I don't really know.

'But you must know. Did your policeman see him too?'

'No, I don't suppose he did. My policeman!' And she went off into a long ripple of laughter. 'He is by no means mine. But I *must* go downstairs and see him.'

'It's certainly made you very strange,' March-banks said. 'You've got no *soul*, you know.'

'Oh, thank goodness for that!' she cried. 'My policeman has one, I'm sure. *My policeman!*' And she went off again into a long peal of laughter, the canaries pealing shrill accompaniment.

'What's the matter with you?' he said.

'Having no soul. I never had one really. It was always fobbed off on me. Soul was the only thing there was between you and me. Thank goodness it's gone. Haven't you lost yours? The one that seemed to worry you, like a decayed tooth?'

'But what are you *talking* about?' he cried.

'I don't know,' she said. 'It's all so extraordinary. But look here, I *must* go down and see my policeman. He's downstairs in the sitting-room. You'd better come with me.'

They went down together. The policeman, in his waistcoat and shirt-sleeves, was lying on the sofa, with a very long face.

'Look here!' said Miss James to him. 'Is it true you're lame?'

'It is true. That's why I'm here. I can't walk,' said the fair-haired young man as tears came to his eyes.

'But how did it happen? You weren't lame last night,' she said.

'I don't know how it happened—but when I woke up and tried to stand up, I couldn't do it.' The tears ran down his distressed face.

'How very extraordinary!' she said. 'What can we do about it?'

'Which foot is it?' asked Marchbanks. 'Let us have a look at it.'

'I don't like to,' said the poor devil.

'You'd better,' said Miss James.

He slowly pulled off his stocking, and showed his white left foot curiously clubbed, like the weird paw of some animal. When he looked at it himself, he sobbed.

And as he sobbed, the girl heard again the low, exulting laughter. But she paid no heed to it, gazing curiously at the weeping young policeman.

'Does it hurt?' she asked.

'It does if I try to walk on it,' wept the young man.

'I'll tell you what,' she said. 'We'll telephone for a doctor, and he can take you home in a taxi.'

The young fellow shamefacedly wiped his eyes.

'But have you no idea how it happened?' asked Marchbanks anxiously.

'I haven't myself,' said the young fellow.

At that moment the girl heard the low, eternal

laugh right in her ear. She started, but could see nothing.

She started round again as Marchbanks gave a strange, yelping cry, like a shot animal. His white face was drawn, distorted in a curious grin, that was chiefly agony but partly wild recognition. He was staring with fixed eyes at something. And in the rolling agony of his eyes was the horrible grin of a man who realizes he has made a final, and this time fatal, fool of himself.

'Why,' he yelped in a high voice, 'I knew it was he!' And with a queer shuddering laugh he pitched forward on the carpet and lay writhing for a moment on the floor. Then he lay still, in a weird, distorted position, like a man struck by lightning.

Miss James stared with round, staring brown eyes.

'Is he dead?' she asked quickly.

The young policeman was trembling so that he could hardly speak. She could hear his teeth chattering.

'Seems like it,' he stammered.

There was a faint smell of almond blossom in the air.

STACY AUMONIER

Juxtapositions

'WHERE we are all mixed up,' said my friend,
Samuel Squidge, vigorously scraping down the
'portrait of the artist, by himself,' with a palette-
knife, 'is in our juxtapositions. It's all nonsense, I
tell you. People talk about a bad colour. There's no
such thing as a bad colour. Every colour is beautiful
in its right juxtaposition. When you hear a woman
say "I hate puce," or, "I love green," she might as
well say "I hate sky," or, "I love grass." If she had
seen puce used in a colour-print as Hiroshige the
Second used it—green—fancy *loving* green! The
idiot! Do you remember what Corot said? He said
Nature was too green and too badly lighted.   Now
the old man was quite right——'

When Squidge starts talking in this strain he is
rather apt to go off the deep end. I yawned and
murmured sweetly:

'We were talking about Colin St. Clair Chasseloup.'

'Exactly! And I'm trying to point out to you how,
with Colin St. Clair Chasseloup, it's all a question
of juxtapositions. You say that Colin is a frozen
drunkard, a surly bore, a high-pressure nonentity.
Listen to me. We're all nice people, every one of us.
Give a man the right air he should breathe, the right
food he should eat, the right work he should do, the
right people he should associate with, and he's a
perfect dear, every one of him. There isn't a real
irreconcilable on the earth. But the juxtaposition—'

'What has Chasseloup to complain of?   He has

money, a charming wife, children, a place in the country, a flat in town. He does exactly what he likes.'

Squidge surveyed me with amazement.

'You ass! You prize ass! I thought you wrote about people. I thought you were supposed to understand people! And there you go and make a smug, asinine remark like that.'

I blushed, fully conscious that Squidge was being justifiably merciless. It was an asinine statement, but then I was merely putting out a feeler, and I could not explain this to the portrait painter. After all, I did not really know St. Clair Chasseloup. He was only a club acquaintance, and a very un-clubbable acquaintance he was. He appeared to dislike club life. To a stranger he seemed to reek of patrician intolerance. He was an aristocrat of aristo-crats. His well set-up, beautifully groomed figure, clean-cut features, well-poised head were all in the classic tradition of a ruling caste. It was only about the rather heavy eyelids and the restless mouth that one detected the cynic, the disappointed man, the disillusioned boor. Why? . . . It was no affair of mine, the secret troubles of this man's heart. But it was his business to behave himself to me decently. To hell with Colin St. Clair Chasseloup! I disliked the man. But then we all dislike people whom we feel nurture an innate sense of superiority to us. Added to this trying exterior of complete self-absorp-tion and superiority, one had also to allow for the vanity of the cripple.

St. Clair Chasseloup had lost his right leg just below the knee. It happened before the War. Indeed, at the time when he was a naval cadet at Osborne, skylarking with other young cadets, he had slipped

from a pinnace on a rough day and his right foot had
been crushed against the stone wall of a jetty. The
leg had to be amputated. That was the end of his
naval career. And his father had been a commodore
before him, and his father's father was in the battle
of Trafalgar, and so on right away back to the
spacious days of Elizabeth—all naval men. Devilish
bad luck, you may say! Of course, one had to allow
for the bitterness that this misfortune must have
produced. At the same time it doesn't excuse a man
not answering when he's spoken to by a fellow-
member at the club, or for looking at one—like
Chasseloup did!

Squidge's championship of the thwarted seaman
amused me. You could not conceive a more remarkable contrast. I was not even aware that they knew
each other. In spite of his missing limb, St. Clair
Chasseloup was the kind of man who always looked
as though he had just had a cold bath, done Swedish
drill, and then passed through the hairdresser's on
his way to your presence. He was aggressively fit.
Squidge looked as though a walk to the end of the
street would have brought on valvular disease of the
heart. From the centre of a dank beard, limp ends
of cigarettes eternally clung. Physically, he was just
comic. It was his vivid eyes and his queer excitable
voice that told you that he was a person of no mean
vitality. He was just as sociable and optimistic as
Chasseloup was taciturn and moribund. And yet
they met on some old plane, it appeared. Well, well,
I could understand Squidge finding merit in Chasseloup, indeed in any one, but what would Chasseloup's
opinion of Squidge be? It made me shudder to
contemplate. On the occasion I am recounting it
was almost impossible to extract any further intimate

details out of Squidge, for he had flown off on one
of his pet theoretical tangents.

'It's a queer rum thing,' he was saying, 'why
people ever get married at all. You simply can't get
level with it—the most unlikely, most outrageous
combinations! The more outrageous the more
likely they are to be a success. You see some
scraggy goat of a woman and you think to yourself,
"Poor wretch! whatever sort of chance has she got
of getting married?" and the next thing you hear
is that she's married to some god who adores her,
and they have a large family of boys at Harrow and
girls at Girton. Queer! Another woman breathes
sunlight and the men pursue her, and nothing
happens. She's unhappy. I know a woman who is
married to a man she is apparently in love with, and
he with her. They have two jolly kids, a boy and a
girl. They are a most delightful, happy family.
They have money and are bursting with health and
good spirits, and yet nearly every year the mother
gets fits of melancholia, and has to go away to a
nursing home and lie up for months. Some genius
has said that when contemplating marriage, what
you want to seek in common is not intellectual
ambitions and tastes, it's recreations. It's quite
right. Generally speaking, a man's at work all day,
so is a woman. When they meet in the evening they
want to get away from it. It's the time when they
spread their feathers. If they can play and fool
around they can be happy. Life for the most part is
a drab monologue. It's when you come to the
accents you want each other. . . . If you can share the
same tooth-brush with a woman for twenty-five
years and she can still surprise you, then you're all
right, both of you——'

'My dear Squidge, what has your disgusting notion with regard to the tooth-brush to do with St. Clair Chasseloup?'

'Nothing. I'm talking.'

'I noticed that. Tell me frankly. Would you say that he and his wife—Aimée, isn't it?—have recreations in common?'

'Yes.'

'What are they?'

'Bach.'

'Bach! what are you talking about? Colin St. Clair Chasseloup! Bach!'

'It seems funny to you, doesn't it? You know him and you've seen her. You know him, all beef and phlegm, the immovable mass. A man who thinks of nothing but dumb-bells and double Scotches. And you've seen her, the daughter of a hundred earls, highly strung, æsthetic, a little queer, passionately devoted to ultra-modern music, Coué, Montessori, anything and everything that crops up. They've nothing in common, you might say. He's out all day, playing a surly game of golf, or loafing in a club. She's playing the piano, Ravel, Debussy, or some of those queer Russian Johnnies. Or else she's inventing cute devices for the upbringing of the precious children. He lets them rip. She spoils them. When you see them together you would say that they were two people who had just missed their last bus and had to walk home, each thinking it was the other's fault. And yet I tell you they are the only two people suitable to each other. They have a mutual appreciation of accents—the same accents. They meet in the solemn tonal climaxes of Bach——'

'I can't believe that Colin likes Bach.'

'I didn't once. I found out through my pal, Paul

Furtwangler, the 'cellist. He goes there several nights a week—she pays him well, too—and he just plays Bach. It soothes the savage beast. It keeps him at home, quietens him, stays his hand from the whisky bottle. It's marvellous. He can't abide Chopin, or all the jolly tuneful stuff barbarians like you and I enjoy. There's something about it, I suppose, the orderliness, the precision, the organic building up of solemn structures that just fills the kink in his life made by his tragic defection. She hoiks him to St. Anne's, Soho, to hear the oratorios. They chase the Bach choir hither and thither. She plays it herself, although she's not much of a performer. That's why she gets Furtwangler and sometimes the Stinzel quartette. When they are listening to Bach together, they meet on a plane of complete satisfaction. Of course, the War didn't do him any good. He used to hobble backwards and forwards to Whitehall doing some ridiculous anti-aircraft intelligence stuff, and he used to look bitterly at his pals when he saw them prancing backwards and forwards, with the salt of the North Sea bitten into their faces. He was a good boy in those days, though. He left the bottle alone, and only groused and grumbled. Weren't we all doing that? . . . That's what I mean about people—married people especially—you can never tell whether they are happy or not. We all have to live our own lives in our own way. The breezy couple who go about singing "La, too, te rum, tum, tumple, rum, tum, tootle, tootle, lay," and who kiss in public, and say "darling this" and "darling that", you generally find that one or both parties are carrying on a secret liaison with a cook or a chauffeur. Colin has just got to be like that, and the woman understands him. She doesn't want

him different. While he is like that she has a more
complete grip over him, because she knows that no
other woman will understand or tolerate him. And
they don't. Of course, they quarrel sometimes, and
he goes off and makes no end of a beast of himself.
But she knows she is secure. He will come whining
back to her like a whipped puppy. And he will grope
for her in the darkness, and she will hold his hand,
and they will listen to the solemn chords of a Bach
fugue, and will feel horribly melancholy, and tre-
mendously moved, and somehow completely satisfied. That's just people, they're like that. It's no
good arguing about it. I must be going. I'm going to
have a Turkish bath with Smithers.'

The contemplation of Squidge in a Turkish bath
talking to Smithers, who is enormously fat, held me
for the moment, and then my mind reverted to
Chasseloup.

Dash it! you couldn't help being interested in the
beast. I had to acknowledge that, in spite of his
rudeness and indifference to me, the man had somehow always attracted me. I suppose because I
wanted to know him, his rudeness and indifference
piqued me all the more. And his wife—well, there it
was, I had only seen her in concert-halls and theatres,
and riding about in taxis with him, but that peculiarly wistful face would have enslaved any one. She
was slight and fragile, with pale face and very red
lips, and that curious gleaming blue-black hair that
so often accompanies a pallid complexion. Her
eyes were wonderful, large, reflective, dark, with
terrific things going on in them all the time. At the
same time I shouldn't describe them as altogether
unhappy eyes. They reflected too much vital movement for that. The woman was living, and of how

many of these hard-bitten society women can you say the same?

It happened that a few nights after my talk with Squidge, I met Chasseloup at the club. He was sitting in a corner of the smoking-room, drinking whisky and being talked to by one of the pet club bores. He occasionally growled a monosyllabic reply. After a time the club bore retired and I was left alone with him. I sat back and smoked, but did not speak. We must have sat like that for nearly twenty minutes. There must have been something about this conspiracy of silence which appealed to Chasseloup. I was aware of him occasionally glancing at me, and at length he actually ventured to address a remark. He said:

'This club whisky gets worse every day.'

I believe I must have blushed with pleasure as I hastened to acquiesce.

'Yes, it's awful stuff.'

(Did you ever know a club where the members didn't all agree that the food and drink supplied was the worst in town?)

After a few snappy sentences about the club whisky Chasseloup even went so far as to generalize. He said:

'Fancy reaching the stage of Colonel Robbins, a man who led a brigade in South Africa, and now there's nothing left for him in life but to serve on wine committees.'

I was startled by this sociable reflection, and before I could reply, he had capped it with:

'Even over that he's come to the end of his tether. His palate is worn out.'

He rose abruptly and rang the bell and ordered some more of the inferior stuff. This insignificant

conversation seemed to form a bond between Chasseloup and myself. From that evening onwards his
attitude towards me underwent a change. It was not
that he talked much, but I was aware that I was one
of the few members who didn't get on his nerves. It
was extremely flattering.

'All right, my friend,' I thought. 'I'll find out all
about you yet.'

Nevertheless, there was a long interval of time
between that conversation and the eventful Sunday
evening, when I met him and his wife at the Minerva
Musical Society's function at the Grafton Galleries.

Now it is not of the slightest importance, except
as it affects the chronicle of the events I am about to
describe, but I have to say that my own tastes with
regard to music are catholic, cosmopolitan, and
undistinguished. I like Chopin and Schumann, and
most of the Old Masters. I like Bach when I'm
in the mood. I even like Jazz music sometimes, and
foxtrots, and barrel-organs, and Old Bill playing his
mouth-organ. But I must confess that what is known
as the Modern British composer leaves me cold.
Perhaps I'm not educated up to him. And the
activities of the Minerva Musical Society are almost
entirely concerned with the modern British composer. Crowds of very precious overfed and under-
fed people meet together, and they sit on little gilt
chairs and burble with delight about the productions
of Mr. Cyrus P. Q. H. Robinson, or the tone poem
of Ananathius K. Smith. I know nothing about it.
They may be right. The only thing I have to record
is that it bores me. The only reason I went to this
particular evening was—and it is a weakness common to many weak-minded creatures like myself—
that my wife took me. She is more eclectic about

these matters than I am. She knows more, and so probably she is quite right in believing that Cyrus and Ananathius are geniuses. That isn't the point. The point is, I was frankly bored. And early in the evening, looking round the room, and confessing to myself that I was frankly bored, I suddenly happened to notice that the two people who had just come in and were sitting just behind us were Mr. and Mrs. Colin St. Clair Chasseloup. Immediately my boredom vanished. Here was a human problem of more interest than the scherzo movement of Mr. Cyrus P. Q. H. Robinson's F minor sonata. I looked round and fidgeted, and my wife said: 'Hush!'

And then without any question I heard Chasseloup say in a rather rude, abrupt voice:

'I'm not going to listen to any more of this drivel.'

And he got up and walked to the back of the room.

With two per cent. of his aplomb I got up and whispered:

'I don't care for this very much, dear. I'll just go and smoke a cigarette.'

I strolled out and found Chasseloup in the corridor. He was looking thoroughly irritable. I went straight up to him and said:

'What about a drink, Chasseloup?'

His face cleared perceptibly. He gave me quite a friendly nod, and muttered:

'Yes.'

I must now pay a tribute to that most sound of all social conventions—namely, that of evening dress. It will carry one through almost any difficulty. Chasseloup and I were both in evening dress.

We wandered out into Grafton Street just as we

were, without hats or coats. He had gone barely twenty yards when I had to exclaim:

'Good God! It's Sunday night! Everything is shut. We are just five minutes too late. I'm awfully sorry, old boy.'

It was interesting to watch the play of expression on Chasseloup's face. The jolt of irritation, the attempt to control a recognition of the jolt, and then the sudden ugly thrust of the chin. He merely said:

'Let's see what we can do.'

But there was in that thrust all the perverse tendency of a man who meant to get a drink, not because he particularly wanted it, but because he was annoyed at being thwarted.

We took two sharp turns to the left—or the right— and we came to a street, the name of which I musn't tell you, otherwise the whole story becomes almost libellous. In any case, we were not five minutes' walk from the Grafton Galleries, and we were going down a world-renowned street, consecrated chiefly to very swell private clubs. Suddenly Chasseloup jerked out:

'That looks a good place. Let's try it.'

From the exterior it was quite obvious what it was. It was a very select private club, probably an exclusive ornithologist's club, or a club consecrated to men who had won honours for discovering the secrets of subaqueous plant-life. I don't know. Chasseloup didn't know; but without the slightest hesitation we strolled casually into the smoke-room. The commissionaire glanced at us questioningly, but one look at Chasseloup convinced him that he was wrong in his doubts. With a proprietary air, Chasseloup flung himself into an easy chair on the right of the fire, and I occupied the left. There were only two old gentlemen in the room, and they were so absorbed in a conversation about goitres they didn't notice us. An ancient waiter appeared—a man who must have been there at least thirty years—and he came timidly forward. He was about to take orders in a mechanical way, and then he looked at us, and a curious sense of misgiving seemed to creep over him, not as though he were suspecting us, but as though he were suspecting his own memory. Chasseloup, with his white waistcoat and gilt buttons, his braided trousers and commanding atmosphere, couldn't be anything but a most distinguished member.

The waiter fumbled clumsily with a tray, and murmured defensively:

'You gentlemen are stopping the night, I presume?'

An expression of unctuous indignation settled on Chasseloup's features.

Of course,' he said.

The old waiter almost crawled on the carpet and took our order for two double whiskies. Thus, you may see what a domineering personality, backed up by evening dress, may accomplish. I could not possibly have done this by myself, but in the presence of Chasseloup I felt quite like an old member of this club of which I did not even know the name.

Chasseloup was not by any means a drunkard. But I discovered—at least, I have discovered later— that he considers three double whiskies his right and lawful due for an evening. They do not appear to have the slightest effect on him. We had two in this club—we were in there less than ten minutes—and then he said:

'We'll have one more somewhere else and then toddle back.'

It appeared to me to have been a sufficient triumph to have broken the laws of the land so successfully and speedily, without challenging Fate farther. Indeed, if we wanted one more drink we could easily have obtained it where we were. But it was quite patent that it was the very facility which was the obstacle in Chasseloup's case. It was all too dead easy. There was no fun in having a drink unless you had to fight for it. We had risen and walked to the door. Just as we reached the entrance hall, a man who looked like a butler came stealthily in from the street. He glanced anxiously at us, and then going up to Chasseloup, he whispered:

'Limpo?'

Now Chasseloup naturally had got a limp, and I expected to see this piece of impertinence drastically handled. Whatever was the fool getting at? But Chasseloup gave no sign. He just stared hard at the other, who quickly added:

'Her ladyship says will you come across immediately? I'll show you the way.'

Chasseloup hesitated for a fraction of a second, then, squaring his shoulders, he said:

'Come on, then.'

It was quite apparent that he had not the faintest idea what adventure he was committed to. Crossing the street, I whispered:

'What's it all about?'

And he whispered back:

'I don't know, but I guess we'll get our third drink.'

We went into a palatial block of flats and entered a lift. We were whisked up five floors and ushered

into a heavily carpeted hall. The butler left us and
did not return for three or four minutes. When he
did he seemed all on edge. He said nervously to
Chasseloup:

'Er—would you mind your friend waiting outside,
sir?'

Chasseloup spoke emphatically:

'No, tell her ladyship that where Limpo goes
Blotto follows.'

There was another interval, and then the butler
returned and asked us both to follow him.

We went into a large smoking-room, sparsely
furnished. The room was occupied by three men.
They were all big men, and they were all standing.
On the hearthrug stood one of the most sinister-
looking individuals I have ever seen. He was very
tall, with heavy shoulders and a fierce black moustache and wicked eyes. There was something about
the way the men were standing I didn't like. It
appeared to be all carefully planned. The big man,
whose voice seemed surprisingly thin for his bulk,
said banteringly:

'Oh, come in, Mr.—er—Limpo. Julius Lindt,
perhaps I should say. It pains me to tell you that her
ladyship is not present, unavoidably detained—see?'

Chasseloup bowed formally, and said in an ice-
cold voice:

'I regret to hear it.'

'Um—um—yes. Yes, quite so. I can quite believe
it. I presume you are a great reader of *The Times*,
Mr.—er—Limpo, Lindt I should say.'

'I always read *The Times*,' answered Chasseloup
politely.

'Yes, and write for them, advertise, too, Mr—er—
Lindt. Nice friendly, loving little paragraphs, eh?'

He held out a copy of *The Times*, the outside sheet
showing. Round one paragraph some one had put a
blue pencil line. The big man thrust it in Chasseloup's face and said:

'Just read that out, Mr—er——'

There was a nasty dangerous tone in his voice.
I didn't like it at all. I began to think lovingly of the
Minerva Society, the little gilt chairs, and Cyrus
P. Q. H. Robinson's F minor sonata. Chasseloup
was perfectly calm. He never took his eyes off the
other man's face. He said coldly:

'My friend, Blotto, will read it.'

The paper was handed to me, and I read out from
the agony column:

'Molly. Am yearning for you. Shall be at the
Club Sunday night. If the Dragon is away, send over
for me. All my love. Limpo.'

I was too nervous to see the humour of the situation. Here was the outraged husband and by great
guile he had captured the wrong *tertium quid!* How
could one explain? Chasseloup's regrettable limp
appeared damning evidence. He had gone there,
and deliberately put his head through the noose.
The situation was appalling. The worst of it was,
that under such circumstances men do not stop to
think and reason. Passion and mob-law are old
confederates. This fact was brought home during
the ensuing seconds. Everything seemed to happen
in a flash. I was conscious of the Dragon stretching
out his hand towards a short, stocky riding-whip,
which had been concealed by the fire-place; of he
other two men stealthily closing in on Chasseloup.
And then a fourth man—was it the butler?—gripped
me by the throat from behind, and I was jerked
towards the door. The idea was to get me out of the

way whilst the other three men horsewhipped Chasseloup. I fell backwards into the hall, and the door slammed to. At least it nearly did. It was slammed with terrific violence, but just in the nick of time a leg was thrust through. Now the force with which it was pushed would have broken any ordinary leg, but as it happened the leg that was thrust through was made of wood and steel framing.

The arms above were apparently engaged else-where. The sight of that upturned boot spurred me to action. I drove my elbows violently into the ribs of my attacker. I heard him groan, and I leapt forward to the door again, I think he must have been the butler. I never saw him again. When I forced my way back into the room, I think the moral effect of my presence was more valuable to our side than any physical exploit I was likely to offer. Three men against two are not overwhelming odds. The man just in front of the door, who was gripping Chasse-loup by the waist, hesitated, and paid the penalty by getting a blow over his left eye. The other two men were closing in, when Chasseloup ducked and got free. It was then that I saw the man as he really was. His eyes were gleaming with exultation. He was thoroughly enjoying himself. With a sudden unex-pected swerve he seized a vase and smashed the electric light globes. The room was in darkness.

Now for a mixed body of men to fight in the dark is a dangerous and difficult game. You do not know who is with you or against you. Oaths were ex-changed rather than blows. And the Dragon called out:

'Where's Dawson? Where's that —— butler?'

Then he gave a curse which showed that he was foolish to reveal his whereabouts. One fool struck a match, which served no better purpose than to reveal the point of his jaw, a fact that was promptly taken advantage of. He went down and out. We were now two against two, and one of them had a black eye that would last many a week. The Dragon was blind with rage. He roared:

'Come out into the hall!'

And he stumbled out there and waved his arms challengingly. We all followed him. The man with the black eye had had enough, and I sat on the opposite side of the hall also a spectator. For it seemed to be suddenly mutually agreed that this was an affair between the Dragon and Chasseloup. They both wanted to fight. I could have yelled out that the whole thing was a mistake, a misunderstanding, that Chasseloup was not the man who had liaisons with the other man's wife; but if I had done so I felt that Chasseloup would never forgive me. He had already taken his coat off, and so had the Dragon. And they fought. An affair of this nature between two heavyweights seldom lasts long. It depends so much on who gets in the first good blow. And in this case the fight certainly didn't last three minutes. It was horrible. I don't know whether the Dragon was much of a boxer. He certainly seemed to have some knowledge of the game, but he never landed a blow. After a few exchanges he received a punch on the nose, and the blood ran down all over his dress shirt. Then he hit wildly, and suddenly received three terrible blows in rapid succession; one on the chin, one on the jaw, and then a fearful thump over the heart, which laid him out. We were now in complete possession of the field, the man with the black eye being the only conscious enemy in the flat, and he had done with fighting for the day.

'Now, where's that butler?' said Chasseloup.

'Oh, come on, for God's sake!' I exclaimed, foreseeing more blood-letting. 'Leave the butler alone. Let's get away.'

'I'm not going till I get what I came for.'

'What's that?'

'That drink.'

The man with the black eye, who appeared to be some sort of hired ruffian, grinned in a sickly manner.

'All right, guv'nor,' he said; 'I can fix that for you.'

He went into the dining-room and returned with a tantalus and some glasses.

Chasseloup poured himself out his double whisky, just the exact amount, and no more. Then he put on his coat and readjusted his hair in the mirror. His face was unscratched.

'There's something perfectly disgusting about you,' I thought.

When he left the flat the Dragon was partly conscious, and he was mumbling something about the police and fire-arms and vengeance. We went down in the lift. Just as we were going out through the entrance hall a typical young-man-about-town came up the steps. He was limping. Chasseloup raised his hat.

'Mr. Lindt, I presume?'

The young man started. Chasseloup smiled quite graciously.

'Her ladyship is expecting you in the smoke-room,' he said.

'Oh! thank you, thank you, sir.'

The dude blushed and hurried on.

'But, good Lord!' I exclaimed, when we were in the street. 'It's a bit unfair. They'll half murder him.'

'That's his affair,' said Chasseloup.   'Besides, it serves him right—to go fooling about with another man's wife.'

To look back on it, it seems almost unbelievable, but from the moment when we left the Minerva Musical Society to the moment we returned marks the lapse of rather less than an hour. And when we returned nothing might have happened at all. There they all were, the same people, the same little gilt chairs. Everybody looked quite unconcerned, but nobody looked more unconcerned than Colin St. Clair Chasseloup, lolling indolently on a stuffed settee at the end of the room.

As it happened, they were just finishing some modern work, and then there was an interval.   Both our wives joined us and were introduced. Mrs. Chasseloup was charming. She said:

'You bad men! where have you been?'

Without waiting for a reply, she added excitedly:

'Colin, you'll be pleased. Paul Tingleton's ill, and he can't lead his quintette. And I've persuaded Mr. Oesler to end up with the Bach fugue you love so much.'

Queer fish, people are. A few minutes later we were drinking lemonade and coffee and talking of such precious intimacies as the colour of a musical phrase, and only a quarter of an hour ago—— Then we were back in the concert hall, Chasseloup and his wife and my wife and I, and the great Mr. Oesler began to play Bach.

And then the queerest thing of all—Chasseloup! Chasseloup, whose face I had seen but a few minutes before ablaze with anger and cruelty, suddenly mellowing, becoming gentle and wistful. And he leaned forward with his lips parted, and his wife sat beside him with an identical expression on her face. And then I saw his hand steal towards her lap, and she took it in both of hers and gripped it greedily. And they sat there, side by side, perfectly oblivious to their surroundings, perfectly happy, like two children listening to a fairy-tale.

KATHERINE MANSFIELD

Sun and Moon

IN the afternoon the chairs came, a whole big cart
full of little gold ones with their legs in the air. And
then the flowers came. When you stared down from
the balcony at the people carrying them the flower-
pots looked like funny, awfully nice hats nodding
up the path.

Moon thought they were hats. She said: 'Look.
There's a man wearing a palm on his head.' But she
never knew the difference between real things and
not real ones.

There was nobody to look after Sun and Moon.
Nurse was helping Annie alter mother's dress which
was much-too-long-and-tight-under-the-arms and
mother was running all over the house and tele-
phoning father to be sure not to forget things. She
only had time to say: 'Out of my way, children!'

They kept out of her way—at any rate Sun did.
He did so hate being sent stumping back to the
nursery. It didn't matter about Moon. If she got
tangled in people's legs they only threw her up and
shook her till she squeaked. But Sun was too heavy
for that. He was so heavy that the fat man who
came to dinner on Sundays used to say: 'Now, young
man, let's try to lift you.' And then he'd put his
thumbs under Sun's arms and groan and try and
give it up at last saying: 'He's a perfect little ton of
bricks!'

Nearly all the furniture was taken out of the
dining-room. The big piano was put in a corner and
then there came a row of flower-pots and then there

came the goldy chairs. That was for the concert. When Sun looked in a white-faced man sat at the piano—not playing, but banging at it and then looking inside. He had a bag of tools on the piano and he had stuck his hat on a statue against the wall. Sometimes he just started to play and then he jumped up again and looked inside. Sun hoped he wasn't the concert.

But of course the place to be in was the kitchen. There was a man helping in a cap like a blancmange, and their real cook, Minnie, was all red in the face and laughing. Not cross at all. She gave them each an almond finger and lifted them up on to the flour bin so that they could watch the wonderful things she and the man were making for supper. Cook brought in the things and he put them on dishes and trimmed them. Whole fishes, with their heads and eyes and tails still on, he sprinkled with red and green and yellow bits; he made squiggles all over the jellies, he stuck a collar on a ham, and put a very thin sort of a fork in it; he dotted almonds and tiny round biscuits on the creams. And more and more things kept coming.

'Ah, but you haven't seen the ice pudding,' said Cook. 'Come along.' Why was she being so nice, thought Sun as she gave them each a hand. And they looked into the refrigerator.

Oh! Oh! Oh! It was a little house. It was a little pink house with white snow on the roof and green windows and a brown door and stuck in the door there was a nut for a handle.

When Sun saw the nut he felt quite tired and had to lean against Cook.

'Let me touch it. Just let me put my finger on the roof,' said Moon, dancing. She always wanted to touch all the food. Sun didn't.

'Now, my girl, look sharp with the table,' said Cook as the housemaid came in.

'It's a picture, Min,' said Nellie. 'Come along and have a look.' So they all went into the dining-room. Sun and Moon were almost frightened. They wouldn't go up to the table at first; they just stood at the door and made eyes at it.

It wasn't real night yet but the blinds were down in the dining-room and the lights turned on—and all the lights were red roses. Red ribbons and bunches of roses tied up the table at the corners. In the middle was a lake with rose petals floating on it. 'That's where the ice pudding is to be,' said Cook.

Two silver lions with wings had fruit on their backs, and the salt-cellars were tiny birds drinking out of basins.

And all the winking glasses and shining plates and sparkling knives and forks—and all the food. And the little red table napkins made into roses. . . .

'Are people going to eat the food?' asked Sun.

'I should just think they were,' laughed Cook, laughing with Nellie. Moon laughed, too; she always did the same as other people. But Sun didn't want to laugh. Round and round he walked with his hands behind his back. Perhaps he never would have stopped if Nurse hadn't called suddenly:

'Now then, children. It's high time you were washed and dressed.' And they were marched off to the nursery.

While they were being unbuttoned mother looked in with a white thing over her shoulders; she was rubbing stuff on her face.

'I'll ring for them when I want them, Nurse, and then they can just come down and be seen and go back again,' said she.

Sun was undressed first, nearly to his skin, and dressed again in a white shirt with red and white daisies speckled on it, breeches with strings at the sides and braces that came over, white socks and red shoes.

'Now you're in your Russian costume,' said Nurse, flattening down his fringe.

'Am I?' said Sun.

'Yes. Sit quiet in that chair and watch your little sister.'

Moon took ages. When she had her socks put on she pretended to fall back on the bed and waved her legs at Nurse as she always did, and every time Nurse tried to make her curls with a finger and a wet brush she turned round and asked Nurse to show her the photo of her brooch or something like that. But at last she was finished too. Her dress stuck out, with fur on it, all white; there was even fluffy stuff on the legs of her drawers. Her shoes were white with big blobs on them.

'There you are, my lamb,' said Nurse. 'And you look like a sweet little cherub of a picture of a powder-puff?' Nurse rushed to the door. 'Ma'am, one moment.'

Mother came in again with half her hair down.

'Oh,' she cried. 'What a picture!'

'Isn't she,' said Nurse.

And Moon held out her skirts by the tips and dragged one of her feet. Sun didn't mind people not noticing him—much. . . .

After that they played clean tidy games up at the table while Nurse stood at the door, and when the carriages began to come and the sound of laughter and voices and soft rustlings came from down below she whispered: 'Now then, children, stay where you are.' Moon kept jerking the table-cloth so that it all hung down her side and Sun hadn't any—and then she pretended she didn't do it on purpose.

At last the bell rang. Nurse pounced at them with the hair brush, flattened his fringe, made her bow stand on end, and joined their hands together.

'Down you go!' she whispered.

And down they went. Sun did feel silly holding Moon's hand like that but Moon seemed to like it. She swung her arm and the bell on her coral bracelet jingled.

At the drawing-room door stood mother fanning herself with a black fan. The drawing-room was full of sweet smelling, silky, rustling ladies and men in black with funny tails on their coats—like beetles. Father was among them, talking very loud, and rattling something in his pocket.

'What a picture!' cried the ladies. 'Oh, the ducks! Oh, the lambs! Oh, the sweets! Oh, the pets!'

All the people who couldn't get at Moon kissed Sun, and a skinny old lady with teeth that clicked said: 'Such a serious little poppet,' and rapped him on the head with something hard.

Sun looked to see if the same concert was there, but he was gone. Instead, a fat man with a pink head leaned over the piano talking to a girl who held a violin at her ear.

There was only one man that Sun really liked. He was a little grey man, with long grey whiskers, who walked about by himself. He came up to Sun and rolled his eyes in a very nice way and said:

'Hullo, my lad.' Then he went away. But soon he came back again and said: 'Fond of dogs?' Sun said: 'Yes.' But then he went away again, and though Sun looked for him everywhere he couldn't find him. He thought perhaps he'd gone outside to fetch in a puppy.

'Good-night, my precious babies,' said mother, folding them up in her bare arms. 'Fly up to your little nest.'

Then Moon went and made a silly of herself again. She put up her arms in front of everybody and said: 'My daddy must carry me.'

But they seemed to like it, and Daddy swooped down and picked her up as he always did.

Nurse was in such a hurry to get them to bed that she even interrupted Sun over his prayers and said:

'Get on with them, child, *do*.' And the moment after they were in bed and in the dark, except for the nightlight in its little saucer.

'Are you asleep?' asked Moon.

'No,' said Sun. 'Are you?'

'No,' said Moon.

A long while after Sun woke up again. There was a loud, loud noise of clapping from downstairs, like when it rains. He heard Moon turn over.

'Moon, are you awake?'

'Yes, are you?'

'Yes. Well, let's go and look over the stairs.'

They had just got settled on the top step when the drawing-room door opened and they heard the party cross over the hall into the dining-room. Then that door was shut; there was a noise of 'pops' and laughing. Then that stopped and Sun saw them all walking round and round the lovely table with their hands behind their backs like he had done. . . . Round and round they walked, looking and staring. The man with the grey whiskers liked the little house best. When he saw the nut for a handle he rolled his eyes like he did before and said to Sun: 'Seen the nut?'

'Don't nod your head like that, Moon.'

'I'm not nodding. It's you.'

'It is not. I never nod my head.'

'O-oh, you do. You're nodding it now.'

'I'm not. I'm only showing you how not to do it.'

When they woke up again they could only hear father's voice very loud, and mother, laughing away. Father came out of the dining-room, bounded up the stairs, and nearly fell over them.

'Hullo!' he said. 'By Jove, Kitty, come and look at this.'

Mother came out. 'Oh, you naughty children,' said she from the hall.

'Let's have 'em down and give 'em a bone,' said father. Sun had never seen him so jolly.

'No, certainly not,' said mother.

'Oh, my daddy, do! Do have us down,' said Moon.

'I'm hanged if I won't,' cried father. 'I won't be bullied. Kitty—way there.' And he caught them up, one under each arm.

Sun thought mother would have been dreadfully cross. But she wasn't. She kept on laughing at father.

'Oh, you dreadful boy!' said she. But she didn't mean Sun.

'Come on, kiddies. Come and have some pickings,' said this jolly father. But Moon stopped a minute.

'Mother—your dress is right off one side.'

'Is it?' said mother. And father said 'Yes' and pretended to bite her white shoulder, but she pushed him away.

And so they went back to the beautiful dining-room.

But—oh! oh! what had happened. The ribbons and the roses were all pulled untied. The little red table napkins lay on the floor, all the shining plates were dirty and all the winking glasses. The lovely food that the man had trimmed was all thrown about, and there were bones and bits and fruit peels and shells everywhere. There was even a bottle lying down with stuff coming out of it on to the cloth and nobody stood it up again.

And the little pink house with the snow roof and the green windows was broken—broken—half melted away in the centre of the table.

'Come on, Sun,' said father, pretending not to notice.

Moon lifted up her pyjama legs and shuffled up to the table and stood on a chair, squeaking away.

'Have a bit of this ice,' said father, smashing in some more of the roof.

Mother took a little plate and held it for him; she put her other arm round his neck.

'Daddy. Daddy,' shrieked Moon. 'The little handle's left. The little nut. Kin I eat it?' And she reached across and picked it out of the door and scrunched it up, biting hard and blinking.

'Here, my lad,' said father.

But Sun did not move from the door. Suddenly he put up his head and gave a loud wail.

'I think it's horrid—horrid—horrid!' he sobbed.

'There, you see!' said mother. 'You see!'

'Off with you,' said father, no longer jolly. 'This moment. Off you go!'

And wailing loudly, Sun stumped off to the nursery.

Submarine

THERE was a loud squealing in her ears and it was
like the translation into sound of the hurried green
twilight about her. Her head felt as if it was padded
with vacuum like a thermos, but—also like a thermos filled with iced lemonade—cool, acid, and
lucid inside. She watched Amos in front of her,
cannon-ball-headed, waddling grotesquely, sticking
out a large creased behind, like an offended rhinoceros, planting his immense feet on gardens and
moving creatures and swaying flowers, flapping a
portentous hand like a drunkard. 'That's the man
I love,' she thought, gaping at him through streaked
unflattering space, and as she thought this, his foot
moved carelessly and he sprang, sprawling askew, to
a point outside her range of vision. She could only
see a blinkered view through the window in her
helmet.

She was not wearing the full diving-suit but only
a headpiece with a rubber 'bertha' and her own
bathing-dress. She felt like a top-heavy pawn on a
drunken chess-board. The air-pipe was under her
arm. The helmet was like a diving-bell with only a
certain allowance of bubbling squealing air trapped
inside it. When she bowed forward to look at a little
crab, the air receded up to her mouth; in fright she
bent backward and the crisp line of the water slipped
down at once to her Adam's apple. Now she felt
braver; she could bend her nervous weightless body
a little—not too much—to allow her window to
command a view of white coral branches, white

craters, anemones like pianists' fingers, green-black patches of matted weed, crabs and smiling open mussels, little glassy splinters of fish that moved off round her ankles like sun-touched midges round the pillars of a cathedral. Looking at her ankles, slim and pearl-green under a body that felt so top-heavy and undisciplined, she tried to dance a step or two. Instantly she soared by mistake—sideways—back-wards—outspread like a spider—outspread like a little boy lifted by the seat of the trousers. . . . She landed on one heel, unable for a moment to retrieve her aspiring right leg, in a white coral crater.

'Who *was* that man like?' came suddenly into her mind as she waved and slanted in the urgent water, unable to stand, unable to fall. She was thinking of the man in charge of the raft above her. 'Who *was* he like?' Her eyes remembered the man, standing in his shirt-sleeves in the sun on the raft, scowling at the negroes who worked the pump, turning with an apologetic smile to her and Amos. Her ears remem-bered him. . . . 'It's not often we get a lady on this raft, wanting to dive for the fun of the thing, too. But you couldn't wear the outfit, lady, well, look, you couldn't move it—try one of the shoes . . . well, look, there, you see—why, you couldn't carry the weight over the side—three hundred and twenty-five pounds—of course it feels like a feather once you're under water, but it'd be the getting there. Still . . . well, look, I'd like you to go down and see the *Will o' the Wisp*—she lies so pretty, just twenty-eight feet under that buoy there; we shall get the whisky out of her hold by to-morrow night, I guess, if there really are only a hundred cases. No—she's not worth salving, herself—she was only a dot-and-carry-one old schooner and she crumpled her bows right in, running into that rock there—the sea was pretty high and the old man must have lost his head. . . . It's only the whisky the owners want out of her; well, look, right here, within a hundred miles of the Yankee buyers, whisky's worth something, I can tell you. Well, look, lady, I'd like you to see her—well, why don't you go down in this gadget here, what the niggers use when they don't want to bother with the whole caboodle?—nothing but the helmet and the tube, you see—works just as well for a short trip.'

Well, look, he said so often—who *was* that like?— with that mumbled *well*, like *wll*, and the open throaty *look*—'*wll lok*'. It was like *Nana*—he might be Nana's son—that was why the connexion—or disconnexion—in her memory had made her so uncomfortable. Everything connected with Nana was wounding. The thought of Nana brought in a rush into her mind a young lifetime of croonings and hummings and comfortings and scoldings and rockings and forgivings . . . and then—*crash*—a day when Amos discovered that Nana, turned from nurse to housekeeper, had during these twenty years stolen eight hundred and thirty pounds out of the money given her for her charge's upkeep. The widow profiting by the orphan's trust. Nana turned out of the house. Amos shouting, 'You're lucky we don't care to prosecute. . . .' Nana's sailor son—who happened to be in Harwich—sent for in a great uproar. 'Call yesself a gentleman—this is how you reward my old mother's lifetime of service. . . . Wait till I get you alone—I'll get a chance to get even with you some day. . . .' She had only seen Nana's son on that occasion—she had looked over the bannisters and seen him shaking his fist. The man on the raft *was* like him. Amos would not notice it—he was so

short-sighted. Besides, it was ten years ago. But
'*wll lok*'—it was Nana's exact intonation. Surely
the coincidence could be *too* extraordinary. She and
Amos were only here by chance, yachting in the West
Indies—had come here idly to this lonely lagoon,
having heard of the wreck of the little smuggler.
'Why, there's diving—oh, what fun, Vi, let's
dive. . . .' So here they were, by chance, at the
bottom of the sea, at the mercy of a man on a raft—
who was like Nana's son. By chance. 'I'll get a
chance to get even. . .' *Was* it Nana's son? Now,
suddenly, she remembered that he had said to Amos,
'Some people like diving, and some do it once and
never do it again.' Amos had said, 'We shall never
get a chance to do it again, whether we like it or not.'
And Nana's son had replied, 'Probably not.' (It *was*
Nana's son.) Then, to the negroes, 'You goggling
idiots, can't you—aw hell—well then, get to hell
out of here. I'll do it myself.' He would work the
pump himself.

The young woman, alone in a squealing bubbling
silence in the crater, looked about her in a panic,
moving jointlessly like a cheap puppet. She thought
thirstily of the safe dry air—of the light sky—of
birds—of England—Oh, to be in England now that
April's here; there's the wise elm he grows each
twig twice over. . . . She tentatively pulled her air-
tube—the signal for help from the raft. There was
no answering pull. She could probably swim upward
unaided—indeed she had some difficulty in remaining
down. But Amos in his leaden armour. . . . Where
was Amos? Where was the wreck of the *Will o' the
Wisp*—?—he would be there. She began to climb
prancingly up the side of the crater, a mild slope of
perhaps six feet but as difficult as a mountain to her

unwieldy feet. At the edge of the crater at last, she could see the wreck quite near, looking very different from her expectation. It looked like a little leaning house with a swinging door; the mast, with flags of blackish sea-weed, was like a dying tree over the little house, and the ominous green light added to its menacing look. A waltzing inverted Spanish onion bowing to the crushed bows of the ship was identifiable as Amos. As his wife approached, the unsuspicious Amos, in one flying stride like a slow-motion cinema study, aimed himself at the sloping deck of the schooner, reached it, slipped and fell, and lay in the scuppers. He did all this with absurd suspended ponderousness; his helmet, of course, could not change its expression to a smile, and this immobility gave him the earnest look of a puppy trying unsuccessfully for the first time to climb steps. His wife, however, did not smile at his antics inside her own soberly grinning mask. Somehow she reached the lower side of the ship, bruising her shoulder against a stanchion. She could reach her Amos' foot as he cautiously tried to get up. She pulled his foot! he sat down again as abruptly as the supporting water would allow him to, and bounced once. (What a field there is for a submarine low comedian!) Amos made a flapping gesture of irritation, like the 'Don't bovver me' of a baby.

'Amos—come quickly—that's Nana's son, we're in danger,' yelled his wife. Her ears cracked. The squealing in her headpiece changed its note and crackled; she felt almost suffocated; she reeled. Amos could not hear a sound. He flapped foolishly again. 'Amos—Amos—' She pulled his ankle in panic—it was all she could reach of him. He tried to draw it away. There was asperity in his flapping.

She pointed upward like a Salvation Army preacher. He turned his mask towards her! she half saw his mouth moving behind the glass. He pointed at her and pointed upward as he lay along the rail at an impossible angle. He was evidently saying, 'Go up yourself then, but leave me alone.' This squealing instead of silence was a more frightful answer than silence. There he was, wrapped away in his own squealing sound-proof world. A fish swam between him and her. 'Amos—Amos!' she screamed, and once more was checked by semi-suffocation. Was the air being cut off from above? Amos withdrew his leaden foot from her reach. He regained a kind of perpendicularity and signed to her once more, peremptorily, that she should soar away from him. He took one step away from her. As a step, it failed. As a flight, it was unexpectedly successful; the steep deck seemed to launch him backwards into space; he flew towards his wife and, for a second, sat lightly on her iron face. She clasped him round the middle; he doubled up like a jointed foot-rule. She was saving him. She bounded about frantically. Amos managed to twist himself out of her grasp but she caught his arm. 'It's Nana's son up there—an enemy.' She clung with both hands to his rubber wrist, dragging him. Amos, she could see, was now quite alarmed—not suspicious of foul play but dumbfounded by the frenzied behaviour of his wife. He pulled his safety cord. They were instantly caught up to heaven together, floating sideways, inter-twined, through the blowing current, like G. F. Watts' *Paolo and Francesca*. Their two round steel heads collided at the surface, at the foot of the raft's ladder. Some one lifted our young woman's false head off; she was herself again—she was herself in her bathing-suit, unarmoured, safe, as though coming aboard after a common swim. A face bent over her. Nana's son? What *had* she been thinking of? This man was not in the least like Nana's son; he was short and broad—Nana's son had been tall and knock-kneed; this man on the raft was obviously Australian—he greeted her with an unmistakable accent, and his first words were not *wll lok*, but *lok here, lidy*. . . . What madness of memory had caught her, down there in that new senseless shadowed world?

Amos was being helped up the ladder. Some one opened his little window and his voice leapt out like a bird out of a cage. 'Good Lord, Vi, what in the world . . .?' as the raftman helpfully wrenched his iron head off.

ALDOUS HUXLEY

The Tillotson Banquet

I

Young Spode was not a snob; he was too intelligent for that, too fundamentally decent. Not a snob; but all the same he could not help feeling very well pleased at the thought that he was dining, alone and intimately, with Lord Badgery. It was a definite event in his life, a step forward, he felt, towards that final success, social, material, and literary, which he had come to London with the fixed intention of making. The conquest and capture of Badgery was an almost essential strategical move in the campaign.

Edmund, forty-seventh Baron Badgery, was a lineal descendant of that Edmund, surnamed Le Blayreau, who landed on English soil in the train of William the Conqueror. Ennobled by William Rufus, the Badgerys had been one of the very few baronial families to survive the Wars of the Roses and all the other changes and chances of English history. They were a sensible and philoprogenitive race. No Badgery had ever fought in any war, no Badgery had ever engaged in any kind of politics. They had been content to live and quietly to propagate their species in a huge machicolated Norman castle, surrounded by a triple moat, only sallying forth to cultivate their property and to collect their rents. In the eighteenth century, when life had become relatively secure, the Badgerys began to venture forth into civilized society. From boorish squires they blossomed into *grands seigneurs*, patrons of the arts, virtuosi. Their property was large, they were rich; and with the growth of

industrialism their riches also grew. Villages on
their estate turned into manufacturing towns, un-
suspected coal was discovered beneath the surface of
their barren moorlands. By the middle of the nine-
teenth century the Badgerys were among the richest
of English noble families. The forty-seventh baron
disposed of an income of at least two hundred
thousand pounds a year. Following the great
Badgery tradition, he had refused to have anything
to do with politics or war. He occupied himself by
collecting pictures; he took an interest in theatrical
productions; he was the friend and patron of men
of letters, of painters, and musicians. A personage,
in a word, of considerable consequence in that
particular world in which young Spode had elected
to make his success.

Spode had only recently left the university. Simon
Gollamy, the editor of the *World's Review* (the 'Best
of all possible Worlds'), had got to know him—he
was always on the look-out for youthful talent—had
seen possibilities in the young man, and appointed
him art critic of his paper. Gollamy liked to have
young and teachable people about him. The possession of disciples flattered his vanity, and he found it
easier, moreover, to run his paper with docile col-
laborators than with men grown obstinate and case-
hardened with age. Spode had not done badly at his
new job. At any rate, his articles had been intelligent
enough to arouse the interest of Lord Badgery. It
was, ultimately, to them that he owed the honour of
sitting to-night in the dining-room of Badgery House.

Fortified by several varieties of wine and a glass
of aged brandy, Spode felt more confident and at
ease than he had done the whole evening. Badgery
was rather a disquieting host. He had an alarming

habit of changing the subject of any conversation that had lasted for more than two minutes. Spode had found it, for example, horribly mortifying when his host, cutting across what was, he prided himself, a particularly subtle and illuminating disquisition on baroque art, had turned a wandering eye about the room and asked him abruptly whether he liked parrots. He had flushed and glanced suspiciously towards him, fancying that the man was trying to be offensive. But no; Badgery's white, fleshy, Hanoverian face wore an expression of perfect good faith. There was no malice in his small greenish eyes. He evidently did genuinely want to know if Spode liked parrots. The young man swallowed his irritation and replied that he did. Badgery then told a good story about parrots. Spode was on the point of capping it with a better story, when his host began to talk about Beethoven. And so the game went on. Spode cut his conversation to suit his host's requirements. In the course of ten minutes he had made a more or less witty epigram on Benvenuto Cellini, Queen Victoria, sport, God, Stephen Phillips, and Moorish architecture. Lord Badgery thought him the most charming young man, and so intelligent.

'If you've quite finished your coffee,' he said, rising to his feet as he spoke, 'we'll go and look at the pictures.'

Spode jumped up with alacrity, and only then realized that he had drunk just ever so little too much. He would have to be careful, talk deliberately, plant his feet consciously, one after the other.

'This house is quite cluttered up with pictures,' Lord Badgery complained. 'I had a whole wagonload taken away to the country last week; but there are still far too many. My ancestors would have

their portraits painted by Romney. Such a shocking
artist, don't you think? Why couldn't they have
chosen Gainsborough, or even Reynolds? I've had
all the Romneys hung in the servants' hall now. It's
such a comfort to know that one can never possibly
see them again. I suppose you know all about the
ancient Hittites?'

'Well . . .' the young man replied, with befitting
modesty.

'Look at that, then.' He indicated a large stone
head which stood in a case near the dining-room
door. 'It's not Greek, or Egyptian, or Persian, or
anything else; so if it isn't ancient Hittite, I don't
know what it is. And that reminds me of that story
about Lord George Sanger, the Circus King . . .'
and, without giving Spode time to examine the
Hittite relic, he led the way up the huge staircase,
pausing every now and then in his anecdote to point
out some new object of curiosity or beauty.

'I suppose you know Deburau's pantomimes?'
Spode rapped out as soon as the story was over. He
was in an itch to let out his information about
Deburau. Badgery had given him a perfect opening
with his ridiculous Sanger. 'What a perfect man,
isn't he? He used to . . .'

'This is my main gallery,' said Lord Badgery,
throwing open one leaf of a tall folding door. 'I must
apologize for it. It looks like a roller-skating rink.'
He fumbled with the electric switches and there was
suddenly light—light that revealed an enormous
gallery, duly receding into distance according to all
the laws of perspective. 'I dare say you've heard of
my poor father,' Lord Badgery continued. 'A little
insane, you know; sort of mechanical genius with a
screw loose. He used to have a toy railway in this

room. No end of fun he had, crawling about the floor after his trains. And all the pictures were stacked in the cellars. I can't tell you what they were like when I found them: mushrooms growing out of the Botticellis. Now I'm rather proud of this Poussin; he painted it for Scarron.'

'Exquisite!' Spode exclaimed, making with his hand a gesture as though he were modelling a pure form in the air. 'How splendid the onrush of those trees and leaning figures is! And the way they're caught up, as it were, and stemmed by that single godlike form opposing them with his contrary movement! And the draperies . . .'

But Lord Badgery had moved on, and was standing in front of a little fifteenth-century virgin of carved wood.

'School of Rheims,' he explained.

They 'did' the gallery at high speed. Badgery never permitted his guest to halt for more than forty seconds before any work of art. Spode would have liked to spend a few moments of recollection and tranquillity in front of some of these lovely things. But it was not permitted.

The gallery done, they passed into a little room leading out of it. At the sight of what the lights revealed, Spode gasped.

'It's like something out of Balzac,' he exclaimed. 'Un de ces salons dorés où se déploie un luxe insolent. You know.'

'My nineteenth-century chamber,' Badgery explained. 'The best thing of its kind, I flatter myself, outside the State Apartments at Windsor.'

Spode tiptoed round the room, peering with astonishment at all the objects in glass, in gilded bronze, in china, in feathers, in embroidered and painted silk, in beads, in wax, objects of the most fantastic shapes and colours, all the queer products of a decadent tradition, with which the room was crowded. There were paintings on the walls—a Martin, a Wilkie, an early Landseer, several Ettys, a big Haydon, a slight pretty water-colour of a girl by Wainewright, the pupil of Blake and arsenic poisoner, and a score of others. But the picture which arrested Spode's attention was a medium-sized canvas representing Troilus riding into Troy among the flowers and plaudits of an admiring crowd, and oblivious (you could see from his expression) of everything but the eyes of Cressida, who looked down at him from a window, with Pandarus smiling over her shoulder.

'What an absurd and enchanting picture!' Spode exclaimed.

'Ah, you've spotted my Troilus.' Lord Badgery was pleased.

'What bright harmonious colours! Like Etty's, only stronger, not so obviously pretty. And there's an energy about it that reminds one of Haydon. Only Haydon could never have done anything so impeccable in taste. Who is it by?' Spode turned to his host inquiringly.

'You were right in detecting Haydon,' Lord Badgery answered. 'It's by his pupil, Tillotson. I wish I could get hold of more of his work. But nobody seems to know anything about him. And he seems to have done so little.'

This time it was the younger man who interrupted.

'Tillotson, Tillotson. . . .' He put his hand to his forehead. A frown incongruously distorted his round, floridly curved face. 'No . . . yes, I have it.' He looked up triumphantly with serene and childish brows. 'Tillotson, Walter Tillotson—the man's still alive.'

Badgery smiled. 'This picture was painted in 1846, you know.'

'Well, that's all right. Say he was born in 1820, painted his masterpiece when he was twenty-six, and it's 1913 now; that's to say he's only ninety-three. Not as old as Titian yet.'

'But he's not been heard of since 1860,' Lord Badgery protested.

'Precisely. Your mention of his name reminded me of the discovery I made the other day when I was looking through the obituary notices in the archives of the *World's Review*. (One has to bring them up to date every year or so for fear of being caught napping if one of these old birds chooses to shuffle off suddenly.) Well there, among them—I remember my astonishment at the time—there I found Walter Tillotson's biography. Pretty full to 1860, and then a blank, except for a pencil note in the early nineteen hundreds to the effect that he had returned from the East. The obituary has never been used or added to. I draw the obvious conclusion: the old chap isn't dead yet. He's just been overlooked somehow.'

'But this is extraordinary,' Lord Badgery exclaimed. 'You must find him, Spode—you must find him. I'll commission him to paint frescoes round this room. It's just what I've always vainly longed for—a real nineteenth-century artist to decorate this place for me. Oh, we must find him at once —at once.'

Lord Badgery strode up and down in a state of great excitement.

'I can see how this room could be made quite perfect,' he went on. 'We'd clear away all these cases and have the whole of that wall filled by a heroic fresco of Hector and Andromache, or "Distraining for Rent", or Fanny Kemble as Belvidera in "Venice Preserved"—anything like that, provided it's in the grand manner of the 'thirties and 'forties. And here I'd have a landscape with lovely receding perspectives, or else something architectural and grand in the style of Belshazzar's feast. Then we'll have this Adam fire-place taken down and replaced by something Mauro-Gothic. And on these walls I'll have mirrors, or no! let me see . . .'

He sank into meditative silence, from which he finally roused himself to shout:

'The old man, the old man! Spode, we must find this astonishing old creature. And don't breathe a word to anybody. Tillotson shall be our secret. Oh, it's too perfect, it's incredible! Think of the frescoes.'

Lord Badgery's face had become positively animated. He had talked of a single subject for nearly a quarter of an hour.

II

Three weeks later Lord Badgery was aroused from his usual after-luncheon somnolence by the arrival of a telegram. The message was a short one. 'Found.—SPODE.' A look of pleasure and intelligence made human Lord Badgery's clayey face of surfeit. 'No answer,' he said. The footman padded away on noiseless feet.

Lord Badgery closed his eyes and began to contemplate. Found! What a room he would have! There would be nothing like it in the world. The frescoes, the fire-place, the mirrors, the ceiling. . . . And a small, shrivelled old man clambering about the scaffolding, agile and quick like one of those whiskered little monkeys at the Zoo, painting away, painting away. . . . Fanny Kemble as Belvidera, Hector and Andromache, or why not the Duke of Clarence in the Butt, the Duke of Malmsey, the Butt of Clarence. . . . Lord Badgery was asleep.

Spode did not lag long behind his telegram. He was at Badgery House by six o'clock. His lordship was in the nineteenth-century chamber, engaged in clearing away with his own hands the bric-à-brac. Spode found him looking hot and out of breath.

'Ah, there you are,' said Lord Badgery. 'You see me already preparing for the great man's coming. Now you must tell me all about him.'

'He's older even than I thought,' said Spode. 'He's ninety-seven this year. Born in 1816. Incredible, isn't it! There, I'm beginning at the wrong end.'

'Begin where you like,' said Badgery genially.

'I won't tell you all the incidents of the hunt. You've no idea what a job I had to run him to earth. It was like a Sherlock Holmes story, immensely elaborate, too elaborate. I shall write a book about it some day. At any rate, I found him at last.'

'Where?'

'In a sort of respectable slum in Holloway, older and poorer and lonelier than you could have believed possible. I found out how it was he came to be forgotten, how he came to drop out of life in the way he did. He took it into his head, somewhere about the 'sixties, to go to Palestine to get local colour for his religious pictures—scapegoats and things, you know. Well, he went to Jerusalem and then on to Mount Lebanon and on and on, and then, somewhere in the middle of Asia Minor, he got stuck. He got stuck for about forty years.'

'But what did he do all that time?'

'Oh, he painted, and started a mission, and con-
verted three Turks, and taught the local Pashas the
rudiments of English, Latin, and perspective, and
God knows what else. Then, in about 1904, it seems
to have occurred to him that he was getting rather
old and had been away from home for rather a long
time. So he made his way back to England, only to
find that every one he had known was dead, that the
dealers had never heard of him and wouldn't buy his
pictures, that he was simply a ridiculous old figure of
fun. So he got a job as a drawing-master in a girls'
school in Holloway, and there he's been ever since,
growing older and older, and feebler and feebler, and
blinder and deafer, and generally more gaga, until
finally the school has given him the sack. He had
about ten pounds in the world when I found him.
He lives in a kind of black hole in a basement full
of beetles. When his ten pounds are spent, I suppose
he'll just quietly die there.'

Badgery held up a white hand. 'No more, no
more. I find literature quite depressing enough. I
insist that life at least shall be a little gayer. Did you
tell him I wanted him to paint my room?'

'But he can't paint. He's too blind and palsied.'

'Can't paint?' Badgery exclaimed in horror.
'Then what's the good of the old creature?'

'Well, if you put it like that . . .' Spode began.

'I shall never have my frescoes. Ring the bell,
will you?'

Spode rang.

'What right has Tillotson to go on existing if he
can't paint?' went on Lord Badgery petulantly.
'After all, that was his only justification for occupy-
ing a place in the sun.'

'He doesn't have much sun in his basement.'

The footman appeared at the door.

'Get some one to put all these things back in their places,' Lord Badgery commanded, indicating with a wave of the hand the ravaged cases, the confusion of glass and china with which he had littered the floor, the pictures unhooked. 'We'll go to the library, Spode; it's more comfortable there.'

He led the way through the long gallery and down the stairs.

'I'm sorry old Tillotson has been such a disappointment,' said Spode sympathetically.

'Let us talk about something else; he ceases to interest me.'

'But don't you think we ought to do something about him? He's only got ten pounds between him and the workhouse. And if you'd seen the black-beetles in his basement!'

'Enough—enough. I'll do everything you think fitting.'

'I thought we might get up a subscription amongst lovers of the arts.'

'There aren't any,' said Badgery.

'No; but there are plenty of people who will subscribe out of snobbism.'

'Not unless you give them something for their money.'

'That's true. I hadn't thought of that.' Spode was silent for a moment. 'We might have a dinner in his honour. The Great Tillotson Banquet. Doyen of British Art. A Link with the Past. Can't you see it in the papers? I'd make a stunt of it in the *World's Review*. That ought to bring in the snobs.'

'And we'll invite a lot of artists and critics—all the ones who can't stand one another. It will be fun to see them squabbling.' Badgery laughed.

Then his face darkened once again. 'Still,' he added, 'it'll be a very poor second best to my frescoes. You'll stay to dinner, of course.'

'Well, since you suggest it. Thanks very much.'

III

The Tillotson Banquet was fixed to take place about three weeks later. Spode, who had charge of the arrangements, proved himself an excellent organizer. He secured the big banqueting-room at the Café Bomba, and was successful in bullying and cajoling the manager into giving fifty persons dinner at twelve shillings a head, including wine. He sent out invitations and collected subscriptions. He wrote an article on Tillotson in the *World's Review* —one of those charming, witty articles, couched in the tone of amused patronage and contempt with which one speaks of the great men of 1840. Nor did he neglect Tillotson himself. He used to go to Holloway almost every day to listen to the old man's endless stories about Asia Minor and the Great Exhibition of '51 and Benjamin Robert Haydon. He was sincerely sorry for this relic of another age.

Mr. Tillotson's room was about ten feet below the level of the soil of South Holloway. A little grey light percolated through the area bars, forced a difficult passage through panes opaque with dirt, and spent itself, like a drop of milk that falls into an inkpot, among the inveterate shadows of the dungeon. The place was haunted by the sour smell of damp plaster and of woodwork that has begun to moulder secretly at the heart. A little miscellaneous furniture, including a bed, a washstand and chest of drawers, a table and one or two chairs, lurked in the

obscure corners of the den or ventured furtively out
into the open. Hither Spode now came almost every
day, bringing the old man news of the progress of
the banquet scheme. Every day he found Mr.
Tillotson sitting in the same place under the window,
bathing, as it were, in his tiny puddle of light. 'The
oldest man that ever wore grey hairs,' Spode reflected
as he looked at him. Only there were very few hairs
left on that bald, unpolished head. At the sound of
the visitor's knock Mr. Tillotson would turn in his
chair, stare in the direction of the door with blinking,
uncertain eyes. He was always full of apologies for
being so slow in recognizing who was there.

'No discourtesy meant,' he would say, after asking. 'It's not as if I had forgotten who you were.
Only it's so dark and my sight isn't what it was.'

After that he never failed to give a little laugh,
and, pointing out of the window at the area railings,
would say:

'Ah, this is the place for somebody with good
sight. It's the place for looking at ankles. It's the
grand stand.'

It was the day before the great event. Spode came
as usual, and Mr. Tillotson punctually made his little
joke about the ankles, and Spode as punctually
laughed.

'Well, Mr. Tillotson,' he said, after the reverbera-
tion of the joke had died away, 'to-morrow you
make your re-entry into the world of art and fashion.
You'll find some changes.'

'I've always had such extraordinary luck,' said
Mr. Tillotson, and Spode could see by his expression
that he genuinely believed it, that he had forgotten
the black hole and the blackbeetles and the almost
exhausted ten pounds that stood between him and

the workhouse. 'What an amazing piece of good fortune, for instance, that you should have found me just when you did. Now, this dinner will bring me back to my place in the world. I shall have money, and in a little while—who knows?—I shall be able to see well enough to paint again. I believe my eyes are getting better, you know. Ah, the future is very rosy.'

Mr. Tillotson looked up, his face puckered into a smile, and nodded his head in affirmation of his words.

'You believe in the life to come?' said Spode, and immediately flushed for shame at the cruelty of the words.

But Mr. Tillotson was in far too cheerful a mood to have caught their significance.

'Life to come,' he repeated. 'No, I don't believe in any of that stuff—not since 1859. The "Origin of Species" changed my views, you know. No life to come for me, thank you! You don't remember the excitement, of course. You're very young, Mr. Spode.'

'Well, I'm not so old as I was,' Spode replied. 'You know how middle-aged one is as a schoolboy and undergraduate. Now I'm old enough to know I'm young.'

Spode was about to develop this little paradox farther, but he noticed that Mr. Tillotson had not been listening. He made a note of the gambit for use in companies that were more appreciative of the subtleties.

'You were talking about the "Origin of Species",' he said.

'Was I?' said Mr. Tillotson, waking from reverie.

'About its effect on your faith, Mr. Tillotson.'

'To be sure, yes. It shattered my faith. But I remember a fine thing by the Poet Laureate, something about there being more faith in honest doubt, believe me, than in all the . . . all the . . . I forget exactly what; but you see the train of thought. Oh, it was a bad time for religion. I am glad my master Haydon never lived to see it. He was a man of fervour. I remember him pacing up and down his studio in Lisson Grove, singing and shouting and praying all at once. It used almost to frighten me. Oh, but he was a wonderful man, a great man. Take him for all in all, we shall not look upon his like again. As usual, the Bard is right. But it was all very long ago, before your time, Mr. Spode.'

'Well, I'm not as old as I was,' said Spode, in the hope of having his paradox appreciated this time. But Mr. Tillotson went on without noticing the interruption.

'It's a very, very long time. And yet, when I look back on it, it all seems but a day or two ago. Strange that each day should seem so long and that many days added together should be less than an hour. How clearly I can see old Haydon pacing up and down! Much more clearly, indeed, than I see you, Mr. Spode. The eyes of memory don't grow dim. But my sight is improving, I assure you; it's improving daily. I shall soon be able to see those ankles.' He laughed, like a cracked bell—one of those little old bells, Spode fancied, that ring, with much rattling of wires, in the far-off servants' quarters of ancient houses. 'And very soon,' Mr. Tillotson went on, 'I shall be painting again. Ah, Mr. Spode, my luck is extraordinary. I believe in it, I trust it. And after all, what is luck? Simply another name for Providence, in spite of the "Origin of Species" and the rest of it. How right the Laureate was when he said that there was more faith in honest doubt, believe me, than in all the . . . er, the . . . er . . . well, you know. I regard you, Mr. Spode, as the emissary of Providence. Your coming marked a turning-point in my life, and the beginning, for me, of happier days. Do you know, one of the first things I shall do when my fortunes are restored will be to buy a hedgehog.'

'A hedgehog, Mr. Tillotson?'

'For the blackbeetles. There's nothing like a hedgehog for beetles. It will eat blackbeetles till it's sick, till it dies of surfeit. That reminds me of the time when I told my poor great master Haydon —in joke, of course—that he ought to send in a cartoon of King John dying of a surfeit of lampreys for the frescoes in the new Houses of Parliament. As I told him, it's a most notable event in the annals of British liberty—the providential and exemplary removal of a tyrant.'

Mr. Tillotson laughed again—the little bell in the deserted house; a ghostly hand pulling the cord in the drawing-room, and phantom footmen responding to the thin, flawed note.

'I remember he laughed, laughed like a bull in his old grand manner. But oh, it was a terrible blow when they rejected his designs, a terrible blow! It was the first and fundamental cause of his suicide.'

Mr. Tillotson paused. There was a long silence. Spode felt strangely moved, he hardly knew why, in the presence of this man, so frail, so ancient, in body three parts dead, in the spirit so full of life and hopeful patience. He felt ashamed. What was the use of his own youth and cleverness? He saw himself suddenly as a boy with a rattle scaring birds

—rattling his noisy cleverness, waving his arms in ceaseless and futile activity, never resting in his efforts to scare away the birds that were always trying to settle in his mind. And what birds! wide-winged and beautiful, all those serene thoughts and faiths and emotions that only visit minds that have humbled themselves to quiet. Those gracious visitants he was for ever using all his energies to drive away. But this old man, with his hedgehogs and his honest doubts and all the rest of it—his mind was like a field made beautiful by the free coming and going, the unafraid alightings of a multitude of white, bright-winged creatures. He felt ashamed. But then, was it possible to alter one's life? Wasn't it a little absurd to risk a conversion? Spode shrugged his shoulders.

'I'll get you a hedgehog at once,' he said. 'They're sure to have some at Whiteley's.'

Before he left that evening Spode made an alarming discovery. Mr. Tillotson did not possess a dress-suit. It was hopeless to think of getting one made at this short notice, and, besides, what an unnecessary expense!

'We shall have to borrow a suit, Mr. Tillotson. I ought to have thought of that before.'

'Dear me, dear me.' Mr. Tillotson was a little chagrined by this unlucky discovery. 'Borrow a suit?'

Spode hurried away for counsel to Badgery House. Lord Badgery surprisingly rose to the occasion. 'Ask Boreham to come and see me,' he told the footman who answered his ring.

Boreham was one of those immemorial butlers who linger on, generation after generation, in the houses of the great. He was over eighty now, bent, dried up, shrivelled with age.

'All old men are about the same size,' said Lord Badgery. It was a comforting theory. 'Ah, here he is. Have you got a spare suit of evening clothes, Boreham?'

'I have an old suit, my lord, that I stopped wearing in—let me see—was it nineteen seven or eight?'

'That's the very thing. I should be most grateful, Boreham, if you could lend it to me for Mr. Spode here for a day.'

The old man went out, and soon reappeared carrying over his arm a very old black suit. He held up the coat and trousers for inspection. In the light of day they were deplorable.

'You've no idea, sir,' said Boreham deprecatingly to Spode—'you've no idea how easy things get stained with grease and gravy and what not. However careful you are, sir—however careful.'

'I should imagine so.' Spode was sympathetic.

'However careful, sir.'

'But in artificial light they'll look all right.'

'Perfectly all right,' Lord Badgery repeated. 'Thank you, Boreham; you shall have them back on Thursday.'

'You're welcome, my lord, I'm sure.' And the old man bowed and disappeared.

On the afternoon of the great day Spode carried up to Holloway a parcel containing Boreham's retired evening-suit and all the necessary appurtenances in the way of shirts and collars. Owing to the darkness and his own feeble sight Mr. Tillotson was happily unaware of the defects in the suit. He was in a state of extreme nervous agitation. It was with some difficulty that Spode could prevent him, although it was only three o'clock, from starting his toilet on the spot.

'Take it easy, Mr. Tillotson, take it easy. We needn't start till half-past seven, you know.'

Spode left an hour later, and as soon as he was safely out of the room Mr. Tillotson began to prepare himself for the banquet. He lighted the gas and a couple of candles, and, blinking myopically at the image that fronted him in the tiny looking-glass that stood on his chest of drawers, he set to work, with all the ardour of a young girl preparing for her first ball. At six o'clock, when the last touches had been given, he was not unsatisfied.

. He marched up and down his cellar, humming to himself the gay song which had been so popular in his middle years:

'Oh, oh, Anna Maria Jones!
Queen of the tambourine, the cymbals, and the bones!'

Spode arrived an hour later in Lord Badgery's second Rolls-Royce. Opening the door of the old man's dungeon, he stood for a moment, wide-eyed with astonishment, on the threshold. Mr. Tillotson was standing by the empty grate, one elbow resting on the mantelpiece, one leg crossed over the other in a jaunty and gentlemanly attitude. The effect of the candle-light shining on his face was to deepen every line and wrinkle with intense black shadow; he looked immeasurably old. It was a noble and pathetic head. On the other hand, Boreham's outworn evening-suit was simply buffoonish. The coat was too long in the sleeves and the tail; the trousers bagged in elephantine creases about his ankles. Some of the grease-spots were visible even in candle-light. The white tie, over which Mr. Tillotson had taken infinite pains and which he believed in his purblindness to be perfect, was fantastically lopsided. He had buttoned up his waistcoat in such a fashion that one button was widowed of its hole and one hole of its button. Across his shirt-front lay the broad green ribbon of some unknown Order.

'Queen of the tambourine, the cymbals, and the bones,' Mr. Tillotson concluded in a gnat-like voice before welcoming his visitor.

'Well, Spode, here you are. I'm dressed already, you see. The suit, I flatter myself, fits very well, almost as though it had been made for me. I am all gratitude to the gentleman who was kind enough to lend it to me; I shall take the greatest care of it. It's a dangerous thing to lend clothes. For loan oft loseth both itself and friend. The Bard is always right.'

'Just one thing,' said Spode. 'A touch to your waistcoat.' He unbuttoned the dissipated garment and did it up again more symmetrically.

Mr. Tillotson was a little piqued at being found so absurdly in the wrong. 'Thanks, thanks,' he said protestingly, trying to edge away from his valet. 'It's all right, you know; I can do it myself. Foolish oversight. I flatter myself the suit fits very well.'

'And perhaps the tie might . . .' Spode began tentatively. But the old man would not hear of it.

'No, no. The tie's all right. I can tie a tie, Mr. Spode. The tie's all right. Leave it as it is, I beg.'

'I like your Order.'

Mr. Tillotson looked down complacently at his shirt front. 'Ah, you've noticed my Order. It's a long time since I wore that. It was given me by the Grand Porte, you know, for services rendered in the Russo-Turkish War. It's the Order of Chastity, the second class. They only give the first class to crowned heads, you know—crowned heads and ambassadors. And only Pashas of the highest rank get the second. Mine's the second. They only give the first class to crowned heads . . ."

'Of course, of course,' said Spode.

'Do you think I look all right, Mr. Spode?' Mr. Tillotson asked, a little anxiously.

'Splendid, Mr. Tillotson—splendid. The Order's magnificent.'

The old man's face brightened once more. 'I flatter myself,' he said, 'that this borrowed suit fits me very well. But I don't like borrowing clothes. For loan oft loseth both itself and friend, you know. And the Bard is always right.'

'Ugh, there's one of those horrible beetles!' Spode exclaimed.

Mr. Tillotson bent down and stared at the floor. 'I see it,' he said, and stamped on a small piece of coal, which crunched to powder under his foot. 'I shall certainly buy a hedgehog.'

It was time for them to start. A crowd of little boys and girls had collected round Lord Badgery's enormous car. The chauffeur, who felt that honour and dignity were at stake, pretended not to notice the children, but sat gazing, like a statue, into eternity. At the sight of Spode and Mr. Tillotson emerging from the house a yell of mingled awe and derision went up. It subsided to an astonished silence as they climbed into the car. 'Bomba's,' Spode directed. The Rolls-Royce gave a faintly stertorous sigh and began to move. The children yelled again, and ran along beside the car, waving their arms in a frenzy of excitement. It was then that Mr. Tillotson, with an incomparably noble gesture, leaned forward and tossed among the seething crowd of urchins his three last coppers.

477   L

IV

In Bomba's big room the company was assembling. The long gilt-edged mirrors reflected a singular collection of people. Middle-aged Academicians shot suspicious glances at youths whom they suspected, only too correctly, of being iconoclasts, organizers of Post-Impressionist Exhibitions. Rival art critics, brought suddenly face to face, quivered with restrained hatred. Mrs. Nobes, Mrs. Cayman, and Mrs. Mandragore, those indefatigable hunters of artistic big game, came on one another all unawares in this well-stored menagerie, where each had expected to hunt alone, and were filled with rage. Through this crowd of mutually repellent vanities Lord Badgery moved with a suavity that seemed unconscious of all the feuds and hatreds. He was enjoying himself immensely. Behind the heavy waxen mask of his face, ambushed behind the Hanoverian nose, the little lustreless pig's eyes, the pale thick lips, there lurked a small devil of happy malice that rocked with laughter.

'So nice of you to have come, Mrs. Mandragore, to do honour to England's artistic past. And I'm so glad to see you've brought dear Mrs. Cayman. And is that Mrs. Nobes, too? So it is! I hadn't noticed her before. How delightful! I knew we could depend on your love of art.'

And he hurried away to seize the opportunity of introducing that eminent sculptor, Sir Herbert Herne, to the bright young critic who had called him, in the public prints, a monumental mason.

A moment later the Maître d'Hôtel came to the door of the gilded saloon and announced, loudly and impressively, 'Mr. Walter Tillotson.' Guided

from behind by young Spode, Mr. Tillotson came
into the room slowly and hesitatingly. In the glare
of the lights his eyelids beat heavily, painfully, like
the wings of an imprisoned moth, over his filmy
eyes. Once inside the door he halted and drew
himself up with a conscious assumption of dignity.
Lord Badgery hurried forward and seized his hand.

'Welcome, Mr. Tillotson—welcome in the name
of English art!'

Mr. Tillotson inclined his head in silence. He was
too full of emotion to be able to reply.

'I should like to introduce you to a few of your
younger colleagues, who have assembled here to
do you honour.'

Lord Badgery presented every one in the room to
the old painter, who bowed, shook hands, made
little noises in his throat, but still found himself
unable to speak. Mrs. Nobes, Mrs. Cayman, and
Mrs. Mandragore all said charming things.

Dinner was served; the party took their places.
Lord Badgery sat at the head of the table, with Mr.
Tillotson on his right hand and Sir Herbert Herne
on his left. Confronted with Bomba's succulent
cooking and Bomba's wines, Mr. Tillotson ate and
drank a good deal. He had the appetite of one who
has lived on greens and potatoes for ten years
among the blackbeetles. After the second glass of
wine he began to talk, suddenly and in a flood, as
though a sluice had been pulled up.

'In Asia Minor,' he began, 'it is the custom,
when one goes to dinner, to hiccough as a sign of
appreciative fullness. *Eructavit cor meum*, as the
Psalmist has it; he was an Oriental himself.'

Spode had arranged to sit next to Mrs. Cayman;
he had designs upon her. She was an impossible

woman, of course, but rich and useful; he wanted to bamboozle her into buying some of his young friends' pictures.

'In a cellar?' Mrs. Cayman was saying, 'with blackbeetles? Oh, how dreadful! Poor old man! And he's ninety-seven, didn't you say? Isn't that shocking! I only hope the subscription will be a large one. Of course, one wishes one could have given more oneself. But then, you know, one has so many expenses, and things are so difficult now.'

'I know, I know,' said Spode, with feeling.

'It's all because of Labour,' Mrs. Cayman explained. 'Of course, I should simply love to have him in to dinner sometimes. But, then, I feel he's really too old, too *farouche* and *gâteux*; it would not be doing a kindness to him, would it? And so you are working with Mr. Gollamy now? What a charming man, so talented, such conversation . . .'

'*Eructavit cor meum*,' said Mr. Tillotson for the third time. Lord Badgery tried to head him off the subject of Turkish etiquette, but in vain.

By half-past nine a kinder vinolent atmosphere had put to sleep the hatreds and suspicions of before dinner. Sir Herbert Herne had discovered that the young Cubist sitting next him was not insane and actually knew a surprising amount about the Old Masters. For their part these young men had realized that their elders were not at all malignant; they were just very stupid and pathetic. It was only in the bosoms of Mrs. Nobes, Mrs. Cayman, and Mrs. Mandragore that hatred still reigned undiminished. Being ladies and old-fashioned, they had drunk almost no wine.

The moment for speech-making arrived. Lord Badgery rose to his feet, said what was expected of

him, and called upon Sir Herbert to propose the
toast of the evening. Sir Herbert coughed, smiled,
and began. In the course of a speech that lasted
twenty minutes he told anecdotes of Mr. Gladstone,
Lord Leighton, Sir Alma Tadema, and the late
Bishop of Bombay; he made three puns, he quoted
Shakespeare and Whittier, he was playful, he was
eloquent, he was grave. . . . At the end of his
harangue Sir Herbert handed to Mr. Tillotson a
silk purse containing fifty-eight pounds ten shillings,
the total amount of the subscription. The old man's
health was drunk with acclamation.

Mr. Tillotson rose with difficulty to his feet. The
dry, snake-like skin of his face was flushed; his tie
was more crooked than ever; the green ribbon of
the Order of Chastity of the second class had somehow climbed up his crumpled and maculate shirt-
front.

'My lords, ladies, and gentlemen,' he began in a
choking voice, and then broke down completely. It
was a very painful and pathetic spectacle. A feeling
of intense discomfort afflicted the minds of all who
looked upon that trembling relic of a man, as he
stood there weeping and stammering. It was as though
a breath of the wind of death had blown suddenly
through the room, lifting the vapours of wine and
tobacco-smoke, quenching the laughter and the
candle flames. Eyes floated uneasily, not knowing
where to look. Lord Badgery, with great presence of
mind, offered the old man a glass of wine. Mr.
Tillotson began to recover. The guests heard him
murmur a few disconnected words.

'This great honour . . . overwhelmed with kindness . . . this magnificent banquet . . . not used to
it . . . in Asia Minor . . . *eructavit cor meum.*'

At this point Lord Badgery plucked sharply at one of his long coat tails. Mr. Tillotson paused, took another sip of wine, and then went on with a newly won coherence and energy.

'The life of the artist is a hard one. His work is unlike other men's work, which may be done mechanically, by rote and almost, as it were, in sleep. It demands from him a constant expense of spirit. He gives continually of his best life, and in return he receives much joy, it is true—much fame, it may be— but of material blessings, very few. It is eighty years since first I devoted my life to the service of art; eighty years, and almost every one of those years has brought me fresh and painful proof of what I have been saying: the artist's life is a hard one.'

This unexpected deviation into sense increased the general feeling of discomfort. It became necessary to take the old man seriously, to regard him as a human being. Up till then he had been no more than an object of curiosity, a mummy in an absurd suit of evening-clothes with a green ribbon across the shirt-front. People could not help wishing that they had subscribed a little more. Fifty-eight pounds ten—it wasn't enormous. But happily for the peace of mind of the company, Mr. Tillotson paused again, took another sip of wine, and began to live up to his proper character by talking absurdly.

'When I consider the life of that great man, Benjamin Robert Haydon, one of the greatest men England has ever produced . . .' The audience heaved a sigh of relief; this was all as it should be. There was a burst of loud bravoing and clapping. Mr. Tillotson turned his dim eyes round the room, and smiled gratefully at the misty figures he beheld. 'That great man, Benjamin Robert Haydon,' he continued, 'whom I am proud to call my master and who, it rejoices my heart to see, still lives in your memory and esteem,—that great man, one of the greatest that England has ever produced, led a life so deplorable that I cannot think of it without a tear.'

And with infinite repetitions and divagations, Mr. Tillotson related the history of B. R. Haydon, his imprisonments for debt, his battle with the Academy, his triumphs, his failures, his despair, his suicide. Half-past ten struck. Mr. Tillotson was declaiming against the stupid and prejudiced judges who had rejected Haydon's designs for the decoration of the new Houses of Parliament in favour of the paltriest German scribblings.

'That great man, one of the greatest England has ever produced, that great Benjamin Robert Haydon, whom I am proud to call my master and who, it rejoices me to see, still lives on in your memory and esteem—at that affront his great heart burst; it was the unkindest cut of all. He who had worked all his life for the recognition of the artist by the State, he who had petitioned every Prime Minister, including the Duke of Wellington, for thirty years, begging them to employ artists to decorate public buildings, he to whom the scheme for decorating the Houses of Parliament was undeniably due . . .' Mr. Tillotson lost a grip on his syntax and began a new sentence. 'It was the unkindest cut of all, it was the last straw. The artist's life is a hard one.'

At eleven Mr. Tillotson was talking about the pre-Raphaelites. At a quarter-past he had begun to tell the story of B. R. Haydon all over again. At twenty-five minutes to twelve he collapsed quite speechless into his chair. Most of the guests had already gone away; the few who remained made haste to depart.

Lord Badgery led the old man to the door and packed him into the second Rolls-Royce. The Tillotson Banquet was over; it had been a pleasant evening, but a little too long.

Spode walked back to his rooms in Bloomsbury, whistling as he went. The arc lamps of Oxford Street reflected in the polished surface of the road: canals of dark bronze. He would have to bring that into an article some time. The Cayman woman had been very successfully nobbled. 'Voi che sapete,' he whistled—somewhat out of tune, but he could not hear that.

When Mr. Tillotson's landlady came in to call him on the following morning, she found the old man lying fully dressed on his bed. He looked very ill and very, very old; Boreham's dress-suit was in a terrible state, and the green ribbon of the Order of Chastity was ruined. Mr. Tillotson lay very still, but he was not asleep. Hearing the sound of footsteps, he opened his eyes a little and faintly groaned. His landlady looked down at him menacingly.

'Disgusting!' she said; 'disgusting, I call it. At your age.'

Mr. Tillotson groaned again. Making a great effort, he drew out of his trouser pocket a large silk purse, opened it, and extracted a sovereign.

'The artist's life is a hard one, Mrs. Green,' he said, handing her the coin. 'Would you mind sending for the doctor? I don't feel very well. And oh, what shall I do about these clothes? What shall I say to the gentleman who was kind enough to lend them to me? Loan oft loseth both itself and friend. The Bard is always right.'

T. O. BEACHCROFT

She was Living with his People

From the very first Emerald had never taken to her mother-in-law. And certainly she was an odd little woman; so cold and distant. Em liked people who gave you a bit of a welcome, and made you feel at home, as if they were pleased to see you.

But the first time Emerald had met 'Ma', as all the family called her, she had had quite a shock. Ma had just said, 'How do you do?' and had gone on talking almost as if she wasn't there. How different it was when Em had taken Percy round to see her own mother; and how happily they had all got on together.

Em went over all these things in her mind, as she often did since they were married. She had bought a large bunch of chrysanthemums cheap up at the market, and was arranging them in one or two vases round their sitting-room, before Percy came in from work.

She heard a loud knock at the front door, and put her head out of the window to see who it was. Down in the street, three floors below, she saw Mr. Blakeney, a breezy man of forty or so, who was one of the machine-shop foremen from Percy's works.

'Good evening, Mrs. Matthew!' he shouted. 'Your Perce up there?'

''E ain't come in yet,' Em called out.

'Well, I should 'a thought he'd come running back, so soon in his married life,' said Blakeney. 'Never mind, you'll do. I've got——' He seemed quite prepared to carry on a ten minutes' conversation by shouting up from the street.

'Wait a minute,' said Em, 'I'll come down and let you in.'

She ran as quietly as she could down the stairs. Six months ago she had jumped at the idea of their having two rooms at the top of her mother-in-law's house so cheap. Mr. Blakeney followed her up into the sitting-room and looked round admiringly.

'Well, Mrs. Matthew,' he said, 'this is a snug little place you've got here. Haven't you made it all look nice, too! You wait till you've got a baby, though: then you won't have so many sixpences to spend on flowers, I'll bet.'

'They look nice, don't they?' said Em.

'Ever so nice,' said Blakeney. 'Quite reminds me of the Assembly Rooms on a dance night. However, I'll tell you what I came round about. I'm getting up a sort of Christmas Club at the Works, and seeing it's Friday and pay-day, I'm just calling round about. Every one takes a two-bob ticket, and then we share out the prizes a week before Christmas. Just adds a little excitement, you know. The first prize is a fiver, and there's lots of little ones.'

Em studied the little book of names and tickets hesitantly.

'Ought I to?'

'You ought if you want to,' said Blakeney. 'But there ain't no sort of duty about it. I bet your Perce would want one, though: that's why I came.'

'Right you are, then,' said Em, 'and mind you draw me that five pounds.'

'Ah,' said Blakeney, 'that's what they all say. Got your two bob ready? Well, there's good management for you: before Perce comes back with his Friday money and everything. First year I was married, we always used to run out about Wednesday.

Well, it's a life, isn't it? Good night, Mrs. Matthew,' he said, opening the door. 'So pleased to have seen your little place. I must tell Mrs. Blakeney all about it.'

'Good night,' said Em. 'How's Perce doing at his job?'

'Oh, he's doing all right. He's quite a clever workman, is your Perce.'

'I knows 'e's clever,' said Em, 'but we mustn't tell him so.'

'That's right,' Blakeney shouted from the landing below, and rattled off down the stairs.

Em turned and looked round the room with pleasure. It was nice of Blakeney to notice and talk to her about it. She began to get Percy's tea ready. In a minute or two the door opened and she turned round to greet him—but it was Ma.

'Come in,' said Em, brightly.

Ma was a frail-looking little woman of fifty or so: her hair had already turned white. She was small and slight in every way, with neat features and a bright spot of colour on each cheek. Em was larger altogether, with black, rather untidy hair and wide dark eyes. Ma always made her feel too big and awkward.

Ma looked round the room for a moment, half humming under her breath a few notes that never quite became a tune. Em knew quite well that she wanted to be told who the visitor had been.

'Won't you sit down?' said Em.

Ma still paused uncertainly. 'I just looked in to see if Perce was back,' she said.

'No, he's late, isn't he?'

'I thought I heard you talking to him just a minute ago.'

'No,' said Em.

'Well,' said Ma, 'it's a queer thing I should have heard some one so plain.'

Em felt angry. Why couldn't she ask right out who it was, if she was so nosy and curious, instead of always hinting all round? She always managed to put Em in the wrong without seeming inquisitive herself.

'Oh, that wasn't Perce you heard,' said Em. 'I had a visitor.'

Ma went on with her humming, and began to look at the flowers.

'It was Mr. Blakeney from the factory,' said Em.

'Oh,' said Ma, immediately affecting indifference. 'However much did all those chrysanthemums cost you?'

'Very little,' said Em. 'I got 'em cheap, up at the market.'

'Too many flowers in a room don't look well,' said Ma. 'Just a few looks much better.'

'Mr. Blakeney said how nice they looked,' said Em.

'And too many flowers ain't healthy. That's what the doctors say,' said Ma, as though she were communicating a well-known fact to some one very ignorant indeed. 'You ought to put some of them out on the landing. Let me do it for you.'

'I'll do it later,' said Em, busying herself about her cooking arrangements. As Ma watched her, without saying anything, she became more and more uncomfortable and awkward.

'What's that for?' said Ma distastefully, as Em put a couple of cooked pig's trotters in a pie-dish to heat them up.

'Them's for Perce and me,' she said. 'One each.'

There was a long silence.

'What men really need when they come in is a good bit of steak or something with some nourishment in it. Them things may be all right for *you*.'

'But Perce likes these very much.'

'Well, 'e didn't used to,' said Ma, implying that she knew far more about her son's likes than his wife did.

'Well, he asked for them,' said Em. 'He did really. Why should you think I'd go givin' him anything he don't like? Besides, we often 'ave a good piece of steak; we did last night.'

'Oh, well,' said Ma, 'we all have different opinions. I should have thought your bit o' money was better spent on good food than on *chrysanthemums*. But you know best.'

Em could have screamed with exasperation. The old woman was so artful. She said the most outrageous things without ever saying them at all. Ma waited for a few moments, and finding Em made no reply, turned towards the door. On her way she caught sight of the Christmas Club ticket which Em had left on the table.

'I suppose this is what that fellow Blakeney come round about,' she said. 'Perce wasn't having any, so he thought he'd try you. Seems a pity when the husbands have got too much sense they has to come round and try the wives. They find it pays, I suppose.'

'Why, what's the harm?' said Em. 'It's just an ordinary Christmas Club. We may get a five pound prize.'

'Yes,' said Ma, as she closed the door. 'But it's Perce's money. It's 'im what does the work for it and brings it in. That's what you've got to think of. And if you take my advice, don't you let father ever get to hear of that ticket. He'd call it sheer *madness*.'

She was gone. Why should Ma accuse her of wasting all the money and not feeding Percy properly, and make everything she did look wrong? Only ten minutes before Mr. Blakeney was telling her how well she managed; and that was what ordinary people thought about it. When Percy arrived, rather late, she began to pour it all out to him. She told him everything that Ma had said.

'Oh, don't mind it,' said Percy. 'She's just a bit like that. That's all: just a bit narky.'

'But I do mind. Why don't you stand up for me a bit more, Perce? Why don't you tell 'er I am a good wife, and I do feed you properly, and how happy we are?'

'Oh, she knows it really.'

'She doesn't say so. I should have thought you'd like to have stood up for me. Any one'd fancy you wanted her to go on thinking I was a bad wife to you.'

'Oh, I couldn't go saying things like that to her,' said Percy.

'Why not?' said Em.

'Oh, she'd think I was a soft fool.'

'Oh,' said Em, tearfully, 'I don't seem to under-stand any of you. If you're happy with me, why can't you go and tell her so? The truth is you're absolutely under both their thumbs, and you'd do anything they say, regardless of me. Can't I even take a two-shilling ticket in a club draw without their leave?'

'All the same,' said Percy rather gloomily, 'I wish you hadn't taken it.'

'Why ever not?'

'Look,' said Percy, 'I'm afraid I've got some bad news.'

'What?' said Em, with a horrible premonition of what was coming.

'They've gone and closed down the whole of my shop at the factory. I've lost my job. I'm one of the three million now.'

'But only just now Mr. Blakeney said how well you were doing.'

'Did 'e?' said Percy. 'Well, I believe I was. But what's the good? You can do as well as a living marvel, and still lose your job these days. What's happened is simply this: I and a few other chaps were making ball joints, and now they've suddenly decided they can buy all their ball joints cheaper outside. So out we all go—and that's the end of it. There's no arguing at all. Blakeney doesn't know. It may be his own shop next time.'

'Oh,' said Em, 'I've been telling you my troubles, and you've had this on your mind all the time. Why didn't you tell me straight away?' She began to kiss him, and after awhile they felt much happier.

During the next weeks Em found things more and more difficult. With Percy no longer earning they seemed to have no more independence than children. She thought Percy was silly to be so cautious and careful always to do what his father and mother wanted. 'It's no good looking at it any other way,' he said to her many times. 'He's paying for us; he's supporting us; and the brass tacks of it is I've just got to do what he wants.'

'Then he oughtn't to expect,' said Em. 'Why don't you tell him right out you aren't a child now and you've got a will of your own?'

'Because I can't possibly, and there you are. It's

no good, Em; it really isn't. What's the point of having a row? It will only go on a few months, and then I'll be in work again.'

'It seems it's going on for ever. Aren't we ever to do anything that *I* want?' she said plaintively.

Percy sighed and swung the blind cord about.

Ma seemed to have more and more of a finger in everything they did. Now Em hadn't a penny of her own, she had no way of doing or buying anything that was hers. She tried all she knew to get a job, but the factories were all running short-handed shifts; the shops needed no help; she wasn't a skilled needlewoman; she put her name down as a daily, but she had no reference or experience of any kind, and she was told there were hundreds waiting.

There were long, rain-sodden days, and she leant against the window sill gazing into the little yard and the other little yards all round, and grew more and more depressed. Percy was out a good deal, and he seemed unwilling to tell her just what he was doing all the time.

One day Ma said to her: 'You and Perce better come down and eat with us. It's silly you cooking your own meals up here now.'

'Oh,' said Em, taken aback, 'we'd rather——'

Ma interrupted her. 'Then I can make certain he gets something proper to eat instead of those pig's feet things.'

Em felt she would like to hit Ma for saying that.

'I've spoken to Perce about it,' the old woman said, 'and he thinks it would be best—he wants it.'

Afterwards Em said to Percy, 'Why can't you sometimes speak up for yourself? Why do you let her always say it's you wanting it, when it's only her really? You never think of me, and always of her.

Soon she'll be saying we'd better sleep apart, and you'll just agree.' She began to cry, and when Percy put his arms round her she pushed him away.

'And she's always nagging me about that Christmas ticket,' she said. 'She hints I was careless with money, and threw it about. I wish I'd never seen it.'

At meal-times now she felt more than ever a stranger among the family. They were always quite a large party, as there was an unmarried brother and a sister of Percy, and two grandchildren living at home. Father used to grumble at his food. Sometimes he would push it aside and go out in a fury. The children would stare hard at their plates, not daring to catch his eye, and Ma used to say nothing at all, but her cheeks would turn very pink.

At other times Em would hear him ranting and going on at one or other of the two young motor drivers who were in his employment. He evidently enjoyed threatening them with the sack, and finding fault with everything they did. He would haul them by the lapels of their coats over the front doorstep, back them up against the wall of the narrow passage and yell with his face very close to theirs. Outside, Em would see one of the cars standing at the kerb; and passers-by would glance in hurriedly to see what was happening. Yet he kept his business going very well, paid good wages, and had many regular customers who always used his cars for a long trip.

Ma told Em that this was the only way you could run a job, and that the young men would always be slacking and letting him down if he didn't keep girding at them.

'He's got a tongue in his head it does you good to listen to,' she said with a sour smile.

In his jocular moods father cracked jokes with Em

and treated her better than he did his own family; but she never felt safe with him. Once he caught her suddenly and roughly by the arm and said to her, half in fun and half threatening: 'What's this about spending two shillings on a blasted Christmas draw?'

'I'm sorry,' she said, 'I didn't mean——'

'Well, just you remember, it's my money now,' he said. 'All these club draws and sweeps is a lot of damn silliness.'

He stared into her face and Em suddenly felt frightened.

She began to see that he was often at the back of Ma's oddness. She began to see that Ma's digs and taunts at her were not always her own fault-finding at all, but a kind of reproach because she had never been allowed by her own husband to do this or that: a kind of envy. Nice flowers in the room, pig's trotters for dinner, Christmas Club tickets, all these things would have thrown father into one of his rages or 'bust-ups' as Ma called them.

And Ma would talk as if Percy, as if all husbands, were just the same.

'I'll give you a piece of advice,' she said to Em one day. 'Never say "no" to your husband.'

'But you must sometimes,' said Em.

Ma looked annoyed. 'I'm merely telling you what thirty years of married life has taught me,' she said. 'Know better if you must.'

Em was silent.

Ma hummed in her tuneless way for a moment or two, and then went on 'Never say "no". Not however tired you are, or whatever he wants, because if you won't, there's plenty others as will. I dare say you'll find that out.'

All day Em thought of this, and it seemed to her

more and more horrible. She went up to her room and stood for a very long time looking out into the streaming night, watching the blurred lights of the streets and other houses all round. A dark shadow seemed to hang over her happiness and marriage. She wanted to run down and tell Ma she was all wrong. Percy wasn't like that. Her marriage with him was different altogether. That's what Ma seemed incapable of seeing.

It was a week or so before Christmas. Em was out one evening bringing home some things from the shops for Ma. She could not help feeling cheery at the approach of Christmas. Even when Ma had said: 'We don't take much notice of Christmas in this 'ouse—holly and overeating and all that silliness,' it had not depressed her.

A woman she knew, the wife of one of the men up at Percy's old job, said to her: 'You're lucky, Em. Heard about that Christmas draw?'

'No.'

'Your Perce has won the five pounds prize.'

Em rushed home as fast as her legs would carry her.

'Perce!' she cried. 'At last we've 'ad something nice happen. The five pounds! Isn't it splendid!'

Percy was quite silent. 'But Em,' he said after a while, 'you know we told you that wasn't really our money if we won. It's father's by rights.'

'But you don't really mean he'd take it?' said Em.

'Why not?'

'Well,' said Em, 'it's so—so—— Doesn't he want you to have anything?'

'As a matter of fact,' said Percy, 'I've settled the question beforehand. I've lost it.'

'You've what?'

'I've had it stolen. Some one in the crowd on the way home; must have taken it out of my pocket.'

Em was too stupefied to say anything at all.

'Don't be cross with me,' said Percy. 'It wouldn't have been ours anyway.'

Later on Percy said to her, 'Look—if father hears I've lost that five pounds I don't know what he won't do. Could I possibly tell him it was you as lost it?'

'Well——!' said Em.

'You see, he won't lose his temper with you. If it's me, there'll be a bust-up, and Ma will come into it as well as me. If it's you, he'll just pass it over.'

'It's always Ma you're thinking of,' said Em. 'But go on—I don't mind. If it's lost, it's lost. We shan't get anything of it anyway. We shan't ever get any luck or fun or anything at all. I don't mind what you say.'

'After all,' said Percy, 'it's only been a month or two. I'm sure to get work after Christmas. Don't be unhappy, Em.'

'It's all right for you,' said Em, 'I shan't ever be happy in this place. Your Ma doesn't want nor like me. It'll be Christmas in a few days, and things ought to be so nice.'

'Don't cry,' said Percy, 'please don't cry.'

But on Christmas Eve Em felt she could bear things no longer. Father had gone out after dinner. Percy was off for a long walk with his brother, and she felt Ma had deliberately encouraged Percy to go without her; saying they would walk too far for her, and it did the men good to go out by themselves.

Em saw Percy off: then instead of going to help Ma with the washing up, ran up to her own room and burst into tears. She thought about her own parents and their country home. How much better it would

have been if they could have lived there—how much
nicer her parents would have been to Percy.

Last time her mother had come up to London Em
had told her about everything. Her mother had
sympathized and comforted her, but Em could see
it made her unhappy. Suddenly her mother's very
kindness struck her as rather silly and annoying. It
wasn't any good her getting unhappy too. She
couldn't really understand. She couldn't help her.
No one, she thought, could help her but herself.

On a sudden impulse she ran down the stairs to the
kitchen, where Ma was just beginning to wash up the
dinner things.

'I want to say something,' said Em. 'I've been
thinking. I never seem to please you, nor do the
right thing. Can't we get on better? I'm sorry if I'm
wrong.'

For a moment Ma made no answer at all, then
she said, looking very hard at the sink: 'I don't
know what you mean. We get on all right as far as I
know.'

Em began to feel baffled, as she always did when
she tried to have anything out with Ma. 'Well,' she
said, 'I feel I don't please you. I don't see what I've
ever really done wrong.'

'Perfect,' said Ma, with emphasis, 'is a thing we
none of us are, and I never asked or expected of *you*.
Do you want me to go about pretending I think
you're perfect?'

'No,' said Em, 'but I don't see why you think
everything I do is wrong.'

Percy had often told her it was no good talking to
Ma like this, and she began to wish she'd never tried.

'I don't think everything you do is wrong,' said
Ma, 'but young ones can't be always right. We all

see things different, and you want me to say I see everything your way. What's the sense? I think you were silly to go and buy that ticket, and as for losing the five pounds, you can't expect me to come and kiss you on both cheeks, can you? I'm sure I feel I've been very forbearing about it. But you don't seem never to 'ave been crossed nor criticized in your life.'

It was a long speech for her, and all the time she was talking in her calm, biting way, Em felt more and more angry.

'Well, then,' said Em, her colour rising with her temper, 'I'm not the only person round here as can lose things. You'll find there may be others too, if you keep on at me so.'

'I wasn't keeping on at you,' said Ma, 'and there's no call to get angry. That's a nasty temper of yours.'

'What I mean is this, see?' said Em, breaking in. 'I've heard enough lectures and rows and snaggling away at me about that ticket because I never lost the money at all. I ain't the guilty one. And if you want to know, it's Perce all the time as lost it, though he's got such wind up about what his pa would do I let him think it was me: so there. And I was quite willing to. Poor Perce is so under your thumbs, that's what it is. But if I'm to hear nothing but ticket, ticket, ticket, all the rest of me life, always ticket for breakfast, ticket for dinner, and ticket to tuck meself up in bed with, well then, I thought it was time you knew the truth. I'd have kept it secret, but it ain't worth suffering like a martyr for, all the rest of me life. It's bad enough having to live in this house as it is, with nothing but rows and disagreeablenesses.'

Em suddenly realized she'd gone pretty far, so she stopped. There was a moment's silence, and Ma began to pick up some dirty plates and carry them to the sink. As she did so she hummed a little tune in the back of her throat that never developed more than two or three notes.

'It makes no difference,' said Ma, with her back to Em, 'who lost that money. You, or that fool boy. And if you feel like that, you'd better go upstairs and cool your head. You've been very rude.'

'I'm sorry,' said Em. 'Let me help you with all this washing up.'

'I don't want help, thank you.'

But Em still hung about. Having worked off her anger, she felt, as violent-tempered people often do, rather friendly and anxious to make it up.

'Let me help,' she said, 'I'd like it. Really. I'm sorry, really.'

'Hadn't you better go upstairs?' said Ma in her most icy tones.

'Oh, all right,' said Em, and began to flounce out.

But as she reached the door it opened abruptly. Em was almost knocked over as father pushed violently in. He threw the door to with a slam that made the kitchen ring.

Em began to go out again as quietly as she could.

'Here,' said father, 'I want you. And you,' he said to Ma, speaking as if they were both criminals, and he some kind of avenging officer.

For a moment he stood and said nothing, but merely glowered. His face had turned very red, and his eyes too looked red. One grizzled curl, from his short-cropped hair, hung over his forehead like a bull's forelock. His leather driving coat was open, showing an old khaki muffler hanging down inside, and the fleshy bulk of his chest. He looked immensely strong and awkward, as if he were cobbled up in too many clothes, which hindered the movements of his short arms and neck.

He stood planted massively, glaring at them, like some weighty and fierce old bull or stallion, gathering its bulk for an attack. In the silence created by himself he breathed aloud.

Em made a movement to escape, but he caught her by the arm.

'Come back,' he said. 'I want to see you, my girl.'

Em felt really frightened. This was the kind of thing she had always feared from him. All the time Ma went on quietly with her washing up, walking from the table to the sink and back again to the table, pretending nothing was happening.

'Yes,' he said, still holding Em's arm, and rubbing in the threat slowly and nastily, 'I want to see you.' He turned to Ma. 'Think I'm going to be made a bloody fool of in my own 'ouse?' he suddenly shouted. 'I tell you there are ways of stopping that. Think that little brat there's going to make a fool of me? There are ways of stopping that she won't like. She's got to learn if she lives with me.'

Em felt her heart beating. Ma still went on very calmly washing up her dishes.

'Well,' she said, 'there's no need to go on with all this bluster. What's the girl done? I dare say she'll be sorry.'

'You've been telling me all this time,' he said, turning to Em, 'that it was you who lost this club ticket money?'

Em tried to speak, but nothing came out.

'Go on, answer me!' he shouted.

'Yes,' Em managed to say.

'And all the time it was done on purpose to deceive me. Think you're going to live under my roof and think of me last in the house, do you? Thought you could make a fool of me in public, did you?'

'I'm sorry,' Em said, 'I really meant——'

'Nice thing for me,' he shouted. 'I was sitting up at the "Gardener's Arms" with some friends of mine, and found they all knew it was that damn fool Perce, all the time, as lost or *spent* every penny of that five pounds. And I'd been made to think it was you lost the money. You've been making people laugh at me, haven't you?' He shook her arm. 'Well, I'm going to make you laugh the other way round; see that? When I come through the hall, I had a look to see if there was a good stick there that'd do for you. And there is. If I'd had the upbringing of you properly we'd have had this out ten years ago.'

Em felt as if she were having a nightmare.

'Once'll be enough, I dare say,' he said, pulling her towards the door.

'Wait a minute, wait a minute,' said Ma, polishing a spoon very hard as she spoke, and not looking at them, 'don't talk like that.'

'Oh, you're coming into it now—taking her side, I suppose.'

'Never mind about that,' said Ma. 'You can't talk to Em like that. She's a married woman, twenty years of age. She's acted for the best, and if she's done wrong, she's sorry. Don't be so silly.'

'Oh, it's silly, is it,' he shouted, 'just to take a few steps to prevent her deliberately making the whole street make fun of me? Why don't you call 'em all in here right away to laugh at me? Come on, let's do it! Come on!' He put his face close to hers and shouted into it.

'Don't be a big looby,' said Ma promptly, and Em could see that though she spoke quietly, two bright red spots of colour had flamed up high in her cheeks, and the pupils of her eyes were dilated till the whole iris was black. 'You keep your hands off Em, or you will 'ave the whole street down on you. And as for that silly deceiving you about the five pounds, it was *me* that put her up to it all along. It was me made her think it was the best thing to do. So there.'

'What!' said father. 'You mean you——'

'Why don't you go and lie down?' said Ma, in her iciest voice. 'No wonder you lose your temper, if you will go drinking so much. It always upsets you.'

'Calling me drunk!' began Father, but the words were lost in a sheer bellow of rage. He caught Ma roughly by the arm and dragged her across the room.

Em involuntarily shrank away, but by the look on Ma's face she could see that anything might happen now. He began hitting Ma with his closed fist. She saw it raised like a club and smash deliberately down in the old woman's face.

Then suddenly Em's temper flared up again, and she found she was joining in the fight herself. She pulled Ma away, and pushed father back as hard as she could. Taken off his balance, he stepped heavily backwards into the dresser. One hand, groping for support, knocked a large dish off the table, and it smashed on the tiled floor. Then there was a splintering crash as his fourteen stone lurched into the dresser, and for a moment it seemed that all the china would fall about his ears. Half-dazed, he turned and fended off the tottering dresser.

Em knelt down by Ma and put her arm round her shoulders. The dresser, with a final crash, fell back against the wall again. Father looked round him, and without saying another word walked out of the

kitchen. He left a breathless silence behind him. In
a moment Ma got up, and almost pettishly twitched
herself away from Em's arms.

'Silly old fool,' she said, and returned to her
washing up. 'Pick up them broken plates,' she said
to Em, 'don't stand about doing nothing.' Her voice
quavered slightly. Em picked up the plates, and,
without saying anything further, began to help Ma
finish off the work. After it was done, Em saw the
kettle was still boiling.

'Wouldn't it be nice to sit down quietly for a few
minutes and drink a cup of tea,' she said.

'You have one if you like,' said Ma. 'But don't
go doing it on my account.'

Em handed her a cup, and Ma sat down at the kitchen table and began to sip it, putting both hands
round it and staring in front of her. Em saw that the
two scarlet spots were still on her cheeks. Her eyes
were still bright and black. It was plain that her lip
was already beginning to swell up and turn colour,
and blood was coming from her mouth.

'It's a shame,' said Em suddenly. 'Does your lip
hurt you?'

'Of course it hurts,' said Ma. 'My whole head
hurts.' Then after a pause she added slowly, 'But it
isn't that as really 'urts. I'm too old to be knocked
about now,' she went on. 'My bones feel too old.
I'm over fifty-five, you know. He oughtn't to 'ave
done it. Going on like a great schoolboy. It's five
years since he hit me; five years next February.'

She said all this in a flat, level tone, and stopped as
abruptly as she had begun. Em saw that her eyes
were brighter than ever, glistening with tears which
refused to drop. Ma smiled a wry smile at her.

'It makes you feel a bit queer,' she said. 'Fancy

his behaving so bad, in front of you; and at you, too.
I'm ashamed of him, letting you see him act so. But I
know what it is, Em, he treats you as one of the family
now, that's what it is. You're in it with us now.'

Ma chuckled. 'If only some of his friends could
'a sometimes seen him,' she said, 'every one speaks
so well of him all the time. It's been better, of course,
since the boys have grown up, but I've always wanted
a daughter.' She paused, and went on sipping.
'Don't think I'd say a word against him really,' she
said, 'not to any one outside of just us. But there,
you've seen for yourself now. I've had some times
with him these thirty years, I can tell you. He broke
my collar-bone once in one of his silly bust-ups.
We all had to keep telling the street I'd fallen downstairs.'

'Did you really?'

'But you'll do him good, you will, with that little
dander of yours. It does him good to be stood
up to.'

Em looked at her, and Ma looked back thought-
fully. For once Ma met her gaze and didn't stare at
something that she was doing. Suddenly Em realized
that she had found a friend. Suddenly she saw the
whole point of this crabbed old woman. She saw the
fascination of her tartness and wry humour, and her
loyalty to her violent husband. Suddenly she began
to admire Ma intensely, and felt proud of having won
her approval. She knew that she had found in her
something that would be stronger and more helpful
through her life than the gentleness and sweetness of
her own mother. She wanted for a moment to put
her arm round Ma, or to make some impulsive expression of affection. But she knew that Ma's straight
look into her eyes and her sour smile was the closest

physical sign of affection or approval she could ever give.

It was an hour later that Percy came back from his walk, and Em was still in the kitchen talking to Ma.

Without saying a word he walked up to the table and with a mysterious look spread first five pound notes upon it; then another five pounds. Em clapped her hands. Ma looked at the notes as if she thought they were imitations.

'What's this?' she said. 'A nice time we've been having with your stories about Em having taken that money, I can tell you.'

'Well,' said Percy, 'I'm sorry. As a matter of fact, no one lost it at all. I had it all the time.'

'But Perce——' said Em.

'I'm sorry,' said Percy. 'It couldn't be 'elped. I simply had to find a way of stopping father from laying hands on it. I'll tell you what we've been up to.'

'When Blakeney heard they'd shut up the shop I was working in, he told the management as he could make all those ball joints off his own bat, and supply them at a cheaper cost than ever they'd made them for themselves. He'd already got an uncle as owned a small factory right out of the town where rents and overheads are low. He only had to have a little capital to start off on, and get just one or two lathes and things. But the management of our works wouldn't advance it. So Blakeney tried to get going on his own, and all of us, who possibly could, came forward with a few pounds to help him. And our five pounds was one.'

'And now I suppose he's closed down and lost everybody's money,' said Ma.

'Not a bit of it,' said Percy. 'He's doing fine—supplying our own factory and another one besides. And he may take up with other small parts besides the ball joints, too. He knows the job inside out, you see. And I've been working up there for the last two weeks, off and on, though I didn't want to tell you and Em for fear of its just being a disappointment. He's given me this money to be going on with, and after Christmas I'm going to start in a regular job. At foreman's wages, too.'

'Oh, well,' said Ma, her eyes twinkling with pleasure, 'sounds a risky, cranky sort of idea to me. But there, nowadays I suppose you 'aves to be content with anything you can get.'

H. E. BATES

The Revelation

My great-uncle Silas was a man who never washed himself. 'God A'mighty,' he would say, 'why should I? It's a waste o' time. I got summat else to do 'sides titivate myself wi' soap.' The housekeeper washed him instead.

Every morning, winter and summer, he sat in the high-backed chair under the window of geraniums waiting for that inexorable performance. He would sit there in a pretence of being engrossed in the newspaper of the day before, his waistcoat on but undone over his collarless blue shirt, his red neckerchief dangling on the arm of the chair, his face gloomy and long with the wretchedness of expectation. Sometimes he would lower the corner of the newspaper and squint out in the swift but faint hope that she had forgotten him. She never did. She would come out at last with the bowl of water and the rank cake of yellow soap that he would say she had been suckled on, and the rough hand-flannel that she had made up from some staunch undergarment she had at last discarded. In winter the water, drawn straight from the well, would be as bitter and stinging as ice. She never heated it. And as though her own hands had lost all feeling she would plunge them straight into it, and then rub the soap against the flannel until it lathered thinly, like snow. All the time he sat hidden behind the newspaper with a kind of dumb hope, like an ostrich. At last, before he knew what was happening, the paper would be snatched from his hands, the flannel, like a cold compress, would be smacked against his face, and a shudder of utter misery would pass through his body before he began to pour forth the first of his blasphemous protestations. 'God damn it, woman! You want to finish me, don't you? You want to finish me! You want me to catch me death, you old nanny-goat! I know. You want me . . .' The words and their effect would be drowned and smothered by the renewed sopping of the flannel and he would be forced at last into a miserable acquiescence. It was the only time when the look of devilish vitality and wickedness left his face and never seemed likely to return.

Once a week, also, she succeeded in making him take a bath. She gave him that too.

The house was very old and its facilities for bathing and washing were such that it might have been built expressly for him. There was no bathroom. My uncle Silas had instead a small iron bath, once painted cream and never repainted after the cream had turned to the colour of earth, which resembled some ancient coracle. And once a week, generally on Fridays and always in the evening, the housekeeper would drag out the bath from among the wine-bottles in the cellar and bring it up and get it before the fire in the living-room. Once, in early summer, as though hoping it might make that miserable inquisition of bathing impossible, he had filled the bath with a pillow-case of cowslip heads and their own wine-yellow liquor. It did not deter her. She gave him his bath in a pudding-basin instead, sponging him down with water that grew cooler and colder as he stood there blaspheming and shivering.

Very often on fine winter evenings I would walk

over to see him, and once, half-forgetting that it was his bath-night, I went over on a Friday.

When I arrived the house was oppressively warm with the heat and steam from the copper boiling up the bath-water in the little kitchen. I went in, as I always did, without knocking, and I came straight upon my Uncle Silas taking off his trousers unconcerned, before a great fire of hazel-faggots in the living-room.

'Oh! It's you,' he said. 'I thought for a minute it might be a young woman.'

'You ought to lock the door,' I said.

'God A'mighty, I ain't frit at being looked at in me bath.' He held his trousers momentarily suspended, as though in deference to me. 'Never mattered to me since that day when . . .'

He broke off suddenly as the housekeeper came running in with the first bucket of boiling water for the bath, elbowing us out of her way, the water falling into the bath like a scalding waterfall. No sooner had the great cloud of steam dispersed than she was back again with a second bucket. It seemed hotter than the first.

'Out of my way!' she ordered.

'Git us a glass o' wine,' said Silas, 'and don't vapour about so much.'

'You'll have no wine,' she said, 'until you've been in that bath.'

'Then git us a dozen taters to roast. And look slippy.'

She was already out of the door with the empty bucket. 'Get 'em yourself!' she flashed.

'I got me trousers off!' he half-shouted.

'Then put 'em on again!'

This relentless exchange of words went on all the

time she was bringing the remaining buckets of water in and he was undoing the tapes of his pants, he shouting for the wine and the potatoes and she never wavering in her tart refusals to get them. Finally, as he began to roll down his pants and she began to bring in the last half-buckets of water, he turned to me and said:

'Git a light and go down and fetch that bottle o' wine and the taters. Bring a bottle of elderberry. A quart.'

While I was down in the cellar, searching with a candle in the musty wine-odoured corners for the potatoes and the bottle, I could hear the faint sounds of argument and splashing water from above. I was perhaps five minutes in the cellar, and when I went back up the stone steps, with the wine in one hand and the candle in the other and the potatoes in my pockets, the sound of voices seemed to have increased.

When I reached the living-room Silas was standing up in the bath, stark naked, and the housekeeper was shouting:

'Sit down, man, can't you? Sit down! How can I bath you if you don't sit down?'

'Sit down yourself! I don't want to burn the skin off me behind, if you do!'

While he protested she seized his shoulders and tried to force him down in the bath, but his old and rugged body, looking even stronger and more imperishable in its nakedness than ever, was stiff and immovable, and he never budged except to dance a little as the water stung the tender parts of his feet.

'Git the taters under!' he said to me at last. 'God A'mighty, I'll want summat after this.'

Gradually, as I was putting the potatoes in the ashes under the fire, the arguments quietened a little, and finally my Uncle Silas stooped, half-knelt in the water and then with a brief mutter of relief sat down. Almost in silence the housekeeper lathered the flannel she had made from her petticoat and then proceeded to wash his body, scrubbing every inch of it fiercely, taking no more notice of his nakedness than if he had been a figure of wood. All the time he sat there a little abjectly, his spirit momentarily subdued, making no effort to wash himself except sometimes to dabble his hands and dribble a little water over his bony legs. He gave even that up at last, turning to me to say:

'I never could see a damn lot o' use in water.'

Finally, when she had washed him all over, she seized the great coarse towel that had been warming on the clothes-horse by the fire.

'You're coming out now,' she said.

'I don't know as I am.'

'Did you hear what I said? You're coming out!'

'Damn, you were fast enough gittin' me in—you can wait a minute. I just got settled.'

Seizing his shoulders she began to try to force him to stand up just as she had tried to force him, only a minute or two before, to sit down. And as before he would not budge. He sat there luxuriously, not caring, some of the old devilish look of perversity back in his face, his hands playing with the water.

'He's just doing it on purpose,' she said to me at last. 'Just because you're here. He wants us to sit here and admire him. That's all. I know.'

'Don't talk so much!' he said. 'I'm getting out as fast as you'll let me.'

'Come on, then, come on!' she insisted. 'Heaven knows we don't want to look at you all night.'

The words seemed to remind my Uncle Silas of something, and as he stood up in the bath and she began towelling his back he said to me:

'I recollect what I was going to tell you now. I was having a swim with a lot o' chaps, once, in the mill-brook at . . .'

'We don't want to hear your old tales, either!' she said. 'We heard 'em all times anew.'

'Not this one,' he said.

Nevertheless her words silenced him. He stood there dumb and almost meek all the time she was towelling him dry and it was only when she vanished into the kitchen to fetch a second towel for him to dry his toes that he recollected the story he had been trying to tell me, and came to life.

'I was swimming with these chaps, in the mill-brook, and we left all our clothes on the bank . . .'

'Mind yourselves!'

The housekeeper had returned with the towel, and my Uncle Silas, as though he had never even heard of the tale he was so anxious to tell and I was so anxious to hear, said solemnly to me:

'Next year I'll have peas where I had taters, and taters where I had carrots. . . .'

'Dry your toes!' said the housekeeper.

'Dry 'em yourself and don't talk so much!'

At the same moment she thrust the towel in his hand and then began to scoop the water out of the bath with an enamel basin and put it into a bucket. When the bucket was full she hastened out of the room with it, her half-laced shoes slopping noisily in her haste. Almost before she had gone through the door and long before we heard the splash of water in the sink my Uncle Silas said swiftly, 'Tot out,' and I uncorked the wine-bottle while he found the glasses in the little cupboard above the fire.

We were standing there drinking the wine, so red and rich and soft, Silas in nothing but his shirt, when the housekeeper returned. She refilled the bucket quickly and hastened out again. No sooner had she gone than he turned to me to continue the story, and standing there, his thick blue-striped flannel shirt reaching below his knees, the hairs on his thin gnarled legs standing out as stiff as the bristles on his own gooseberries, the wine glass in one hand and the towel in the other, he looked more wicked and devilish and ugly than I ever remembered seeing him. Going on with the story, he had reached the point when the men, coming out of the mill-stream, had found their clothes gone, when the housekeeper returned.

'I think I s'll have peas along the side o' the wood,' he said, serenely, while she refilled the bucket, 'and perhaps back o' the well.'

'You get your toes dried and get dressed!' she ordered.

'And you mind your own business and get the supper. And look slippy!'

As soon as she had left the room again he resumed the tale, but no sooner had he begun than she returned. It went on like this, he telling a sentence of the tale and she returning and he interspersing some angelic and airy remark about his peas and potatoes until at last she came in to spread the cloth on the table and lay the supper. She was in the room for so long, laying out the plates and the cutlery, that at last he gave it up, turning to me with an air of satanic innocence to say:

'I'll tell you the name o' the tater when I can think of it. My memory ain't so good as it was.'

After that he proceeded meekly to put on his pants, tucking in the voluminous folds of his shirt before tying up the tapes. While the tail of his shirt was still hanging loose he remembered the potatoes I had put in the hot ashes under the fire and seizing the toasting-fork he began to prod their skins. 'Damn, they'll be done afore I get my trousers on,' he said. And standing there, with the toasting-fork in his hand, his pants tight against his legs and the tail of his shirt protruding, he looked more than anything else like the devil of tradition, prodding the roasting sinners.

That veritable air of devilishness was still about him when, finding a moment later that the house-keeper had left the room again, he turned swiftly to me to say:

'Give us another mouthful o' wine. I'll tell you what happened.'

I had hardly begun to pour the wine into his glass before he began to say, in a devilish, husky voice that was hardly more than a whisper: 'Some gals had got the clothes. They stood up on the bridge and dangled our trousers over and threatened to drop 'em in the mill-pond. What d'ye think of that? There we were swimming about wi' nothing on and they wouldn't give us the clothes.'

He went on to tell me how gradually they grew tired and desperate and at last angry at the three girls dangling over the bridge while they grew colder and colder in the deep mill-pool and how finally he himself climbed out of the water and ran up to the bridge, stark naked, and frightened the girls into dropping the clothes and retreating. Long before he

had finished I noticed that the housekeeper had
returned and was standing in the doorway, unseen
by my Uncle Silas, attentively listening.

'God A'mighty, you should have seen 'em drop
the clothes and run when they see me. All except
one.'

'What did she do?'

'Run off across the meadow with my clothes
under her arms. What d'ye think o' that?'

'What did you do?'

'Run after her.'

He ceased speaking, and taking a slow drink of
his wine he moistened his thick red lips with his
tongue, as though the tale were not finished and he
were trying to remember its end. A strange almost
soft expression of reminiscence came over his face,
flushed with the bath and the wine, as though he
could see clearly the river, the meadow, and he himself
running across the summer grass, naked, pursuing
the girl running away with his clothes.

'Rum un,' he said at last. 'I never did find out
who she was. Never did find out.'

At that moment the housekeeper came in from
the doorway, moving so quietly for once that he
scarcely heard her, the sound of the cheese-dish
being laid on the table startling him so much that
he could only turn and stare at her, fingering the
tapes of his pants and at a loss for words.

'Didn't you ever find out?' she said.

'No. I was just telling the boy. It's been so damn
long ago.'

She looked at him for a moment and then said:
'I know who she was. And so do you.'

It was the only time I ever saw him at a loss for an
answer and it was almost the only time I ever saw

her smile. He stood there slowly licking his lips in uneasy silence until at last she snapped at him with all the old habitual tartness:

'Get yourself dressed, man! I ain't running away with your clothes now, if I did then.'

She began to help him on with his clothes. He still had nothing to say, but once, as she was fastening the back buttons of his trousers and he stood with his face turned away from her, he gave me a half-smiling but inscrutable look, rich with devilry, his eyelids half-lowered and his lips shining wet with the wine.

And I began to understand then something I had not understood before.

CONSTANCE HOLME

The Last Inch

THE woods were wet, that morning. Horses and
men scrambled and slithered on the steep river bank,
and when finally the butt of the big beech was drawn
out into the open park, it left a deep trench to mark
its course. Buck Drummond set his men to 'tidy'
the big log with the cross-saw, while he himself
snigged the tops across to the timber-carriage, which
had been left standing on the drive so as to disfigure
the turf as little as possible.

It had taken six horses to fetch the butt out, six
horses straining and scrambling, with chains clanking
and brasses swinging. Buck Drummond had only a
man and a boy to help him, but then Buck was a host
in himself. He was not only a waggoner born, his
father having been one before him, but he was also
a born organiser; he was, moreover, an artist. Ted
Hutchinson, the timber-merchant, counted him his
best man—Ted Hutchinson, who could turn out
thousands of pounds' worth of Shire horses from his
various stables, but was content for his own part to
race about the country in a ramshackle Ford.

Buck was young for a foreman, being only about
thirty, but his capacity could be gauged by that
quaint air of wisdom beyond his age which is also
to be seen in a good young dog. He was slightly
above middle height, with curly sandy hair and a
pleasant Scotch face on a beautiful body. He was
slim but not thin, hard but not stiff, supple but not
sinuous. His small feet lifted themselves lightly in
their heavy boots. His fustians, ungaitered, but tied

below the knee like those of his men, took on a grace of their own from the grace of his figure. Their soft golden-brown was so exactly suited to the woods that it might have been provided by Nature by way of protective colouring.

Good timber-hauling, however, is not only a matter of body but of brains, demanding a knowledge of angles and stresses, together with an eye for delicate adjustments and distribution of weight. The born waggoner in Buck came out in the way he sized up his loads before he touched them; the artist in the ease and grace with which he assembled them; the efficient organiser in the fact that he wasted neither time, strength, nor speech. He could fetch, lift, and place a log within five minutes, and without even the slightest appearance of effort or hurry. He was unusually quiet, both with his horses and his men, giving few orders, and those almost in an undertone. And he never gave an order twice. . . .

Even apart from these things, he was no mere ignorant carter. He knew the market value of the 'wood', as he called it, that he hauled; where it was going, and what it would be used for at the other end. His job had taken him on to various estates up and down the country, and he knew a good many interesting facts about each of them. He could make a pretty shrewd guess, too, as to why the timber was coming down, and whether the proceeds would go into Government pockets or those of others.

He used only three of his team for taking the tops up the slight incline that led to the timber-waggon— Lauder, Elspie, and Haig, with Lauder leading as usual. The leader of a timber-team corresponds to the foreman of the gang in that he must have brains, and in this case it was Lauder who had them. He was a brown, about nine years old and as clever as paint, but nothing to look at either from a timber point of view or any other. He was rather undersized for a timber-horse, to begin with, and he was thin and rat-tailed, and looked like a bad feeder. Beside Elspie, the chestnut mare, and Haig, the big, placid bay wheeler, he looked like something that ought to have been carting manure on a second-rate holding.

Probably because of his extra intelligence, he was inclined to be temperamental, apt to excite himself if he had a man at his head, and to pull too fiercely; so, because of this idiosyncrasy, Buck worked him by voice alone. Backing up the slope, he called to him by name, and the three horses, taking a circular 'cast' like that of a sheep-dog, followed him with a rush, the log dragging inertly at their heels. If they narrowed the cast by attacking the slope too directly, the log would roll over and refuse to follow, and they would have to be sent back to straighten it up again. Then once more they would make their rush at the little hill, their coats and brasses gleaming in the fresh sunlight that had followed the wet night.

Arrived at the timber-waggon already stationed under the triangular 'legs', the young waggoner loosed Elspie and Haig, afterwards harnessing Lauder alone to the lifting tackle. Here again he worked him only by voice, often without even glancing in his direction. 'Come to me, Lauder!' he would call, and Lauder would turn to him like a child; or, 'Another inch!' and the brown horse would move backwards or forwards, lowering or lifting the load as the foreman fitted it into position.

The first two 'tops' settled themselves comfortably enough, but the third, a heavy, curved bough, with a tiresome twist in it both to right and left, promised to give trouble. Buck lowered it once or twice, only to swing it up again, climbing about the load with that peaceful sureness of his that neither loitered nor hurried. He moved carefully as he prised the logs apart to make a safe resting-place for the awkward customer, for both his boots and the smooth skin of the beech were slippery with the wet. Lauder, harnessed at right angles to the load, moved forward or yielded a step according to order. The big curved limb, swung on block and pulley and clipped by great hooks, hung suspended between the 'legs' like an unusually clumsy sword of Damocles. Buck studied it first from one point and then another; once, when he was on the ground, catching the end of it as it was hauled upwards, and allowing it to lift him completely over the waggon.

Presently, however, he got things as he wanted them, and, climbing back on to the load, steadied the bough as Lauder lowered it for the last time. He lowered it gingerly, as if conscious, even with his back to it, of the delicacy of the operation, and stopping for further orders at discreet intervals. 'Another inch!' Buck called, as the bough still hung, and, slipping at that moment on the logs beneath, fell forward across them. Lauder backed obediently without hesitation, lowering the great limb lightly on to the prostrate waggoner.

It was so neat and efficient an accident that the neat and efficient mind of Buck Drummond must surely have appreciated it if he had been in a position to do so. That little slip had dropped him face downwards across the load, with the bough not yet wholly in place pinning him across back and elbows. It was pressing on him, but not heavily enough to hurt him; it merely held him there a complete captive. He could neither raise himself by his hands to lever the weight off him, nor turn himself ever so slightly to swing it aside. He felt about cautiously with his feet, but could find no foothold. He was as helpless and as neatly pinned as a trussed chicken. And if Lauder moved again, feeling the weight of the log still more or less on the pulley—well, Buck did not need telling what several tons of 'wood' were capable of doing to you if you happened to be beneath them.

He found presently that he could lift his head just a very little, and by turning his eyes up he could watch the movements of the horse in front of him. He would have called to him to move forward and free him, but he felt too uncertain of his voice in his constricted position. Lauder knew as well as he did that the log ought to be in its place by now, and if he did not recognise his voice, might possibly misinterpret the order. Buck finally decided to wait until the men came up after finishing their crosssawing, trusting to Lauder's training to keep him motionless in the meantime.

It was wiser to wait—he had settled on that; but however wise it might be, it was certainly not pleasant. Each time his glance climbed from the brown hocks to the brown quarters, he expected to see them giving under the strain. A great stillness seemed to have fallen upon the world, which had lately been so full of cheerful and musical movement —a stillness in which the only sound was the faint buzzing of the cross-saw. The men were still at work, then, he thought to himself, and there was no knowing how long they would be. Certainly, they might wonder, after a while, why he did not return, and climb the little slope to see what kept him. But they were as well aware as he that the last load would probably be difficult to tackle, and so would not expect him to be through with it very soon. And by the time they did begin to think he ought to be finished, it would probably be too late. By that time Lauder would probably have yielded the last inch, letting down the full weight of the big bough upon Ted Hutchinson's best waggoner.

The tiny sound of the cross-saw seemed to go on interminably. It seemed to Buck, listening, that they must have cut the whole of the butt to pieces by now, instead of just trimming off the limb-sockets that would have made it awkward to handle. 'I'll hae to tell 'em off aboot that,' he said to himself mechanically, forgetting for the moment that he was not in a position to 'tell off' anybody. He remembered it at once, however, because he tried to move a leg, and found that he was beginning to get cramp. But by this time, indeed, he hardly dared to move at all in case Lauder, wondering at the silence and wearying of the whole business, should take the least motion of the log as an excuse for that last inch.

And still the infinitesimal sound of the cross-sawing went on. . . . Other sounds came to him presently, equally disturbing, though after another fashion. Elspie and Haig, he could hear, were beginning to fidget, evidently becoming puzzled by the continued lull. Like all well-trained timber-horses, they would stand for hours while work was in progress, but no doubt they found something sinister in this particular pause. He could hear them stamping and fussing behind him, and knew that they were moving about by the sound of the chains. He began to be afraid that they might wander

round the waggon in search of amusement, and
so irritate or startle Lauder into yielding that last
inch. . . .

But still Lauder stood quietly, awaiting the final
order. . . . His head was slightly bent as he braced
himself against the continued strain. Once he bent
it lower still, and the log quivered in response,
lifted a useless fraction and settled itself again. Once
he switched his rat-tail as if getting impatient, and
Buck caught his breath, or would have caught it if
the log had not caught it for him already. Once,
too, he turned his brown head, though carefully,
without moving his body, sending a questioning
glance in the direction of the waggon. Buck saw him
do it, and was stirred by the humanness of the action
into trying to call to him, only to find that his voice
remained in his throat. And still over the little hill
the buzz of the cross-saw went on. . . .

Buck did not hear it stop. By that time he was
engaged in trying to twist his neck to watch Elspie
and Haig, as they came, blundering and inquisitive,
round the timber-carriage. The first that he knew of
the men was when they were right upon him with
frightened shouts, sending his heart into his mouth
for fear they should startle Lauder. But Lauder still
stood, unstartled, unstirred. He stood while the
load was swung aside and the foreman helped into
an upright position; while the men, getting no
answers to their questions, stood back panting;
and when Elspie and Haig had come up and were
nosing him fondly but interferingly, Lauder was still
standing. . . .

Buck slipped off the waggon without vouchsafing
any information to his puzzled underlings. He was
a trifle stiff, a trifle red in the face, but otherwise he

seemed exactly as usual. Once on the ground, he signalled his men to swing the log back to its former angle. Then—'Another inch!' he called to Lauder, and the horse stepped back instantly.

The big bough dropped delicately into place.

VIOLA MEYNELL

The Pain in the Neck

1

THE names inscribed on the small brass tablet beside
the bell on the street door were Skeat and Wylie.
John Skeat? Christopher Wylie? Guess again, no
doubt. There was no clue. They must *have* Christian
names. The bell underneath theirs was labelled: Mr.
Douglas Jefferson; the one underneath again: Mr.
and Mrs. Alfred Bannister. Though the stucco house
was disproportionately tall for its width, there were
only the three floors. The flight of steps from the
pavement led to a ground-floor that was already quite
high in the world, so that Mr. and Mrs. Bannister's
ground-floor flat was no more on a level with
passers-by than the apartments of the caretaker and
his wife in their shallow basement. And Skeat and
Wylie from their third-floor windows would have
quite a lofty view of other people's chimneys.

For the house was on one of London's hills, that
survive almost imperceptibly beneath their covering
of houses and of streets that strap them down, as a
bulging cart-load is strapped down by cords. It was
a compact hill, surmounted by a water-tower. Skeat
and Wylie sometimes held forth to the effect that they
did not live in London at all; they lived in the village
of Campden Hill, with its water-tower for parish
pump, and situated conveniently close to the market-
town of Notting Hill Gate. There were still trees and
gardens and blackbirds and cottages on Campden
Hill, which detached it from Oxford Street by more
than the two-penny 'bus drive.

Entering by the three-belled door one was aware of a certain sumptuousness. Mr. and Mrs. Alfred Bannister's occupation of their present flat was evidently something of a misfit. More of their large handsome pieces of furniture than they might have wished to bestow on a hall which was also used by other people (and more than those other people might have wished) were ranged against the walls. And even up the first flight of stairs, massive frames took steps upwards parallel with the stairs, like a heavy gilt staircase on the wall. All this stopped abruptly on the first landing, where Mr. Jefferson was monarch, whose comfortable bachelor quarters could not boast such married opulence, but could lend some sporting prints to the landing. Upwards from there, a still barer spirit prevailed. In the Skeat and Wylie domain there was the same economy of objects as of initials on the door-plate. Only the maid's room was embellished with knick-knacks. But there was more air and more light than in the rest of the house. In fact, these were bright country rooms, befitting their village situation.

Not that its occupants were not in close connexion with London town. Camilla (or 'Mill') Wylie acted as secretary to Sir Joseph Sandford, the economist, and presented herself at his door in Chelsea every morning at ten o'clock, returning early in the afternoon to type at home from her shorthand notes. In the meantime, Jane Skeat had been the deft housewife, perpetuating the bright, light-coloured charm of their quarters and providing for their simple, hygienic and yet elegant housekeeping.

Few people are consciously, confessedly happy, but this condition really was achieved in the top flat at 17 Campden Hill Terrace. Jane had an income,

Mill a salary. They had leisure to do whatever they wanted. They went abroad every year; they had been to France, Italy, and Spain; they were going next year to Ragusa. They had friends—not indispensable, but valuable. They had security in each other, after each had emerged from college to embark on a solitary existence. The sound of life in their flat was a blithe, major-key one. Since each had so much to gain from the other's society, discordances were as unlikely as they were in Jane's beautiful playing on her Blüthner cottage-grand. Their possessions and arrangements had become precious to them just because they were no longer entirely their own, but shared. Their temperaments were well-suited, even the differences between them being complementary ones. They both liked Bach and salads. Mill could not sew, Jane could and did; such a convenient discrepancy almost amounted to a bond. Of characteristic divergences of opinion there were, indeed, plenty. Jane was proud that England had a Society for the prevention of cruelty to children, Mill scorned it for needing one. Jane would press on Mill the latest thing in throat-gargles; Mill would declare that the better the gargle the worse for the throat's natural power of resistance; and so on, up to the larger affairs of life. The two-sidedness of things was well represented by them. Life was not all insipid agreement. And it seemed as if the amicable differences in their outlook existed really only to give point to the luxury and certainty of their tie, the infinitely contented consciousness of I—have—you, and you—have—me. If they had not been two in some things, how could they have been conscious of being one?

Their appearance was interestingly dissimilar, but

even so achieved a certain unity. Jane was tall, had fair curls, considerable gracefulness and, without being pretty, an oddly charming face. Mill was lower, sparer, hardier, with fine eyes and a rather noble forehead. Together they gave an impression of each supplying what the other lacked, and of forming a unit that was well equipped for varied and successful living.

They were, by phases, soberly or gaily, placidly or excitedly, conscious of the extraordinary good fortune of their intimacy. Who now thought of coming home to an empty flat? Not they. Who might be compelled to endure bores for sheer companionship's sake? No longer they. They had become that social unit which one person cannot be, and which only begins with the number two. Married couples had few advantages over them. They had some enormous advantages over married couples. They were much happier than Mr. and Mrs. Bannister below. While Mr. Bannister downstairs was deciding that if his wife was late again for the theatre that evening he would simply go without her, upstairs Mill was calling from one room to another:

'What are you doing? Don't forget we're to look in on the Swannicks this evening.'

'I'm washing my hair.'

'You haven't got much time.'

'I haven't got much hair!'

Or while Mr. Bannister took strong exception, in a voice which could almost have been heard upstairs, to his wife's opening the window, pointing out that he did not buy coals to warm the street, Mill, above, was saying to Jane: 'Why don't you sit right *on* the fire?' and Jane was saying: 'I'd love to.'

2

The little dinners they gave were delightful. Mill's cocktails, Jane's courses, Mill's satirical comments on whatever foibles of human nature she had encountered during the day, Jane's good hostess-ship, combined to make their invitations acceptable ones. They kept late hours, and sometimes it was one o'clock before the last amused or amusing word had been spoken and the guests let out on to the country-quiet of the tree-sprinkled street. With some visitors the end always came too soon; with others stray thoughts of delightful bed might be the stimulation behind Mill's last sallies.

One night there were two guests. Nora Granger, the original *invitée*, had replied that she had an acquaintance on her hands who was new to London, and it was finally decided that she should bring him along.

Nora Granger, who was a neighbour, left at eleven, the young man lingering for a few minutes which were stretched incredibly into over an hour. It was not because he had much to say that he stayed; he merely seemed to neglect to go. His name was Arthur Phelps. His father, they understood, had gone out to Johannesburg as a young man to edit a newspaper and had remained ever since. The son had evidently been a problem. Various occupations in Johannesburg had been begun and abandoned, and now in an 'anything-that-comes-along' manner, he was filling a job as reporter for a London newspaper at three pounds a week. His appearance was in no way striking, but was agreeable. He was slightly below medium height, had a small dark moustache, and slow enunciation. Mill and Jane managed with some effort to find sufficient subjects of conversation that were not alien to him. Jane played the piano. Mill gave an amusing enough idea of the kind of correspondence with which her employer had been deluged after being over-persuaded to write an article in the press. But, in fact, she was tired by an arduous day's work and would have been glad to be made to forget it rather than talk about it. She watched Phelps somewhat expectantly. He was a chain-smoker, and each cigarette was like a new little peg to keep him fastened down to his chair for so much longer. In lighting up, if he chanced to be speaking he would pause in the middle of an already slow sentence, his audience having to wait, while the match did its work, for the leisurely conclusion of the phrase. He would even stop in the most improbable places in a sentence, as 'When I was once in—(leisurely pause for lighting)—'Natal. . . .' Even when he at last went, he nearly did not go; it seemed almost by a miracle that his gradual departure was really consummated.

Mill's fine tired head fell dramatically forward. 'What a crashing bore!' she moaned; 'what a pain in the neck!'

3

During their three years together there had been certain social or family duties they kept apart. Mill had a tenacious aunt: naturally Jane was not called upon to participate in dutiful visits to Cadogan Square. Jane took an old nurse to the theatre once in a while. They also had their individual charities. Otherwise, though they had originally planned, on high-sounding principles, to respect their separate

friends, they had never in the least wanted to do so.
In the beginning they had discussed elaborately how
they could have their friends to see them without
interfering with each other. Supposing Jane had
some one in the main room, Mill could easily occupy
the room at the back; it was itself a nice room, and
she could even entertain some one there at the same
time. They need never be in the least on top of each
other. What an imaginary situation all this was! In
actual fact, as it proved, they liked seeing people
together or not at all. Friends were shared or faded
out.

There had been three years of enjoying nothing
that was not shared, and enjoying doubly everything
that was. And then something a little different
happened. Arthur Phelps had rung up, Mill heard
one day when she came in at lunch-time, and had
invited Jane to spend the morning at a skating rink.
'You remember he had been skating the day he came
here?' Jane added in telling her.

'But imagine his mistaking you for a sporting
young woman!'

'But I think I must be, after all!—it was such fun.'

'You went?'

'Oh yes I went.'

High boots fitted with skates soon occupied a
place in Jane's boot-chest. Morning skating was
so pleasant an occupation that the only wonder was
what she had ever done with her seemingly employed
mornings before. Mill was tentatively, warily pleased
at the diversion for her. This action of Jane's certainly had a slightly suspect element of change in it;
but on the other hand it was an action they would
both have spoken of as 'going skating' rather than
'going out with Arthur Phelps.'

But the time came when Jane put on her hat at non-skating times.

'Whither?'

'I'm going out. . . .' The reply was a little unprepared and flustered.

'You don't say.'

4

Skating alone, she was clenched in her body, holding her skates on with her toes, her arms rigid, her eyes fixed on the ice in front of her, though unhappily certain that when she fell it would be backwards. When he came, and her hand rested however lightly upon his, she was firm like the rock of ages, her muscles relaxed, her eyes disengaged. It was not that he could yet skate so very much better than herself, but his lack of fearfulness was sufficient for two. As for when they had their hands crossed in front, her right hand in his right and left in his left, they could have skated like that across whole continents.

When they had parted outside the rink, or at the tube-station, or at her house door, she felt as she did when she had not his support on the ice. This strange thing happened to her. In the ordinary daily course of her life she was now at a loss, bewildered, unsafe, incomplete, as if she were skating alone.

5

Spring had begun; almond trees were in blossom; life was transformed.

Mill knew what was coming.

There are some things so overwhelmingly right that one cannot suffer over them; to do so even in one's inmost thoughts would be pure treachery. Not only was suffering impossible, but there was even something specially welcoming in Mill's attitude to Phelps. She often quoted him. 'Isn't Arthur amusing when he describes his interviews with film stars!' She introduced him flatteringly into conversations with other people. 'We used not to be great experts on flying records, but we know some one now, don't we, Jane, who makes it all interesting.' Or when some visitor spoke of advancement in careers: 'I wonder if real talent *does* get overlooked; we have a friend who a few months ago was doing police court reporting for his paper, and already he's covering most of the big things.'

She did not overdo it, but she lost no opportunity. She showed assiduously how much she liked him. She had to prove to Jane many times a day that she never *could* have dropped her head forward and exclaimed, 'What a crashing bore!' For that she had done so was now too bad to be true. Besides, he was not a bore. He had a slow manner which might allow one to say such a thing of him if one was not already fond of him. But that same manner might even prove an attraction to any one who loved him.

Mill would have liked to laugh to Jane about that old incident, saying outright: 'Do you remember that I ran him down the first time he came? Well, we know now who the fool was that evening.' But for two reasons she did not speak. The first was that she knew that a disclaimer does not wipe out a past expression of opinion. Something new is added— —another opinion—but the original opinion is a fact in itself, and, as such, unchangeable for ever.

The second reason for not referring to the incident was that such speech would have intruded too

clumsily on the separate trembling world in which
Jane lived, in which her imagination was dazzled
by something almost too bright to look at, and
appalled by possible abysses of pain never conceived
of before.

And when Jane actually announced that she was
engaged to Arthur, Mill could further atone for her
unhappy words by transporting herself into the
region of their happiness, with no thought of her
own loss.

And, for that matter, would not a light mention
of the incident to Arthur himself be enough to banish
it from her mind for ever? That was a good idea—
to tell Arthur, to confess to him, and then never
think of it again; to get rid of it that way. They got
on well together, so she would have no difficulty in
speaking.

'To think that the first time I saw you I thought
you a most ordinary young man, and said so!' she
took occasion to remark to him when they were
alone. 'It gets me down quite badly sometimes when
I think of that.'

He gave one short shout of laughter. 'I shouldn't
lose any sleep over that if I were you.' His thoughts
did not remain a moment on the subject. He had
not sufficient conceit to make him interested. It
seemed, indeed, as if his laugh, which was always a
pleasant one, had been produced on this occasion
by the thought that any one should be expected to
think anything else of him.

He was killed a week later. A giant airship, taking
notable people on a far trip, glided into a mountain
in a fog. Ravines and woods in France were strewn
with charred bodies, and Arthur Phelps, reporting
the trip for a newspaper, was among them.

6

The early afternoon sun entered the room where sunshine seemed naturally to belong. The bare walls of this room had been painted pale yellow last year, and the yellow had actually proved to be exactly as they wanted it. A mellow wicker bird-cage, which must have once brought a canary from Madeira, hung above the stiff-chintzed window-seat. The cage contained a rag bird of silky feathers and glass-bead eyes, and Jane had always feared that some short-sighted person might think they really kept a bird in a cage. A large bunch of helicrysum of all colours hung head downwards elsewhere; the brass fender and scuttle were like amateur suns. When the true sunshine entered the room it magically touched to completion all that had been like latent sun already.

Mill sat alone, expecting Jane. Jane's condition had gradually improved. After lying prostrate for some days she had begun by rising one day to go and see an aunt of Arthur's in the country whom he had once taken her to visit.

Once on her feet again she had resumed at least life's superficial routine, though it was strange to see her put sugar in her tea, or take up a book or paper—and painful to observe her hands occupied inter-mittently with her knitting while her eyes forgot to move their gaze from some spot on the wall. To-day she had probably gone for one of the long walks with which misery tries to blunt itself by fatigue. As Mill now awaited her return, and noticed how benevolently the sunshine had come into the room, she could not but feel that a little light might soon shine again in Jane's life.

It was just at such moments as these that her words when she first saw Phelps would flash back into her mind. How she hated them! They had long seemed unfortunate. Since his death they had an irretrievable quality of shameful abuse. Luckily, she never had to think of them long, for she could feel sure that they now echoed only in her own mind. She remembered when she was almost a baby helping her nurse to lay the cloth for tea. There is a slight spot on the cloth: the bread-and-butter plate goes over that, she knows quite well that it does. Another spot, and the cake covers that; it is the nursery tea-table procedure; now the cloth is clean. Who does not cover and conceal? Who does not rely on making this or that episode as if it had never been? Dark deeds are forgiven and pass into oblivion; it would be a hard world indeed if a slight involuntary offence were remembered.

But perhaps it *is* such a hard world?

No, even Jane herself, though her nature was to a rare degree void of the means to offend, must sometimes be glad to earn forgetfulness for some slight injury committed.

But on the whole she would prefer to have done some real wickedness towards Jane, who would have forgiven it. For those words she had uttered had a more deadly quality than wickedness. No such good luck for her as some ugly forgivable crime. *Her* fault was slight, blameless—and potentially fatal. But now that the days and weeks had passed since Arthur's death, Mill could be sure the remark was forgotten.

Because otherwise things would be different now. Jane would be—not resentful, oh no, not her!—but merely *conscious* in some acutely sensitized spot of

her. Would she not have said (Mill could hear her
in dark imaginings): 'Mill I am going away.' 'Going?
Where?' 'Don't mind, don't regret it. Somehow I
have to go.' 'Usen't we to be happy?' '*Rather!*'
'Have I ever been unkind to you?' 'As if you could
be!' 'How can you go? To whom? To strangers?
But think what we have shared. Think, too, how I
knew *him* and liked him. Others you go to will have
neither known nor cared for him.' 'I know, I know.'
'You see, you can't go. Didn't I rejoice with you?
Was I ever mean or disloyal?' 'Never, never for a
moment. But—I must go.'

Having let her thoughts run away with her in this
particular gloomy fashion, Mill at any rate had the
consolation of contrasting such fantasies with facts
as they were.

When Jane came in the tea-hour had arrived, and
by the open window their cups soon steamed faintly.
From the moment of Jane's entry Mill could see
that she, too, was aware of the gentle charm of the
afternoon indoors, the tempting look of one of their
famous little home-made wholemeal loaves, the
golden butter stamped with a sheaf of corn. The
bird-cage, oddly shaped like the unfamiliar hay-
stack of another country, swayed faintly in the
window embrasure. Their cigarette smoke floated
slowly to the window, then darted out. They lingered
in the kind of dalliance which Mill could never resist,
though typing till midnight might be the price she
paid for it. The maid Rose, who liked Mill but
adored Jane, and whom Mill approved for the very
reason of that preference, came to remove the tea-
things, and something peaceful and familiar in the
scene as she entered made her think: 'It's beginning
to be like before.' She felt that the time had come

when it would be quite all right for her to enter the room as briskly and cheerfully as she used. A child's voice called outside, for it was sounds like boys' and girls' voices, and birds' singing, and trees in a breeze, rather than of traffic, that rose in the gardened street outside.

Mill felt a deep distant thankfulness. Without treachery, she could not help knowing that as she and Jane had been happy in the past they would be happy once more. Their life would always be second-best for Jane, but good for all that. Life would not be held down, it thrust itself up again. It was thrusting itself up now before her very eyes. For Jane was even talkative, it was to be noticed, bent on communicativeness, telling very deliberately, in her sweet and rather tired voice, the incidents of her walk.

'I called in at the Swannicks,' she was relating, and Mill, not to be behind in interest in any detail, broke in:

'Haven't they gone yet? I remember the Colonel remarking skittishly that they would soon be "going places and seeing things."'

'They go on Saturday.'

'To see that all's well with the Empire.'

'Oh well—they're going to heaps of places.'

'He likes places that are red on the map, does the Colonel. Wouldn't it be dreadful to have to go—'

But Jane interrupted in her turn. 'They intend eventually to settle somewhere quite fresh, they don't know where.'

'Good luck to them.'

'Would you like to see where they are going? They gave me this route.' She stretched her hand for her bag. Mill, looking at her, saw in her fair face an intention greater than was warranted by what they were saying. And suddenly she knew that they were not talking about a mere nothing, as would have appeared. It was like those occasions when Jane was at the piano and Mill thought she was still playing a few preparatory runs on the keys, but imperceptibly she had passed into the piece itself. Jane with quiet purpose was now actually in the process of imparting some information. Reluctantly, inevitably, she was coming to it. And in the meantime, forestalling her, as she opened her bag, her Cook's ticket, a stiff, rubber-banded booklet, fell out on the table between them.

ELIZABETH BOWEN

Joining Charles

Everybody in the White House was awake early that morning, even the cat. At an unprecedented hour in the thick grey dusk Polyphemus slipped upstairs and began to yowl at young Mrs. Charles's door, under which came out a pale yellow line of candle-light. On an ordinary morning he could not have escaped from the kitchen so easily, but last night the basement door had been left unbolted; all the doors were open downstairs, for the household had gone to bed at a crisis of preparation for the morrow. Sleep was to be no more than an interim, and came to most of them thinly and interruptedly. The rooms were littered with objects that had an air of having been put down momentarily, corded boxes were stacked up in the hall, and a spectral breakfast-table waiting all night in the parlour reappeared slowly as dawn came in through the curtains.

Young Mrs. Charles came across to the door on her bare feet, and, shivering, let in Polyphemus. She was still in pyjamas, but her two suit-cases were packed to the brim, with tissue paper smoothed on the tops of them: she must have been moving about for hours. She was always, superstitiously, a little afraid of Polyphemus and made efforts to propitiate him on all occasions; his expression of omniscience had imposed upon her thoroughly. His coming in now made her a little conscious; she stood still, one hand on the knob of the dressing-table drawer, and put the other hand to her forehead—what must she do? Between the curtains, drawn a little apart, light kept coming in slowly, solidifying the objects round her, which till now had been uncertain, wavering silhouettes in candle-light. So night fears gave place to the realities of daytime.

Polyphemus continued to melt round the room, staring malignly at nothing. Presently Agatha tapped and came in in her dressing-gown; her plaits hung down each side of her long, kind face, and she carried a cup of tea.

'Better drink this,' said Agatha. 'What can I do?' She drew back the curtains a little more in her comfortable, common-sense way to encourage the daylight. Leaning for a moment out of the window she breathed in critically the morning air; the bare upland country was sheathed but not hidden by mist. 'You're going to have a beautiful day,' said Agatha.

Mrs. Charles shivered, then began tugging a comb through her short hair. She had been awake a long time and felt differently from Agatha about the day; she looked at her sister-in-law haggardly. 'I dreamed and dreamed,' said Mrs. Charles. 'I kept missing my boat, saw it sliding away from the quay; and when I turned to come back to you all England was sliding away too, in the other direction, and I don't know where I was left—and I dreamed, too, of course, about losing my passport.'

'One would think you had never travelled before,' said Agatha tranquilly. She sat down on the end of the narrow bed where Mrs. Charles had slept for the last time, and shaking out Mrs. Charles's garments, passed them to her one by one, watching her dress as though she had been a child. Mrs. Charles felt herself being marvelled at; her own smallness and youth had become objective to her at the White

House; a thing, all she had, to offer them over again every day to be softened and pleased by.

As she pulled on the clothes she was to wear for so long she began to feel formal and wary, the wife of a competent banker going to join him at Lyons. The expression of her feet in those new brogues was quite unfamiliar: the feet of a 'nice little woman.' Her hair, infected by this feeling of strangeness that flowed to her very extremities, lay in a different line against her head. For a moment the face of a ghost from the future stared at her out of the looking-glass. She turned quickly to Agatha, but her sister-in-law had left her while she was buttoning her jumper at the neck and had gone downstairs to print some more labels. It had occurred to Agatha that there would be less chance of losing the luggage (a contingency by which this untravelled family seemed to be haunted) if Louise were to tie on new labels, with more explicit directions, at Paris, where she would have to re-register. Agatha was gone, and the cup of tea, untasted, grew cold on the dressing-table.

The room looked bare without her possessions and withdrawn, as though it had already forgotten her. At this naked hour of parting she had forgotten it also; she supposed it would come back in retrospect so distinctly as to be a kind of torment. It was a smallish room with sloping ceilings, and a faded paper rambled over by roses. It had white curtains and was never entirely dark; it had so palpably a life of its own that she had been able to love it with intimacy and a sense of return, as one could never have loved an inanimate thing. Lying in bed one could see from the one window nothing but sky or sometimes a veil of rain; when one got up and looked out there were fields, wild and bare, and an unbroken skyline to emphasize the security of the house.

The room was up on the top floor, in one of the gables; a big household cannot afford a spare bedroom of any pretensions. To go downstairs one had to unlatch the nursery gate at the head of the top flight. Last time Charles was home it had been very unfortunate; he had barked his shins on the gate and shouted angrily to his mother to know what the thing was *still* there for. Louise fully realized that it was being kept for Charles's children.

During that first visit with Charles she had hardly been up to the second floor, where the younger girls slept in the old nursery. There had been no confidences; she and Charles occupied very connubially a room Mrs. Ray gave up to them that had been hers since her marriage. It was not till Louise came back here alone that the White House opened its arms to her and she began to be carried away by this fullness, this intimacy and queer seclusion of family life. She and the girls were in and out of each other's rooms; Doris told sagas of high school, Maisie was always just on the verge of a love-affair, and large grave Agatha began to drop the formality with which she had greeted a married woman and sister-in-law. She thought Agatha would soon have forgotten she was anything but her own child if it had ever been possible for Agatha to forget Charles.

It would have been terrible if Louise had forgotten, as she so nearly had, to pack Charles's photograph. There it had stood these three months, propped up on the mantelpiece, a handsome convention in sepia, becomingly framed, from which the young wife, falling asleep or waking, had turned away her face instinctively. She folded back a layer of tissue paper before shutting her suit-case and poked down a finger to feel the edge of the frame and reassure herself. There it was, lying face down, wrapped up in her dressing-gown, and she would have seen Charles before she looked again at his photograph. The son and brother dominating the White House would be waiting on Lyons platform to enfold her materially.

Mrs. Charles glanced round the room once more, then went downstairs slowly. Through the house she could hear doors opening and shutting and people running about because of her. She felt ashamed that her packing was finished and there was nothing for her to do. Whenever she had pictured herself leaving the White House it had been in the evening, with curtains drawn, and they had all just come out to the door for a minute to say good-bye to her, then gone back to the fire. It had been more painful but somehow easier. Now she felt lonely; they had all gone away from her, there was nobody there.

She went shyly into the morning-room as though for the first time and knelt down on the rug in front of a young fire. There was a sharp smell of wood-smoke; thin little flames twisted and spat through the kindling. A big looking-glass, down to the ground, reflected her kneeling there; small and childish among the solemn mahogany furniture; more like somebody sent back to school than some one rejoining a virile and generous husband who loved her. Her cropped fair hair turned under against her cheek and was cut in a straight line over the eyebrows. She had never had a home before, and had been able to boast till quite lately that she had never been home-sick. After she married there had been houses in which she lived with Charles, but still she had not known what it meant to be home-sick.

She hoped that, after all, nobody would come in for a moment or two; she had turned her head and was looking out at the lawn with its fringe of trees not yet free from the mist, and at the three blackbirds hopping about on it. The blackbirds made her know all at once what it meant to be going away; she felt as though some one had stabbed her a long time ago but she were only just feeling the knife. She could not take her eyes from the blackbirds, till one with a wild fluty note skimmed off into the trees and the other two followed it. Polyphemus had come in after her and was looking out at them, pressing himself against the window-pane.

'Polyphemus,' said Mrs. Charles in her oddly unchildish voice, 'have you any illusions?' Polyphemus lashed his tail.

By midday (when she would be nearly at Dover) the fire would be streaming up briskly, but by that time the sun would be pouring in at the windows and no one would need a fire at all. The mornings were not cold yet, the girls were active, and it was only because of her going away that the fire had been lighted. Perhaps Agatha, who never hurt anything's feelings, would come in and sit not too far away from it with her basket of mending, making believe to be glad of the heat. 'I don't suppose there'll be fires at Lyons,' thought Mrs. Charles. Somewhere, in some foreign room, to-morrow evening when the endearments were over or there was a pause in them, Charles would lean back in his chair with a gusty sigh, arch his chest up, stretch out his legs and say: 'Well, come on. Tell me about the family.'

Then she would have to tell him about the White

House. Her cheeks burnt as she thought how it would all come out. There seemed no chance yet of Agatha or Maisie getting married. That was what Charles would want to know chiefly about his sisters. He had a wholesome contempt for virginity. He would want to know how Doris, whom he rather admired, was 'coming along'. Those sisters of Charles's always sounded rather dreadful young women, not the sort that Agatha, Maisie, or Doris would care to know. It seemed to Charles funny— he often referred to it—that Agatha wanted babies so badly and went all tender and conscious when babies were mentioned.

'She'll make no end of a fuss over our kids,' Charles would say. The White House seemed to Charles, all the same, very proper as an institution; it was equally proper that he should have a contempt for it. He helped to support the girls and his mother, for one thing, and that did place them all at a disadvantage. But they were dear, good souls.—Mrs. Charles knelt with her hands on her knees and the hands clenched slowly from anger and helplessness.

Mrs. Ray, the mother of Charles, suddenly knelt down by his wife and put an arm round her shoulders without saying a word. She did these impulsive things gracefully. Mrs. Charles relaxed and leant sideways a little against the kind shoulder. She had nothing to say, so they watched the fire struggle and heard the hall clock counting away the seconds.

'Have you got enough clothes on?' said Mother after a minute. 'It's cold in trains. I never do think you wear enough clothes.'

Mrs. Charles, nodding, unbuttoned her coat and showed a ribbed sweater pulled on over her jumper. 'Sensible of me!' she proudly remarked.

'You're learning to be quite a sensible little thing,' Mother said lightly. 'I expect Charles will notice a difference. Tell Charles not to let you go out in the damp in your evening shoes. But I expect he knows how to take care of you.'

'Indeed, yes,' said Mrs. Charles, nodding.

'You're precious, you see.' Mother smoothed back the hair from against Mrs. Charles's cheek to look at her thoughtfully, like a gentle sceptic at some kind of miracle. 'Remember to write me about the flat: I want to know everything: wallpapers, views from the windows, sizes of rooms——We'll be thinking about you both to-morrow.'

'I'll be thinking of you.'

'Oh, no, you won't,' said Mother, with perfect finality.

'Perhaps not,' Mrs. Charles quickly amended.

Mother's son Charles was generous, sensitive, gallant, and shrewd. The things he said, the things he had made, his imprint, were all over the White House. Sometimes he looked out at Louise with bright eyes from the family talk, so striking, so unfamiliar that she fell in love with the stranger for moments together as a married woman should not. He was quiet and never said very much, but he *noticed*; he had an infallible understanding and entered deeply, it seemed, into the sisters' lives. He was so good; he was so keen for them all to be happy. He had the strangest way of anticipating one's wishes. He was master of an inimitable drollery— to hear him chaff Agatha! Altogether he was a knightly person, transcending modern convention. His little wife had come to them all in a glow from her wonderful lover. No wonder she was so quiet; they used to try and read him from her secret, sensitive face.

A thought of their Charles without his Louise troubled them all with a pang when Louise was her dearest. Charles in Lyons, uncomplaining, lonely, tramping the town after business to look for a flat. The return of Louise to him, to the home he had found for her, her room upstairs already aghast and vacant, the emptiness that hung over them, gave them the sense of pouring out an oblation. The girls were heavy, with the faces of Flemish Madonnas; Doris achieved some resemblance to Charles, but without being handsome. They had cheerful dispositions, but were humble when they considered themselves; they thought Louise must have a great deal of love in her to give them so much when there was a Charles in her life.

Mrs. Ray, with a groan at her 'old stiff bones', got up from the hearthrug and sat on a chair. She thought of something to say, but was not quite ready to say it till she had taken up her knitting. She had hoped to have finished this pair of socks in time to send out by Louise with his others: she hadn't been able to—Mrs. Ray sighed. 'You're making my boy very happy,' she said, with signs in her manner of the difficulty one has in expressing these things.

Louise thought: 'Oh, I love you!' There was something about the hands, the hair, the expression, the general being of Mother that possessed her entirely, that she did not think she could live without. She knelt staring at Mother, all in a tumult. Why be so lonely, why never escape? She was too lonely, it couldn't be borne; not even for the sake of the White House. Not this morning, so early, with the buffeting strangeness of travel before her, with her wrists so chilly and the anticipation of sea-

sickness making her stomach ache. The incom-
municableness of even these things, these little ills of
the body, bore Mrs. Charles down. She was tired
of being brave alone, she was going to give it up.

It is with mothers that understanding and comfort
are found. She wanted to put down her head on a
bosom, this bosom, and say: 'I'm unhappy. Oh,
help me! I can't go on. I don't love my husband.
It's death to be with him. He's grand, but he's
rotten all through——' She needed to be fortified.

'Mother——' said Louise.

'Mm-mm?'

'If things were not a success out there—— If one
weren't a good wife always——' Mother smoothed
her knitting out and began to laugh; an impassable,
resolute chuckle.

'What a *thing*——' she said. 'What an idea!'

Louise heard steps in the hall and began kneading
her hands together, pulling the fingers helplessly.
'*Mother*,' she said, 'I feel——'

Mother looked at her; out of the eyes looked
Charles. The steady, gentle look, their interchange,
lasted moments. Steps came hurrying over the flags
of the hall.

'I can't go——'

Doris came in with the teapot. She wasn't grown
up, her movements were clumsy and powerful, more
like a boy's. She should have been Charles. Her
heavy plait came tumbling over her shoulder as she
bent to put down the teapot—round and brown with
a bluish glaze on it. Sleep and tears in the dark had
puffed up her eyelids, which seemed to open with
difficulty: her small eyes dwindled into her face.
'*Breakfast*,' she said plaintively.

Rose, the servant, brought in a plate of boiled

eggs—nice and light for the journey—and put them down compassionately.

'Even Rose,' thought Mrs. Charles, getting up and coming to the table obediently because they all expected her to, 'even Rose——' She looked at the breakfast-cups with poppies scattered across them as though she had not seen them before or were learning an inventory. Doris had begun to eat as though nothing else mattered. She took no notice of Louise, pretending, perhaps, to make things easier for herself, that Louise were already gone.

'Oh, Doris, not the *tussore* tie with the *red* shirt.' Whatever White House might teach Mrs. Charles about common sense, it was her mission to teach them about clothes. 'Not,' said Mrs. Charles, with bravado rising to an exaggeration of pathos, 'not on my last day!'

'I dressed in the dark; I couldn't see properly,' said Doris.

'You won't get eggs for breakfast in France,' said Maisie with a certain amount of triumph as she came in and sat down.

'I wonder what the flat'll be like?' said Maisie. 'Do write and tell us about the flat—describe the wallpapers and everything.'

'Just think,' said Doris, 'of Charles buying the furniture! "*Donnez-moi une chaise!*" "*Bien, Monsieur.*" "*Non. Ce n'est pas assez confortable pour ma femme.*"'

'Fancy!' said Maisie, laughing very much. 'And fancy if the flat's high up.'

'There'll be central heating and stoves. Beautiful fug. She actually won't be chilly.' Mrs. Charles was always chilly: this was a household joke.

'Central heating is stuffy——'

Doris broke away suddenly from the conversation. 'Oh!' she said violently, 'Oh, Louise, you are lucky!'

A glow on the streets and on the pale, tall houses: Louise walking with Charles. Frenchmen running in blousey overalls (Doris saw), French poodles, French girls in plaid skirts putting the shutters back, French ladies on iron balconies, leaning over, watching Charles go up the street with Louise and help Louise over the crossings; Charles and Louise together. A door, a lift, a flat, a room, a kiss! 'Charles, Charles, you are so splendid! Mother loves you and the girls love you and I love you——' 'Little woman!' A French curtain fluttering in the high, fresh wind, the city under the roofs—forgotten. All this Doris watched: Louise watched Doris.

'Yes,' smiled Louise. 'I *am* lucky.'

'Even to be going to France,' said Doris, and stared with her dog's eyes.

Louise wanted to take France in her two hands and make her a present of it. 'You'll be coming out soon, Doris, some day.' (It was not likely that Charles would have her—and did one, anyhow, dare let the White House into the flat?)

'Do you really think so?'

'Why not, if Mother can spare you?'

'*Louise!*' cried Maisie reproachfully—she had been sitting watching—'you aren't eating!'

Agatha, sitting next her, covered up her confusion with gentle comforting noises, cut the top off an egg and advanced it coaxingly. That was the way one made a child eat; she was waiting to do the same for Charles's and Louise's baby when it was old enough. Louise now almost saw the baby sitting up between them, but it was nothing to do with her.

'You'll be home in *less* than the two years, I shouldn't be surprised,' said Mother startlingly. It was strange, now one came to think of it, that any question of coming back to the White House had not been brought up before. They might know Mrs. Charles would be coming back, but they did not (she felt) believe it. So she smiled at Mother as though they were playing a game.

'Well, two years at the very least,' Mother said with energy.

They all cast their minds forward. Louise saw herself in the strong pale light of the future walking up to the White House and (for some reason) ringing the bell like a stranger. She stood ringing and ringing and nobody answered or even looked out of a window. She began to feel that she had failed them somehow, that something was missing. Of course it was. When Louise came back next time she must bring them a baby. Directly she saw herself coming up the steps with a child in her arms she knew at once what was wanted. Wouldn't Agatha be delighted? Wouldn't Maisie 'run on'? Wouldn't Doris hang awkwardly round and make jokes, poking her big finger now and then between the baby's curling pink ones? As for Mother—at the supreme moment of handing the baby to Mother, Louise had a spasm of horror and nearly dropped it. For the first time she looked at the baby's face and saw it was Charles's.

'It would do no *good*,' thought Mrs. Charles, cold all of a sudden and hardened against them all, 'to have a baby of Charles's.'

They all sat looking not quite at each other, not quite at her. Maisie said (thinking perhaps of the love-affair that never completely materialized): 'A great deal can happen in two years,' and began to

laugh confusedly in an emotional kind of way.
Mother and Agatha looked across at each other.
'Louise, don't forget to send us a wire,' said Mother,
as though she had been wondering all this time she
had sat so quiet behind the teapot whether Louise
would remember to do this.

'Or Charles might send the wire.'

'Yes,' said Louise, 'that would be better.'

Polyphemus, knowing his moment, sprang up on
to Mrs. Charles's knee. His black tail, stretched out
over the tablecloth, lashed sideways, knocking the
knives and forks crooked. His one green eye sardonically penetrated her. *He* knew. He had been given
to Charles as a dear little kitten. He pressed against
her, treading her lap methodically and mewing
soundlessly, showing the purple roof of his mouth.
'Ask Charles,' suggested Polyphemus, 'what became
of my other eye.' 'I know,' returned Mrs. Charles
silently. '*They* don't, they haven't been told; you've
a voice, I haven't—what about it?' 'Satan!' breathed
Mrs. Charles, and caressed fascinatedly the fur just
over his nose.

'Funny,' mused Agatha, watching, 'you never
have cared for Polyphemus, and yet he likes you.
He's a very transparent cat; he is wonderfully
honest.'

'He connects her with Charles,' said Maisie, also
enjoying this interchange between the wife and the
cat. 'He's sending some kind of a message—he's
awfully clever.'

'Too clever for me,' said Mrs. Charles, and swept
Polyphemus off her knee with finality. Agatha was
going as far as the station; she went upstairs for her
hat and coat. Mrs. Charles rose also, picked up her
soft felt hat from a chair and pulled it on numbly, in

front of the long glass, arranging two little bits of hair at the sides against her cheeks. 'Either I am dreaming,' she thought, 'or some one is dreaming me.'

Doris roamed round the room and came up to her. 'A book left behind, Louise; *Framley Parsonage*, one of your books.'

'Keep it for me.'

'For two years—all that time?'

'Yes, I'd like you to.'

Doris sat down on the floor and began to read *Framley Parsonage*. She went into it deeply—she had to go somewhere; there was nothing to say; she was suddenly shy of Louise again as she had been at first, as though they had never known each other—perhaps they never had.

'Haven't you read it before?'

'No, never, I'll write and tell you, shall I, what I think of it?'

'I've quite forgotten what I think of it,' said Louise, standing above her, laughing and pulling on her gloves. She laughed as though she were at a party, moving easily now under the smooth compulsion of Somebody's dreaming mind. Agatha had come in quietly. 'Hush!' she said in a strained way to both of them, standing beside the window in hat and coat as though *she* were the traveller. 'Hush!' She was listening for the taxi. Mother and Maisie had gone.

Wouldn't the taxi come, perhaps? What if it never came? An intolerable jar for Louise, to be deprived of going; a tear in the mesh of the dream that she could not endure. 'Make the taxi come soon!' she thought, praying now for departure. 'Make it come soon!'

Being listened for with such concentration must have frightened the taxi, for it didn't declare itself; there was not a sound to be heard on the road. If it were not for the hospitality of *Framley Parsonage* where, at this moment, would Doris have been? She bent to the pages absorbedly and did not look up; the leaves of the book were thin and turned over noisily. Louise fled from the morning-room into the hall.

Out in the dark hall Mother was bending over the pile of boxes, reading and re-reading the labels upside down and from all aspects. She often said that labels could not be printed clearly enough. As Louise hurried past she stood up, reached out an arm and caught hold of her. Only a little light came down from the staircase window; they could hardly see each other. They stood like two figures in a picture, without understanding, created to face one another.

'Louise,' whispered Mother, 'if things should be difficult—— Marriage isn't easy. If you should be disappointed—I know, I feel—you do understand? If Charles——'

'Charles?'

'I do love you, I do. You would tell me?'

But Louise, kissing her coldly and gently, said: 'Yes, I know. But there isn't really, Mother, anything to tell.'

STELLA GIBBONS

Saturday Afternoon

ONE o'clock on Saturday afternoon.

Suddenly the sirens began. Their sound swooped into the basement kitchen at 46 Marling Street, Camden Town, and put Mrs. Spenk in mind of an air-raid, as they did every Saturday. She was scuttling round the kitchen laying the stained cloth with three places when the noise began, and when she heard the first uncouth howl from Sheer's Tobacco Works just round the corner she glanced despairingly at the clock and darted across to the stove, and thrust a knife down into the potatoes.

They were not done. Nor was the cabbage. Nor was the stew. And in ten minutes Spenk would be home from Sheer's wanting his dinner, and young Cissie too. Oh, what was the matter with Saturday, that everything went wrong and made you want to scream the place down? It was the same every Saturday (slap! went the vinegar down on the table beside the crusted egg-cup that held the mustard)— try as she might, nothing would go right of a Saturday.

'All be'ind, like the cow's tail, I am this morning,' muttered Mrs. Spenk, rummaging in the bread crock under the mangle. She looked like a cross goblin in the dim kitchen, with her hair lifted off her worried little face and her hollow temples, and coiled on the top of her head in the style of thirty years ago.

'Eat—eat—eat—like a lot of 'orses. Cloth never gets off the table, Saturdays.'

She shoved a vase of marigolds, withering in stale water, into the middle of the table. Even the flowers looked dull in the kitchen, where the only vivid thing was the beautiful red and gold fire, roaring proudly behind its bars like a lusty lion. The shiny brown walls, brown oilcloth, and grey ceiling were nets for darkness, and outside there was no sunlight.

To and fro scurried Mrs. Spenk, pitching wet potato peelings into the dustbin, opening a tin of peaches. In the midst of her dartings (and the cabbage stems still hard as wood!) slow steps began descending the area steps, and glancing angrily out between the lace curtains she saw the large silhouette that was more completely familiar to her than any other in her narrow world.

He came into the kitchen, and his experienced eye took in the bare table, the agitated saucepans, and his wife's angry face. His own, tired and dirty and already sullen, became lowering.

'Ain't it ready yet, then?'

'No, it isn't. I'm all be'ind this morning. You know I 'ad to take Georgie down to the Ear 'ospital and they kep' me there the best part of an hour. You're early, aren't you? 'Tisn't more than ten pars'.'

'I'm orlright. You 'urry up them saucepans.'

He pushed past her across the room, and went into the little scullery, where she heard him having a bit of a wash while she slopped some stew onto a half-warm plate.

The sound of his leisurely preparations made her furious.

She called sharply:

'Where are you off to, s'afternoon?'

'Down to the Bridge with Charlie Ford.' His

sullen voice beat back her shrill irritation with a flat wall of secrecy. She muttered something about a waste of money, but he pretended not to hear.

He came back into the room with his face washed clean and looking startlingly different. He was fifty, and flabbily stout, but his unfulfilled youth seemed petrified in the immature curves of the lips behind his moustache and in the uncertain expression of his eyes.

He glanced furtively across at his wife as he sat down to his plate of stew, but said no more. He kept looking up at the alarm clock on the mantelpiece between his half-masticated mouthfuls, for the match began at 3.15, and it took a good hour to get down to Stamford Bridge. At twenty to two he got up, putting on his bowler. Mrs. Spenk, who had started on her own stew, neither looked up nor spoke. The air of the kitchen was charged with waves of resentment that rolled from the taut, raging little woman to the big sullen man.

The monotonous hours of the week, spent by him in a vast air-cooled impersonal room shaken by machines, and by her in a little underground room smelling of stale food, had fused once again into the mutual nervous hatred of Saturday afternoon. Every week it was the same. Neither knew what was the matter. They only felt angry and tired out. By Saturday afternoon Mr. and Mrs. Spenk were no longer a man and a woman. They were the results of a fact called the social system.

Another piece of the system came slowly down the steps as Mr. Spenk was going up; his daughter Cissie, aged sixteen, who earned thirty shillings a week as a junior-typist-cum-switchboard-operator in a paper-pattern shop in the Strand. Usually Cissie was cheerful, but now Saturday afternoon had got her too. She was coiled in on herself in a satisfying fit of temper about nothing.

'Ullo, Dad.'

'Ullo. You been sacked yet?' he asked, disagreeably.

This was a sore point, for Cissie was impertinent, and seldom kept a job longer than three months. But she was too depressed to flare back at him. She turned her face away, muttering, 'Oh, shut up, do,' and slouched past him down the steps and in at the dark door.

Outside the light was so lowering that dusk seemed only just round the corner. The pavements were greasy. The sticks of celery in the baskets at street corners shone white as bones. Mr. Spenk bought a paper, and settled down to half an hour's strap-hanging in a carriage full of men in spotty suits and cloth caps. Charlie Ford had failed to turn up; and he was alone. He felt no better. His pipe tasted sour, and there was nothing much in the paper. A fool trod on his corn in the scramble at Charing Cross. He hated everybody.

His face was set in sullen lines as he climbed the grass-grown steps to the shilling tiers. He felt that if he didn't get a good position against the barriers he would kick up a shine, demand his money back, raise blasted hell. But he got a good place all right, plumb opposite the grand-stand. A huge, massed semicircle of pink dots curved away from him on either side, topped by thousands of cloth caps of pinkish-grey, greeny-brown, speckled grey. The air was warm and heavy, and did not carry the flat roar of thirty-five thousand voices.

After an unseeing stare round, Mr. Spenk settled down to his paper, and to wait.

Cissie went straight over to the glass by the window and began squeezing earnestly at an invisible spot on her white chin, staring into her face with passionate interest as though she had not seen it for six months.

She was still staring, and pawing the spot discontentedly with one finger, when her mother came in, dressed to go out. Cissie did not turn round.

'Well, my lady! What's the matter with you? Got out of bed the wrong side this morning, like your father? Don't you want no dinner?'

'Don't fancy stew. 'S always stew, Saturdays. I'm not 'ungry.'

'Go without, then. Only don't go pickin' about in the safe after I'm gone out. I want this 'ere for supper.'

Cold stew and vegetables were being slammed into the safe.

'Where's Georgie?' asked Cissie, who wanted to be sure the house would be empty that afternoon.

'Upstairs with Mrs. P. 'E don't want no dinner, neither. 'Is ear's too bad, 'e says.'

Coals were shot noisily into the range and damped down with the colander of tea-leaves from the sink, while Cissie stood in maddening idleness with all this energy whirling round her, trying how her hair looked with a centre parting.

Not until she heard the door slam, and her mother running angrily up the area steps, did she turn round. Then she turned suddenly, staring at the kitchen already settling into winter twilight, with the red eye of the fire now burning sulkily. Cissie gave a loud and animal yawn, stretched, stared again, and suddenly tore across the kitchen and upstairs into the bathroom which the Spenks shared with the rest of the house.

She began to let hot water furiously into the bath, twizzling the taps round and round, using up the Saturday night bath water. Her round face was youthful and tired as a cross fairy's under its paint. Every few minutes she yawned extravagantly, and the steam, which was already warming the tiny, dank cell deliciously, was drawn down into her lungs.

She locked the door. She lit the gas. She crumbled a twopenny packet of bath salts into the discoloured bath, and began to undress.

Mrs. Spenk, fussing up the steps of the house next door, found young Mrs. Judd waiting; dark, severe, and like a gipsy.

'There you are,' she exclaimed, 'I was just wondering if I wouldn't come along and fetch you. But there, I said to myself, I expect she's been kept. I know what Saturday is.'

They ran down the steps rapidly together, as though no precious second must be wasted.

'There's a 47,' said Mrs. Spenk, as they crossed the road. 'We'd better take it. The big picture starts at a quarter to three, and if there's anything I do hate it's coming in in the middle of the big picture.'

The Majestic Cinema was already lit up when they arrived; and the lights were on inside the hall, diffusing that languid, warmly coloured glow which prepares the mind of the audience to receive dreams. Outside, the greasy streets were lost in cold shadows. Inside, the tall gold curtains streamed to meet the benign glow and the walls were stippled with a gold on whose bland expanse shone ruby and amber lights.

Mrs. Spenk and Mrs. Judd were shown into two good seats in the middle of the hall, and they sat down. Mrs. Spenk, with lips pressed bitterly together, sat upright in her ruby-covered seat. Nevertheless, its curves caressed her taut spine. Neither woman spoke as they sat waiting for the lights to fade; and the eyes of both were turned upwards to the rich, mysterious folds of the curtain hiding the screen.

Mr. Spenk, waiting under a lead-coloured sky with fifty thousand other spectators (for the ground had filled rapidly) still felt no better. He huddled himself up with his pipe and stared sourly in front of him. The idle roar from the crowd poured up to the dim clouds; it was waiting, no more; relaxed as an enormous animal.

Suddenly, at ten past three, there was a satisfied stirring and a murmuring. The teams were running down the sloping alley-way underneath the grandstand, pretty as a ballet in their blue and red and white shirts, and white shorts. They scattered across the grass, livid green in the lowering light, and began to punt the ball about. The satisfying dull 'ponk!' as they kicked it whetted the crowd's appetite; it was in the very mood that once presaged gladiatorial combats.

The visiting team won the toss. Mr. Spenk stolidly watched the preliminary punting, saw even the kick-off without settling down comfortably to a critical absorption in the game, as he usually did at once. Play began badly. It was not good football. Lowther, the squat, dark Scotsman in whom the crowd was most interested, scurried down the field like a crab, hugging the ball when he should have passed and passing when he should have shot.

Backwards and forwards swayed the crowd, following the ball. Now the bright figures clotted in front of one goal, now in front of the other; now they spread out along the grass; but still the play did not improve. The crowd began to feel famished, like an animal with forbidden food dangled before its eyes. It wanted the food of swift, accurate, triumphant action expressed through the bodies of the players. It could feed on such action, and release through it the energy imprisoned in its own myriad devitalized bodies. Still such action did not come.

But suddenly the game improved. The crowd began to rock faster. Loud, short roars broke its watching silence. The crowd-animal was at last eating its food of swift, fierce action. Excitement began to pump into the dead air above the stadium.

'Oh, angel boy! Oh, pretty!' cried a lyric voice above the long roar as Charlton, the visiting goal-keeper, leapt four feet in the air, striking the ball yards out of the net.

Mr. Spenk was really watching now. He was eating his food with the rest of the crowd. Presently he, like the rest of the crowd, would begin to feel better.

The lights were fading. A long beam shot across the darkness and ghostly words shone suddenly behind the curtains, which parted with a rippling noise. Dreams were about to be made.

Neither Mrs. Spenk nor Mrs. Judd saw the notice of the censor's approval, the names of the author, director, and photographers, or the names of the cast.

For them the big picture did not begin until a lovely giantess appeared on the screen, petulantly asleep in a billowing bed. Gerda Harbor in 'Gay Lady.'

Their eyes followed her awakening as solemnly as the eyes of children, while their ears accepted without offence the disdainful nasal cadences of her voice. The luxury of her bedroom, which their eyes had scarcely time to absorb, pointed no contrast between itself and the rooms in which they slept. They were like two children listening to a story.

Mrs. Judd, better informed, nudged Mrs. Spenk when the hero appeared.

'That's Orme Roland. 'E always acts with Gerda Harbor. Isn't 'e a lovely feller?'

'Nice-lookin', but a bit thin on top, ain't 'e?' objected Mrs. Spenk. In spite of the dream-weaving silver beam and the shadows that were created to absorb into themselves all the tiredness and vague discontent in the audience, the taint of Saturday morning still soured Mrs. Spenk's tongue. But her pose was less rigid in her seat. No one else was sitting upright. The audience was chiefly young men and women; and each girl rested her head on the thin shoulder of her boy. Darkness, lies and dreams fed these children of the machine age like the pictures in the crystal of a Persian magician. The machines wove dreams; their children watched; and forgot their slavery to the weavers.

''E's been married three times,' observed Mrs. Judd.

''As 'e now? Fancy! It's a wonder any one in 'Ollywood would 'ave 'im, after that. Still, I suppose it don't mean the same to Americans as it does to us. 'E is a nice-lookin' feller, and no mistake. She's lovely, too. I like that way of doin' 'er hair.'

Mrs. Spenk, also, was beginning to feel better.

Just before half-time, United equalized. Now, at twenty past four, the Pensioners wanted a goal to win. They attacked like vigorous yet cold-thinking demons. Each rush was planned. Lowther, at last, was awake. His crab-like scurries, in which the ball seemed tied by an invisible wire to his toes or his heel, brought roars of ecstasy from the crowd. Mr. Spenk roared with the rest. He stood on tiptoe to roar and see the better. When Fordy, the visiting team's inside-right, steadied himself—shot—shot too high and struck the bar, Mr. Spenk joined in the terrible impatient groan that went up.

''Ow's Lowther doin' now?' asked a voice, triumphantly.

''E ain't doing so badly,' admitted another voice. 'Seems a bit too fond of the ball, though. Might 'ave treacle all over it, the way it sticks to 'im.'

'Half an hour ago you said 'e was afraid of it. Cor! there ain't no pleasin' some people.'

'Orlright, don't upset yerself. Fact is, you take football too seriously. It ain't like 'orse-racin'.'

The moonlight rippled on the lake in the millionaire's garden. There was a party, and the house was lit up, and distant music in the ballroom floated from the windows. But outside on the terrace they were alone—those two—the mocking beauty in black velvet and the tall man in faultless evening-dress. His hand slipped over hers—he bent towards her. . . but she slipped from him, lightly as her own scarf that waved in the moonlit air.

'Shall we dance?'

'I never cared for dancing—until now.'

Arm in arm, they passed into the great house, the woman smiling dazzlingly into the man's eager eyes.

'Leadin'' 'im up the garden,' murmured Mrs. Spenk, and Mrs. Judd, watching raptly, nodded.

At last! Over his head and slam into the net! The visiting goalkeeper sprawled on his face; and then, across the dusky field, skirred the whistle for 'time'. The crowd rocked and roared for nearly a minute while the teams were going off the field, but already people were working their way towards the exits.

Mr. Spenk, having re-lit his cold pipe (it tasted good again), ambled up the tiers and joined the slowly swaying herds of people on their way to the gate. He stopped for a moment or two at the stone barrier along the top tier and stood looking down on the crowd; a large, amiable chap at whom no one would look twice. He had seen some good football. That was worth seeing, that was.

He sleepily adjusted his bowler and pipe, and stumped down the steps. The satisfied crowd-animal, swaying home under the darkening sky into the lit streets, ate him up.

They began the kiss.

Slowly, very slowly, so that the audience might savour in its full strength this moment for which it had been unconsciously longing, his hands fell upon her shoulders. She stared up into his suffering face, with a tender smile at the corners of her lips. Tears brightened her great eyes, and her hair was adorably disordered. She had been crying. He had been mad with rage. Now he was angry no longer. The strain between them had relaxed, deliciously, and the

audience relaxed as well. He drew her close to him.
Her head went tilting back, with its fleece of fairest
angel hair. His arms drew her closer, closer. Slowly,
in deliberate ecstasy, their lips touched at last. The
curtains swung together to a burst of music as the
two figures faded out.

'Lovely!' sighed Mrs. Spenk, groping for her hat.
'I *did* enjoy that. 'Aven't enjoyed anything so much
for months.'

Back through the streets where the mud now shone
in the lamp-light like a paste churned from jewels
came Mr. and Mrs. Spenk by their separate ways,
both soothed, rather sleepy, and amiable.

But as Mrs. Spenk and Mrs. Judd turned out of
the jolly rattle of Camden Town High Street into
Marling Street, where it was darker and quieter,
Mrs. Spenk's spirits fell. She remembered that
Cissie was sulky, and Tom had the rats, and there
was the tea to get. There was no end to it. Whenever
you had a bit of fun, you had to pay for it. Oh, well,
it was all in the day's work.

She said good night to Mrs. Judd at the top of the
area steps and ran down. A light shone in the
kitchen, and the blind had been pulled down over
the lace curtains.

Cissie was standing exactly where she had stood
three hours ago, in the same position; in front of the
glass, with her face screwed sideways the better to
pick at the invisible spot on her chin.

''Ave you been there all the afternoon?' asked her
mother, good-naturedly, hanging up her coat and hat
behind the door. 'You won't 'ave no face left if you
pull it about much longer; you'll wear it away.'

Cissie did not turn round. But her thin back,

whose shoulder-blades showed under a clean pink blouse, looked friendly. She said, mildly:

'The kettle's boiling. I got tea for you.'

'That's a good girl. Dad 'ome? Where's Georgie?'

'Still upstairs with Mrs. P. He says his ear's better. Dad won't be home for another half an hour, I shouldn't think. The paper says there was nearly fifty thousand down at the Bridge this afternoon.'

Mrs. Spenk was putting four heaped spoonfuls of tea into the brown pot, and glancing critically over the table to see if Cissie had forgotten anything. The table looked nice. Cissie had put on a clean cloth and fresh water in the marigolds. There was a new pot of jam and half a pound of yellow cake. The gaslight softened the rusty colours in the kitchen into warmth, and the kettle was singing. The fire was gold.

Mrs. Spenk poured the water on the tea, murmuring: 'We won't wait for Dad,' and sat down opposite Cissie, kicking off her shoes. She stared across at her daughter.

'Well—you *are* all dressed up like a dog's dinner. Where are you off to, to-night?'

'Nowhere, reely,' putting up a small red hand, with pointed shiny nails, to her hair. 'I may be goin' out with Millie Thomson a bit later.'

'Your eyebrows, Cissie Spenk! 'Oo are you supposed to look like—Anna May Wong or what?'

'Oh, I wish they'd grow quicker, so's I could pluck 'em more often,' said Cissie, earnestly. 'I love pluckin' 'em. I like to make 'em so thin you can't hardly see I've got any at all.'

Mrs. Spenk's caustic rattle of laughter was interrupted by Mr. Spenk.

'Ready for tea, Dad?'

'I could do with a cup. You never saw such a sight as there was down at the Bridge; must have been over sixty thousand down there. Took me the bes' part of an hour, getting away.'

Mrs. Spenk and Cissie looked interested, but each woman wondered how men could so waste their time and money.

Tea was then eaten, in a warm, comfortable silence. It was half-past six. The nervous misery of Saturday morning had gone over into the repose of Saturday night. In front of the Spenk family lay a fair prospect twenty-four hours long, called 'termorrer's-Sunday'; a day on which no one need get up early, and huge meals were eaten all day.

After tea Cissie went off mysteriously to meet Millie Thomson. Mrs. Spenk piled the dishes up in the scullery with one eye on the clock, for her shopping was not yet done. The second kettle had boiled while they finished tea, and she now splashed the water over the dirty dishes.

Mr. Spenk had drawn his chair to the fire, with a paper and his pipe. But there was an uneasy thought at the back of his mind which interrupted his comfort. He tried to ignore it, but it came back. It was the memory of Saturday morning, blent with another emotion too vague to name.

At last he got up heavily, and went out into the scullery. He held out his hand to his wife for the drying-cloth. She, flushed and busy in the candle-light and the steam, stared at him blankly.

'Give you a 'and,' said Mr. Spenk.

'Well, I never! Miracles will never cease!' cried Mrs. Spenk ironically.

But she smiled at him as she flipped across the drying-cloth.